"Classic fantasy elements get a fresh take in this expertly crafted, Arabian-inspired world that is dark, romantic, and entirely enchanting. With complex characters that tug on your heartstrings and a story that is lush in both its beauty and prose, Hafsah Faizal's *We Hunt the Flame* is not to be missed!"
—KATIE STUTZ,
bookseller at Anderson's Bookshop

"*We Hunt the Flame* is a lush and vibrant epic fantasy immersed in ancient Arabian culture that will leave you wanting more. Perfect for fans of Roshani Chokshi and Renée Ahdieh."
—MELISSA LEE,
bookseller at Blue Bunny Books

"In her incredible debut, Hafsah Faizal has crafted a whirlwind Arabian-inspired fantasy, filled with heart-stopping twists; powerful friendships; a steamy, well-developed romance; and lyrical prose that left me breathless. Fans of *The City of Brass* or *Children of Blood and Bone* will devour this tale that left me with my jaw on the floor, distressed that the story was over."
—SHAUNA SINYARD,
bookseller at Park Road Books

"Hafsah Faizal's *We Hunt the Flame* is a gorgeously written, exquisitely built world that you will want to stay in forever. Nasir and Zafira are epic protagonists, and the entwining of their stories results in one of the most stunning pieces of YA fantasy literature."
—RACHEL STROLLE,
librarian at Glenside Public Library District

We Hunt the Flame

HAFSAH FAIZAL

FARRAR STRAUS GIROUX · NEW YORK

To my mother,

for shaping my heart,

and my father,

for hardening it to steel

Farrar Straus Giroux Books for Young Readers
An imprint of Macmillan Children's Publishing Group, LLC
175 Fifth Avenue, New York 10010

Text copyright © 2019 by Hafsah Faizal
Map credit © Virginia Allyn
All rights reserved
Printed in the United States of America
Designed by Elizabeth H. Clark
First edition, 2019

fiercereads.com

Library of Congress Cataloging-in-Publication Data
Names: Faizal, Hafsah, author.
Title: We hunt the flame / Hafsah Faizal.
Description: First edition. | New York : Farrar, Straus and Giroux, 2019. |
Summary: In a world inspired by ancient Arabia, seventeen-year-old
huntress Zafira must disguise herself as a man to seek a lost artifact
that could return magic to her cursed world.
Identifiers: LCCN 2018035775 | ISBN 9780374311544 (hardcover)
Subjects: CYAC: Fantasy. | Magic—Fiction. | Blessing and cursing—Fiction. |
Impersonation—Fiction. | Middle East—Fiction.
Classification: LCC PZ7.1.F347 We 2019 | DDC [Fic]—dc23
LC record available at https://lccn.loc.gov/2018035775

Our books may be purchased in bulk for promotional, educational, or business use. Please contact
your local bookseller or the Macmillan Corporate and Premium Sales Department at
(800) 221-7945 ext. 5442 or by email at MacmillanSpecialMarkets@macmillan.com.

ISBN 978-0-374-31154-4 (FSG hardcover edition)
1   3   5   7   9   10   8   6   4   2

ISBN 978-0-374-31348-7 (OwlCrate edition)
1   3   5   7   9   10   8   6   4   2

ISBN 978-0-374-31351-7 (Indigo edition)
1   3   5   7   9   10   8   6   4   2

ISBN 978-0-374-31364-7 (international paperback edition)
1   3   5   7   9   10   8   6   4   2

ISBN 978-0-374-31366-1 (ShelfLove edition)
1   3   5   7   9   10   8   6   4   2

ISBN 978-0-374-31378-4 (B&N exclusive edition)
1   3   5   7   9   10   8   6   4   2

Love is for children, said the girl.
Death is for fools, said the shadow.
Darkness is my destiny, said the boy.
Allegiance is my undoing, said the eagle.
Suffering is our fate, said the beauty.
And they were all horribly wrong.

Arawiya

Azraa

Sarasin

Sultan's
Keep

Leil

Daama River

Dancali Mountains

Tenama Pass

Afya

Demenhur

Thali

Selah

The
Empty Forest

N

Asma

ACT I

SILVER AS A CRESCENT MOON

CHAPTER 1

People lived because she killed. And if that meant braving the Arz where even the sun was afraid to glimpse, then so be it.

On the occasional good day, Zafira bint Iskandar mused that she was braver than the sun itself. Most days, she couldn't wait until the evernight Arz was behind her and she was firmly rooted in the plains of her caliphate, daama snow and all.

Today was one of those days, despite the antlers rough against her hands. She stepped free of the cursed prison of a forest, pretending her sigh was due to her task being complete rather than a product of the tightly coiled fear unwinding in her heart. The morning sun kissed her cheeks in welcome.

Marhaba to you, too, coward.

Sunlight was always faint in the caliphate of Demenhur, because the sun didn't know what to do with the snow that should be sand.

Before her, the sea of white rolled out smooth and pristine, gifting her a moment's contentment in her solitude, even as her toes numbed and the air crippled her nose. For in a caliphate where a woman's actions were always in danger of being turned against her, there was nothing easy about pretending to be a man. Not when she had the curves of a woman, and the voice and gait of one, too.

She dragged the deer carcass along, a trail of steam in her wake, the sullied snow an eerie crimson. There was a promise in the air. A stillness in the earth and in the whispering trees.

It's nothing. Paranoia had a way of visiting when he was least desired. She was a bundle of emotions because of the impending wedding, that was all.

Sukkar nickered from the rotting post where she had tethered him, blending in with his near-white coat. While she made quick work of tying the deer to her stallion's saddle, he remained still, as sweet as the name she had given him.

"We had a good hunt today," she said to the horse who hadn't helped, and swung onto his back.

Sukkar didn't react, content with staring across the distance into the Arz as if an ifrit would leap out and swallow him whole.

"Dastard," Zafira said, a smile on her numbing lips.

Though everyone was a coward when it came to the forest—each of the five caliphates that made up Arawiya were afraid of the Arz, for it rimmed those lands, too. It was a curse they'd shared ever since the land had been robbed of magic. Baba had taught Zafira that the Arz was, in many ways, simply a forest. He had taught her of ways to use it to her benefit. Ways to believe she could tame it, when in reality she could not. No one could.

His death had proved as much.

Zafira steered Sukkar away from the forest, toward the clearing and deeper into Demenhur. But the Arz was such that it always demanded one last glimpse. She paused and turned.

It watched. Breathed. Its skeleton trees reached with gnarled fingers steeped in swirling shadow.

Some said it devoured men like vultures on the dead. Yet Zafira returned, day after day, hunt after hunt. She was aware each venture could be her last, and though she swore she didn't fear much, finding herself lost was her biggest fear of all.

Still. There was a pulse deep inside her that relished those visits into the depths of darkness. She hated the Arz. She hated it so much, she craved it.

"Akhh, plenty of time to stare at the Arz every daama day," she said to Sukkar, a quiver to her voice. "We need to get back for the wedding, or Yasmine will have our heads."

Not that Sukkar cared. Zafira clucked her tongue and urged him forward, the tension escaping his taut muscles as the distance between them and the Arz grew.

Until the air heavied with another presence.

The small hairs on the nape of her neck lifted, and she threw a wary glance over her shoulder. The Arz stared back, as if with bated breath. No—whoever it was stood here in Demenhur, imitating the silence almost as well as she did.

Almost.

If there was one thing she feared more than losing herself within the Arz, it was being caught unaware by a man who could prove she was no hunter but a *huntress*, a girl of seventeen concealed beneath the weight of her father's hooded cloak every time she hunted. Then she would be shunned, her victories derided. Her identity, viciously unraveled. The thought closed hands around her heart, the *thud, thud, thud* racing a little bit faster.

She spun Sukkar to face the Arz, kicking against the strains of his hesitation as a low command drifted on the wind, words undecipherable.

WE HUNT THE FLAME

"Yalla." She urged him to hurry, voice tight.

He shook out his mane and cantered forward without protest. The air darkened as they neared the forest. Funny, Zafira was heading *toward* the unknown at the first sign of mortal danger.

The cold bit at her face. A blur of black sped from her right, a second blur from her left. *Horses.* She bit her lip and swerved Sukkar between them, ducking when something swung for her head.

"Qif!" someone yelled, but what kind of idiot would *stop*?

Sukkar. He froze at the border of the Arz and Zafira jerked in her saddle—a slap, reminding her that he had never ventured this close. Wood and sour decay assaulted her cold senses.

"Laa. *Laa.* Not now, you dastard," she hissed.

Sukkar threw his head but didn't budge. Zafira stared into the hushed darkness, and her breath faltered. The Arz wasn't a place to turn one's back to; it wasn't a place to be caught unaware and unsuspecting and—

With a curse, she veered Sukkar around, despite his protests.

The wind howled, cold and harsh. She was painfully aware of the Arz breathing down her back. Until she took in the two horses snorting a mere four paces away, coats dark as the night sky, powerful bodies cloaked in chain mail. War horses.

Bred in one place alone: the neighboring caliphate of Sarasin.

Or possibly Sultan's Keep. It was hard to tell which, when Arawiya's sultan had recently murdered Sarasin's caliph in cold blood, unlawfully seizing control of land and armies the sultan had no need for—not when Arawiya rested under his control, and not when he had the Sultan's Guard at his beck and call. The caliphs existed for balance. He wasn't supposed to *kill* them.

Atop their horses, the men's bare arms were corded with muscle, faces cut with harsh lines. They were the color of people who knew life beneath a sun, the ebb and flow of the desert Zafira longed for.

"Yalla, Hunter," the larger man said, as if she were cattle to be herded, and her eyes fell to the scimitar in his grasp.

If Zafira had any doubts on where they were from, the timbre of his voice was enough. Her throat closed in on itself. Being tracked by gossiping Demenhune was one thing; being attacked by Sarasins was another.

She lowered her head so that her hood obscured more of her face. She braved the darkness; she slew rabbits and deer. She had never stood before a blade.

But for all their might, the men held their distance. Even they were afraid of the Arz. Zafira lifted her chin.

"Whatever for?" she drawled over the sudden hiss of the wind. She had people to feed and a bride as beautiful as the moon to say goodbye to. *Why me?*

"To meet the sultan," the smaller man said.

The sultan? Skies. The man had shorn more fingers from hands than hair from his head. People said he had been good once, but Zafira found that hard to believe. He was Sarasin by birth, and Sarasins, she had been told all her life, were born without a shred of good in their hearts.

Panic flared in her chest again, but she lowered her voice. "If the sultan wanted to see me, he would respect me with a letter, not his hounds. I'm no criminal."

The small man opened his mouth upon being likened to a dog, but the other shifted his blade and drew closer. "This isn't a request." A pause, as if he realized his fear of the Arz wouldn't allow him to move any farther, and then, "Yalla. Come forward."

No. There had to be a way out. Zafira pursed her lips in realization. If there was one thing other than barbarism Sarasins were known for, it was pride.

She whispered sweet nothings to Sukkar. Maybe it was the men, or maybe it was the war horses, mighty and intimidating, but her loyal horse took a step back. It was the closest he had ever gone to the Arz, and Zafira was going to torture him with much more. She gave the men a crooked smile, her lips cracked and likely colorless from the cold. "Come and fetch me."

"You have nowhere to go."

"You forget, Sarasin. The Arz is my second home."

She stroked Sukkar's mane, steeled her heart, and steered him into the dark.

It swallowed her whole.

She tried, tried, tried not to acknowledge the way it welcomed her, elated whispers brushing her ears. A surge in her bloodstream. Hunger in her veins.

Dark trees stood eerie and unyielding, leaves sharp and glinting. Distantly, she heard the gallop of hooves as the Sarasins shouted and followed. Vines crunched beneath Sukkar's hooves, and Zafira's sight fell to near blindness.

Except for his panicked breathing, Sukkar was mercifully quiet as Zafira listened for the men, her own heart an echoing thud. Despite their fear, they *had* followed, for pride was a dangerous thing.

Yet only silence drummed at her ears—like the moment after a blade's unsheathing. The halt after the first howl of wind.

They were gone.

For once she appreciated the fearsome, incalculable strangeness of the Arz that made the men disappear. The two Sarasins could be leagues away, and neither she nor they would ever know it. Such was the Arz. This was why so many people who entered never returned—they couldn't *find* their way back.

A soft hiss sounded from the east, and she and Sukkar froze. She could see little of his white coat, but years of returning again and again had sharpened her hearing better than any blade. She saw with her ears in the Arz. Footsteps echoed, and the temperature careened downward.

"Time to go home," Zafira murmured, and Sukkar shivered as he edged forward, guided by her hand, by that rushing whisper in her heart. Sated only when she moved.

The darkness ebbed away to a soft blue sky and the distant throb of the sun. At once, she felt a yawning emptiness as the cold stung her nostrils, scented with metal and a hint of amber.

The Sarasins, it seemed, hadn't been so lucky. How long ago had the three of them ridden into the Arz? It couldn't have been more than twenty minutes, but the position of the sun claimed it had been at least an hour.

Zafira didn't want to know whether the sultan had really sent for her. Or, if so, *why*. It was the *why* that caused Sukkar to snort beneath her, ever aware. *One thing at a time*, he seemed to say.

Where the war horses had stood, the snow was now smooth and—

She yanked on Sukkar's reins.

A woman stood against the plains of white.

A heavy cloak of gray, no, shimmering *silver* sat on her slender shoulders above a sweeping red gown. Her raised hood barely covered the top of her stark hair, as white as the snow. Her lips were crimson, a curve of blood.

Zafira swore the woman hadn't been there a moment ago. A gallop began in her chest.

The Arz depraves an idle mind.

"Who knew you could kill so swiftly," the woman said in a voice of silk.

Did the Arz conjure voices to its illusions, too?

"I am no assassin. I only evaded them," Zafira said, realizing a beat later that she shouldn't respond to an illusion. She hadn't killed those men— *had she?*

"Clever." The woman smiled after a pause. "You truly do emerge sane and in one piece." A gust billowed her cloak. Her dark eyes drifted across the first line of the Arz trees with an odd mix of awe and—*skies*—adoration.

The woman wavered and solidified. Real and not.

"It's a lot like Sharr, isn't it?" Then she shook her head, every movement deliberate.

Fear simmered beneath Zafira's skin at the mention of Sharr.

"Oh, how could I ask such a tease of a question?" she continued. "You haven't been to the island yet."

Are you real? Zafira wanted to ask. She demanded instead, "Who are you?"

The woman fixed her with that glittering gaze, bare hands clasped. Did she not feel the sting of the cold? Zafira tightened her fingers around Sukkar's reins.

"Tell me, why do you hunt?"

"For my people. To feed them," Zafira said. Her back ached and the deer was beginning to smell.

The woman clucked her tongue with a slight frown, and Sukkar trembled. "No one can be that pure."

Zafira must have blinked, for the woman was suddenly closer. Another blink, despite her best efforts, and the woman had moved away again.

"Do you hear the roar of the lion? Do you heed its call?"

Where did this loon crawl from? "The tavern is in the sooq, if you're looking for more arak." But Zafira's usual candor was hindered by the tightening in her throat.

The woman laughed, a tinkling that stilled the air. Then Zafira's vision wavered, and the snow was suddenly clothed in shadow. Black bled into the white, tendrils reaching for Zafira's ankles.

"Dear Huntress, a woman like me has no need for drink."

Huntress. The reins slipped from Zafira's hands.

"How——" The words died on her tongue.

A smile twisted the woman's lips, and with it, Zafira's heart. It was the type of smile that meant she knew Zafira's secrets. The type of smile that meant no one was safe.

"You will always find your way, Zafira bint Iskandar," the woman said.

She sounded almost sad, though the glint in her eyes was anything but. "Lost you should have remained, cursed child."

The silver of her cloak flashed when she turned, and then Zafira must have blinked again.

Because the woman had vanished.

Zafira's heart clambered to her throat. Her name. That smile. There was no sign of the bleeding black or the silver cloak now. The snow was pristine as the claws in her brain loosened.

Then Sukkar was off before she could regain her hold on his reins.

She fumbled with a shout, sitting tall to keep from tumbling to the snow. He continued on a mad dash until they crested the slope and stumbled to a stop.

Zafira jerked back, cursing until Sukkar ducked his head with a dignified snort. *Breathe. Assess.* She looked back at the evernight forest once more, but the woman was nowhere to be seen. It was almost as if Zafira had imagined the entire encounter.

Perhaps she *had*. Zafira knew the Arz better than most, which was to say she understood that no one could *ever* know its secrets. To trust in its wickedness was to court a tortured death.

Do you hear the roar of the lion?

It wasn't a roar Zafira heard. Something else beckoned from the darkness, enticing her. Growing with her every visit. It was as if a thread of her heart had snagged in the forest and was trying to reel her back in.

She drew in a sharp breath. Exhaustion had conjured the woman, that was all.

And now she was late. She veered Sukkar around with a huff. She had a dress to don and a wedding to catch.

CHAPTER 2

PEOPLE DIED BECAUSE HE LIVED. AND IF THAT WAS the only way to carry forward in this life, then so be it.

There had been a particularly strong blizzard in the neighboring caliphate of Demenhur three nights ago, and Sarasin was chillier because of it. The combination of desert heat and the wayward cold rattled Nasir's bones, yet here he was, far from his home in Sultan's Keep, the small portion of land from which the sultan ruled Arawiya's five caliphates.

Nasir's missions to Sarasin always gave him a sense of nostalgia he never could understand. Though he had never lived here, it was the caliphate of his lineage, and it felt familiar and strange at once.

He came here for one act alone: murder.

Leil, the capital of Sarasin, was crawling with armed men in turbans of azure. Three stood guard at the entrance to the walled city. Billowing sirwal, instead of tighter-fitting pants, hung low across their hips, vain muscled arms glistened bronze. A gust of desert air carried the musky odor of hot sands, along with the chatter of children and their scolding elders.

Nasir studied the sentries and slid from his mare's back with a heavy sigh. He had no need for a skirmish with a horde of lowborn men.

"Looks like I'll be taking the long route," he murmured, rubbing a hand across Afya's flank. She nickered a reply, and he tethered her beside a sleepy-eyed camel. She was his mother's horse, named after her favorite of the Six Sisters of Old.

He climbed a stack of aging crates and leaped from awning to awning of the surrounding structures, balancing on jutting stones, his ears still ringing with orders from the Sultan of Arawiya. He likened the sultan's voice to a snake, softly creeping into his veins and penetrating his heart with venom.

He scaled the wall and leaped onto the nearest rooftop with practiced ease, sidestepping the ornate rug sprawled in its center, jewel-toned cushions strewn to one side.

Sarasin's open skies were as bleak as his thoughts and forever downcast in gray, brightened only by the expectant hum of the upcoming camel race. He had little interest in the race itself——he was here for the cover it provided and the man it promised.

He vaulted to the next rooftop and swayed when a blade arced down a mere fraction from his face. A girl of about thirteen leaped back with a gasp, dropping one of her twin scimitars to the dusty limestone, her concentrated drill broken. Nasir's gauntlet blade thrummed, but the last thing he needed was to kill unnecessarily. *As if your kills are ever necessary.*

He lifted a finger to his lips, but the girl stared slack-jawed at his hooded attire. An assassin's garb of layered robes in black, etched with fine silver. His fitted sleeves ended in the supple leather of his gauntlets, blades tucked beneath the folds. The traditional gray sash across his middle was shrouded by a broad leather belt housing smaller blades and the sheath of his scimitar. The ensemble had been engineered in Pelusia, the caliphate as advanced in mechanics as in farming, so there was nothing finer.

"Hashashin?" the girl whispered in a way that promised his presence would be kept secret. A winding cuff resembling a snake encircled her upper arm, blue jewels studding its eyes.

No, Nasir wanted to say to that voice of awe. *An assassin lives an honorable life.*

There was a time when a hashashin danced and the wicked perished, merchants rose to power, trades fell to dust. The glint of a blade turned the tides of the world. They had been poets of the kill, once. Honor in their creed.

But that was long before Nasir's time. He didn't live. He existed. And no one understood the difference between the two until they ceased to live.

The girl grinned. She was too fair for Sarasin standards, with white hair stark against her brow, but it wasn't uncommon for the snow-brained Demenhune to turn up here, particularly womenfolk. Demenhur's caliph was a biased crow who would blame women for old age, if he could.

She picked up her scimitar, continuing with praiseworthy maneuvers that would guarantee her a sought-after place in a house of assassins, but Nasir didn't comment. Fewer words worked best in his world, where a person encountered today could be a maggot's feast tomorrow.

He swept past her and leaped to the next rooftop, which overlooked houses of tan stone. The streets below were empty, except for the rare camel being pulled along. Dusty lanterns hung from eaves, the glass long ago shattered into the desert.

The rooftops ended and Nasir dropped down to Leil's sooq. Stalls with rickety legs spread across the expanse, tattered cloth in an array of colors shading goods from the meager sun. The stench of sweat and heat stirred the air. Bare-chested urchins ducked beneath tables and between swaths of fabric as a good-size crowd meandered the stands. Here, the ghostly landscape was alive.

It would be even busier at noon, when the sharp scents of nutmeg and sumac would entwine with meat-filled mutabaq as merchants catered to the workers who mined for coal and minerals in one of the worst places of Arawiya: the Leil Caves.

Now vendors extolled other wares—bolts of fabric in bright colors muted by the dull skies; spices in enough hues to paint papyrus; carved stone platters with designs so intricate, Nasir did not see the point.

He shoved past a gaggle of women and nearly stepped on a salt merchant cross-legged on a rug, sacks of the precious commodity perched around him and a sharp-eyed falcon on his shoulder. The weathered man looked up with a toothy smile, excited at the prospect of a new customer.

Until he saw Nasir's garb and the gleam in his eyes turned to fear.

Others had begun to take notice. A woman dropped her newly purchased sack of grain. Nasir lowered his head and pressed forward. If he passed close enough, their whispers brushed his ears. If he passed closer still, they would dare to look at him. They knew what Nasir strode for, dressed the way he was.

So he pretended not to notice when a bag of dinars fell from his side and scattered across the dusty ground, sand muting the glimmer of the silver coins.

It was better this way. It was better for Nasir to be as evil as Sultan Ghameq in their eyes. Because in many ways, he was. Maybe even worse.

Still, the people of Sarasin had become hardened to the life that grew more desolate by the day. Their caliph had just been murdered, their lands wrongfully seized by their own sultan. Yet no one seemed any more disturbed than they had been before.

Stand up, he ordered them in his head. *Defy. Fight.*

Self-derision tore a sound from his chest. *Not even you defy the sultan.*

And the ones who dared to raise their heads: Nasir killed.

He finally reached the alley at the end of the sooq. A girl blinked wide gray eyes and limped into the shadows, dust stirring in her wake. Sand qit ducked into the rubble, paws silent, tails curling. Ragged papyrus covered the crumbling stone walls, lathered with scrawling lines of poetry from some romantic fool with too much hope in his hands.

His mother used to say that a person without hope was a body without a soul. It was the loss of the Sisters nearly a century ago that had left the people this way, bereft of the magic Arawiya depended on. And here, where the sand was soot and the sky was forever dusk, there was no hope for anyone, especially Nasir.

A guard stepped from the shadows, sand scraping beneath his boots. Nasir stared down his drawn sword with cool disinterest.

"Halt," the guard said, puffing out his chest and, subsequently, his gut. *Where do these fools find so much food?*

"A bit too late for that," Nasir said smoothly. He flicked his wrist and extended his gauntlet blade.

"I said, *halt*," the guard repeated. He stood tall, a little too new and eager for a world that would set him crooked soon enough.

Nasir would spare him the experience. His blade flashed in the meager light. "Such pitiful last words."

The guard's eyes bulged. "No! Wait. I have a sister—"

Nasir pivoted a full turn to avoid the guard's sword and slashed his blade across the man's neck. He dragged the gurgling corpse to the shadows before straightening his robes and returning to the alley, hands sliding over the gritty stone wall to find a hold. *I'll be an old man by the end of this.*

He scaled the wall to the rooftops north of the sooq, vaulting from terrace to rooftop until he reached the most extravagant limestone construction of the city, taller than the rest. The prestigious quarters of Dar al-Fawda. The owners of the camel race were one of the finer groups of notoriety the dead caliph had turned a blind eye upon.

Lattice screens and lush cushions sprawled across the creamy stone in soft sighs of color. A dallah pot and a set of handleless cups lay to the side, stained with dark rings. Strewn sheets and silken shawls littered the expanse. He knew what occurred on these rooftops, and he was glad for his timing.

He pushed aside a pile of silken cushions and crouched at the roof's edge. The gray skies told nothing of the time of day, but below, the wadi where the race would take place was beginning to attract crowds—Sarasins, with dark hair, olive skin, and rueful eyes. *His* people.

Foolish people, come to empty their coffers with damning bets placed upon camels. He made a dismissive sound and looked to the tents beyond.

Any moment now.

Nasir reached into the folds of his clothes for the sweet he had saved from the night before, but his fingers touched the cool surface of a disc. He brushed his thumb over the camel-bone mosaic adorning the flat circle. Inside, a sundial lay dull with age and veins of turquoise patina, the glass long since cracked. It had once gleamed in the palm of a sultana, and he thought—

Not the time for memories, mutt. He flinched at the echo of his father's voice and pulled out the crinkling wrapper of the date cake.

These were the small ways in which he could feel like the human he was born as. A leftover cake saved for later. An aging sundial from moments past.

Where was that damned boy? Camels were being pulled forward, and Nasir needed to be down there before the crowds became impenetrable. He drummed his fingers on the stone, coating his fingers in creamy dust.

I am going to rip his—

The trapdoor creaked open and Nasir turned as a boy with knobby elbows climbed onto the roof. A sand qit meowed and curled around the child's dirty feet.

Nasir lifted an eyebrow. "You took your time."

"I—I'm sorry. I couldn't get away from Effendi Fawda." The page boy's brown skin was smeared with dirt. The owner of Dar al-Fawda was no respectable one, but if the boy wanted to respect him with the title of effendi, Nasir did not care.

"Everything is ready for you," the boy said, as if he had been given a tremendous task other than telling Nasir where to find the man he sought. Nasir liked that the boy wasn't afraid to speak to him. Afraid of him? Most likely. But not afraid to *speak* to him.

Nasir played along with a small nod. "You have my shukur."

At his thanks, the boy looked as surprised as Nasir felt, and before his pride could stop him, Nasir held out the date cake. A gasp wheezed past the boy's chapped lips and he reached with careful fingers, unfolding the wax sheet with awestruck features. He licked the sugar from his dirty fingers and Nasir's stomach clenched.

All he ever saw were blood, tears, and darkness. The hope in the boy's eyes, the dirt on his face, the jutting of his bones—

"Can you . . . bestow another favor?"

Nasir blinked at the boy's poise. He and "favor" never sat in the same sentence.

"The children slaved to the races," he ventured. "Can you free them?"

Nasir looked to the wadi, to the children. His voice was flat, uncaring. "If they don't die in the races, they're bound to die elsewhere."

"You don't mean that," the boy said after a long pause, and Nasir was surprised to find anger aflame in his dark eyes. *Let it burn, boy.*

"Salvation is for foolish heroes who will never exist. Help yourself and leave the rest."

It was advice Nasir should have followed years ago. He turned without another word and dropped from the rooftop, swiftly lowering himself to the ground.

Dar al-Fawda guards in sirwal and black turbans loitered nearby. The higher-ups wore plain, ankle-length thobes and sported thick mustaches as they shuffled past. Nasir could never understand the horrid fashion of a mustache without a beard, but these men believed the bigger the better.

He waited in the shadows of a date palm and, head low, slipped into a group of drunkards on their way to the race. They passed bookies on short stools and people cheering for their bets, damning their meager earnings for the thrill of a short-lived gamble.

More camels ambled into the wadi. Children, too, dressed in nothing but dusty sirwal. Nasir's fingers twitched when a man used a whip on a boy whose cheeks streamed with tears as he rubbed an already reddening shoulder, eyes murderous.

Only in Sarasin could vengeance start so young.

Very few protested the use of children in the races, for the lighter the rider the faster the camel, and so the atrocity carried on. Nasir's blood burned black, but he stilled his fingers.

Monsters bore no duty to the innocent.

When his drunk companions finally reached the throngs in the sidelines, Nasir slipped away, clenching his teeth against the stench. He pushed past cheering people and sidestepped sand qit and children searching for scraps.

He reached the tents.

The few he peered inside were empty. They held traditional majlis seating, with cushions spread out across the floor for private negotiations or more intimate happenings. The page boy's marker, a red shawl pinned beneath a stone, lay at the seventh tent as promised.

Nasir dropped his hand to the scimitar at his side.

The mark could be young or near death. He could have children who would stare into his lifeless eyes and scream for a soul that would never return.

He's a name. A scrap of papyrus, rolled and shoved into Nasir's pocket.

He slipped inside. The beige walls of the tent dressed the place with forlorn, wan light that stole through tears in the fabric and illuminated swirls of dust. Scrolls and books were scattered across the carpet that covered the sand, and a gray-haired man was bent over them, scribing by lantern.

The shouts and cheers of the crowd grew louder as the races began, echoing with the grunts of camels and the cries of the children upon them. The man rubbed his beard, murmuring to himself.

Nasir used to wonder why he stopped feeling sorrow for the people he was sent to slay. At some point, his heart had ceased to register the monstrosity of his deeds, and it had nothing to do with the darkness tainting the lands. No, it was his own doing.

He was turning his heart black, no one else.

Nasir paused at the man's calm demeanor and considered killing him without his knowledge. But amid the scrolls he spotted titles written in the ancient tongue of Safaitic—even an account of the deceased Lion of the Night, a man of two bloods who had set his mind upon Arawiya's throne, doling death in his wake during the horrific Black Massacre.

A historian. This man was a historian. *That* was why Nasir had to kill him?

He pressed his foot deeper into the sand, crunching it beneath his boot.

The man looked up. "Ah, you have come. It took you long enough to find me."

Irritation stirred in Nasir's chest. It wasn't always that his marks spoke to him, that they didn't fight him. "I am no hunter. I kill when ordered."

The man smiled. "Right you are, hashashin. But once the head falls, the rest is destined to follow. You tore down our caliph, and as his advisor by name, I have been waiting for you since."

A warmth filled the man's eyes, and Nasir darted a wary glance behind, only to realize it was directed at *him*. Like the page boy's gratitude at the rooftop. But this, *this* was a hundred times worse.

No one should show kindness to their murderer.

"Owais Khit," Nasir pronounced quietly. The name in his pocket. His voice held a sense of finality, and bitter hatred sank fangs into his heart.

Owais was here for the children of the races, rallying to free them. It was unfortunate that he had another agenda, too. One that had nothing to do with the dead caliph and that made Nasir curious, as treasonous as it was. For in Arawiya, strength meant death, unless it was in allegiance to the sultan.

The man dipped his head. "Him I am. Make it quick, but know that this will not end with me."

"You speak of treason. Your very work is treason." Nasir should not have indulged him. He should have killed him before he had glimpsed the brown of the man's eyes and curiosity got the best of him. What treason was there in the study of history?

"Who delivers justice to a treasonous sultan?" Owais asked. "The sultan had no place murdering our caliph, as cruel as he was. He has no right taking our land and controlling Sarasin's army. We are one of five caliphates to govern. Think, boy. With five caliphates under his thumb and the Sultan's Guard at his call, what need does he have to take over an army?

"The people remain silent out of the fear that taxes may increase. The peace is temporarily ensured—for what? My work was merely unearthing the reason for change. For why a tyrant emerged in place of our good sultan. Our sultana would not have brought him into the fold if he were so dark a man. Something stirs in the shadows, boy. Soon, death will be the least of our horrors." Owais lifted his chin, exposing his wizened neck. "Be swift. Know that my work will continue through others. Perhaps, one day, it will continue through you, and Arawiya will return to the splendor it once was."

Impossible, for a boy whose hands were steeped in blood. Whose heart was as dark as the one Owais sought to rectify. Whatever this man and his people were trying to accomplish, it would live a short life. Their numbers dwindled with each passing day—Nasir ensured it.

His scimitar sang as he pulled it free. Owais exhaled and wound his turban around his head, eyes flashing in the glint of the blade, a brilliant chestnut hidden beneath the folds of aging skin. A smile curved the man's lips once more, and Nasir thought of the sultan passing him the fold of papyrus. He thought of Owais's warning and realized the absurdity of killing a man for the mere act of reading.

But he never left a job unfinished.

There was a hitch in the man's breath when the metal touched his skin. One last spike of emotion before Nasir shifted his arm and blood oozed free. Somewhere, children were losing their father. Grandchildren were losing their greatest love.

He pulled a feather from the folds of his robes and touched it to the blood. It settled on the dead man's chest, its black vane tipped glimmering red.

Anyone who saw it would know Owais's killer. They would know vengeance was impossible.

The hashashin in Nasir crouched. He closed the man's eyes and straightened his turban. "Be at peace, Owais Khit min Sarasin."

Then Nasir filled his lungs with the familiar stench of blood, and left.

He pinned the flap open so that the people would know. It was the one lenience he could leave them—a marker to help them bury the dead. The people would never consider Nasir an ally, but in that moment he almost felt like they could.

They were right to hate him, for Nasir had killed more than he could count. It used to matter, before. Now it was nothing more than a swipe of his sword. Another felled soul.

To the people, he was not Nasir Ghameq, crown prince of Arawiya, no. He was the purger of life.

The Prince of Death.

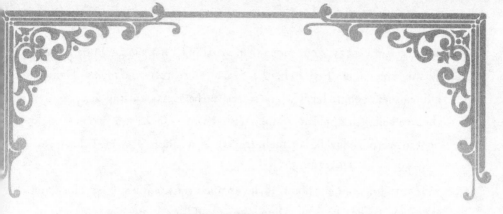

CHAPTER 3

I<small>N</small> D<small>EMENHUR</small>, <small>THEY BLAMED WOMEN BECAUSE OF THE</small> Six Sisters. Zafira carried the knowledge like a wound that could never heal.

That word—*Huntress*—was a thorn dragged across the wound, fresh pain gritting her teeth. She had always been the Hunter. She had always referred to *herself* as the Hunter. And though she was convinced she had imagined the silver-cloaked woman, the illusion was a reminder that no matter what she did, she could always be brought to blame.

Just like the Six Sisters of Old, who had staked their lives to bring daama Arawiya to fruition and now lay as parables of shame.

Had the Sisters been men, Arawiya would still have magic. Had the Sisters been men, the caliphates would not be cursed. Had the Sisters been men, everything would be as it once was. Or so the Demenhune caliph preached.

Zafira believed otherwise.

As she and Sukkar crested the last hill that stood between her village and the Arz, she wished, more than anything, that she could be herself. That women didn't have to be the incapable creatures the men of Demenhur claimed them to be. The one solace she had was knowing that not all of the five caliphates held the same twisted views. In Zaram, women could fight in arenas, equal beside men. In Pelusia, a calipha governed alone, surrounded by her Nine Elite.

Zafira fingered her hood. If she escaped the confines of her cloak and the masquerade of a man, Demenhur would not praise her. Her accomplishments would shift into a cause for blame. A twisted foreboding of a predicament to come.

Gloomy thoughts for a wedding day.

A lone figure came into view, and Zafira had a fleeting moment of panic before she registered the soft features and sunlit curls. Deen. One of four souls who knew she was the Arz Hunter. He waited with a blade in his hands, unflinching against the cold winds.

Zafira dismounted and nudged his shoulder. "One day, you will venture the darkness with me."

Deen smiled, eyes trained upon the Arz as he spoke his favored line. "But today is not that day." Flakes of snow dusted his curls. His dimpled cheeks were pink from the cold, and his green coat bulged around his arms, muscled from his months in the army. "You were gone quite a while." He wrinkled his nose. "Yasmine is going to have your head."

Zafira scrunched the side of her mouth. "Not when she sees the deer I caught for the wedding feast."

Deen and his sister, Yasmine, shared the same soft beauty—hair that shone like burnished bronze, rounded features, warm hazel eyes. He was beautiful, inside and out. Yet after his parents' deaths, he had plastered on a smile that Zafira loathed, barely masking the torment floundering in his eyes.

A crease marred his forehead now. She knew he couldn't see much of her beneath her hood and scarf, but his concern said he saw enough.

"Are you all right? Something happened in the Arz, didn't it?"

"A little scare," she said with a smile because he knew her so well. "You know how it is."

He hummed and his eyes drifted to the dark forest again. "It's getting closer, isn't it?"

She didn't need to answer. The Arz crept closer with each passing day, spearing their borders with bladed roots and swallowing the land. If the Demenhune thought they were dying with the endless snow, it was only a matter of time before the Arz swept across their caliphate—the entire *kingdom*—leaving them for the whispers of nightmares and monsters within the absolute black.

"Last night I dreamed I was on Sharr."

Zafira froze at his words. *Sharr.* What were the odds, hearing the name of that forsaken place twice in one morning? It was an island of evil, a place warned of in the dead of night beneath the flicker of a lantern. A fear just out of reach because it lived beyond the Arz.

It had been a prison fortress before it had stolen the Sisters and magic. Now it was wild and untamed, with oases run rampant, and it reached for Arawiya with the Arz, each tree another sentinel in its army.

"In the prison it once was?"

Deen shook his head, his gaze distant. "I was trapped inside a massive tree. Darkness like smoke. Whispers." He grimaced and looked at her. "So many whispers, Zafira."

She did not tell him of the whispers that shadowed her every waking moment.

Deen sighed. "I don't know what it means, but did it have to plague me today of all days?"

"At least today you'll have a distraction to help take your mind off it." She reached for his hand, and he slipped his gloved pinkie around hers.

"Dear snow, is that you being optimistic?"

She laughed and his face sobered as they turned back to the village, ice crunching beneath their boots.

"Do you remember Inaya?"

"The thin baker's daughter?" Zafira asked. No one baked bread in the western villages as scrumptiously as the thin baker did. His daughter was a soft-spoken girl with watchful eyes and a mane of hair as wild as a lion's.

He nodded. "The baker took a fall a few days back, and it doesn't look like he'll walk again. So word spread that she was going to take the reins."

Zafira's stomach dropped.

"The za'eem's men came this morning when she was opening shop." Deen's jaw was tight, and Zafira wanted to smooth the tension away with her fingers. "I was right there, selling skins to old Adib. One of them dragged her out. Another ordered some squat to take over and stand behind the counter, likely a man who's never kneaded bread in his life."

"And Inaya will be married in a few days to someone for whom she'll make a *good wife*," Zafira finished.

Deen murmured an affirmation.

This za'eem headed their village alone, but nearly every village head was the same. Everyone listened to the drivel of the caliph—drivel their useless sultan should have shut down but couldn't care less about. Most days, Zafira didn't even understand the point of the sultan if the caliphs were allowed to command so freely.

Worse, most villagers believed every twisted word—if the men, desperate in their need to pin blame, said the villagers would starve with a woman taking ownership of a bakery, they would believe it. The mere definition of superstition.

"Akhh, Deen, why?" Zafira's vision pulsed red, and Sukkar snorted in concern. "Then there was that other girl last month, the one caught chopping wood in the Empty Forest, where every daama man and his grandfather chops wood. As if her hands would kill those trees any more than the snow does."

Deen cast her a look. "Are you worried?"

"Worried?" Zafira almost barked out.

He smiled. "Sometimes I forget you're not like me. Just be more cautious, eh?"

"Always," she promised as they came to his and Yasmine's house.

He nodded at the door. "She doesn't know. Today doesn't feel like the right time to tell her. Especially with that goat of a za'eem coming to the wedding."

He was right. Yasmine would rip the za'eem to shreds herself. Zafira handed Sukkar's reins to Deen, and he left to take care of the deer. She trudged up the two short steps, but before she could knock, her friend yanked open the warped door, worry and fury written across her face.

"I was hoping you'd be smiling," Zafira said wryly, stepping inside.

Yasmine's scowl deepened. "Oh, I'm smiling. Kharra, I'd be smiling even wider if you had missed the wedding altogether."

Zafira clucked her tongue and shivered when the warmth of the fire touched her. "Such a foul mouth."

"It's nearly *noon*." Yasmine pressed her lips into a flat line, never one for patience, unlike Deen.

"Sabar, sabar. I have a good reason." Zafira thought of the baker's daughter, Inaya, whose wedding would not be as happy as Yasmine's. She dropped her hood and shook her dark hair free, rubbing her arms to loosen the cold that had rooted in her bones.

Baba had said the heat used to be sweltering once, with sand rising in dunes across the oasis-like caliphate. Snow had been a once-in-a-year treat, until the blizzards came and never left. It was the same day they, and those in the other caliphates, had lost the magic once housed in each of the five royal minarets.

Zafira had never known that life. When aquifers once summoned water, healers aided the injured, and ironsmiths manipulated metal. Magic was as distant as a mirage now, and the lands lay in ruin, worsening as the Arz grew.

Each caliphate had been left with some sort of curse: snow for Demenhur, desolation in Sarasin, soil destruction in once-fertile Pelusia, untamable sands in Zaram. Only Alderamin lived as it once did, selfishly isolating itself from the rest of the kingdom.

Zafira accepted a warm bowl of shorba from Yasmine and stirred the soft lentils, settling before the fire. She rubbed at the ache in her chest that panged whenever she thought of the magic she had never had the chance to experience. Of the sand that had never trickled between her fingers or shifted beneath her feet.

Yasmine sat down and tucked her sweeping ankle-length gown beneath her thighs. It was unadorned and threadbare, but Yasmine glowed even in her rags. Zafira could only imagine how she would look dressed for the wedding.

Skies. This very evening.

"I'm expecting a believable reason for your delay, but guess what?" Yasmine asked as lentils melted on Zafira's tongue.

"I don't know if I should play this on your wedding day," Zafira said. They'd been preparing for weeks, but she still wasn't ready to see Yasmine with another, with beautiful half-Sarasin Misk Khaldun. There would be no sleeping over when the loneliness in her own house became too heavy to bear. There would be no curling herself against Yasmine's side like a lost child.

"Such a bore. I pity anyone who dreams of the mysterious Hunter every night."

"I am not a bore."

Yasmine barked a laugh. "Sometimes." Then she dropped her voice to a whisper. "*Most times.*"

Zafira scowled.

"I hate it when you play safe, old woman. But," Yasmine teased, "rumor has it the caliph is in the House of Selah. So close to us!"

"I don't see how that's exciting," Zafira said. In fact, her blood started to boil when the murmur of the silver-cloaked woman's voice echoed in her head again. *Huntress.* Along with the thought of the baker's daughter. Had Ayman, the Caliph of Demenhur, heard of the Hunter? It wasn't as though anything exciting ever happened in Demenhur that might overshadow her.

Yasmine pushed her shoulder. "Oi. What if he's here for the wedding?"

Zafira laughed at that. "Yes, I'm sure the old man traveled all the way here to watch you get married." She leaned into the fire, inhaling the warmth.

"And if he— Wait. What happened?" Yasmine fixed Zafira with her feline stare, laughter diminished.

Zafira sat back with a blink. "What do you mean?"

Yasmine leaned closer, burnished bronze hair shimmering in the firelight. "Your face is like Deen's terrible meat wraps; you can never hide anything. What happened?"

Zafira licked her lips. The Ra'ad siblings knowing she was the Arz Hunter came with its own headaches, like the one forming right now.

"I caught a pretty large deer. Should feed more people tonight if we can get it cooking." Zafira downed her shorba and slipped her tongue out to catch the last of the lentils. Yasmine shouldn't have to worry on her wedding day. "Let me help Deen."

She started to get up, but Yasmine pulled her back down with a sharp yank on her cloak, and Zafira sat with an exaggerated sigh.

"You never help Deen when you get home—he must be taking care of it right now," Yasmine snapped. "Tell me what happened."

"Let's talk about something else. Like Misk," Zafira suggested hopefully.

Yasmine snorted and pulled a cushion onto her lap. It was one of three, worn and holey. They once belonged to Yasmine and Deen's parents, apothecaries who had died years ago when the Sarasin caliph launched an attack on Demenhur's borders. He was always leaving behind leagues of dead, or ghostly homes, their inhabitants stolen as prisoners of war. Yasmine and Deen's parents had been of the former group.

Deen had fallen in the depthless between. He was a ghost of the living, a prisoner who roamed free.

He had been a soldier then, but never since. Watching loved ones die would make even the worst of men desert an army destined for death. Not that he *had* deserted. Not that the rest of the army cared.

"Zafira, please," Yasmine said, the ache in her voice pulling a cord in Zafira's heart. Firelight cast shadows on her face. "You know we might not get a chance like this for some time. To sit here side by side. Alone."

Zafira squeezed her eyes closed. Skies, she knew. Yasmine madly loved Misk, and he promised a life far better than this. Zafira didn't envy their love; she had learned to accept it during the many moons Misk spent courting Yasmine. But a wedding was different. *Final*, somehow, and she just didn't know how to continue without her friend being hers alone anymore.

She opened her eyes. Yasmine was staring, waiting.

"I know, Yasmine. I know." Zafira bit her lip and picked a handful of words. Lying wasn't her greatest asset, so the short truth would have to suffice. "I was ambushed by a couple of Sarasins on monstrous horses that made Sukkar look like a dog. So I . . . led them into the Arz and escaped. I don't think they're dead." *Yet.*

Yasmine's eyes glowed like Zaramese honey in a ray of light.

"You escaped and they didn't? That's it? Why were they even there? They could've been assassins, Zafira."

She doubted that. "They seemed a little too big for hashashins."

"Oh, so you're an expert on hashashin sizing now? Sarasins know what they're doing."

"If they knew what they were doing, they wouldn't have been trying to capture me for the sultan," she said. "I've done nothing wrong to be persecuted."

Yasmine's eyebrows rose. "Kharra. Zafira, the sultan. Imagine if he had sent his son. You wouldn't stand a chance against the Prince of Death."

Zafira shivered. Whenever she wished the sultan would die, she was slapped with the reminder of his successor: the crown prince, whose death count was so high, he was said to have stopped washing the blood from his hands.

"Why?" Yasmine's voice rose. "Why can't you stop this foolishness? Stop pretending to be a man—stop hiding yourself. Meet with the caliph and his officials, show them who you are, and I'm certain they'll send aid for the hunts. You're helping your people. There's no shame in that."

"I never said there was," Zafira lashed out. "But who's a caliph to stop a sultan?"

Yasmine's eyes flashed. "Who knows if the sultan actually sent the Sarasins? We don't know what's happening up north, now that the sultan has killed the Sarasin caliph. You don't know what they truly wanted."

Perhaps word was spreading of what she could do when so many could not. That a mysterious man was entering the absence of light and returning sane and in one piece. The fire hissed and shadows danced across the room.

"Do you really think the caliph will hate you for being a woman?" Yasmine asked.

This argument was one they'd had far too often, and Zafira was daama tired of it. Yasmine knew what happened in the villages—why couldn't she understand that Zafira was no different from a girl baking bread?

"He won't hate me, but he will twist my very existence. Do you think seeing a woman won't make them rethink my every accomplishment? I'm no different than the scores of other girls frowned upon. Look at how they point fingers at the Six Sisters. Look at our women. They listen to this drivel that we are incapable, that we are to blame for every wrong, that we must lose all freedom when we marry—" Zafira stopped, skin burning.

She couldn't shame marriage on Yasmine's wedding day, not when the sister of her heart had wanted this for so long.

"I'm losing nothing by marrying Misk," Yasmine said, voice soft. "I'm *gaining* something."

But Zafira, and most women, didn't have what Yasmine did: a man who loved her more than the word could express. A man who treated her as an equal, maybe even more.

"I don't know, Yasmine," she whispered, digging her nails into her palms and leaving little crescent moons in her skin. She dropped her gaze to the henna curling along Yasmine's arms, her smooth skin aglow in the firelight. This was what was expected of women. To look pretty, to be married. Not for them to hunt in the darkness of the Arz. Not for them to gut bloody meat and feed the people of her village.

Yasmine shook her head. "*I* do. It doesn't matter what you are. You are your strength. Why must you prove the lie that they are better than us by deluding yourself and hiding beneath a man's clothes? Think of all the women you can help by being *you*."

Silence, and then Yasmine's voice in a harsh whisper.

"What are you waiting for, Zafira?"

She grabbed the empty bowl and made for the kitchen. Zafira opened her mouth. The women Misk had promised to send to help Yasmine dress for the wedding would be here any moment now. She didn't want the conversation to end like this.

She didn't know what she was waiting for. But there was something, wasn't there? Something more she needed to prove.

Conquering the Arz wasn't enough.

Zafira wasn't like Yasmine, who wore confidence like a second skin. Whose generous curves were the envy of the masses *because* she was proud of them. Zafira shied from pride; she shied from herself.

The door flew open.

"I've skinned the deer, Yasmine," Deen called. He trudged inside and smiled when he saw Zafira by the fire. "Ah, you're still here."

His right sock was torn, revealing one of his toes as he crossed the scarred stone floor. "Akhh, Zafira. You look like you've been given Yasmine's infamous mincing."

Zafira's laugh was shaky. His eyes sparkled and fell to her lips before he looked down at his hands. Her breath hitched.

"I just came to grab a few things," he said. "The deer is a little bigger than usual."

"Are you complaining?" she teased. Or tried to. Everything felt heavier with Yasmine's words and the intent in Deen's eyes.

"Never," he said, finding what he needed. He held up a heavy-toothed knife. "I'll see you later?"

"If the bride allows. You know how she is."

He laughed as he closed the door behind him, the fire crackling in the silence.

She exhaled and looked up to find Yasmine leaning against the hallway entrance, half draped in shadows. Watching her.

"One day, someone will bring color to those dead cheeks of yours." She looked wistful.

"Don't count on it, Yasmine. I've never blushed," Zafira said, suddenly tired. She arranged the cushions again, tracing a fading pattern with her finger. She didn't see marriage in her future, or love. "Demenhune rarely do. *You* don't, and Misk looks at you like he could light the entire village on fire."

Yasmine shook her head. "There are things a person knows. I know he's out there, that someone. Probably as grumpy as you. He'll look into those icy eyes of yours and make you blush and wish you could begin all over again. I just know it." Yasmine's forlorn tone didn't match her hopeful words.

Zafira's mother once had someone like that. Umm had stood by Baba until his death, and now she existed without living. Alive, yet dead. It was thoughts of Umm and Baba that wrenched at Zafira's soul and reminded her that she was nothing but a broken girl pretending to be someone else, trying to raise a sister in a place too cold for life. Her heart still struggled to pull the shattered pieces of itself together again, to make her whole.

The blood that ran through her veins rushed with dispassion, not love, not a desire for life in a place where everyone smiled and laughed while the cold ate at their bodies and the lack of magic withered their cores. Where even the eminent Bakdash parlor was still open and bustling, serving iced cream to the people even as they shivered and craved warmth.

Zafira gathered the shards of her broken heart. She lifted her hood, and Umm and Baba faded away. Yasmine was wrong. Zafira would never make the mistake of falling in love.

There was no point to a feeling that fleeted. To a love she would be destined to lose.

CHAPTER 4

NASIR FELT LIGHTER, DESPITE THE NEW DEATH ON his growing list. He supposed he should feel guilt for killing a man whose only crime was curiosity. But he had killed for less.

Afya seemed subdued on the ride back, as if she knew what act he had committed. They passed buildings and houses in a blur of dark sand and then a single flag bearing the Sarasin emblem, an eclipsed sun with a sword through its center, before they crossed the border between Sarasin and Sultan's Keep. The difference was stark—the skies brightened, the sun heavied. The sands churned flaxen.

The homes on the outskirts of Sultan's Keep were cobbled together with tan stone and flat roofs, doors of dark wood with copper-accented arches desperately shrouding the truth of the slums. The inhabitants had flocked here to Arawiya's grand capital for a better life close to the sultana, the immortal safi who had saved Arawiya from collapsing after the Sisters disappeared.

The sultana was dead now, and her husband—Nasir's father—was a monster. He was *now* a monster.

Closer to the palace, the houses were fewer and larger, sprawling with their own minarets and pointed copper domes, latticed stone leading to immaculate courtyards. Nasir doubted the people who lived in them were any happier than those in the slums.

His route didn't take him through the sooq. A mercy, for the last thing he needed was the streets to fall silent and the overzealous to drop to their knees. This route was quieter, though he passed several roaming merchants. One barreled a wagon full of Pelusia's bright persimmons and dusky grapes, sacks of olives running low. Another pushed a smaller wagon with wares of silver, his path set on the richer end of the sultan's city.

The familiar shadows of the Sultan's Palace fell upon the road. Unlike the heart of the man sitting upon the throne, the palace was an object of beauty. It stretched in a mass of limestone and detailed carvings, trelliswork giving glimpses of the shadows within. The tan stone had been polished to a gleam, competing with the minarets rising to the skies. The golden domes were cut with rays of obsidian from the volcanic mountains of western Alderamin, their spires ending in curves shaped like water drops. A reminder that without water, the people were nothing but carcasses for the hungry sands.

The guards surrounding the black gates leaped to attention when the sentry announced Nasir's arrival. He swung from Afya's back and dropped his hood, running his fingers through his unruly hair to clear it of sand before tossing the reins to whichever man scrambled forward to catch them.

"Ensure she's tended for."

"Yes, my prince," the guard hurried to say.

Nasir stepped through one of the pointed arches and into the tiled courtyard. Out of habit, he dipped a finger into the fountain in its center, staining the waters pink. Why the sultana had commissioned a fountain in resemblance to a lion, Nasir never knew. He had never questioned his mother, only appreciated her existence until she was taken from him.

He paused before the double doors and noted the undulation of the guards' throats as they grasped the copper handles. *Fear.* Carefully cultivated, easily sustained.

Inside, the air was still and his footsteps echoed. Darkness wrapped a suffocating cloak around him. On the gilded balcony above, maids and servants bowed and scurried away like the rats they were, darting in and out of rooms. The palace was so dark, one couldn't tell the difference between rat and man anyway.

The only refuge from the shadows were dim torches lit along the way, and nothing stood in the light for long.

Nasir made his way to the stairs as a servant ambled from the opposite corridor, carefully balancing a platter of qahwa. Surprise struck the servant's solemn features when he saw the prince, and the tray tipped. Too late, the man pitched forward to steady it, crashing into Nasir in the process.

The servant dropped to his knees and whimpered—*whimpered*—beside the tarnished silver platter. Dark qahwa bled from the brass dallah.

A thousand memories flickered through Nasir's mind, flashes he had long since filed away. Coffee spilling. Cups shattering. A burning slap. He swallowed and blinked—a weakness, there and gone between heartbeats.

"Forgive me," the servant half squeaked.

Nasir's thoughts stumbled to a halt. *Don't think, mutt,* he imagined the sultan saying.

"Silence. Get this cleaned." His words were low, carefully neutral, but his pulse had quickened like a spooked child's. Two nearby maids hurried to help, and Nasir stepped over them. He didn't have to look back to know that the starved servant was nodding, eyes closed in gratitude—gratitude that Nasir hadn't ordered to have him beaten for the heinous act of spilling coffee. He clenched his jaw. Every daama time a servant associated him with the sultan, he only loathed himself more.

"Nasir! You have returned so soon," a cheery voice called. Nasir screwed his eyes shut before cooling his features. *When did that damned staircase get so far away?*

Sultan Ghameq's prized General al-Badawi wore a wolfish grin, oblivious to the servants mopping at the floor.

"Did you enjoy seeing the children in the camel races?" he asked, dusky blue eyes bright in the dim foyer. Anger feathered his jaw, revealing how he felt about those helpless children thrown atop the camels. At last, rage for something that wasn't Nasir's doing.

"I don't have time for this, Altair." Nasir turned to leave.

"So excited to see the sultan, eh? No doubt eager to put your tongue to his sandal."

Nasir wanted to tear Altair's carefully styled turban off his hair—which brushed the back of his neck as Nasir's did, the copycat—and shove it down his pretty throat. He was a person one would call beautiful, but the parts of his interior that bubbled to the surface were hateful. As if he had been *born* to hate Nasir.

But Nasir couldn't hate Altair back, for his hateful words tended to hold truth.

"Another word and you'll find my sword at your throat," Nasir growled.

"Easy, hashashin," Altair said, raising his hands. "Speaking of hashashins, the ones your father sent to bring back the Demenhune Hunter failed miserably. They never even returned! Who knew the Hunter was a cold-blooded murderer much like yourself?"

"So I'm to retrieve him?" Nasir's lips dipped into a frown. He had never been tasked with bringing back the people he found. He killed them.

Altair shrugged and placed a hand on the dagger at his waist. He couldn't have been much older than Nasir, but he acted as if everything were a jovial affair. "The sultan has moved on to plan *ba* and wants to see you. Something about a man named Haytham?"

This was how their every conversation passed: with gibes Nasir ignored as best as he could. If it was his status Altair hated him for, Nasir would have given him princedom with a smile.

Altair watched with the eyes of a hawk, noting the exact moment his words struck, before he laughed and strode down the hall with the ease of a prince himself. The last Nasir heard was his rich voice calling to one of the few courtiers idling about.

"Yalla, fetch my falcon. I'm hungry for a hunt."

——◆——

"Nasir."

Sultan Ghameq's voice floated from the balcony above. Nasir looked to where emirs usually waited for entrance into the upper throne room, but there were no officials in sight now, only his father.

Ghameq's copper skin was shadowed by a beard shorter than his fist, whereas Nasir's was cut close to his skin. The sultan studied his son, turban swallowing light. He had completed the job much too soon, hadn't he?

"You are getting better at this."

Much too soon, indeed.

"Do you have another?" Nasir asked in a toneless voice that had taken years to perfect.

"Bloodthirsty, are we?" the sultan asked, raising one dark eyebrow. A thousand answers rose to Nasir's lips, but only silence stretched between them. This was the palace of Arawiya. The center of power for five caliphates and hundreds of thousands of people. But it was empty. Ghostly. It had been *missing* something ever since the sultana's death.

A glint caught his eye—the inscribed, rusted medallion that always hung from the sultan's neck, partially shrouded by his layered black thobe. Nasir stiffened his shoulders against a shudder. He was a hefty man, the sultan. Bulked with muscle and strength.

Nasir knew all about that strength.

"Are you just going to stand there, mutt?" Ghameq watched for Nasir's flinch, which never came. As disgusted as it made him feel, the word was practically Nasir's nickname.

"Wash the blood from your hands and fetch the boy. We have a meeting with Haytham."

Old news, Sultani. For there was one thing Nasir could always count on Altair to do: never lie.

"I've received news a Sarasin contingent is missing," Nasir said quickly, referencing a report he had received earlier that morning. He wouldn't bother mentioning the men sent to find the Demenhune Hunter, a fool's errand from the start. A contingent, however, was too big a disappearance to ignore.

"And?" the sultan asked, nostrils flaring. That anger, increasing.

"They were my responsibility," Nasir said, limiting his words. "Now they are missing."

"Only you could lose an entire contingent of the greatest army in Arawiya." More insults and not a hint of surprise. There wasn't even a shift in the man's features.

He knows. Nasir exhaled. "Where have you moved them? We had no right touching Sarasin in the first place. Why haven't you appointed another caliph? Do you intend to rule as caliph and sultan?"

In the silence, a flicker of fear burned in Nasir's stomach before he strangled it to death.

Finally, the sultan spoke. "Do not question me, boy. They are my blood. I will do as I please."

"You lost claim to Sarasin blood the moment you sat on Arawiya's throne." Nasir clenched his jaw, knowing he had depleted his allotted words.

"When will you pay heed to your own concerns?" the sultan thundered.

Nasir kept his voice level. "I'm the prince, Sultani. An entire body of armed men gone missing is cause for my concern."

"No, scum. You are nothing."

Nasir touched two fingers to his brow and left to fetch the boy. Sometimes he wondered why he even tried.

———◆▶

No one had ever expected the Sisters to die—not even they *themselves* expected to. Had the sultana not arrived at that crucial moment of ruin, Arawiya would have collapsed entirely. She had lifted the ropes and held their kingdom together, ensuring some sense of order. She had been just, smart, wise. Strong. Yet Nasir never understood how Ghameq had forced her to leave him the crown that should have been Nasir's by succession.

Not that Nasir wanted it. He wasn't ready for such a responsibility; he doubted he would ever be.

Scarcely a year after her announcement of the succession, the sultana was pronounced dead from a grave illness that spurred the people into a panic, for safin were immortal. Their hearts slowed once they reached full maturity, and they didn't die from mortal ailments.

Safin rarely died without a blade to their throats.

Nasir agreed, for he knew how his mother had breathed her last.

And now more than Arawiya's crown lay in the sultan's grasp. A caliphate did, too.

The dungeon lock fell away with an echoing *clang*, and the door swung into a barren room where a boy of eight huddled against the wall. As Nasir's eyes adjusted to the bleakness, he wondered if Altair knew of the boy shivering in the damp cold of the dungeons. Nasir hadn't even known until a few days ago. Then again, Nasir knew very little about the royal agenda.

When he stepped within the clammy confines of the palace dungeons, they fell silent. Despite the dark, they always knew when he entered, and no one breathed a sound.

If he were truly his father's son, he would have basked in their fear, but he was his mother's son, too, and it only sickened him.

He stepped into the boy's cell, clenching his teeth against the stench of rot and feces. "Get up."

The young Demenhune eyed the lash in Nasir's hand and stood, teetering on his feet. He had been here for half a moon, no more, but already his bones jutted, his hair lay lackluster, and his skin was duller. He shuffled forward, the grit of sand scraping stone loud in the hushed silence. Nasir threw a dusty cloak around his shoulders.

"Baba?" the boy said.

"You will see him," Nasir replied softly, and in the harsh darkness, the curve of the boy's small shoulders relaxed, content with the mere chance of seeing his father.

Beside the door, the guard glanced at the boy's cloak, then dared to flick his gaze to Nasir, who paused without turning his head.

"Something wrong, guard?" he asked, looking ahead. He made the word sound like a curse.

"N-no, my liege," the guard murmured.

Nasir cut his gaze to him, and the guard dropped his head. He waited a touch longer, until he caught the flare of the guard's nostrils, fear reinstated. Then he tightened his grip on the lash and pushed the boy toward the stone stairs.

Yalla, he wanted to snap as the boy's palm slid along the onyx railing. At the top, Nasir removed the cloak and shoved it behind a cupboard. The boy's small chest rose with a deep inhale before the door to the sultan's chambers opened.

The sultan was seated on the black majlis sofa that covered half of the main room. He was barefoot and cross-legged, his sandals a hairbreadth away on the ornate Pelusian rug. He looked less kingly, seated on the floor. A scribe was kneeling before him.

Black scrolls were in the sultan's hands.

Every week, the scrolls were brought to the sultan, a new record of Arawiya's dead. Most of the scrolls listed out the men who had perished while mining in the Leil Caves of Sarasin because of a collapsed wall, a beating, or worse—the quiet deaths in which entire groups were attacked by invisible fumes that blocked their lungs, suffocating them until they heaved their last.

Until this day, the scrolls had sat untouched in a basket beside the sultan's throne, boiling Nasir's blood. Now, he stilled at the impossible sight before him.

The sultan tapped a finger on a scroll. "I want these fumes harvested."

"Sultani?" stammered the scribe, stilling his hand across the papyrus. Ink dripped from his reed pen.

"These fumes. The vapors that suffocated these men," the sultan said thoughtfully.

The scribe nodded, jerky and fervent.

"I want them harvested or replicated and then contained and brought to me."

Ah. That was more like his father.

"I do not think we know how, Sultani," the scribe said quietly.

Disgust twisted the sultan's face. "I know you're all witless. Have 'Uday take the coterie of Pelusians to the caves and give them what they need. I want this done quickly." Nasir doubted the delegation of Pelusians living in Sultan's Keep enjoyed being ordered about. "Now get out."

The scribe murmured his respects and hurried from the room, thobe shuffling.

"Fumes," Nasir said when they were alone. He wanted to pronounce the word as a question, but his pride refused.

"Set the fire," Ghameq said instead, and met his gaze when Nasir didn't move at once. Nasir clenched his teeth, wanting to demand an answer, but the little boy was a risk.

So after one lengthy moment, Nasir left him shivering by the door and lit the fire. *Coward. Coward. Fool.*

There was only one reason for a fire in the midday heat. And the more Nasir played with magic, the more dangerous the line he trod. Rarely a day passed in which the sultan didn't order Nasir to assist him with its use.

Perhaps the magic that once lit the royal minarets was clean and good, but this anomaly was nothing near it. This was a hell of its own.

And he did not know where it came from.

The sultan toyed with the antique circle at his chest. Nasir had touched it once, that medallion. Darkness had seized his mind, whispers and half-crazed screams echoing in his ears when his fingers passed over the inscriptions in the ancient tongue. It was a darkness wrought with pain, a darkness that could never end.

It was a darkness that despaired in itself.

The medallion was special, and the fact that it was with the sultan at all times made it even more so. And if Ghameq saw the same darkness, he welcomed it.

The fire roared to life, and the sultan stood. Sweat trickled down Nasir's back when he reached for the poker, his palm slick against the metal. He was very well capable of using it himself, but he passed it to his father.

The poker. Burning flesh. A scream. He squeezed his eyes shut and released a quivering breath. It was a weakness he wished he didn't have to display, and with it came a lick of shame at his neck.

"You are still weak," the sultan murmured as he stoked the fire.

Nasir quelled the ire that quaked at the tips of his fingers. "I'm worn out, Sultani." *And there will come a time when I won't be.*

"Hmm," the sultan said absently, as if he had heard Nasir's unspoken words. "One day, you will see the flaw in your ways, in your curse of compassion, and understand what I've wanted for you from the beginning."

But his father *hadn't* wanted this from the beginning. There was a time when he, too, had valued compassion. Nasir thought he remembered the curve of a smile and a palace flooded with light. He held that flickering memory close, but with each passing day, it only withered further. Was this what Owais had been trying to understand?

The boy crouched and reached a careful hand for a grape in the bowl by the sultan's sandals, and Nasir waited until he swallowed his stolen prize before handing Ghameq the leather folder.

He stepped back. The farther from this abomination of magic he could be, the better.

Ghameq flipped open the sleeve and tossed a strip of papyrus into the fire, its surface covered in words the near-black of blood.

Dum sihr. Blood magic, punishable by death and forbidden by the Sisters, for it allowed a person to practice magic of their choosing with the price of blood. Without it, the masses were restricted to the one affinity they were born with. But Ghameq was the sultan. He could do as he wished. What Nasir didn't understand was *how* he could use magic if it no longer existed.

He knew the Silver Witch was somehow involved—that woman who frequented the palace as if she were a sultana herself. She was the one who provided Ghameq with the strips of papyrus wrought with blood. Blood that somehow played the part of both wielder and vessel itself.

The flames crackled and burst open, fading to the color of Pelusian eggplants. The room exploded in hue and heat as a silhouette rose from the flames, giving shape to a pale face with dark eyes and the stringy beard of a man who was alive and whole in Demenhur: Haytham, wazir to the Caliph of Demenhur.

Rimaal. The Demenhune never failed to spook him; they looked like ghosts—pale, ethereal, and strangely beautiful. Like Altair, they were full of light, but *too* much light, as if snow flowed through their delicate veins.

"Where is he?" Haytham, unwilling traitor to his caliph, rasped. He darted quick glances behind him, to a room unseen.

"Here," Nasir said.

"Baba!" the boy whimpered when Nasir guided him closer.

Haytham's strangled cry sent a sob through the boy, and Nasir tightened his grip around his shoulders.

"Give him to me, I beg you," said the wazir. *Pathetic.*

"Begging changes nothing," Nasir said, and the sultan stepped forward.

Men cowered before Haytham. His strength as wazir was the only reason the Caliph of Demenhur still stood. Yet even with an entire caliphate between them, Haytham's fear was instant. Nasir noted it in the stilling of his form and the tightening of his jaw.

Haytham dropped to his knees. "Sultani."

"Get up," Ghameq said in staid condescension. "Has the Silver Witch approached Ayman?"

Nasir stiffened. Those were not two people to appear in the same sentence, let alone the same room. Ayman was a good caliph, if there was one. He wouldn't tolerate a meeting with the likes of the silver-cloaked witch. Even so, she was familiar enough. Ghameq could have asked her himself.

He doesn't trust her.

Haytham stared at his son. His loyalty to his caliph ranked higher than loyalty to his sultan, but his love for his son exceeded all else. He closed his eyes and the answer was *yes*, or there would be no hesitation. The sultan turned to the boy, and Nasir wanted to shove him into the shadows, away from that malevolent gaze.

"She has," Haytham said. "They met in the House of Selah by the western villages. We do not know to whom her letter was delivered, but we hope it was the Hunter. I know nothing else, Sultani."

At the mention of the Hunter, the sultan's eyes lit up. If there was anything more unnerving than the Demenhune, it was the Hunter. Nasir didn't know if everyone in Arawiya knew of him, but Nasir knew enough.

No one else could do what the Hunter could. Nasir had tried it himself. On an assassination errand, he had detoured to the Arz. The moment he set both feet into the forest, an impossible darkness had swarmed and the way out had disappeared. It had taken him hours to get back, and he had been breathless for days, heart stuttering at every little sound.

He was an assassin, stealthy, deadly, feared. Yet he had never felt such fear in his life—he had very nearly drowned from it.

The magic of the Arz and the magic of the medallion around Sultan

Ghameq's neck *had* to be one and the same. It wasn't fueled by what once lit the minarets. This magic was limitless, dark, endless.

"Does the quest begin in two days?" the sultan asked.

"We believe so," answered the wazir.

What quest? Haytham's fiery body wavered, flames casting long shadows in the room. Nasir tugged at the neckline of his thobe as sweat beaded on his skin.

"My son, Sultani. Why have you taken my son?" Haytham blustered.

Not even Nasir, the daama crown prince, knew the answer to that.

"Ensure the caliph will stand before the Arz when the quest begins, and your son will be returned to you unharmed."

"Before the Arz? But——" Haytham stopped, and Nasir made the realization as he did. "You mean to kill him."

The sultan denied nothing. First the Caliph of Sarasin. Then the army and the gas from the Leil Caves, and now this mysterious quest. The Demenhune caliph. Haytham looked at his son again, and amid the fire, the pain in his eyes shone.

"Accidents happen often in these strange times, wazir," the sultan mused. "And if you find your throne cold and empty, sit on it."

Understanding dawned in Haytham's eyes. He was to be a pawn. Because a throne with a pawn upon it was infinitely more useful than an empty one. The sultan could control Sarasin easily enough from Sultan's Keep, but Demenhur was much too far and expansive, and the people less in favor. With his son in danger, Haytham would be the perfect, obedient puppet.

Haytham threw a glance at something behind him, his hair glowing purple. The shift bathed the room in purple, too, and the boy drank in the sight with wide eyes and parted lips. Nasir loathed his childish innocence.

"Will you or will you not do as I've asked?" The sultan's voice was hard.

Haytham paused. His son leaned closer, catching every word.

"He will be there." Haytham's voice cracked with his oath. "Please— please don't hurt my boy."

If Ayman was soft, Haytham was hard. He was the one who kept Ayman standing, who kept order in Demenhur, one of the largest caliphates of Arawiya. But in that moment, Nasir had never seen a weaker man. *Love makes men weak.*

"He is safe so long as you cooperate," the sultan said, as if promising Haytham he would water his weeds.

Safe? In a damp, cold dungeon that would kill him before anything else?

Haytham opened his mouth, to beg again by the look in his eyes, but the sultan threw a single black seed into the flames. The Demenhune and the fire disappeared.

"Take him back," Ghameq said in the sudden silence.

There were a million things Nasir wanted to say. A million words and a hundred questions. "He will come prepared," he managed finally. Haytham. Ayman. They weren't fools.

The sultan didn't even spare Nasir a glance. "He will come prepared for you, not for an entire contingent of Sarasin forces armed without blades."

Nasir froze. Slaughter and suffocation. That Sarasin contingent hadn't gone *missing*; Ghameq had merely given them a new order. He was already commanding the army he lawfully could not.

The Sultan of Arawiya planned to have them suffocate the innocents of Demenhur's western villages and make sure the caliph was among them.

With the attack coming from a caliphate, rather than the sultan, there would be no more skirmishes for expanding borders. There would be war.

The caliphs existed to hold the sultan in check, just as the sultan existed to hold the caliphs in order. They were very nearly kings themselves, the sultan merely stewarding them all. A fail-safe left by the Sisters to ensure balance.

What was Ghameq trying to do?

Nasir opened his mouth, but he was an assassin, and his hands were steeped in blood—how could he argue against the death of innocents? He pressed his lips together.

And like the mutt that I am, I will do everything he says.

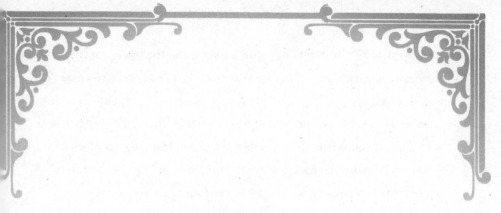

CHAPTER 5

ZAFIRA'S HOUSE WAS THE LAST IN THE VILLAGE AND closest to the Arz, making it easy for her to switch between herself and the Hunter. Still, she breathed a relieved sigh when she snapped the latch of her front door into place.

A fire crackled in the hearth, and Lana was sprawled across the cushions of their majlis, asleep. The village news scroll lay in her lap, along with the latest edition of *al-Habib*. The periodical was worn and tattered from the many hands that had perused it before hers. It was full of gossip, short stories, and the latest happenings from around the kingdom. The faltering caliphates and lack of magic meant the editions were few and far between, but that only made them more cherished.

Al-Habib was aniconic and abstract, rife with calligraphic art. Zafira never had the patience for them, but she had always wished for depictions giving faces to the names, if only so she had an image of the caliph and the sultan in her head to hate. The crown prince to fear. The immortal safin to understand.

Light freckles dusted Lana's glowing skin, and the orange of the flames danced in her dark hair. If life were simpler, Zafira might have envied her sister's beauty.

She slipped out of her boots and crossed the foyer, digging her heels into the little bumps so she could feel the stone. Hanging her cloak on the polished knob by the hall, she went to remove her satchel and froze. A square was tucked between the folds. *Parchment.*

Silver as a crescent moon, crimson as fresh blood.

She threw a quick glance at Lana and pulled it out with careful fingers. The silver winked in the frail firelight. It hummed. Beckoned like the Arz. Her breath escaped haltingly.

Open me, the parchment seemed to whisper. The dangerous curve of the silver-cloaked woman's smile flashed in her mind, and she turned it over slowly. Angled creases and an unbroken seal—a letter, reminding her of a woman who did not exist.

The words *bint Iskandar* were wrought upon the silver. Daughter of Iskandar.

A hammering started in her chest, yet she held deathly still when Lana shifted on the cushions, murmuring something about Deen in her sleep. Zafira pursed her lips and broke the seal, brushing her thumb over the geometric emblem, the slender curve of a crescent moon in its center. Arawiyan script scrawled across the page.

Peace unto you, esteemed one.

You have been invited upon a journey of a lifetime. To an isle where nature has no limits and darkness holds all secrets.

Why should you desire to venture to such a place, you ask? Oh, dear one. For the retrieval of magic in the form of an ancient book known as the lost Jawarat.

Glory and splendor. The past once more.

Your quest begins two dawns hence, at the mouth of the Arz.

Zafira read it again and again, finding it harder to breathe with each pass. The words coiled in her, strangled her heart.

Magic. A journey to Sharr, for there was no other island in existence. To retrieve *magic*. To restore Arawiya to its former glory and do away with the Arz. With this *lost Jawarat*. She racked her brain for the meaning in the ancient tongue. *Lost Jewel.*

She dropped the letter back in her bag with trembling fingers.

Was this why the caliph was in the House of Selah, a quarter-day's ride from here? The western villages were small, the poorest in Demenhur, especially when compared to the majestic capital of Thalj, four days from the outskirts where Zafira lived.

Sweet snow below. *Two days from now.* Sharr and magic and—

Her thoughts screeched to a halt: the silver-cloaked woman *was* real. *She* had left this in Zafira's satchel. There had been no one else in crimson and silver. But how real was this invitation, this quest? The existence of magic?

As much as the woman spooked her, Zafira would endure another meeting just so she could make sense of everything.

She pulled the letter from her satchel again. She needed to hold it. Feel it. Read the words again and again, drunk on something unseen. The shuffle of a blanket broke the silence, and she deftly slipped the silver parchment away again as Lana sat up.

"Okht!"

Zafira would never grow weary of hearing that sweet voice say "sister."

"How's Umm?" she asked with a smile, eyeing their mother's closed door. The letter called to her racing heart.

"Asleep. I don't think she'll be coming to the wedding," Lana said. She had Baba's eyes, soft and brown, but a more haunted version of them. Lana was the one who soothed Umm's nightly episodes of denial, restless by her side. Zafira harbored an endless chasm of guilt because of it, and it suffocated her now until she broke away from her sister's gaze.

The Hunter and the Nurse. That was what Baba had called his girls when he would accompany Zafira into the Arz and little Lana would assist Umm in gathering Demenhur's scarce herbs. Little did he know how much of a nurse Lana would be after their mother's nightmares began.

"You look tired. How was the hunt?" Lana asked, making room for her.

"Good," Zafira said with a shrug, but she didn't miss how Lana's eyes narrowed. As much as she loved Yasmine, Zafira didn't always adore her adamant questioning and her demeaning of the Hunter's masquerade. It was far easier with Lana, who looked at Zafira as something akin to a hero. "All right, all right. Maybe a little exciting, too."

She settled beside Lana and recounted her confrontation with the Sarasins, adding a few more extraneous details to spice up the tale. The letter called from the satchel on her lap, but again, she made no mention of the silver-cloaked woman. Lana's eyes danced as she hugged her tasseled blue pillow to her chest.

Zafira had gifted it to her long ago. Thanks to the skins from her hunts, they weren't the poorest people in the village, but they didn't always have dinars set aside for extravagance.

She tapped a finger to Lana's nose. "Now, we have a wedding to get to. If you're there before everyone else, you might be able to persuade the servers to give you a larger piece of dessert. You know," Zafira teased, singing her last words with a waggle of her eyebrows, "like aish el-saraya."

Lana's eyes lit up at the mention of the famous bread pudding with pistachios and cream. "Will you braid my hair?"

"And I'll even burn Umm's bakhour so you'll be the best-smelling girl at the wedding," Zafira promised, to Lana's glee. At times like these, Zafira marveled at her sister's childish antics. Her laughs and awe. Her grins and sweet words. It was hard to imagine this was the same girl of fourteen who managed the household by herself and woke in the dead of night to soothe their mother's eerie whimpers. But she was one of many girls forced to age before her time, and it was everyone's fault but little Lana's.

Oblivious to the change in Zafira's mood, Lana grabbed her hand and led her away. Zafira's bag slid to the floor, the letter within.

But first, the wedding.

———◄●►———

The sun began its descent as the crowds grew in the jumu'a. The circular, soft gray stone was heated from beneath and surrounded by the market. Rhythmic patterns leaped from its center, reaching tendrils toward the border, telling a story no one could decipher. Jumu'a stones were scattered across the five caliphates, laid by the Sisters themselves.

Baba said water used to sit beneath this stone once, cooling the ground. That was before the sand became snow. A time now foreign to every Demenhune alive, and to nearly all Arawiyans—unless they were immortal safin, with elongated ears and pride to rival a peacock's. Or more than ninety years old.

Zafira sat cross-legged on a cushion on the ground while the bride lounged regally on a decorated dais. She nudged Yasmine every so often to point out another person they hadn't seen in months.

Most of the western villagers were here in a colorful array of dazzling gowns and dark-hued thobes, hair tucked beneath wool shawls or tasseled turbans, thin bodies bulked by coats, beads and jangling jewelry. Children darted between adults, laughing and shouting. The surrounding shops had closed for the celebration, grimy windows dark, and though ornate carpets and cushions were spread generously across the expanse, most of the people hovered near the low tables laden with food.

It wasn't every day the western villages could boast a wedding, so when the occasion arose, everyone partook—lending decor, delicacies, and furnishings. Especially when it was a beauty like Yasmine, beloved by the children she tutored, admired by the women she inspirited, envied by the men who knew of her closeness to the Hunter.

Warmth from the stone crept to Zafira's cheeks, and she was torn between wanting to blend in with the crowds and wanting to savor every last moment before Yasmine was bound to another.

Her heart stuttered every time the reminder struck.

Steam curled from the roasted venison in the center of each low table, and the smell of rosemary, cinnamon, bay leaves, and garlic reached Zafira's nose even from her distance. Her mouth watered, despite her dislike for garlic. Surrounding the large platters were smaller ones: oily dolma stuffed with onions and roasted eggplants, rounds of baked kibbeh garnished with mint, the flattest of manakish laden with tangy zataar and olive oil.

It had taken many dinars, helping hands, and days of hunting to gather it all, but the look on Yasmine's face when she knew it would feed so many starving stomachs had been worth the tiring effort.

"Lana is alone," Yasmine said, ever watchful from her seat. There was an empty space beside Yasmine for her husband. *Husband.* That was going to take some getting used to.

A little ways away, Lana sat like a queen in a gown of midnight bedazzled with tiny mirrors, her shawl clutched in nervous fingers. A plate of aish el-saraya, half eaten, was balanced on her lap. Zafira had hoped the wedding would be a distraction for her sister, but it seemed more of a reminder of Lana's loneliness as a group of girls her age whispered among themselves right in front of her.

As Zafira watched, someone settled beside Lana in a close-fitting thobe, so finely spun it shimmered in the waning light, offsetting his bronze curls. Deen. Only he was as watchful as Yasmine. Only he could coax a smile so true on Lana's face.

"Not anymore," Zafira said to Yasmine, trying to make sense of the sudden barge of emotion climbing up her throat. Leave it to Deen to love someone else's sister as much as his own.

A young man sauntered up to the dais, his embroidered thobe as vain as the smirk on his face. He dragged his gaze down Yasmine's curves, and Zafira wanted to pluck his eyeballs out.

"Settling for second best because the Hunter kicked you out of his bed?" he asked the bride.

Yasmine only smiled, a picture of elegance with her hands folded in her lap. "Come close. Let me tell you a secret."

He lifted an eyebrow before latching onto his chance to near the beauty.

"I kicked him out of mine, actually," Yasmine said, ever pleasant. "He got a little boring, you know? And I'll happily kick *you* out of my wedding, if it's so hard for you to be polite."

He opened his mouth, but Yasmine wasn't finished.

"Or, the next time little Bishr comes for classes, I could tell him all about his older brother's exciting endeavors. Wait until that makes its way to your parents, hmm?"

He jerked back as if she had slapped him and awkwardly hurried away.

Yasmine lifted an eyebrow at Zafira. "And that is how you take care of them. *Without* getting your hands dirty—I could see you readying to rip his head off."

"My solutions don't involve me being insulted, but by all means, please continue," Zafira drawled.

The Hunter's secrecy had given the Ra'ad siblings a sort of prominence, for there was no better way to learn about him than through the two people who knew him—*her*.

There should never have been enough to feed the roughly three hundred people of the western villages, but there always was. Some said it was the Arz that created abundance in the small morsels, that the animals held a little bit of *other*ness, making their meat seem more. Zafira decided it was

Deen's expert distribution skills, ensuring everyone was fed at least once every few days.

Of course, Demenhur *had* livestock, but the sheep and cattle were rarely enough. And for the ones better off, nothing was more special than game from the dangerous Arz. Some traveled from around the caliphate for a piece of the Hunter's prize. They were the ones who disgusted her the most.

"Stop looking at my guests like you're about to shoot them. There's no bow in your hands *and* you're wearing a dress," Yasmine reminded her.

Zafira looked at her friend's laughing eyes, stunned once again by her ethereal beauty. Her pale gold bell-sleeved dress shimmered with iridescent beads, bronze hair pinned behind her skull. A lace shawl and a weave of white flowers sat regally atop her head. The pink brushed onto her cheeks and the dark kohl lining her eyes made her look older than her seventeen years.

"Sorry, Yasmine. There are so many eyeballs turning my way," she teased. *And a silver letter on my mind.*

Her pulse quickened. Against reason, she *wanted* to go on the quest. To claim this victory for herself. At the very least, she wanted answers. Could a book really bring back magic? Was the caliph involved? He wasn't *bad.* If, somehow, he found out she was a woman, she would find her way around. He wouldn't chop off her head.

At least, she didn't think he would.

Yet who would feed her people if she went? She *could* ask the silver-cloaked woman for venison, or money. If that mysterious woman wanted Zafira on this quest, she would need to do more than drop a letter in her bag. Then Yasmine and Deen could—

"Zafira, don't."

"Don't what?" Zafira asked, feigning innocence.

"I can see you thinking about something you don't need to think about." Yasmine sighed when Zafira didn't answer, and changed the subject. "You look nice today."

Zafira chortled and a woman nearby stared, taken aback. Nosy dunce. "*Today*, hmm? Maybe because I'm seated beside the bride and stuffed in a dress that happens to be a little too tight."

Yasmine snorted and the woman's eyeballs nearly popped out of their sockets at the girls' rogue behavior.

"I knew we should have bought you a new gown," Yasmine said. But Zafira's dress, though older, was one of her favorites. The sweeping hem was black, the fabric lightening to deep blue as it neared the neckline, which was laced with black filigree. Bold strokes of gold capped and wound down the shoulders, each swirl ending in fine points. The design was why she had spent the extra dinars on it—it reminded her of her arrows. Sleek, fierce, *and* beautiful.

Zafira opened her mouth to argue, but Yasmine continued. "And with that hair of yours done up the way it is, I'm being overlooked."

Zafira touched her hair with a careful hand. She liked the way the women had put it up in a crown, forcing her to leave her shawl at home. It made her feel pretty for once, regal even. To call Yasmine either word, however, would be a sore understatement. "Not even the moon will dare to rise tonight. How could she, in the face of such beauty?"

Yasmine dipped her head, oddly shy. She fiddled with the moonstone in her hands, the Demenhune gem she would gift Misk when the ceremony was complete. The heady scent of bakhour and the aroma of food carried on the slow breeze. Fresh snow began to fall, dusting the sooq around them, though the heated stone and flames surrounding the jumu'a kept the ground snow-free and warm.

Steam no longer rose from the platters and the venison shrank as people ate. Zafira's heart sank. It was merely food, she knew. But proof, too, that nothing good ever lasted long.

After a long moment, Yasmine said, "What if . . . tonight . . . ? I don't know."

Zafira thought about how lucky Misk was and shook her head. "You'll be perfect. He loves you, Yasmine, and you love him, and you both know it. Nothing can go wrong."

Yasmine traced a finger over the floral swirls and geometric patterns of henna offsetting her skin. Somewhere in the design, Misk's name could be pieced together. "Love. What a silly thing."

Zafira met Yasmine's eyes, and another name rose unspoken between them. *Deen.* He had given her everything, and still would, but she couldn't hand over her heart. Not after what had happened to Umm because of Baba.

"There he is!" someone shouted, and Zafira jolted, half expecting Deen to materialize before her. But the crowds were parting for Misk, dressed in a trim black thobe and deep blue turban, tassels swaying with his steps. His eyes were on Yasmine, and Zafira averted her own from the intensity in that heated look.

"You won't lose me, you know," Yasmine said softly. "I'll still be yours."

Yasmine wasn't supposed to be looking at Zafira when Misk was giving her a look like that.

"I know. I'm just being selfish."

Yasmine's lips quirked up. "You've got a lot to compete with. He *is* devilishly handsome."

Zafira's insides warmed, glad for the change in conversation. Misk *was* handsome. More so because he was different. His mother hailed from Sarasin, so with his ink-black hair and darker skin, he stood out among the Demenhune. It was a good thing he hadn't inherited the more notorious Sarasin qualities, too.

"Heart of my heart. Moon of my soul," Misk said to Yasmine, and Zafira took her friend's answering smile and locked it between her ribs. Despite their penchant for violence, Sarasins had a more soothing lilt to their tongue than the Demenhune did. Throatier and silvery at once.

Deen stepped to the other side of Misk, the shimmer of his thobe dazzling in the light. A rust-colored turban obscured almost all of his rogue curls, the fringed edge feathering his neck.

He caught her looking, and his lips curved into a hesitant smile, obscuring the haunted look in his eyes. Zafira offered a tentative smile back and wondered if he had told Yasmine about his dream, and if his dream and the letter were connected.

A pair of guards in the gray-and-blue livery of Demenhur gently parted the crowds. Heavy cloaks shrouded outfits made for the ease of running, warmth, and quick mounting. Their belts bore the seal of Demenhur—a sharp-edged snowflake in antique silver—and two sheaths. One for a jambiya, and another for a scimitar.

Pointed snowflakes aside, an ensemble like that would make for one happy Hunter. If only Zafira were as handy with a needle as she was with a bow.

The village za'eem stepped to the stone mimbar, and everyone stood. Zafira gritted her teeth at the sight of his beady eyes. Warm hands closed around hers, and she eased her clenched fists. Deen murmured her name as he pulled her to his side, and only then did she notice that everyone else had stepped back in the silence. Lana crept to Zafira's other side and grasped her hand.

"We have gathered here today for the promise of unity," began the za'eem. "Unity brought Arawiya to fruition, and unity will carry us beyond these dark days. Without it, we would still be nomads, roaming the endless sands and evading the sweltering sun, when every waking day tasted of danger."

"Akhh, the za'eem should write a book," Deen said, crossing his arms, and Zafira almost smiled at the rare appearance of his irritation.

"The Six Sisters of Old rose from chaos and disruption. They wielded magic from the unimaginable power housed in their hearts. With it, they brought us together, forging caliphates and ruling justly through the council seated in the place we now call Sultan's Keep. They gifted us their good hearts, imbuing the royal minarets with their magic, amplifying their powers so that magic extended to human- and safinkind. Giving us a greater purpose, in which our natural affinities were allowed to define our lives. A healer could heal, a fireheart could call flame."

The ache Zafira felt at the mention of magic slipped into her heart, and the letter winked in her thoughts. Her mind flashed to the Arz, and she rubbed at her chest with the back of her knuckles—would she have wielded fire or water? The ability to heal with a touch or see shards of the future?

"During that golden age, which lasted centuries, the Sisters gave each caliphate a strength the others needed to survive, furthering our unity. Demenhur provided Arawiya with herbs and remedies found nowhere else, along with the appreciation of the arts. Sarasin shared coal and minerals. Pelusia fed us every fruit imaginable and provided us with unmatched engineering, advancing us beyond imagination. Our neighbors in Zaram sailed the seas, trained our fighters, and brought back delectables from the depths of saltwater. The esteemed safin of Alderamin recorded our pasts, studying our faults to help us better ourselves, infusing Arawiya with the spirit of creativity to expand our hearts. They forbade the uncontrollable dum sihr, placing limits on magic to protect us further. Arawiya, our great kingdom, flourished."

The za'eem's voice rumbled to a stop and Zafira rocked back on her heels. *Skies. Calm down.*

Murmurs made the rounds, making it clear Zafira wasn't the only one who yearned for what they had lost and felt pride for what they had accomplished. They had lost more than magic that day. Their lands had become untamable beasts. Walls rose between the caliphates, and now a dark forest was creeping closer with each passing day.

"It was unity that gave us everything. Solidarity and love. So much has been taken from us, dear friends, for when the Sisters disappeared, they took magic with them—the very magic through which they had rooted within every caliphate a reliance so strong. We were left adrift with its disappearance. Our minarets stand in darkness. Arawiya suffers." The za'eem's lips twitched into a sad smile.

That was the one part of history Zafira refused to believe. The Six Sisters wouldn't—*couldn't*—rule steady and just for years upon years and then simply disappear, leaving their people and the land to ruin. None of that made sense.

"Despite this, we persevere," the za'eem continued. "Today's ceremony will unite not only two hearts, but, in their own small way, two caliphates, as well. Mabrook, young souls. May your hearts remain entwined beyond death."

Others echoed his congratulations, and with one last nod, the za'eem stepped away with his guards.

"Not bad, for a biased cow," Zafira said, and Deen murmured his agreement.

But instead of being inspired by the za'eem's speech, the people settled into the same small talk, as if the man had interrupted to say they would serve mint tea at the end.

They had accepted their fate of endless cold and creeping darkness. They didn't desire anything more than what they had. What life would remain to maintain if the Arz swallowed them all?

A village elder stepped forward to perform the marriage ceremony, and a hush fell over the guests when the man raised his arms. A baby cooed, and a mother quieted the little one's happiness.

Yasmine passed the moonstone to Misk, whose eyes never left hers. Deen's fingers brushed Zafira's, and she stiffened, but he merely looped his smallest finger with hers, settling the tide rapidly rising in her chest.

The elder continued, droning with slow, stretched words. Yasmine caught Zafira's gaze across the distance and rolled her eyes. Zafira cut her a glare and smothered a laugh.

"Will marriage change that, you think?" Deen asked.

She canted her head. "What?"

"Her. Her silliness. Her knack for mischief. That unbreakable stubbornness."

Zafira chose her words carefully. "He loves her as she is. Why would she need to be any different?"

"I don't know," he said, tightening his grip around her finger. "I just think that once you're bound to another, you change. That for the happiness of the one you love, and for your own, you change without knowing it."

Like Umm. Like Baba.

The elder was nearly finished. Lanterns flickered to life as the sun dipped away, the musty odor of oil clogging the air. Zafira tilted her head, wanting and not wanting to know more. "How?"

He looked at her, but she couldn't turn her face to his, because now, there were other words involved. Questions and pleas. Thoughts and futures. Invitations and denials.

His answer was soft, a brush of words against the small hairs at the shell of her ear as ululations and song permeated the still air. "I wish I knew."

CHAPTER 6

WHEN NIGHT FELL, NASIR DID NOT EXPECT TO FIND THE lanterns lit and the curtains parted, a late breeze chilling his chambers. Nor did he expect to find Altair lounging on his bed, calfskin sandals resting on his sheets.

The filthy scum.

"What are you doing in my rooms?" Nasir growled. "Who let you in? Don't you have some poor soul to seduce?"

Altair opened his mouth and paused, lifting a finger. "Which question do you want me to answer first?"

He took his time sitting up, fluffing up the pillows behind his back, making Nasir feel like *he* was the one trespassing.

The general was dressed in a deep blue turban and a russet thobe, the cuffs embroidered in gold. He caught Nasir surveying his attire. "There's a party flourishing in the Daama Faris, and I've come to ask you to join me."

You. No respect, no etiquette, no princely titles. Just *you.*

"I will not dabble in debauchery, let alone set foot in a tent full of drunkards," Nasir said as calmly as he could. "Now get off my bed."

Altair swept off the bed with dramatic movements and a heavy sigh. "It will be fun, Nasir. You could use some fun. Why, all that killing must be making you an old man. What are you now, anyway? Two hundred, two hundred and one?"

His voice was cheerful, always loud and carefree, whereas Nasir's was quiet. Too quiet, his mother used to say.

"Twenty," he spat, annoyed at himself for answering.

Altair laughed, deep and slow. And Nasir, failure that he was, remembered that he liked Altair's laugh.

"Akhh, I knew it had those two numbers in there somewhere. Where is that lovely servant of yours, by the way?" Altair clasped his hands together as he peered around the empty room. "The one you stole from your mother?"

A tremor passed over Nasir's fingers. He unclasped the outer layer of his robes, exposing his weapons to Altair's watchful eye. Despite the general's larger size, the two of them were roughly equal in skill, but Altair had his boundaries, and Nasir, hashashin that he was, had noticed them.

Altair repeatedly opened and closed the door of a lantern, filling the room with the exaggerated squeak of its hinges.

"In your own time," Nasir deadpanned.

"Your manners astound, as always," Altair proclaimed. "Where was I? Ah, your servant! I should like to witness her perfection, for she's the reason you don't 'dabble in debauchery,' isn't she?" he drawled in a comical imitation of Nasir's voice.

It wasn't. Nasir hadn't spoken to Kulsum in months. Every time she came near, he would retreat.

"Leave," Nasir said after a long pause filled with the swooshing of steel as he removed his weapons.

"Pity. I thought you might want to know about the mysterious mission, journey, quest—*thing*—the sultan is so keen about."

Nasir felt a vein feather in his jaw. Altair watched carefully, not bothering to even move toward the door as Nasir hung the rest of his weapons on the wall above his bedside table. The bastard always knew what to dangle in front of his face.

"What do you know about it?" he asked carefully, pouring himself a glass of water. Though he could have a throng of servants pouring him water, helping him change, setting his bath, he had ordered to have no one in his chambers. Monsters preferred solitude.

He sat on the edge of his bed.

Altair leaned down with a conspiratorial whisper. "More than you."

"Start talking, then," Nasir said when the water had laved his parched throat.

"Yes, my liege," Altair said mockingly, a twinkle in his eyes.

Nasir bristled at his tone and nearly tossed the glass at the general's head. "Do I need to pay you to speak? Because I'm afraid that won't be happening."

Altair scoffed. "I have an abundance of gold, shukrun. I find the best payments are always the most difficult to extract. So come with me to the Daama Faris, and we can talk over a drink."

Nasir clenched his teeth as Altair lifted two fingers to his brow in a mock salute and strolled from the room. *Weasel.*

———◄●►———

The traveling tavern slouched across the uneven sands not too far from the palace. How Altair had found this place was beyond Nasir, but that was how soldiers and their betters worked.

Stepping into the Daama Faris was like stepping into a different world, for no other place in the sultan's city was this *alive*. Nasir's ever-present irritation was placated by unfamiliar longing. His step faltered.

Such feelings weren't to be encouraged.

Nasir let the tent flap fall behind him and followed a grinning Altair inside, sidestepping the men littering the worn, faded rugs. The messy sight and the blistering heat, combined with the rowdy crowd, made his head spin. Altair greeted a few of the men by name as they wended through, and Nasir expected the tent to fall silent, to see fear in the eyes of the people surrounding him.

But they only gave him a passing glance. They didn't even recognize him.

Was this flood of freedom what it meant to go unnoticed?

Bodily odors and the stench of drink made him grit his teeth. He would leave the place with a layer of grime on his clothes. The thought of inhaling it nearly made him empty his insides, but that would only add to Altair's endless list of taunts, so he swallowed his revulsion.

The two of them shoved their way to a low table too close to the center of the place. Nasir swept his gaze across the tent, noting the most sober, counting the entrances, and pausing at the tables swathed in shadows. There were at least four men in the silver cloaks of the Sultan's Guard, another handful in the black of Sarasin uniform, and a few darker-skinned men near them who could only be Pelusian, talking heatedly with their Zaramese counterparts. Sultan's Keep had its fair share of Demenhune, too, but the fools probably only drank melted snow wherever possible.

"I'll protect you, my dear assassin. Now stop looking like the world might swallow you whole, hmm?" Altair whispered in his ear.

Nasir closed his eyes, *hearing* Altair's smirk. He might as well have vomited.

Altair had the nerve to grip his shoulders and steer him to the worn carpet, where Nasir folded his legs beneath him and sat like a common peasant. It was all he could do not to flip the general over his shoulder.

Altair laughed, clearly enjoying every heartbeat. "Shall I procure you a bib as well?"

"Keep at it and I'll shove your fancy turban down your throat," Nasir offered, noticing that the carpet beneath him was mottled with dark stains of who-knew-what.

He was here for information. He had seen and done worse than this filth. He would survive.

"Fancy, eh? Feel free. Blue isn't really my color." Altair winked and settled on the opposite side of the table.

Nasir didn't bother with an answer. Someone opened one of the tent's many flaps and the moon peeked in, bringing a gust of the cool desert breeze inside. In the deserts of Arawiya, there was nothing more beautiful and beloved than the moon, bringing with her relief from the relentless sun. One more thing the growing darkness sought to diminish.

"Marhaba," the server girl said in greeting. A green jewel—likely fake—adorned her exposed belly button, arms shimmering with iridescent powder. Altair's smirk spread wider, and she took that as permission to sidle close to him.

"Tell me, habibi, does this turban look good on me?" Altair crooned.

Nasir crossed his arms and sighed.

The girl ran a henna-tipped finger across his turban and smiled with pink lips. "I think it makes you look"—she leaned closer and dropped her voice, dark hair fanning him—"ravishing."

Nasir lifted an eyebrow when she trailed her lips down Altair's cheek.

Altair gave him a stupid grin, hunger darkening his gaze. He was drooling like a dog just praised by his master. The girl tittered and Altair answered Nasir's glare with a calm stare before turning to her with a new smile. *He trades faces quickly.*

"One dallah of qahwa for me, please," the general said.

Nasir was surprised. Coffee? He would have thought the general would be all for drink and get drunk.

"And for my friend here . . ." Altair trailed off, gesturing to Nasir, who scowled at the word "friend."

"Water."

The girl bristled at his order, touched Altair's cheek, and glided away.

Altair's eyes followed the server girl. "I knew you were a boring man,

Nasir, but water? I don't think they even have that here. They might just scoop some for you from the toilets."

Nasir bit his tongue.

Altair continued, "Your restraint astounds me."

As if coffee would make Altair forget anything.

"And your lack thereof abhors me," Nasir replied.

"Some seek ways to forget," Altair said, oddly solemn.

Nasir followed his gaze to a man clearly taken by drink. The fool stared at a glass, lost and unfocused until he blinked—a flash of pain, there and gone again. Nasir did not think Altair saw that pain.

"Some of us can never forget." Nasir didn't know why he said those words to Altair of all people.

As a reminder of his idiocy, Altair gave him a withering look. "Some of us don't deserve to."

The girl returned before Nasir could form a retort. She set a dallah pot and a cup in front of Altair, and a smaller glass of water in front of Nasir. It looked clean, and didn't smell like it had been salvaged from . . . there.

"Shukrun, habibi," Altair said, trailing the backs of his fingers over hers.

Nasir's ears burned when the general leaned into her and murmured against her skin before pressing a scrap of papyrus to her palm.

"Listen," Nasir started, but the girl stood and sauntered away with a parting glare. She stopped before one of the men in black uniform. A Sarasin soldier.

"It's bad manners to stare at a woman when you're with a man," Altair drawled.

Nasir gave him a disgusted look. "Whoever told you that is—"

"I made it up myself, actually," he said.

Nasir saw the flash of something cream-colored pass between the girl and the soldier. The scrap of papyrus.

"Don't be nosy, Prince."

Nasir scoffed and looked again, but only the soldier stood there now, staring back at him with cool indifference. Was he part of the contingent tasked with gassing Demenhur? Nasir didn't know.

"Anything I do is for the good of our kingdom," Altair went on. "Isn't that what our duty dictates? There has to be some reason why you skulk around killing innocent people." He poured a stream of the dark coffee into his cup, out of place in the tent full of drink and rowdy men. He caught Nasir watching his cup. "I'd think you of all people would have noticed me to be above this human tendency to muddle the mind."

Nasir was half safin, and not even he referred to himself as anything other than human. Altair was right, though. Nasir *had* noticed the startling clarity in his gaze whenever he returned from his nights out. He simply hadn't expected the man to drink bitter coffee at a tavern.

"Where were we? Ah yes, the mission." Altair stretched his legs to either side of the table, not bothering to lower his voice.

Nasir opened his mouth to ask about the girl and the papyrus, but the Sarasin soldier had disappeared.

"I'm surprised your bleeding father didn't tell you yet. Him and his grand plans."

Nasir held still. Altair never spoke ill of the sultan.

"The Silver Witch has sent out an invitation. Irresistible. Tailored," Altair began, downing a cup of qahwa. It was always a rueful day when the sultan took counsel from the Silver Witch. She was familiar around Sultan's Keep, but Nasir kept his distance from the fair woman who always watched him too closely. "A glamorous way to get something from Sharr——"

"Sharr?" Nasir repeated before he could stop himself. The island of— kharra. Every thought in his mind scattered like sand in a gust of wind.

"Don't interrupt." Altair scowled. "Whatever this thing is, it will sup- posedly restore magic to Arawiya's minarets. And you're a big part of the plan."

"Me. And this prize is——" Nasir broke off as someone kicked him, but when he flicked his gaze up, the degenerate had already swayed past.

Another dry breeze slipped into the tent, ruffling Nasir's hair and stirring the cacophony of odors.

"I don't know what it is except that the Silver Witch is behind it and only the pure of heart can find it."

"Right. And that means I have to go?" Nasir mocked.

A brawl started not three tables from them, between a mouthy Zaramese and a massive man with streaks of sweat staining his qamis. Nasir rubbed his temples as grunts and crashes and swears rose in the already unbearable din.

"Did you have a moment, thinking you were pure of heart?" Altair said, unperturbed. "Ghameq doesn't trust the Silver Witch—for reasons I can't fathom. Your job is to kill the person who finds the prize and bring whatever it is back to your father."

Ah. Now *that* was a task befitting Nasir.

"See? As much as he hates you, you're the only one Ghameq trusts," Altair explained.

But Ghameq didn't trust *anyone*. Not even his own son, let alone the witch he sought counsel from.

Altair croaked a mirthless laugh, coming to the same conclusion. "Laa, that's not it. You're simply the only one he can force and the only one who won't break while doing his bidding."

The words were a slap. An accusation Nasir had grown accustomed to, but not the overwhelming sense of cowardice that came with it. He snapped his gaze to the general with a clench of his jaw. Self-pity could wait.

"And I fear whatever you'll retrieve will be the last thing he needs," Altair concluded.

For what? Nasir almost asked.

But trepidation crossed Altair's proud features and wavered at his proud mouth. Emotion that Altair, in his collected mind, would never betray.

Something worse than Nasir could imagine was at work.

On the daama island of Sharr, no less.

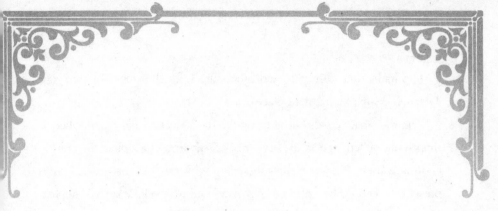

CHAPTER 7

Z AFIRA'S UMM ALWAYS KNEW HER DAUGHTER DIDN'T FEAR the Arz the way other children did. She would usher her to bed with whispers of the Sultana's Guard instead, and Zafira would dream of them chasing after her with their silver hoods and stern faces. Umm was no storyspinner like Baba was, but mothers were always good at spinning fears.

Now the sultana was dead, and Zafira glimpsed a different kind of silver in every slant of shadow.

The letter, and the silver-cloaked woman.

She lay in bed, her skin sore from the tight fit of that infernal dress she had worn at the wedding, just hours before. Yasmine was one house away, as always, but her friend felt somewhere far off and unreachable. *You're selfish, that's all.*

She squeezed her eyes shut and opened them with a groan, clearing her head of Yasmine and Misk. And Deen, carrying his bulky satchel as he disappeared down the street with a bittersweet smile, off to stay with a friend for the next few nights until Yasmine moved to Misk's house.

Sweet snow below.

She had other things to worry about. Like the quest in two days. Through daama Sharr of all places.

The thin mattress did little to muffle the squeak of old wood when she slipped out of bed. She would have to ask Deen to take a look at the creaking bedframe soon. He was always tinkering with random materials, coming up with inventions he dreamed of sharing with the Pelusians two caliphates away.

She threw on a faded tunic and then Baba's heavy cloak. She swung on her smaller satchel, pushing Baba's heftier one away. If she made the trek to Sharr, the lumpy thing would be at her back. With extra clothes, her favorite soap, and the kit of rare medicinal items Baba had put together over the years—strips of fabric, tonics, liniments for wounds, resin for burns, and herbs—all from a time when Demenhur wasn't a cursed chasm of snow, a time Zafira could only dream of.

As she stood with a sigh, she heard the howl of wind and the snap of the front door, but out in the foyer there was only Lana, curled on the majlis, a book in her lap. When Zafira opened her mouth to ask who had come in, she saw what Lana was reading.

Silver glinted in the firelight. *Kharra. Kharra, kharra, kharra.*

"What are you doing?" Zafira asked sharply.

Lana startled, her eyes snaring on Zafira's satchel and hunting clothes. A plate of aish el-saraya from the wedding sat beside her, syrup glistening in the firelight.

"Were you going to tell me and Umm?" Lana asked, accusation in her sweet voice. She held up the letter, and the dip in her forehead bothered Zafira more than she liked.

"I only got it today, and then there was the wedding." *And also the little problem of me not really speaking to Umm anymore.*

Lana was silent a moment. Accusation on her face gave way to hurt, pulling at the cords in Zafira's chest. "But were you going to tell us?"

"Maybe. No. I don't know. It doesn't matter now, does it?" Zafira asked tiredly.

She held out her hand, and Lana folded the invitation before giving it back. The broken seal flashed like the silver-cloaked woman's smile.

Zafira reached for the old blanket hanging by the front door, her fingers brushing the dusty coat beside it. Baba's coat. He had the most elaborate sayings for everything, and he used to describe its color as the waters of the Baransea on the calmest of days beneath the cloudiest of skies, even though he had never seen the Baransea.

Skies, if she went on this journey, she would see it.

Baba had been a collector of stories, a weaver of words. He hadn't been alive before the Sisters fell, but over the years he had gleaned tales from before the Baransea became dangerous, before the Arz sprang up, rimming the caliphates and obscuring the sea from Arawiya. His stories were the reason Zafira knew so much.

Pieces of Baba were scattered throughout their house—his boots, his favorite cup—because Zafira couldn't bear to get rid of them. Even after so many years, she was methodical in her cleaning every evening. It unnerved her to see anything out of place, but in the case of Baba's things, she could only ever run her fingers over their surfaces and gasp away an endless sorrow.

It was her fault. It would always be her fault. If only she had been stronger, *better*.

When Baba had ambled home from the Arz five years ago—months after his disappearance—the first thing Zafira had noticed was his state. His clothes were torn and tattered, shoulders hunched. By the time she saw the blood and understood the expression on his face, he was already moving for her. Readying to attack the very same daughter he had ventured into the Arz to save.

Moments later, he was dead, killed by—

"Okht?"

Zafira flinched. "Sorry. I'm sorry," she said to Lana quickly. She tucked the frayed blanket around her sister's shoulders, stomach clenching at the bones that jutted more sharply than they had one moon ago. "Get some sleep. Umm might start any moment now."

Her words were followed by a soft keening from Umm's room. Something propelled Zafira forward—instinct, perhaps—before she remembered Baba's glassy eyes, blood stretching a horizon across his chest. She clenched her teeth and dug in her heels.

"So much for that." Oblivious, Lana shoved the blanket away with a scrunch of her nose. "Is the trek to Sharr really the day after tomorrow?"

Zafira looked away. "Yes."

Lana's disappointment was a fist to her stomach, and she forced herself to meet those eyes. Baba's eyes, earnest and ancient.

"I'm sorry, Lana."

"Will you take someone with you?" she asked, and glanced wistfully at the novel tucked under her blanket before adding, "A safi would be a good ally to have on your side."

"I don't know who's going. I don't even know if this is real. But you and I both know that safin don't care about us."

The so-called great safin—with their pointed ears, heightened abilities, and endless lives—had abandoned Arawiya when the people needed them most. The caliphates had relied on magic the way a drunk man relied on his glass—except for Alderamin. And now that magic was gone, the safin lived as fine a life as they had before, selfishly hoarding their resources and turning their noses from Arawiya's suffering.

"Maybe they want to help but can't," Lana said. "They have the Wastes on one side and the Arz on the other."

"If they tried hard enough, they would be here."

Lana considered that, her sweet features twisted in thought. "You're a good person, Okht. But you can't do everything you want to do."

Zafira broke into a soft smile, realizing it had been a long time since she'd given anything the benefit of the doubt.

Lana paused on her way to Umm's room. "You don't have to go, though. It's only an invitation."

But every time Zafira thought of *not* going, she felt she was denying herself something she wanted, though she didn't know *how* or *why* she wanted it, except that she did. It felt, somehow, as though she had been waiting for this, and now that the opportunity was finally here, she couldn't let it pass.

It was *Sharr*.

It was danger and death in the worst possible way, yet the very idea made her blood hum, and she couldn't explain that in a way Lana would understand.

So "I do," was all she said, surprising them both.

Lana looked everywhere but at Zafira. She knew that Lana wouldn't press, that Lana trusted her, but she still felt a sinking sort of horrible when her sister nodded and said, "Okay."

"I'll be back soon. I'm just going to the sooq to . . . to think."

Zafira stepped away slowly and then moved quickly. She laced her boots and sheathed Baba's jambiya at her waist. Baba had taught her many things—how to pull back a bow without a whisper of a sound, how to see with her ears and navigate with her heart. After her first venture into the Arz, he had taught her how to protect herself, how the Arz was hers to tame. But *never remain unarmed* was what he stressed the most.

What would Baba say now, about her desire to keep pretending to be a man, which Yasmine called foolish? Which Baba himself had once urged her not to do? Would he want her to venture to Sharr if he knew magic was to be gained?

Zafira lifted the latch.

"Okht." Lana ducked her head and held out a small parcel of food. "To help you think."

Zafira dropped it in her bag. Then she touched a finger to Lana's nose and brushed a kiss to her forehead with a smile, leaving her sister with the mother Zafira refused to see.

CHAPTER 8

WHEN NASIR AND ALTAIR APPROACHED THE TOWERING doors of the palace together, the guards couldn't mask their wide-eyed surprise quickly enough. Nasir still didn't believe it, either. He had gone to a tavern with Altair of all people, for a glass of water and a pot of coffee.

"Sleep well, Prince," Altair murmured as he retreated down another corridor. "Try not to dream of me."

Nasir ignored him and dragged himself up the dark stairs. *Sharr. Sharr. Sharr.* It was as if the word had somehow made him drunk on the arak he refused to drink.

Yet when he stepped into his chambers, he froze, Sharr forgotten.

Someone blocked the air to his right, barely holding back hushed breathing. He flicked his wrist before he remembered that his gauntlet blades were stored uselessly in his bedside drawer, and he almost laughed at his luck. He unsheathed his jambiya with a tug of its onyx hilt and loosed a breath as he took one slow step to his right. Then another. *Inhale.* Two more steps. *Exhale.*

Inhale. He pivoted on his heel, tightened his grip on the blade, and shoved the intruder into a silver beam of moonlight. *Exhale.*

Raven hair, golden skin, depthless eyes. The soft curve of dark lips.

"Kulsum," Nasir breathed. His jambiya clattered to the ground. His hands slid to her face, and he cupped her smooth skin between his palms. He brushed his thumbs over her cheeks and the tension across his shoulders uncoiled. She stared back with the same hunger Nasir had seen when Altair's eyes followed the server girl.

Maybe it was the dark. Or the desire on her face, which he hadn't seen closely in so many months. Or maybe it was the mess in his mind and the way Altair had asked about her.

He didn't stop to consider why she was in his rooms while he had been away with Altair.

No—he kissed her.

His lips slanted down to her mouth, his hands went to her hair, and his body pressed against hers. She kissed him back just as greedily, her hands reaching for his cloak and pulling him closer. In that moment, they weren't a prince and a servant; they were two people, equal and one.

Rimaal, he had missed her. This girl, his mother's servant who had become so much more after the sultana's death. His shard of a heart raced and heat rushed through him. But when her lips parted with his, her hands lost in his hair, he froze. He remembered.

He remembered everything.

He stepped back, and Kulsum stared with wide, unreadable eyes. He wished the moon would reveal more than what he saw.

"Leave," he whispered hoarsely.

She didn't move. Neither of them breathed. This was pain worse than a sword. This was forgetting and then remembering everything afresh, the curse of memories.

"Get. Out." This time, his words were a blade.

Altair was right: some people didn't deserve to forget.

Kulsum tipped her head. She reached up, slowly, as if he might back away, and when he didn't, she trailed her fingers across his right cheek, as she had done so many times before. His eyes fluttered for the briefest moment, and then she left without a word, dress billowing. What could she say?

She no longer had a tongue, and it was because of him that she did not.

CHAPTER 9

NIGHT HAD FALLEN HEAVILY ACROSS DEMENHUR, bringing a phantom silence with it. Snow swirled in wheezing gasps, and Zafira drew her scarf over her face. She was hooded and shrouded, yet it was easy to discern the Hunter, for chances of finding a man in the western villages with a sling of arrows across his back were impossible—she couldn't even count herself. She smirked at her own joke. Yasmine would have snorted. *Skies, she isn't* dead.

Zafira guided Sukkar up the sloping white streets, where houses stood like misshapen teeth. They were the tan stone and colorless mortar common in the desert.

Only, Demenhur was no longer the desert oasis it had been. She sighed, her breath clouding in the cursed cold, and pressed on.

The sooq was ghostly beneath the moon. The forlorn jumu'a boasted no sign of the wedding that had taken place mere hours before. Zafira passed Araby's colorful sweet shop, the shutters pulled tight like those of most other shops in the sooq. Ornaments dangled on shop eaves, swaying eerily in the breeze.

She halted Sukkar before a shop well-known for catering to the jobless superstitious. Through the dark window, she saw grimy glass bottles glinting from the shelves, filled with Arawiya-knew-what. They were meant to be hung in the four corners of a house to deter ifrit, creatures of smokeless fire that could adopt the face of anyone, usually their victim's loved ones. Despite not being able to wield magic the way humans and safin could, ifrit had wreaked havoc worse than either race before the Six Sisters of Old.

Each of the six hailed from the most prominent clans, united by their desire for a better world, rather than by blood. What intrigued Zafira most was what they were: si'lah, creatures mere humans couldn't comprehend. Creatures not even the lofty safin could fathom standing beside as equals, let alone a handful of levels apart.

Once the Sisters had gathered their foes, the insidious ifrit included, they had no place to imprison them, until one Sister stepped forward with a plan. She was stronger than the others, for her heart was pure and she was adamant in her ideals.

On Sharr, the island she was to govern, she created an impenetrable prison where the Sisters jailed the creatures that plagued their people and where she reigned as its warden.

The ornaments hanging from the shop swayed, the strike of metal against metal drawing Zafira out of her thoughts. She eyed those glass bottles and wondered if they worked. If ifrit still roamed Arawiya, invisible to the eye or donning a human's body.

She tugged her scarf back over her mouth and was just about to press Sukkar onward when tiny clay lions in the frontmost display caught her eye, sending a shiver down her spine. She didn't know what the clay felines were supposed to fend off, because the Lion of the Night was dead.

The Lion's mother was ifrit, and his safin father fought to keep him from being banished with the rest of her kind. But life in the safin caliphate of

Alderamin proved more difficult, because pure-blooded safin bore a pride that none could rival. They murdered his father. Banned the Lion from magic. Crushed his core.

Baba always used the example of the Lion whenever he taught Zafira of oppression. Because the Lion did not let the safin crush him. He turned to Alderamin's greatest asset—knowledge. He learned all there was, empowering himself with forbidden blood magic.

Before long, the only creatures more powerful than he were the Sisters themselves, though the fact didn't faze him when he turned his wrath upon the Gilded Throne. Zafira always found it odd that the Lion, with all his knowledge, had made so bold a move. Because the Sisters quickly overpowered him, trapping him on Sharr and putting an end to his reign of darkness.

Decades later, he stirred trouble on Sharr itself, and the warden called for aid. The other Sisters flocked to her, armed with every ounce of Arawiya's magic to defeat him for good.

No one returned.

His roar was the darkness. His den was the shadows. Yet Sharr swallowed them all—the Sisters, the warden, the Lion, even the prison. But the Fall of Arawiya was a victory, wasn't it? Even if the people lost the Sisters and magic, even if the loss gave Demenhur a reason to prove that misfortune followed a woman's actions, Zafira knew, in her heart, that the Sisters had protected them that day.

They had defeated the Lion of the Night with their last breaths.

She pressed her heels against Sukkar's sides. Maybe the tiny lions were merely ornaments, a display of pride for the victory over a man who defied men, only to be slain by women.

"Whoa there." She tugged on Sukkar's reins before a run-down construction, charred black from a fire long ago. It stood behind the sooq, shadowed by the beauty of the House of Selah in the distance.

Zafira tied Sukkar to a beam under a half-broken eave and slipped between the old rails. The creak of the door echoed, and something scurried away in the dark. There was once a time when the hunger was so great, Demenhune of the western villages feasted on the putrid flesh of rats, which killed more than hunger ever would. That was before Zafira had succumbed to the call of the Arz.

She still remembered the bare relief on her parents' faces when she had stumbled from the Arz with three rabbits in hand and a smear of blood on her cheek. Neither Baba nor Umm had known where she had gone, but it was the first time anyone had returned from the forest of no return.

Days later, Baba had shown her how to nock an arrow and how to ensnare a deer, just as his own father had taught him in the forests of northern Demenhur. But when Baba had taken the meat into town and began feeding the villagers, it was Umm who reminded Zafira that, as a woman, she would receive no respect for the work she did. Baba had only smiled, saying Zafira held the power to change the views of the caliph's staunch believers, to give women the equality that was their right. The equality they received in Arawiya's other caliphates.

In the end, Zafira chose fear. She donned a man's clothes and continued to hunt in the Arz with her father, creating a name for herself that was never quite her own. It belonged to a masked figure. A person who, at the end of the day, did not exist.

It was a life Zafira could have lived with, if it meant seeing Baba's proud smile and the villagers' full bellies. Until the day when she, Umm, and little Lana fell ill with the flu that had been spreading throughout Demenhur.

While Zafira lay bedridden at home, food became scarcer. Meat ran low.

Baba had thought he could hunt as his daughter did. Instead, he returned crazed and barely human.

Zafira's breath now puffed in the darkness. She made her way carefully up the stairs reeking of mold, knowing which slats were broken and which were weak. Each of the three stairwells ended in a level of empty rooms. It had been an inn once, welcoming people of other caliphates who used

HAFSAH FAIZAL

to visit for trade and leisure. *Or pleasure*, as Yasmine would say with a suggestive gleam in her eye.

At the top level, Zafira pushed open the door to the roof and tightened her cloak against the sudden gust of air.

This was where she came to be free of the world that expected so much from the Hunter, from herself.

But tonight she was not alone.

A silhouette stood at the end, profile cast in the light of the stars. It seemed someone else couldn't stand enclosed walls, either.

"I just came to—" she started.

"Think," Deen finished for her. He inclined his head, and the clouds parted so the moon could see his smile. "I know. But if you're feeling anything like I am right now, I didn't want you to be alone."

Zafira didn't know what to say. She wanted to wrap her arms around him, but after the way he had looked at her this evening, that didn't feel so good an idea. Instead, she moved to his side, pressing her shoulder to his as she fought the swell of elation in her chest, and together they looked down at Demenhur.

Tiny houses sprawled to their left, shadowed by a crescent of darkness where the Arz encroached. The sooq parted directly below them, and the House of Selah rose to their right, periwinkle in the moonlight.

The House of Selah was a humble name for something akin to a palace. Its stone walls were crumbling, and dark veins of rot stood stark against the cream, for it had been built for the desert, not to withstand an unending wet climate. Yet despite the decay, it was magnificent—twin spires in brilliant ivory rising to the snow-heavy clouds. Between them, the main building arched into the sky.

If this was a beauty, Zafira couldn't imagine the magnificence of the palace in Thalj, where the royal minaret stood, a beacon bathing in shadows ever since magic had disappeared. She couldn't even begin to imagine the palace in Sultan's Keep.

"Do you know what I've always wanted to do?" Deen asked. He slid closer and slipped the hood from her face.

Zafira felt exposed beneath the moon. Out of instinct, she glanced around quickly, but they were alone. "What?" she asked, thinking she knew.

"Explore," he said, expression wistful.

She raised her eyebrows in surprise. He drew lines on the ice-covered railing with one gloved finger, deep in thought. "There's more than Arawiya, Zafira. There has to be. The world can't be just five caliphates, a wasteland, and one deadly sea. I want to travel, discover new places. Meet new people."

She liked that plan, and so did her heart, if the warmth she felt was any indication. If life were simpler, she would want to explore, too. She stared into the distance, where they were blocked by a growing forest. A forest that might be stopped, if she accepted the invitation.

"You've been all over—Zaram, Pelusia, even the barren Wastes to get to Alderamin. You've seen *sand*," she said, a note of envy bittering her tongue. She imagined a world covered in it, baking beneath the sun. Creeping between her toes and scurrying between her teeth. "What's it like?"

"Beautiful. Endless. Freedom wavering beneath the relentless sun," he said softly. "The heat is a pest, but then again, isn't the cold?" He sighed. "I'm content, I am. But there's this . . . this *need* for something more."

It was the first time Deen wanted what she did: *more*. But something else was bothering him. She could see it in the heaviness tugging his lips into a frown. "What is it?"

He dropped his knowing hazel eyes to her, and she felt herself stepping closer. In this space, so close to the moon, anything felt possible. The wind whipped her hair. Deen lifted a careful hand and tucked the ebony strands behind her ear. He inhaled slowly, a shuddering draw that made her keenly aware of their solitude.

"Will you marry me?" The words swooshed past his lips in a rush, as if his heart wanted to savor them but his brain was too frazzled to allow it.

She opened her mouth. Closed it. She had known this was coming. She had known. But *today* of all days? Now of all moments?

His eyes fell from hers. How many times had she watched his lips widen into effortless smiles? How many times had he run after her, snarling and pretending to be the Arz monsters their parents had warned them of as children? How many times had he held her against his chest, sharing his warmth when she shivered in the cold?

He was the one who used what little money he had to buy rich safin chocolate and make the best drink Zafira had ever tasted. He was the one to hold her when Baba had died and her heart had hardened.

She stared into the night until her eyes began to burn.

"Deen, I—" Her tongue felt heavy. *I'm not like Yasmine.* It wasn't that she didn't want marriage. She just wanted *more.* Didn't he just say he wanted that, too? "I'm not ready to marry yet."

Doubt flashed in his beautiful eyes, and Zafira's stomach twisted.

He asked, "And when you *are* ready?"

"I will marry you," she said without a moment's hesitation. Her heart told her brain she was lying, but she ignored it. It wasn't a lie. *It wasn't.* She couldn't think about marriage when the sister of her heart had left her and maybe-assassins had been sent for who knew what. When the Arz had conjured a woman in silver who claimed she was cursed. When an invitation to daama Sharr burned on silver parchment.

Deen exhaled and nodded, but the tension only tightened with the stubborn set of his jaw. "I'm not an idiot, Zafira, asking you to marry me just because my sister's married herself off. But I thought . . ." He paused, and her heart began to pound. "I thought I would be better than a death sentence. I thought marriage would give you another option. Another sense of purpose. Isn't that what you search for in the Arz?"

"What are you talking about?" she whispered. She didn't search for anything in the Arz. She hunted. She didn't know what she wanted any more than she knew what she was waiting for.

But today, the invitation—it had made something rear its head.

"Were you going to tell me?" he asked instead. He sounded tired. Resigned. "About the letter, Zafira. The invitation you have in your pocket right now."

She bit her tongue. *Lana.* Deen was the one who had come when Zafira was in her room.

"I know you," he said. "I saw you at the wedding with that look in your eyes, and I thought it was because of Yasmine. But it wasn't, was it? It's the same look you have when you stare at the Arz, and I should have realized."

She drew her eyebrows together. "What look?"

"Elation. *Adoration*, even," he whispered, and clenched his jaw.

Zafira's pulse fluttered. Hadn't she used the same word to describe the way the silver-cloaked woman stared at the Arz?

"I don't know where it came from, but I know it's an invitation to chaos."

"Deen, it's *magic*. We could have magic again. How can you not want that?" she asked. Sharing the invitation with him opened a spigot inside her, and she wanted to throw back her head and shout. Every story her father had spun could be *real*. Oh, what she would give to feel the rush that the old ones had known. To have magic thrum at her fingertips. "You're less excited than I thought you would be."

"Did you miss the part about Sharr? And before that, you'll need to travel across the Arz."

"I go there every day."

"You don't cross it, Zafira. No one has. Magic might lie at the end of this journey, but that doesn't mean you will attain it. There is no reason to get anyone's hopes up. Least of all yours." He rubbed a hand across his face, and Zafira knew he was upset.

"But think about it," she insisted. "Magic means no more cursed snow. It means the Arz won't swallow us whole, because it won't exist anymore. You can do everything you've always wanted to do."

"At what cost?"

Zafira met his eyes as the cold clouded between them. "At whatever cost it takes. I owe the world this much, don't I? I owe it to the world to try."

"You owe the world nothing. Do you even know where the letter came from? Do you really think magic can be restored with a book?"

Something flickered in his eyes when she didn't respond.

Silence stretched between them until he sighed. "Yaa, Zafira. Will you go, then? Alone?"

"I think so," she said, but felt the need to say more. "How far can we run before the Arz reaches us? Running is not a life."

More silence, in which Deen looked sad, terribly so. She reached for his hand and curled her pinkie around his, but his eyes strayed to her lips and she had to remind herself that he was no longer the boy who cared for her like a sister. That she was no longer a little girl. That he had just asked for her hand in marriage.

Such closeness didn't bode well.

As if hearing her thoughts, he tucked the same wayward strands of hair behind her ear again, admiration in his gleaming eyes, and he leaned closer, barely. Zafira found herself running her tongue over her cold lips. The golden curls at his forehead begged to be touched, but her eyes dropped to the fullness of his mouth.

"Zafira," he whispered.

Marry me. Her daama brain started working again. She took a step back, the words from the letter suffocating her breath.

"Don't," she said quietly, a quake in her voice. The moon was bright enough that she could see desire darkening his eyes.

And the House of Selah, imposing behind him.

Something ached in her heart, but she steeled the shards in her chest and turned away.

CHAPTER 10

WITH EVERY STEP OF SUKKAR'S HOOVES, ZAFIRA found it harder to think. If she was going, she had to decide now. If she was going, every passing moment took her closer to the quest. To Sharr. To leaving her village.

She slid from Sukkar's back with a heavy exhale.

Deen followed close behind on his own horse, Lemun. It had seemed like a peace offering at first, inviting him to spend the rest of the night in her house instead of at his friend's. But now, with him here, all she could do was worry. She had started more than one conversation on the short ride home, but each exchange had dwindled to an uneasy silence with no more than a few words from him.

Meager light illuminated the sloshy alley between her house and that of the Ra'ads, which led to their rickety stable. Zafira trailed her gloved fingers across the crack in her kitchen window, where a trio of potted herbs sat wilted and browned, despite Lana's fervent efforts. Like Demenhur, the caliphate that once grew Arawiya's cures.

It could grow them again. She released a breath and disappeared into the stable. Inside, Deen lit two lanterns and settled Lemun beside Sukkar. Zafira brushed a hand down her horse's neck, and Sukkar nudged her with a small, concerned snort.

A warning she didn't heed.

She thought she saw a flicker of movement to her left, and she instinctively checked to make sure her hood shrouded her face. Discomfort thickened her blood, slowed her mind.

A flash of silver stirred dread into her stomach.

"Peace unto you, Huntress."

Deen drew a sharp breath in the sudden stillness. She knew that voice and the lilt of that word. *Huntress.* She turned.

The stable doors hadn't opened to let anyone in, but why use doors when one could materialize as one wished? Something dark hummed against Zafira's skin, and Deen grabbed her hand. Sukkar and Lemun scrambled back against the wall, snorting in panic.

The woman's cloak shimmered like liquid metal, and only now, free from the fluttering curtain of snow, did Zafira realize her youth.

Skies. She wasn't an illusion. She really had stood before the Arz and murmured those cryptic words. She really had placed the letter in Zafira's satchel.

Why is she here? Zafira lifted her chin. She was not going to cower.

Sukkar and Lemun continued to struggle in fear. Deen tried to soothe them with a distracted hand, but his apprehension only made their protests increase. The woman flicked her wrist, and the very air wavered before the horses quieted.

No.

They stopped breathing altogether.

Deen's eyes were wide. Zafira barely restrained herself from stepping back.

Magic. Magic that shouldn't exist. There was no other explanation for

how the woman had frozen the horses solid. For how she had appeared—
and disappeared—out of thin air.

The rotting walls of the stable suddenly felt like a steel cage.

The woman laughed without mirth, piercing Zafira with startling dark
eyes. Ancient eyes, she realized with a start. Her youthful face was a ploy.
What devilry was this woman capable of?

"Oh, they will live. But for the sake of my hearing, they will remain
this way until I take my leave." Her eyes snared on the black mold staining
the wood, nose wrinkling at the stench of decay. "Which will be soon, I
hope. You wanted to see me, didn't you?"

Zafira wasn't going to react to the fact that the woman had somehow
heard her unvoiced question. She wasn't going to wonder why, out of all
moments, she had chosen the moment when Deen was with her to visit. If
she did, she would go mad.

"Who are you?"

The woman's crimson lips twisted into a one-sided smile. "The Silver
Witch. Fitting, laa?"

More like unimaginative. What happens when you change your cloak? Zafira
thought, surprising herself. It seemed a part of her still hadn't registered the
seriousness of her situation.

"And are you friend or foe?" Zafira asked, and Deen murmured something.

The woman's smile widened. "Someone like you."

Zafira looked at Sukkar. The silk of a shadow whispered against her
skin, reminding her of the Arz, teasing fear into her heart. The lanterns
flickered.

"I am nothing like you," she said darkly. Malevolence spilled from the
woman like morning mist.

The witch hummed but didn't object. "It won't be long before the Arz
descends upon your people."

This, Zafira knew. She woke with the knowledge, she slept with the knowledge. She breathed in dread with every waking day. But she didn't like the way the woman said "your people."

"They are not slaves; they do not belong to me."

The woman—*witch, skies*—looked smug. "Oh, but *you* slave over them. You hunt for them, feed them, worry for them. When you unfolded my letter, your very first thought was of them. Your kingdom may have a king, Huntress, but you are very much its concerned queen."

"The letter," Zafira said through clenched teeth, and Deen had to pull her back. "Tell me about the letter."

The Silver Witch stepped closer with a curious look. "You do not fear me."

You terrify me. Zafira released a quivering breath, hearing Baba's voice. *Fear breeds death. Confidence breeds freedom.*

"The way I see it," she said, "you wouldn't have invited me if you didn't need me. So I have nothing to fear, do I?"

The Silver Witch laughed. "You think yourself irreplaceable? There's many a hunter in Arawiya, girl. I invited you only because you topped my list. Indeed, you have a good deal to fear."

There's no other hunter who can do as I can. But Zafira wasn't about to test that theory. "Why not go to Sharr and retrieve it yourself?"

"If it were so simple, I wouldn't stand amid this rot." Disdain dripped from the Silver Witch's frown.

"If a witch who can wield magic can't retrieve it, what good is a girl with a bow?" Zafira asked, and she could *hear* Deen trying to keep silent.

The witch clucked her tongue. "The more you think about it," she said, leaning close, "the madder you'll become. Wise words, those."

"Baba's," Zafira whispered.

Deen moved then. He wound his pinkie around hers, grounding her.

The Silver Witch smirked. "The one who would not have died if you hadn't been bedridden. I watched him breathe his last. Quite brutal, your mother."

Red pulsed in Zafira's vision. How long had the woman spied upon her and her family? *And why?*

"Thank you for watching," she bit out.

"Not even I can control the Arz." The witch's expression turned wistful. *Adoring.* "There is a certain beauty in chaos, magnificence in the uncontrollable."

"You lie," Deen seethed.

Zafira was frozen with the image of Baba's lifeless body. Deen rubbed his hands up and down her arms, but Zafira wanted to fold into herself.

"Ah, he speaks," the witch said with a smile, and Deen's swallow was audible. "Alas, I cannot lie."

The moment the witch set her sights on Deen, Zafira felt a chill down her spine. She shoved thoughts of Baba away and stood straighter. "If you can't control the Arz, then how would *I* stand a chance in Sharr?"

The witch's dark eyes flashed, and Zafira felt she had pushed too far. If the woman could freeze the very heart of a horse, Zafira did not doubt her own could be shattered in the blink of an eye. And Deen's.

Deen, who was here because of her.

"I am not forcing your hand, Huntress. Come if you wish, or step aside and I'll find another. Pity, I thought you would want to claim such a victory for a woman."

Zafira hesitated.

The witch curled another smile. "Think of it. A life without the shadow of the Arz, with the Baransea at your borders and magic at your beck and call. I will even go so far as to provide passage across the sea. When your caliph comes to see you off, as he will, you'll be in a prime position to strike a bargain or three. You have so much to gain."

She might not be forcing Zafira's hand, but she was certainly guiding it.

"Why the caliph? If this is for all of Arawiya, the sultan should be involved."

"A caliph is as much a king of his caliphate as the sultan is of his kingdom.

And the sultan, as we both know, has had dark notions as of late," the witch replied.

Zafira recalled the men who had ambushed her and, before that, the crown prince who had murdered Sarasin's caliph upon the sultan's orders. Dark notions, indeed.

"As biased as your caliph is, he is a good man. I thought it best to inform him before sending the legendary Hunter of his caliphate on a dangerous mission to Sharr."

"What have *you* to gain?" Deen asked.

The witch's careful expression wavered. Sadness tipped her lips and creased the folds of her dark eyes.

An act. It has to be.

"Is it wrong to seek redemption as any mortal might?"

As any mortal might? Zafira shivered at what that meant the Silver Witch could be. She slid a glance at Deen, but he barely breathed.

"It depends on what you seek redemption from," Zafira said carefully.

"I wronged someone I once loved."

Zafira lifted her eyebrows, and the witch's sorrow vanished as quickly as it had come.

"If you don't believe in redemption, Huntress, then believe this: by the year's end, the Arz will consume every piece of Arawiya. A small risk, embarking on this journey, laa?"

She was right. Sharr might be a sentence of death, but the people of Arawiya had *already* been sentenced to death. It was only a matter of time— so *little* time, too. Less than Zafira had anticipated.

It seemed so simple. Journey to the island, find the Jawarat, end the cursed Arz, and restore magic. But *Sharr.*

"How can a book restore magic?" Zafira asked.

"In the same way a book can reenact the history of civilization, instruct upon a delicious dish, or tell a tale of pleasure," she said, as if Zafira had asked the most obtuse question known to man. "Do you question how a girl like yourself returns from the Arz?"

The witch was adept at answering questions with more questions.

"And you expect her to go alone?" Deen asked. "Why not have the caliph send men with her?"

"If I wanted a party, boy, I would make one," the witch said. She turned, cloak fanning around her. "Death will be her companion. He's kept her safe all this time. Why stop now?"

Zafira shivered at her choice of words. Deen's pinkie tightened around hers, pinching until she tugged away. She heard the woman's voice once more, a hushed whisper in her ear despite the distance between them.

Farewell, Huntress.

An icy fist tightened around Zafira's throat. She struggled to breathe, and when she could, the witch was gone.

CHAPTER 11

NASIR WOKE TO A MANSERVANT BESIDE HIS BED. HE SCOWLED and dragged a hand across his face, stubble scraping his palm. "What is it?" he rasped.

The man looked at his own feet, dark hair cresting his near-translucent skin, an angry scar on his cheek. Demenhune, as far as Nasir could tell. The servants of Sultan's Keep hailed from nearly every caliphate except Alderamin, for safin bowed to no man. It was Ghameq's luck that Alderamin and Sultan's Keep were separated by the Arz and the Strait of Hakim, for Nasir doubted his father would sit on the throne otherwise.

"The sultan—"

"I'm coming," Nasir snapped.

The man flinched and hurried out the door.

Nasir slid from the bed and stepped into the adjoining washroom. His stomach growled, thunderous, but as he finished dressing, he knew he wouldn't have time for a meal, for the sultan didn't tolerate tardiness.

What would it matter if I were late?

His mother was dead. Kulsum had lost her most prized possession. But there would always be something—the sultan could carve out Kulsum's eyeballs, peel the fingernails off Haytham's son. There was always something Sultan Ghameq could do to make one wish he had obeyed, to make one wish for death.

Nasir focused on the soft thuds of his footsteps until his breathing slowed. The massive doors to the throne room groaned as they swung inward, revealing the sultan on the Gilded Throne, receiving emirs. He was always awake, always at work, always sharp-eyed.

Nasir waited, even as the emirs sneered at him while they walked past, proud they were given the sultan's attention before the crown prince was.

When only the two of them remained, Ghameq eyed Nasir's clothing. "Where are you going?"

"You summoned. I thought it was for another kill," Nasir said, realizing his mistake too late.

"How many times have I told you not to think?"

Nasir clenched and unclenched his jaw. "Do you wish for me to change?"

"I don't care what you wear, boy," the sultan said.

I don't care echoed in Nasir's eardrums.

"Fetch something to eat and meet me in my rooms. Make quick."

For the briefest of moments, Nasir couldn't move. The sultan had just told him to *eat.*

His surprise must have been evident on his face, because the sultan scoffed. "Your hunger is pinching your face. I need you clearheaded so that you can remember what I tell you in that ineffective head of yours."

Of course. How could he think, for even a moment, that his father actually cared?

◄ ◆ ►

This time, he shoved his silver circlet on his head, and when a guard let him into the sultan's chambers, Nasir's pulse quickened. The room looked exactly as it had the day before. Even that wretched poker stood as it had after their meeting with Haytham.

He pulled the curtain to the side and entered a smaller room, where Sultan Ghameq lounged on his majlis, legs crossed and a hand on the medallion at his neck. Nasir pulled his gaze away, and his eyes fell on another doorway, beyond which was a bed curtained in ivory, adorned with silver flowers. Nasir froze.

"What?" the sultan asked.

Nasir did not want to answer. "I haven't been here since——"

"Since she died," the sultan enunciated, voice hard.

Nasir released a breath and stared back at his father, waiting. Wishing. Searching. And there it was, the tiniest fissure in the gray stone of the sultan's eyes, gone before Nasir could grasp it.

He knelt, and the moment shattered.

"You're leaving tomorrow," the sultan said.

"For where?"

"Sharr."

If he expected surprise from Nasir, the sultan wouldn't be getting it. "Vicious" was a mild descriptor for Sharr, where the very sand dealt death, yet Nasir felt an odd sense of detachment from the fact that he would soon be deep within the island. Logic told him that he had much to fear: He wouldn't be the dangerous one in the place he was being sent. He wouldn't be in command.

But he had stopped listening to logic when his mother died.

"The Silver Witch is sending the Demenhune Hunter to retrieve the lost Jawarat, a book that will end this drought of magic."

So Haytham's assumption was true. A breeze slipped past the open window, dry and dead, like all of Sultan's Keep.

"The Hunter is a da'ira. A compass. Hunting in the Arz is hard enough, but finding one's way back successfully for five years? There is magic at play. A da'ira is one of the rarer affinities. He has only to set his mind to an object, and he will be led to it. I doubt the man even knows what he is, or he wouldn't so recklessly reveal himself. The two men I sent to retrieve him never returned." The sultan stroked his beard in apparent thought. "So you will have to catch him on Sharr. Use him to find the Jawarat, then kill him. Kill anyone else the witch sends, too."

Kill, destroy. That was what had replaced logic.

"But magic—" Nasir started.

"Did I ask for your thoughts?" the sultan asked, putting him in his place.

He was a lapdog. He couldn't expect to learn more. He didn't *deserve* more.

But how? he wanted to know. How could the Demenhune Hunter have magic when there was none? When it was clear that Ghameq's fire summoning was done through the long-banished dum sihr, magic no one in Demenhur—an ethical caliphate—would, or even *could*, touch?

It meant that everything about magic disappearing was more than black-and-white.

"The witch has wronged me on more than one count," the sultan continued. "Do not let the book fall into her hands. If my assumptions are wrong, and the Hunter is no more than a man with a goal, move on."

Move on. Innocent wording for "kill and be done with it."

"Understood?"

Nasir dipped his head. Whether he wanted to do this or not was unimportant.

"Why me? Why not a contingent?" Nasir asked. He might be the only one who wordlessly did the sultan's bidding, but how was Nasir expected to succeed on an island not even the Sisters had returned from?

"A more strategic option, but we are dealing with a fickle witch, not a mortal rival."

Fickle, indeed.

Nasir thought of the ivory curtains to his left, in that room he doubted even the sultan slept within anymore. The words rushed from his mouth before he could stop them. "And if I don't?"

Sultan Ghameq's answer was immediate. "Your servant girl can stand to lose a few more parts. Then there is the matter of the Dar al-Fawda boy, and Haytham's son. You will never truly be left with no one. You will always find a sick soul to protect. Do you think I can't see that? You are weak. Pathetic.

"And until you murder the sickening leniency festering within, you will never be worthy of being my son."

The vile words echoed in the silence.

Nasir had been a worthy son, once. The sultan was a man he had called Baba once. It was as if something else prowled inside him now, eroding the man Nasir once loved. To see a flicker, a glimmer, a bare *hint* of appreciation in his father's eyes—Nasir would do anything.

Even kill without morals. Murder without regret. Become a monster without bounds.

A servant swept into the room. Nasir heard the swish of her dress around her legs, and he knew, without turning, that it was she. The sultan watched him, so Nasir stoned his features and stared back coolly.

Kulsum glided forward and set a platter of fruit on the floor before the sultan. She crouched, chin tucked to her chest, quiet and expectant, not more than two paces away. Sweet jasmine struck Nasir's senses. He remembered the softness of her skin. The pain.

Ghameq looked down at the tray with silver bowls as if they had appeared on their own. A murmured order to get out—*akhraj*—was the only acknowledgment he gave.

Nasir didn't look at her, though every nerve in his body begged otherwise. Fruits were arranged in the bowls, a multitude of colors sliced delicately and displayed lavishly. They were fresh from Pelusia, the only caliphate with such fertile soil.

The sultan ate. One grape after another, they plopped into his mouth, while Haytham's son shivered in hunger, while the page boy licked his dirty fingers and the children tumbled from the backs of camels. While Arawiya suffered.

Breathe.

"If I may leave, Sultani," Nasir said after a moment.

The sultan chewed on, ignoring him. Darkness edged into Nasir's vision.

Finally, Ghameq grunted. "It's tomorrow, boy. Get ready."

"Assuming I cross the Arz, how will I get to Sharr?" Nasir asked. They had no vessels for sailing the sea. They had no sailors to help them navigate.

"On a ship," Ghameq barked like he was stupid.

Nasir did not think the sultan saw the tic in his jaw. "Yes, Sultani."

He resisted Ghameq's orders, once, for as long as it took before he succumbed to the pain. And he endured it—more than most could. Until the sultan found a better way to ensure Nasir's obedience.

"Will I make the journey alone?"

The sultan smiled, ever a snake, and dread settled in Nasir's stomach. "Take Altair."

Nasir exhaled. What had the sultan's favorite general done to incur Ghameq's wrath?

"And I'm to kill everyone."

"That is what I said, isn't it?" Sultan Ghameq picked up a handful of pomegranate seeds.

Sharr was the land of ghosts, an isle where even the land would be his enemy. Yet Nasir wasn't afraid of that anymore. He was afraid of himself, and the lives he would take, starting with his father's favorite general. For Kulsum. For Haytham's son.

Unless . . . , the voice in his heart began.

He left it at that.

CHAPTER 12

ZAFIRA HAD SPENT THE REST OF THE NIGHT THINKING OF THE woman in the silver cloak—a veritable, magic-wielding *witch*, who spoke of redemption and magic, who looked a handful of years older than Zafira but spoke as if she had lived for centuries. Zafira was not like Deen. She hadn't convened with immortal safin. She hadn't tasted the world beyond Demenhur's western villages. Her knowledge of everything had come through tales spun on quiet nights. A witch was too much to comprehend.

Deen hadn't stayed the night in her house in the end.

After the Silver Witch had vanished, he had slouched against the stable wall with a far-off look in his eyes.

When he had finally gathered himself, Zafira could tell he didn't like what he saw on her face. And when she stretched the silence between them, he took her downcast face in his hands and touched his lips to her forehead.

"Zafira. Zafira, look at me."

But she couldn't. She couldn't look at him, and her eyes had fluttered shut. In the darkness, anything was possible. Baba was alive, Umm was herself, magic still existed. But eyes couldn't stay closed forever, unless one was dead.

And the dead never dreamed.

"This is far beyond us," he had whispered against her skin.

Was it beyond them? *Who decides what's out of reach, if not we ourselves?*

The door to Zafira's room opened now, framing Lana in soft light.

"Okht? I thought I heard the bed creak. I didn't see you come in last night." Her features were lit with relief, and Zafira pulled on a smile. "Ummi asked for you."

The smile slipped from her face. "As she tends to," Zafira said carefully, ignoring the yawning chasm of guilt.

Umm's sanity had been fickle ever since Baba had crawled from the Arz, but she had her rare spasms of lucidity. Moments when Zafira made herself scarce, for it was easier than facing her mother.

"You should go," Lana said quietly, hands clasped. The dying fire angled her face in shadows. Guilt tugged at her mouth. "I . . . I told her about the letter. And Sharr."

With a sigh, Zafira threw the blankets off and stood, the cold going straight through the thin fabric of her old dress and into her bones. Lana padded away, and Zafira heard the shuffle of the majlis pillows by the front door, leaving her to her decision.

Through the threshold, she could see the rust-studded doorknob leading to Umm's room. The same doorknob she brushed past every daama day, guilt searing the fibers of her being.

No more. She was going to Sharr. She could possibly die. She clenched her jaw and crossed over to Umm's door. With every step forward, she felt like the condemned trudging to her beheading.

Approaching the Arz scared her less.

With bated breath, Zafira reached for the door. The wood scraped her bare palms. *Push it open, coward.*

She pushed. The door moaned. *Five years*, it seemed to cry. *Five years.* The woman inside lifted her head immediately, eyes locking on her, fingers twisting with the same disquiet rushing through Zafira's veins.

Umm.

Zafira hadn't exchanged a word with Umm in five years. Five years of having a mother in the same house as her, five years of silence. Some days, before the screaming began, it was easier to think Umm was dead, too.

She looked the same. Head held regally atop a slender neck like a gazelle's. A slim nose that Baba loved. Lips a shade darker than red and eyes bright and cold as Zafira's, feathered by lashes that softened their iciness. Her dark locks were feathered in white.

Those aged strands were a fist to her stomach.

"Zafira," Umm said. Her voice was not the same. It was torn now, wearied by sorrow.

Zafira couldn't move from the doorway. She couldn't breathe.

"You never come to see me."

Umm never ventured through the house, either. These scant walls housed three souls and an abundance of memories. Zafira threw a quick glance behind her, to where Lana was curled on the majlis, dutifully not paying attention.

"I can't," she breathed.

Umm's voice was soft. "It was him or you."

A conversation they should have had five years ago, had the pain not been so suffocating.

"You should have saved him," Zafira whispered. Umm's blankets were strewn about her, even the pale pink one Yasmine had made herself.

"There was no question of whether the child who had lived a fraction of the life he had lived should be spared or not," Umm said, voice cracking in the end. When she drew her next breath, Zafira heard the rattle in her chest. The pain.

Zafira rubbed her face and her fingers came away wet with tears.

Umm lifted her hands. "Yaa, my abal, don't cry for me."

Oh, my wild rose.

Zafira hadn't heard the endearment in years. Everything clawed up her throat, scraping her insides, tearing her resolve. Her father had whispered it last, and then she'd been fighting his iron grasp, gasping for her life.

She remembered that sudden stillness after Umm drove her jambiya through his heart. Red darted across her vision now. Dark red, a line painted down Baba's chest.

Zafira stepped closer. She crouched. Sat. With each movement, her guilt grew as she realized how selfish she had been. She reached for Umm's hands, closing her fingers around the coolness of her mother's. The tears fell now. One after the other, they trickled from a crevice in her chest, turning into a stream flooding from her heart. Umm's eyes wilted into sadness.

"Sometimes I forget his face," Umm whispered.

How could something so painless as the loss of memory hurt so much? The raw despair in her mother's gaze gripped her.

Zafira could never forget Baba's face. She could never forget Baba— khalas, that was that. Yet she had ignored her living parent. She had left her mother to mourn alone. For no matter how much time Lana spent with Umm, it was Zafira who had been there when Baba breathed his last. It was Zafira who understood Umm's grief.

That very mother who had saved her life.

She had allowed her pain to harden into anger. Allowed that anger to fester, blinding her to Umm's suffering. If Zafira grieved from seeing her father die at the hands of her mother, how did it feel for Umm to live with the hands she had used to slay her beloved?

How had it felt for Umm to choose between one love and another?

Zafira forced air into her lungs. She shuttered her selfish, burning eyes and dropped her head to Umm's lap, the gesture foreign. Familiar.

"Forgive me, Ummi. Forgive me," Zafira pleaded. She repeated the words over and over. "For my elusion. For my anger."

Selfish. Childish. Hateful. Skies, there was no daughter in Arawiya worse than her.

"Don't beg, child. I, too, am sorry," Umm lulled, and took Zafira's face in her hands. There was no glint of madness looking back at Zafira from the ice-blue eyes she had inherited. "You did not come to me, and I did not come to you. We are both at fault, are we not?"

No. It was Zafira who was at fault. She had failed her duty as a daughter.

Umm brushed her thumb across Zafira's damp cheek. "Lana tells me you will go to Sharr."

She supposed her tears had to do with more than Umm and Baba. It was everything else, too. Yasmine's marriage. Deen's proposal. This trek to Sharr.

"I won't be like Baba. I won't return to hurt you. I will be victorious, or I will die." There was steel in Zafira's voice.

"I am not trying to stop you, my abal. I only want to know what the search is for."

"The return of magic," Zafira said. "The destruction of the Arz that took him from us."

Umm considered that before she curved her lips into a smile, sending a thousand memories soaring through Zafira. She could see Baba there. She could see warm bread fresh out of the oven. Blankets creating a cocoon. She could see Lana's small hands and Umm's favorite ma'moul cookies.

It was gone now. All of it. Everything.

Because of the Arz.

"Avenge his death, Zafira. Avenge your father and destroy that forest." Umm brushed her thumb across her cheek again, giving her a flicker of light to guide her unknown path. A path Zafira swore to follow.

"Be as victorious as the name I have given you, and bring the desert to its knees."

Zafira took her mother's words, one by one, and swallowed them whole.

——◄●►——

Later, Zafira collected her newly fashioned arrows and slipped them into her sling with soft thuds that mimicked her heartbeat. Lana twirled a white feather between her fingers before gathering the trimmed remnants.

"I'm going to take a wash and meet Simah," she said with a yawn.

"Oh?"

"Lunch," Lana hedged, and when Zafira narrowed her eyes, she said, "Her umm is sick."

"You don't have to run and play doctor every time someone asks. You don't owe—"

"Neither do you," Lana cut her off. Seeing the surprise on Zafira's face, she scrambled closer and took her hand. "I'm sorry, Okht, but it's true, isn't it? I—I'll be back later."

Zafira pulled Lana in for a hug before she could escape, wrapping her arms around her sister and holding her close. She took every word she wanted to whisper and said, "I'm sorry."

Lana pulled back to look at her and pressed a kiss to Zafira's cheek.

"I know," she whispered, and Zafira heard everything in between those letters.

After Lana disappeared down the hall, Zafira sank back into the cushions with a sigh. She picked up Baba's jambiya, weighing it and its straight-bladed cousin, the dagger, in her palms to decide which would be better suited against an enemy.

An enemy. She wouldn't be hunting deer and rabbit anymore. She would be hunting monsters, if the stories about Sharr were to be believed. She would be fighting for her own life.

She jumped at a rap on the door. *Skies, Zafira.* Her pulse quickened as she thought of the Silver Witch, but logic told her the witch would more likely materialize in front of her than knock. Some logic that was.

Zafira pulled open the door.

Deen stood at the threshold, curls dusted in snow. She braced herself for words about how she shouldn't go. Why she should stay.

But instead, he said, "You haven't happened to see the Hunter, have you?"

She smiled, and his eyes sparkled at her relief.

"Last I heard, he was taking the day off," she said.

Deen stepped inside and looked from the strewn feather barbs to the pristine white fletchings of her arrows. He rubbed his hands before the fire and canted his head. "This isn't called 'taking the day off.' Come with me."

She only stared.

"It's been forever since you've stepped out as Zafira."

She tossed the trimmings in the bin. "But then everyone will know how beautiful I am."

His smile was soft. "As they should."

Her skin buzzed, thinking of last night atop the roof, the cold at her neck. Their faces breaths apart. The curve of his lips and the moon running her fingers through his curls. "Where will we go?"

"Hmm, let's see. Maybe Bakdash?" he asked, his tone making it clear he had thought this through.

Zafira pressed her lips into a line and glowered.

He laughed. "I know you hate everything to do with it, but—"

"I hate the *theory* of it," she groused. "The idea of flocking to buy iced cream while carping about how cold the caliphate is."

"You, Zafira, have a very odd way of thinking." Deen picked up her wool shawl and gave it to her. "Bakdash is ours. It's one of the few things that makes Demenhur special. People used to *flock* here from all across Arawiya for a taste. Give it a try, hmm?" His voice softened. "Who knows when you'll have another chance."

His words struck her. This would be her last day in Demenhur for quite some time. Possibly forever.

A voice nagged at her, telling her this journey to Sharr was a lie of an errand that could only bring pain. But she had seen that look on the Silver Witch's features. Zafira knew what it was like to crave redemption, to blame oneself for a moment's weakness.

It was her fault Baba lay with blue lips beneath ice and snow.

Deen watched her, and despite the silence, she knew by the sorrow drowning his beautiful eyes that he had read everything on her face. It was her most damning feature, having her face speak before she did. A thing people never ceased to tell her. An opinion that had been repeated over and over until it had become fact. She wrapped her shawl and tossed her dwindling coin pouch at him before reaching for the door.

"Let's go freeze our lips."

Deen's grin meant more to her than anything coin could buy.

⋅●▶

Zafira folded into herself when they left the house. She noticed, because she didn't have the obscurity of her cloak around her. Her shoulders dipped forward, pulling in her chest. She tucked her chin low, and pressed her lips thin.

She wasn't shielding herself from the cold.

Deen paused. She felt the warmth of his fingers at her chin before he lifted her face to his level. "Zafira. The moon never fears the night. The gazelle doesn't fear the unknown. Why must you, Huntress?"

"But this is not an unknown."

"These are your *fears*, bleeding from the Hunter and into *you*. Don't fear yourself."

She tried. She tried to keep her mind on other things, like the bothersome asymmetry of the houses tucked side by side to her left and the plain of white snow broken by the wheat-like trunks of the Empty Forest to her right. It was a sparse, barren thing. A babe of a forest, compared to the cursed Arz.

Deen stopped before a bush, leafless and near-dead, sprawling in front of a house. Before she could ask, he made a satisfied *aha!* and turned back to her with something cupped in his palms.

A flower. White and whiskered in a fringe of ice. Silken petals held together in a loose grip.

Zafira remembered a dozen wild roses like this, salvaged by Baba. Pressed into her small palms while he hugged her tight and called her his abal. She had known, even then, that Abal was the name of one of the Six Sisters, and it had made her young self feel powerful as much as it made her feel loved.

Deen folded back her shawl and tucked the flower beneath the dark strands of her hair, and she felt the prick of its stem at her scalp before he took her hand in his. "The beauty that withstands all. Stubborn in the harshest of atmospheres."

"Sounds like a bull," Zafira said against the rock in her throat, and he laughed that laugh she loved more than the warmest of fires on the coldest of nights.

When they reached the sooq, Deen squeezed her hand, and she realized how quick she was to mindlessly retreat into herself. She held her chin high as they passed a girl trailing her mother, a shawl around her small shoulders, a steaming cake held reverently in her small fists. They passed a man hauling a wagon of rugs, promising discounts as he barreled on, and another with a trunk full of salves, tinctures, and medicinal herbs, listing prices that made Zafira's eyes pop. Merchants shouted. People bartered. The jumu'a was warm beneath her shoes. Old Adib's stall was busy, the skins of Zafira's hunts being passed from man to woman, woman to Adib, bartering and bickering until they settled on a price.

"Good to know Adib is doing well," Zafira noted.

Deen grunted. "He's getting harder to deal with, that one. We might have to find a new merchant."

He guided her to a small shop tucked behind the one for the superstitious. Unlike the others, this wooden door was a shade of lavender. Zafira touched the smooth surface just as it swung open and a girl burst out, darting through the sooq with an excited shout, her brother behind her.

Deen grinned at Zafira. "Ready?"

"I've never been more excited," she drawled, but she suddenly was. There was a rose in her hair and a smile on Deen's face. There was a pastel door before her and warmth carving a home in her chest. Something thrummed at her fingers, and she wanted to bottle this feeling and cherish it forever.

She did not expect an iced cream parlor to be warm. To be so full of people and wide smiles. Clattering spoons and jeweled metal bowls. Deen tugged her to a corner of the majlis, and she slipped out of her shoes and folded her legs beneath her, setting her arms on the low table. Everything was so . . . *clean*.

"What flavor do you want to try?" Deen asked, unable to dim the light in his eyes.

Zafira slanted her mouth. "Iced cream?"

"Plain it is." He laughed and went to the counter, where two men taking orders greeted Deen by name as he passed them a few dinars. A third figure stood farther back, tugging gooey white cream by the handful. She wore the same outfit as the men.

She. Skies. Zafira studied the workers more closely as Deen returned and sat across from her.

"Who runs Bakdash?" Zafira asked as two girls sat down to their other side and a third went to order for them. The place was bustling, despite the cold. The place was *happy*, reminding her of what she did not have— peace, happiness, a life. All she did was hunt and get ready for the next hunt.

"It's been in the same family for generations. Why the sudden interest?"

"The one in the back," she said, voice low, "is a woman."

Deen looked to the trio, and pride broke across his face. "They are good people."

Zafira made a sound. "Allowing their sister to work with them isn't a glorious feat."

"No—but defying your caliph is," Deen pointed out, and she couldn't argue with that.

A young boy brought them a platter. He set a spoon in front of Zafira, followed by a metal bowl full of fluffy white cream topped with slivered pistachios and an eye-popping candied cherry that could not have been easy to come by.

Deen watched her. "It's called emaa, from the old tongue. It's not the same as iced cream, but it's what makes Bakdash special. They keep it frozen with ice and use their hands to tug it free."

Zafira hadn't eaten iced cream to know the difference. She merely *hmm*ed and tucked her spoon into the white blob, surprised at its softness and the taffy-like pull. It smelled subtly of rose water.

"Don't stare," she commanded.

Deen gave her a sheepish grin and shoved a spoonful of emaa into his mouth with a shrug. She touched her spoon to her lips, the cold chilling her skin. She shivered before dipping it into her mouth, surprised by the burst of honey and rose, the sugar sweetening her tongue, the taffy dulling the cold.

"Well?" Deen asked when she had downed more than a bite.

Zafira could only grin, and Deen's eyes sparkled as he gleaned the rest from her face.

This could be her first and last bowl of emaa. The last time she could feel such unrestrained happiness at so mundane a moment. The last time she could see Deen's smile and freeze her lips.

"Not now," Deen whispered, pushing her bowl closer with his knuckles.

He brushed the backs of his fingers across her cheek, and Zafira didn't even think of the people who could see them. This.

She shoved her heavy thoughts aside and leaned back against the cushion of the majlis, the bowl in her hand, nuts between her teeth, and honey on her tongue. In this moment, it was her and Deen and the iced cream she had once cursed but had now begun to love.

Too soon, the boy returned to take her empty bowl and then they were leaving, picking up a few things from the sooq before heading home. When they neared her house, Deen paused before turning to the street where his friend lived.

He held her gaze, voice soft. "Tomorrow?"

"Tomorrow," she said with a nod, and then he was gone.

The clouds skittered in front of the rising moon, darkening the oncoming night, and the Arz looked like a mouth of jagged teeth, black against blue. Light spilled from their kitchen window, and Zafira was glad Lana was home.

She had just finished checking on Sukkar in the stable when a hand fell on her shoulder. She scrambled back before she caught the shimmer of burnished bronze hair against the moonlight.

"You scared me," Zafira exclaimed in a whisper. The rose in her hair fell to the snow, petals scattering.

Yasmine tipped her head as she stepped closer, birdlike. "Funny. You rarely get spooked." Her voice was flat, and the look on her face told Zafira what was coming next.

Not now, she wanted to say. She wanted to cherish the magic of Bakdash a little longer.

"You're going, aren't you?" Yasmine asked. "To Sharr. Before you ask, yes, I know. Kharra. Everyone in this bleeding, ice-brained village would have known before you told me. If Deen hadn't used his head, I don't think I'd ever know."

"Do you want me to be sorry for not ruining your wedding night?"

Zafira seethed, her good mood shattering. Anger flashed across Yasmine's features. "This is my chance to bring down the Arz. To bring back magic. There's no one who knows the Arz better than I do. Even if the Arz weren't a problem, I can't sit here. You know me, Yasmine. I can't just sit here and do nothing."

The Arz groaned in the lengthy silence as the wind curled through its limbs. How much closer had it grown while Zafira whiled away the evening, eating emaa?

"What of your mother? And Lana?"

Zafira laughed softly. "When I meet the caliph tomorrow, I'm going to ask him to give them a better place to live, along with someone to care for Ummi. If he accepts, Lana will forget within days that she even had a sister."

Yasmine just stared back. *Oh.*

"And you—you have Misk. And your brother. I'll ask the caliph for—"

"You think a gift from the caliph will replace you? Do you think I'm that selfish?" Yasmine snarled, adding a string of curses.

Zafira shook her head, and the silence between them was more painful than anything she had experienced. It stretched like a chasm in the darkness, the bridge across it no wider than a thread.

"You might *die* there, Zafira."

Zafira still didn't reply. She still tasted honey on her tongue.

The bridge collapsed.

"There's nothing I can say, is there?" Yasmine asked, a hysterical laugh bubbling at the end.

Zafira pulled on a weary smile.

Before the tears glistening in Yasmine's eyes could fall, Zafira closed the distance between them. She hesitated and settled on a squeeze of Yasmine's shoulder. "Your husband is waiting for you."

Zafira turned away first, her friend's absence a weight in the depths of her heart, Bakdash far in the past.

CHAPTER 13

"GET UP," NASIR SAID.

Altair was sprawled on his bed, looking nothing like the poised man who reveled in taunting.

"That dull, flat voice. I swear, it's a threat on its own," Altair croaked, pulling a pillow over his head. He wore nothing but a pair of emerald sirwal, his qamis nowhere to be seen.

"You want me to be concerned?" Nasir scoffed. "You're coming, too."

"Sultan's teeth, I wonder why I'm so desolate," Altair droned. "Fetch me some qahwa, will you?"

Nasir threw open the curtains, and a shaft of light hit Altair in the face. It was Nasir's first time visiting Altair's rooms, which he had never expected to be this . . . neat. They were just as monotone as his own chambers. Twin peals of female laughter echoed from the adjoining bathroom, and Altair smiled.

Nasir scowled, ears burning.

"Do I look like one of your girls?" he asked. "Fetch the qahwa yourself.

Drink it, dump it on your head, cry in a corner, I don't care. But we sail at sunrise, which means we have to leave the palace soon. I don't know how long it'll take to cross the Arz, and I don't want to get to that wretched island after the Hunter and whoever else."

Altair peeked over the pillow. "So eager to start killing, aren't you?"

Nasir tossed a satchel at Altair's head. "We ride at dusk. Get ready."

"But of course, Sultani. Can't wait."

Nasir bristled. Altair never bothered with titles when it came to Nasir, and his use now bothered Nasir more than his disrespect ever had. He slammed the door shut on Altair's wheezing laughter.

But his steps faltered when someone new entered Altair's receiving rooms.

"Kulsum?"

Her name alone sent the organ in his chest racing. Her dark eyes lit up as his thoughts came to a halt. *Kulsum in Altair's rooms?* He quickened his pace to the door, putting her behind him. He felt her fingers raking the air, reaching for him. Knifing him.

Mute, always mute.

He didn't look back as the door thudded shut.

———◆———

Nasir took the weapons on his person, along with a rucksack containing a few provisions and a change of clothes.

He expected this journey to be quick, no longer than a few weeks. Head straight through the Arz, sail to Sharr, follow the Hunter, and bring back the lost Jawarat.

Beneath the light of a heavy moon, Nasir saddled a gray stallion, and Altair saddled a roan beside him. The general was an odd sight in hashashin gear, with armor so thin one couldn't imagine it existed at all.

A hashashin's garb was made for blending, for appearing unthreatening, despite the numerous weapons obscured along his body. But in typical Altair fashion, there was something to make one glance at him again. He had discarded the obscuring outer robes in favor of flashing more skin. Though leather gauntlets were wrapped tight around his forearms, the rest of his corded arms were bare, and a turban rimmed in red was styled around his head. The traditional sash around his middle was stark red, too, clashing with his ridiculously colored sirwal.

"Ready to ride the night away, Sultani?" he asked suggestively.

"Save your innuendos for your parties, Altair."

"Ah, so you're not as dumb as your father makes you seem," Altair said with a laugh. "I can't wait until we meet the Hunter. I'll have to introduce you by saying, 'He's not always this grumpy. Then again, he's one of those people who talks less and murders more.'"

"You'll be doing a good job of not frightening him," Nasir said, spurring his stallion forward.

"Shukrun, habibi," Altair called after him. "Endearing as always."

The sands glowed like dying embers in the night. Mansions glittered in the moonlight, and the limestone of the slums loomed eerie and desolate.

No one would be around to see them, not now, when the moon had risen and the cold had begun its sweep across the desert. Nasir's heart stuttered at the thought of crossing the Arz at sunrise, but he didn't have a choice. Kulsum's dark eyes flashed in his mind. The soft curve of Haytham's son's small shoulders.

He never had a choice.

He would cross the Arz and meet the Baransea at sunrise, in whatever condition he stood.

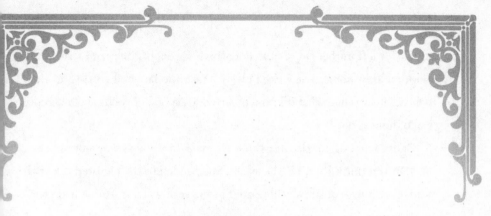

CHAPTER 14

Z AFIRA WOKE TO A PAIR OF CATLIKE EYES STARING INTO HER own. She jerked away. "Yasmine!"

Yasmine answered with a curse. Tears streaked her cheeks, and she looked as though a heavy weight had been set on her shoulders.

"What are you doing here?" Zafira asked, voice rough with sleep. "Shouldn't you be—"

"With my husband? I swear, that's all you ever say when you see me."

Zafira sank back into the pillows and cut a glance at the window before jerking upright again. She had to go. "I have to—"

"Go? Kharra, I know. That's why I came. To see you one last time." Yasmine dropped her gaze to her hands. The henna from her wedding was already fading, the russet now a bright shade of red. She sat on the edge of Zafira's bed, the mattress bowing under her weight.

"Remember when my parents died, and Deen left us to go exploring the kingdom? When he joined that caravan across the Wastes? I still have a little bit left in that tin of hot chocolate he brought back, and I saved the empty vial of honey you licked clean." Yasmine laughed softly and then sighed. "It's strange what I'll remember with a spoon of cocoa and an empty vial of honey, no?"

Zafira tried to puzzle over those words before she swung out of bed.

"Do you think I'll die?" she asked. She padded to the elevated tub with a shiver. Clumps of snow still floated in the cool water Yasmine had probably brought in.

"Do you expect to live? It's scary enough when you disappear into the Arz," Yasmine said, and Zafira heard her recline on the bed.

Zafira glanced at her. "You're awfully optimistic today."

Yasmine shrugged. "It's not every day the sister of your heart settles on a death wish."

"I don't have a death wish, Yasmine. We know I have a better chance at getting through the Arz and, because of it, Sharr. It could be completely different, but I have a *chance* where no one else does. Either way, we won't even see another year before the Arz swallows us whole."

Silence screamed between them as Zafira reached for her clothes and froze. This wasn't the qamis she had left for herself. This was the dress she had worn to Yasmine's wedding, only a lot shorter. She fingered the sharpened swirls along the deep blue shoulder and looked up.

Yasmine smiled. "I know how much you love that dress, and I also know it's a tad tight. So, I . . . shortened it and made it a little looser. If you're going to save the world, you might as well do it in style."

Zafira laughed softly and slipped it over her head, the material soft against her skin. It was lighter, but Sharr wasn't a snowy mess like Demenhur. Her cloak would help her bear the cold until she left.

"Promise me," Yasmine said softly, "that if you die, you will die fighting to return to me."

Zafira struggled to smile. "I would kiss you goodbye, but your husband wouldn't like it."

Yasmine sputtered a laugh and rushed forward, throwing her arms around her. Zafira wasn't certain which of them trembled more. Yasmine pulled away and pressed her forehead against hers, and Zafira inhaled the scent of orange blossom and spice one last time.

"Come back, Zafira. No matter what. Victorious or not, come back."

The cool water had numbed Zafira's skin, but her blood was ablaze as she ruminated her next words, because she was never good at saying goodbye. "I don't plan on dying. I plan on finding that daama Jawarat and coming back."

It was only after she had said the words that she believed them.

Zafira left her room with a sense of finality, Yasmine trailing in silence. But the strength of her words faltered when she glimpsed into Umm's room, Umm's sleeping form denying them a goodbye. Zafira hadn't thought she would miss her mother, but their conversation the day before had left her bereft.

Lana's small shadow crept to her. She was bulked by her coat, dress hem trailing. She gripped her green shawl with fidgeting fingers, knuckles whiter than the cold allowed.

Zafira swung her satchel over her shoulder. "Ready to live somewhere else?" She still wasn't sure how she would put the question to the caliph when she met him. *Skies, the caliph.*

"While you're off dying somewhere?" Lana shrugged and bit her lip.

"There you go! The right questions are finally being asked," Yasmine cheered.

"Why? Why are you doing this?" Lana asked.

"I'm the only chance we have," Zafira said, trailing her knuckles over Baba's blue coat. *The only vengeance Baba will receive.*

"By dying in some cursed place? They'll hail you as a martyr and celebrate you. Talk about you. That's what happens in the books. But you'll be dead and I'll be . . . Okht, I'll be alone," Lana whispered.

Zafira's eyes burned. "It's what Baba would have wanted."

"Don't go in there on Baba's name," Lana pleaded, an edge to her voice. "He's dead."

"She's right," Yasmine said, voice soft. "If you're going to risk your life, it has to be on *your* will. The living can't survive with promises to the dead."

It wasn't just because of Baba. Why didn't they understand? It was magic. It was their *survival*.

"Don't you want magic?" Zafira asked, fervent. She looked at Lana. "Think of Baba's stories—we can experience them, feel them. *Live* them. We'll finally know what we were born with."

"A life without magic isn't so bad."

"A life without magic is what stole the desert from us. And Baba. And Umm. Your parents, too, Yasmine. It's what's causing the Arz to grow."

"Baba is gone, Okht. And Yasmine's parents are dead. The Arz can grow. We can move elsewhere." Lana's eyes glistened with tears. She didn't understand that they couldn't go anywhere the Arz wouldn't follow; no one in Arawiya could. "A life with magic means nothing to me if you aren't in it."

Lana's words carved a chasm in Zafira's heart. She swept her sister's hair from her forehead, tucking it behind the shell of one ear. She brushed her fingers along her freckled skin, still soft as a babe's.

She didn't say all would be right. She did not say she would return. Or that Lana would be safe. She would waste no breath with false promises.

"Let's go meet the caliph."

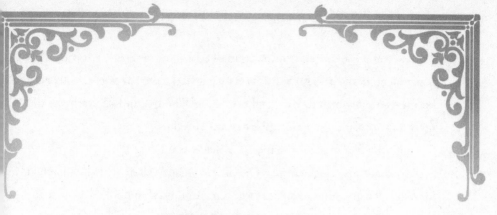

CHAPTER 15

"I'M SURE WE'RE TIRED. ARE YOU TIRED, NASIR?" ALTAIR ASKED, breaking the silence of the howling wind.

Mildly, Nasir registered Altair calling him by his name, not his title. He lowered his sand-dusted keffiyah from his face.

The Arz was . . . gone.

In its place lay a stream of splotched black stones that stretched from east to west. But that wasn't what drew Nasir's gaze. Laa, the water did. A line of azure met the sky, crystalline beneath the beams of the sun. It was harsh, even at this early hour, and the farther Nasir looked, the more the world wavered. There wasn't a man or house in sight to witness it, only endless sands of burnt umber.

The water lapping the stony shore was a foreign sound his mother had murmured stories about, before she was killed—*died*. Before she had died. Surprise was making him slip, making true memories creep past forged ones. Nasir clenched his jaw and tugged on the horse's reins just so the creature would move.

The water's apparent gentleness masked a stark savagery. After the Arz had appeared and the royal minarets went dark, the sea was said to have become a monster in its own right. *Like you.* Though, unlike Nasir, he did not know which master this monster answered to.

Nor who had made it the monster that it was.

"Look at those sleek curves. One fine woman," Altair whistled, hand at his brow. Nasir squinted against the sun. A grand ship bobbed against the current a little ways to his right. Fine indeed. "Perhaps it's all a mirage."

Nasir stilled when movement caught his eye. A flash of silver and a glint of white, and everything suddenly made a sort of sick sense.

"That is no mirage," Nasir said coolly.

Altair's demeanor hardened when he followed Nasir's gaze to the Silver Witch.

She moved in flashes. She was afar, then closer, and then directly before him. Three blinks, and Nasir stared down at her flawless face, his horse rearing, flanks damp with sweat.

He lost control of his limbs and found himself standing on the sand so that the woman wouldn't have to crane her neck. The horses backed away. All of this happened on her call, he knew, but without so much as a twitch from her. Was there no limit to her power?

"Did your father expect you to crawl through the Arz and swim to Sharr?" the witch asked, dark eyes moving from Nasir to assess Altair.

"He is not my father," Altair said, venom in his voice.

"Yet you stand beside your prince as an equal."

"And if that irked him, I'm sure he would make it known," Altair replied curtly. "He does have a way of making a state—"

"Altair," Nasir warned.

The witch's gaze glittered. "Indeed, General, listen to your commander."

The black stones gleamed as the sun rose higher.

"What do you want?" Nasir said, keeping his voice level. They needed to leave.

"What do *I* want? I'm here because Ghameq counted on my interception. Had you set foot in the Arz, you would both be dead. I am not your enemy, princeling."

Nasir bit his tongue—Ghameq *had* promised a ship would be waiting for him. He hadn't even mentioned the Arz.

The witch gave him a knowing look, and with a twist of her crimson lips, she drew an object from the folds of her silver cloak. A disc of deep red, its edges etched in silver filigree. "A compass. To help you find what you desire most."

"The Jawarat," Nasir said, and waited one extra beat before taking it from her. It buzzed in his hand with the barest thrum of *something*.

The witch only smiled. "I'm sure Ghameq sent you here with enough threats to last you the journey. That poor girl has already lost her tongue."

Nasir bristled, remembering Kulsum in Altair's chambers. When Altair was in bed. "She's of no concern to me. She belongs to the general now."

"Ah. So *she's* the reason behind the ink on your arm."

Nasir tugged at his already lowered sleeve and gritted his teeth. *Witch.* Water lapped against the stones. Somewhere a vulture screamed, circling a fresh corpse.

"I've also heard of a young boy in the dungeons. There doesn't seem to be a shortage of souls you'll grow attached to," she *tsk*ed. "Some advice for your journey: Quell your compassion. Stave it. Exploit it. Remember who trained you, hashashin. Do not sour her image."

Nasir paused and lifted his eyes to hers. There was no mirth in her gaze now, only cool assessment.

"Who are you?" he asked.

"Someone like you." She turned, and the curve of her retreating shoulders beckoned, almost a challenge. "You're welcome for the ship."

He blinked, and the Silver Witch vanished.

CHAPTER 16

Z AFIRA OFTEN DREAMED OF THE ARZ BLEEDING THE WAY BABA
had. The dark trees always blossomed red in her dreams.
Now they were gone.

Beneath the shadows of her hood, she blinked a thousand times, but
the Arz had vanished. The crisp cold stung her nostrils and she paused,
expecting a wave of relief. *Then why do I feel loss?*

Shop owners with flour-dusted thobes and grease-splotched dresses
were scattered across the snowy plain. They couldn't know about the trek.
They'd likely noticed the Arz's absence from the sooq and hurried here,
loud voices clouding the cold air. Despite their excitement, no one crossed
the unnatural line where the snow ended like the clean cut of a knife.

Zafira hopped down from Sukkar, helping Lana do the same. When she
placed a hasty kiss on Sukkar's nose, he gave her a curious nudge, for even
he knew Zafira was miserly in her affections.

Beside her, Yasmine and Misk dismounted a mare of their own, and

Deen dug through the satchel strapped to Lemun's saddle before letting out a whistle. "Now that's a sight."

Yasmine hummed in agreement, but she held herself differently. A little fragile, a little delicate.

Because of me. Zafira dragged Lana to the front of the crowd, brushing past a trio of boisterous men and a tiny seamstress, bits of thread clinging to her like worms.

They stopped at a border of black. Where the Arz had once reached for the skies, black pebbles covered the ground, and no sign of the forest remained. No stray tree, no pile of dead twigs, no bush or bramble. Nothing at all to hint at its existence.

It had vanished entirely, the odd stones left in its wake.

Deen stepped to her side, and when she squinted at him against the morning light, she knew that he, too, was reliving their encounter with the Silver Witch. It wasn't *loss* that she felt, she realized. It was the familiar presence of something that was there, despite how it seemed to her eyes.

"Do you feel it?" she murmured to Deen when Lana bent to pick up one of the stones. *The whisper of trees and the brush of leaves.*

He nodded, and she quelled a surge of guilty, selfish elation because she wasn't alone.

Deen lifted his eyes to the skies. "Not even the Silver Witch can be powerful enough to make an entire forest disappear permanently."

"Maybe not, but she's making the start of this journey easy," Zafira said. Unease roiled in her stomach. If the Silver Witch could make an entire forest disappear, why couldn't she retrieve a book?

"Which isn't reassuring," he agreed. "But this is what you've chosen, no? And if she can't lie . . ." He trailed off.

"You believed that? What—if she lies, she'll light up in flames?"

He gave her a mock laugh. "She simply *can't* lie. Some creatures can't. Like safin."

Zafira loosed a slow breath as he meandered away. As if meeting creatures that weren't human was an everyday thing.

A breeze heavy with salt brushed Zafira's skin. She had been so engrossed with the lack of the Arz that she hadn't noticed what its disappearance had given her: the sea. The daama Baransea, where, true to the witch's word, a gleaming ship bobbed in its waters. It looked no more than a quick jog away—a lie, for the Arz was far larger.

Zafira imagined Baba beside her, finally seeing the sea he so loved, the vastness he had spun countless stories about. He had loved the *idea* of the sea, for he had never seen it. He never would.

"It's real," Lana whispered, a tiny thing for fourteen years. She latched her fingers around Zafira's cloak.

"Did you doubt its existence?"

The waves lapped forward, each one imitating the last, and the longer Zafira stared, the more it felt she was moving with them.

"I don't know. It was always a story," Lana said, looking up at her. The melancholy in her eyes knifed Zafira's chest. Finger by finger, Lana pulled away. Zafira felt she had upset her somehow.

She watched her sister show her salvaged stone to Deen and then Yasmine, who looked stunning as always in a pale blue dress laced with white. She watched Misk reach for the pebble, drawing a shy smile from Lana. It would last only a day, that shyness, and then Deen, Yasmine, and Misk would be her family.

Zafira, a memory.

When she turned back to the sea, she was surprised to see it waver before her. She was surprised by the tears that she wiped away, carefully sealing her heart once more.

The sea glistened like liquid jewels, freedom, beckoning as the Arz had. It called to her, a purr across the soft waves that sounded much like her name.

Chimes on the wind. Her name in a breeze.

"Hunter," Yasmine hissed.

Silence fell, and she felt the weight of eyes like countless stones pelted upon her back. Black pebbles lay uneven beneath her boots. Zafira blinked and tried to make sense of the ache in her chest, the racing of her pulse. *That whisper.*

Yasmine looked as if roots were about to sprout out of the ground and swallow Zafira whole. *It's safe*, Zafira wanted to say, but she did not doubt the Silver Witch's smile. That flicker of darkness she felt whenever the woman was near.

She was saved from an explanation when a horn disrupted the silence; ululating and chanting soon followed as a caravan approached with half a dozen camels draped in wool, tan coats spotted with snow.

Zafira made sense of the chanting: *Sayyidi. Sayyidi. Sayyidi.*

The Caliph of Demenhur had come.

Yasmine yanked Zafira to the front of the crowd. A boy tried to look beneath her hood, but she tugged on the fabric, further shrouding her face. She clenched and unclenched her fists by her sides, the smooth leather of her gloves contouring around her fingers. She threw a discreet glance at Deen.

He was already watching her, eyes dark in thought.

Commotion surrounded the caravan as a man hopped down from one of the camels. He wore a red-and-white-checkered keffiyah atop his head. A small beard framed his chin. A slender nose, chiseled cheekbones—he was a good-looking man.

His eyes, however, made the air catch in her throat. Had that same haunted look not been in Lana's eyes, Zafira wouldn't have understood the utter despair. Who hadn't the curse touched? Even the ones better off than she were suffering.

"Who is that man?" Zafira asked, leaning toward Deen.

Something flickered in his gaze. "Haytham. The caliph's advisor. He was one of Demenhur's best falconers before his father, the late advisor, introduced him to the caliph."

"Oh." Zafira couldn't imagine a life in which she did anything for fun and sport, let alone rely on a bird to win something for her.

An older man in a dusky blue turban descended from a traditional howdah—a small, tented seat atop the camel. His layered gray thobe darkened as it trailed the snow, making him seem even more ancient than he was. People dropped to their knees, drenching themselves in snow. Others lifted two fingers to their brows, heads low.

The caliph. The cause of her dress, of hatred toward the Sisters, and of oppression against the hundreds of women in Demenhur.

He was nonplussed by the missing Arz, and she wondered if the Silver Witch had discussed more with him than she had with Zafira. His hooded gaze drifted over the small crowd, pausing on her. The Hunter. She clutched Yasmine's arm.

"Since the loss of magic, you are our one source of light," he called. "At last. Come here, boy."

He knows me, she thought, before her brain reminded her that this was the old nut responsible for the imbalance between men and women. Lana clasped her hand, but Yasmine jerked her head. *Yalla*, her glare shouted. Deen pursed his lips, sharing Zafira's worry tenfold. Misk watched curiously.

Zafira rocked forward on her toes. The ice crackled beneath her boots. The air hung still. Dozens of eyes bored into her cloak, and her heart might as well have hopped into her hands; she felt its thrum in her fingers.

The awkward silence was broken by a group of soldiers dismounting camels. At the distinct lilt of another caliphate's dialect, Zafira jerked her head to a dark-skinned man laughing with his fellows. A Pelusian, though he wore the Demenhune uniform. How had a man born to Pelusia, a half-month's journey away, ended up in Demenhur?

Zafira had a deep respect for the Pelusians. Though their fertile lands were faltering, they nourished all of Arawiya. Without them, the kingdom would lack the mechanical advancements they had, too. Like the chandeliers the rich owned, or the Nimrud lens for magnifying texts and lighting fires.

Zafira stopped. *The caliph, the caliph, the caliph.*

"Sayyidi," she murmured, clearing her throat when she realized she hadn't lowered her voice. Her skin burned and she dropped to one knee, gritting her teeth when the cold seeped through.

The caliph laughed, a low rumbling filled with warmth. It reminded her of that precious vial of honey Deen had brought from Zaram. Try as she might, she couldn't summon her rage.

"Please, rise," Ayman al-Ziya, the Caliph of Demenhur, said.

Zafira stood carefully, hands at her sides, hood throbbing against her scalp. From the confines of it, she studied the caliph without shame. His face sagged with wrinkles, but his brown eyes shone like those of a child's, thrilled at a game. A long beard wound from his chin, wisping at the ends.

"And show some respect." The words were said in that clipped accent— the Pelusian from that group of soldiers. All of Arawiya spoke the same language, with slight variations to each tongue, but Zafira didn't need help reading between the words.

Drop your hood was what he meant.

Silence fell with the sharpness of a blade. Eyes fell upon her, watching, waiting, burning. Countless. Blood roared in her ears.

When she didn't move, the Pelusian grunted and shuffled.

Fingers brushed her hood.

Snow pulsed beneath her boots.

The cold caught in her chest.

"Enough," the caliph thundered. Zafira flinched. "Haytham, rid me of these men. Respect is earned, Pelusian, and you certainly have none of it."

No one moved. No one *breathed.*

Zafira exhaled, and the world spun back into motion. Her fingers twitched to throw down her hood. *Be proud,* Yasmine had said time and time again. But she couldn't be. She wasn't proud. She was *afraid.*

She was afraid of being a woman. Yasmine's disappointment settled heavily on her back.

Sweet snow below. A soldier had just ordered her to drop her hood, and the caliph had snapped at him on her behalf. Zafira watched from the corners of her eyes as Haytham led the group of soldiers away, shouting the entire time. His final command was followed by a reply of which Zafira caught a hiss: "He looks like a daama nisa." Indeed, she *was* a "bloody woman," and it was the Pelusian's loss for not knowing any better.

"When the time is right, Hunter, you will know it. Until then, a hooded boy is fine by me," the caliph said softly. Kindly.

She drew in a breath. She hated the rare moments when she had to speak, and now, in the presence of so many, she found it even harder. Even more so because Deen, Yasmine, and Lana were here, too.

"Shukrun, sayyidi," she said, pitching her voice as low as she could. It rumbled from her throat, barely decipherable.

He stopped her before she could kneel again. Everyone knew the caliph had no royal blood in his veins—none of them did. Not even Sultan Ghameq, with whom the sultana had fallen in love and to whom she had handed the crown of Arawiya. The Sisters had never expected to die, and there was no one in line to succeed to their thrones when they had all but vanished.

Humans were nowhere near as powerful as the Sisters, and a council in Sultan's Keep wasn't enough. So in each caliphate, the people turned to the Sisters' most trusted men. Here, it had been Ayman's father. It was love for the old caliph that kept Ayman on the throne.

"Our minarets may light once again," the caliph said, his voice low, the words meant for her alone. "We might finally be free of this curse. Do you assent to the silver invitation, Hunter?"

Laughter bubbled to Zafira's lips and she swallowed it down. Why did she always want to laugh at the least opportune times? Her heart began rising to her throat.

Say yes. Yes meant undulating waves. Magic for the future. Every tale of Baba's a reality. Vengeance upon the forest that stole him away.

My life forfeit.

A quiver began at Zafira's fingertips. A tic in her neck danced to some frenzied tune. The upper half of her body tipped forward in assent, but the rest of her held back. The people that had gathered from the villages watched, not knowing what was happening, but Haytham's gaze weighed upon her heavily from his place beside the caliph.

Conquering the Arz wasn't enough. Skies. This—*this* was what she had been waiting for.

Zafira inhaled deep and felt the crash of her heart. She nodded. Sealing her life to a miserable cause. For the future of her people. *For magic.*

Haytham's sigh of relief echoed the caliph's.

She was going to do what no man had done before. It meant the people of Arawiya had a chance at survival. A chance to outlive the Arz, to feel magic roar through their veins.

But then.

Boots she knew as well as her own shuffled to her side, filling her with foreboding. She looked to her right as he looked to his left.

Deen.

CHAPTER 17

ZAFIRA TRIED TO STRAIGHTEN HER SHOULDERS, BUT SHE WAS stuck. Like the little birds she sometimes found in the snow. *It's strange what I'll remember with a spoon of cocoa and an empty vial of honey.*

Yasmine knew.

"Deen Ra'ad?" Haytham asked.

The question jerked Zafira from her thoughts. She didn't know Haytham knew of Deen.

"Can I help you?"

"I'd like to join the quest," Deen said, lifting his head.

His voice. His words. Every nerve ending that had frayed when Zafira nodded finally exploded.

"Why would a deserter want to go?" a nearby soldier shouted. It seemed they knew about the quest, too. Murmurs rose through the crowd, polluting the air with wrongful thoughts. "He'd sooner abandon his caliphate than—"

"*Enough!* He was discharged from our ranks with honor!" Haytham shouted.

Deen nearly had been a deserter after his parents' deaths, but he was saved the dishonor when the caliph gave him a discharge that some felt he had taken too readily.

Haytham said, not unkindly, "Only the Hunter was invited."

She could hear Deen's inhale. That shuddering draw she knew so well. The same draw before he had proposed. He was close enough to touch, to beg in a whisper, but the caliph stood before them, and every movement of hers as the Hunter took the strength of a thousand.

"Do you intend to send him alone?" Deen asked evenly.

It was clear Haytham hadn't considered that. "There are many qualified men still in our service."

Deen inclined his head. "They may be superior in strength, but their loyalties lie with Demenhur, with Arawiya."

He spoke loudly, clearly, but Zafira knew that tone, the fear humming beneath the surface. "You need someone like me."

"I don't follow," Haytham said slowly.

"Just as there is no man more likely to succeed than the Hunter"—he stopped, and there was another shuddering draw—"there is no man in Arawiya more loyal to the Hunter than I."

In the silence, the shards of Zafira's heart crumbled.

Fell.

Wept.

Drowned.

She watched as the wheels spun in Haytham's head and the logic of Deen's words struck. People murmured, their whispers buzzing in the air. She wanted to fall to her knees and scream.

Haytham inhaled. He opened his mouth, damning her. Damning *him,* the man who wanted to marry her.

"Very well," he said. He sounded far off. The pound of *Sharr, Sharr, Sharr* in her pulse turned to *Deen, Deen, Deen.* "You may join the Hunter. Sayyidi Ayman, cast your eyes upon the two who will restore glory to Arawiya."

The caliph smiled. Haytham beamed. Neither realized what had just been done.

Zafira felt the heavy silence of a tomb.

She turned away abruptly. Deen trailed her like a child's rag doll, but she was afraid that if she started stringing letters together, she would end with her nails on his beautiful face, so she kept her mouth pressed closed. For here, where she was supposed to be a man, she could not afford mistakes. She stared at Yasmine's tear-stained face and turned, heading to where the Arz had just recently stood on spindly trunks.

It was familiar. It was grounding. It terrified her.

A good distance away, the waves lapped lazily against the black stones, reaching and retreating. The ship tilted and righted.

She knew, then, why the Silver Witch had chosen that moment to arrive in the stable, when Deen and Zafira were together, secluded, thoughts and feelings raw. Pliable. She had sent only one invitation, but she had always intended for Deen to be a part of the journey.

She had promised that the sultan wouldn't know, but there was no doubt he would learn an entire segment of the Arz had disappeared and that the notable Hunter had boarded a ship on the Baransea itself.

What other plans did she spin in her web of silver, deceiving without lying?

"Quite a sight, isn't it?" someone asked, stepping to her side. Haytham. A wicked sword hung from his side, the white hilt carved with words from the old tongue.

Could she describe the sea as beautiful? Yes, very much so. But was that a word a man would use? Her brain refused to think, so she settled with a nod.

This close, it wouldn't be difficult to discern she was no boy, so she held herself carefully. Haytham smiled, his eyes darting a path across her face—her lips, her nose, the hood that concealed the rest of her. She was lucky her delicate features were a commonality in Demenhur, and that—

"You're younger than I thought."

She stopped breathing. *I could* pass for a young boy. Albeit a tall one. Haytham opened his mouth. Zafira swallowed.

"The caliph is an old man," Haytham said finally, and she exhaled in relief. "He is disheartened over the ruin of our lands and the whole of Arawiya. He appreciates what you do for the western villages, but he has not had a chance to reward you for your deeds. This was not how he wanted to meet you for the first time."

Zafira kept her lips thinned and forced a smile. "That's all right, effendi."

"Please, Haytham will do," he said.

Some ways behind them, the caliph hacked a cough that rattled down to his bones.

Haytham looked back at her. "Did you know there is an heir to our ice throne?"

Zafira blinked at his change of thought, and unease skittered across her skin. "I thought the caliph was childless."

"As does the rest of the Arawiya," Haytham said. "You see, the heir is a girl. Cast away by her father, because how can a girl take control of an entire caliphate?"

"How can a woman do anything at all?" Zafira bit out, anger masking her surprise.

"I have always wished for someone to take matters into her own hands," he said, an odd tone to his words. He studied her as he spoke. "To prove to our caliph that a body is only a body and that a soul determines one's actions. Yet here we are, aren't we, Huntress?"

Panic gripped her, climbed her throat. "How?" she whispered.

"Experience. What better way to allow a woman before tutors of politics and battle strategy than to dress her as a boy?"

Zafira thought of that girl, the calipha-to-be.

"You have made a place for a man who does not exist," Haytham continued. "I will do what I can, readying the caliph's daughter for her role by right, but if you can find it in your heart to embrace what you are, the world will be better for it."

Snow flitted from the skies, and anger burned her sight. How could he impose that responsibility upon her? Wasn't she doing enough?

"May I borrow our esteemed Hunter, Haytham?"

The caliph. Haytham froze for the barest of moments before stepping away, and the caliph smiled as he took Haytham's place by Zafira's side. Deen joined them, trying to catch her eye.

She ignored him. One moment he had wanted to marry her and explore the world, the next he was ready to lie down and die like an old man.

But if Deen had a death wish, who was she to stop him?

She had one to match.

The caliph caught a snowflake in his weathered palm. "I have faith you will claim victory over the lost Jawarat. We may not have the brutality of the Zaramese, the cunning of the Sarasins, the wisdom and might of the Pelusians, or the experience of the Alder safin, but we have good intentions, good hearts, and the two of you."

Two men handed Zafira and Deen each a satchel.

"Salves, dates, and preserved meat," the caliph explained.

"I have a request," Zafira said quickly, voice hoarse. "If I may, sayyidi," she added.

He inclined his head, and she took it as permission to continue.

"I-I would like for our families—mine and Deen Ra'ad's—to be given shelter in your palace." She kept her voice in a careful rasp. "In Thalj. And care for my mother, who is ill."

The caliph was silent.

Zafira felt she had overstepped. *Skies, Zafira. Thalj?* She worried her lip and flicked her gaze to Haytham, but he was a picture of nervous emotion now, looking into the distance as if he were expecting someone. Zafira looked away, before his jittery stance could transfer to her.

"Granting your families residence in the palace of Thalj is the very least I could do for saviors with the hearts of lions," the caliph said finally. "And finding a nurse for an ill mother is a simple matter."

She jerked a nod, tamping down her relief before it could twitch her lips into a smile. "There is one more thing. Without my hunts, the western villages won't—"

"We will take care of that, too," he said. "It will not be easy, but we will provide more grain from our stores, and venison when possible."

Zafira exhaled.

"Rest assured, my fearless, we will take care of everything," the caliph promised.

Everything. All she needed to do was get through the Baransea, venture across Sharr, and return with the book. Or die. Simple enough.

Zafira's chest constricted. Deen returned to the others and bumped noses with Misk in farewell, then lingered in a fierce embrace with Yasmine, the look on her face crushing a weight against Zafira's chest. He drew Lana into a hug, straightened her shawl, and gave them some last-minute instructions on caring for Sukkar and Lemun.

Zafira watched from afar, because she couldn't step closer. She might never see them again. She might never grip Lana's hands or hear Yasmine's voice. But she didn't know how to say goodbye. So she looked her fill and closed her eyes and breathed deep.

The caliph smiled, and Zafira wanted to tell him, *laa*, they weren't fearless.

"Whether you return as heroes or succumb as martyrs, you will forever be in our souls." His next words were directed at her. "May Arawiya be with you, lionheart."

It was a kind dismissal. A farewell offered to a soldier not expected to return.

A plank connected the ship to the pebbled shore. Zafira looked back at Yasmine gripping Lana's shoulders, Misk behind them. He held her gaze, despite her heavy hood, and gave her a small nod, the tassels of his turban fluttering in the cold breeze. There was a strange look on his face, as if he was just now seeing her for the first time. *He knows who I am.*

"Farewell," she whispered, before carefully crossing the stones, entering what used to be the Arz. They slid beneath her boots, clattering like fresh bones. Even a quarter of the way across, they were surprisingly clean. Not even a leaf lay on them.

After what felt like forever, she reached the shore, Deen trailing her in silence. She leaned down as if to touch the water, but he guided her to the ship, eyes wide at her antics, and she jerked from his touch. The plank creaked beneath her weight, moaning a goodbye as she furthered from the place she called home.

The ship bobbed in welcome, and though she knew what it was like to be atop a beast that moved of its own accord, this felt different. Like her stomach had come untethered. She gripped the railing.

From the snow in the distance, dozens watched her and Deen. She was too far away to make out the glimmer of tears that shone in Yasmine's eyes. Too far from her family already. She looked away, to the gleaming ship, unnaturally perfect. Zafira knew whom she had to thank.

That woman with a smile of ice, limitless in her power, effortless in her command.

A man carrying a trunk passed in front of them, and Deen nodded in his direction. "There's something wrong with them. I mean, this ship can't be real. It was the Silver Witch's doing. Maybe the men aren't real, either. We don't have a reason for trunks and whatever else they're carrying around. They're moving about, doing nothing, and I have a feeling this ship will sail itself."

Zafira didn't like the idea of a mirage taking them across the Baransea. An illusion full of illusionary men. She suppressed a shudder, but she was still too angry to feel anything else.

Deen sighed after a moment. "You have no right to be angry at me. You decided to do this just as I did."

"No, dolt. You decided to do this *because* I did!" she shouted.

For a long moment, they stared at each other, tensed breaths clouding the chilled air. Her eyes burned, tracing the curve of his mouth, always so quick to smile. The shadow of a beard, darkening his skin. The crease between his brows, now furrowed in anger. Those rogue bronze curls, slipping from his turban to catch the light.

He looked different without a thobe and the bulk of the coat he always wore. His loose trousers were tucked into his calfskin boots. A dark linen shirt complemented the indigo turban loose around his head.

An ax lay against his back—it had been a long time since Zafira had seen him with his weapon of choice. He once prided himself in having been trained by a Zaramese fighter, for only they were skilled with the tabar. But that was before. The past Deen.

He was here now because of her. He had set aside his fears and pledged his daama life because of her. It was her fault.

The fight rushed out of her. "Don't come."

His answering question was immediate. "Why not?"

Zafira looked up at the sky, down at the ship, and then straight at him. "I don't want to lose you."

"You cannot lose what's already lost." Deen shook his head slowly.

Zafira jerked back. "What does that mean?" she asked. Then she thought of his dream and said, "No, no, it's fine. I don't want to know."

She crossed her arms over her chest as if her world hadn't skidded to a halt and begun anew. The tales of Sharr were terrifying, but those of the Baransea were equally so. They told of creatures large enough to swallow ships and the sea itself. Of smaller ones great enough in number to eat away a vessel while its occupants idled unaware. The waters lapped lazily against the ship in false innocence.

"They'll tell stories about us," he coaxed.

She considered ignoring him, but they were in this together now. She begrudgingly cast him a look, pretending something didn't lighten in her chest when relief flickered in his eyes.

"I never thought you vain," Zafira said, raising an eyebrow.

He laughed. "That's how men are."

She smiled. "I see you've been reacquainted with your tabar."

Something flashed across his features before he grinned, and Zafira knew this was the moment in which they forgave each other.

"Indeed. I see you've brought only, what, fifteen arrows?" He punched her lightly on the shoulder, and her heart warmed. "What if you miss, Hunter?"

"You know me, Ra'ad. I never miss."

CHAPTER 18

THE COMPASS IN NASIR'S POCKET WAS HIS ONLY
proof that he hadn't imagined the Silver Witch. He tucked his
keffiyah into his bag and whispered in the gray stallion's ear to
find his way home.

Had the Demenhune Hunter already boarded a ship in his caliphate?
Had Haytham led his caliph to the Arz, where Ghameq's stolen Sarasin
forces would murder everyone in proximity of the western villages?

Children, elderly, innocents. There was no end to death.

Nasir set his jaw. "We need to get moving. The ship isn't going to sail
itself."

"Don't tell me you can sail a ship, princeling," Altair said.

Nasir bristled at the name the Silver Witch had used. "I didn't—"

"Ah, you won't have to do a thing. Look! Men to do your bidding."

The sea breeze tousled Nasir's hair. There *were* men on board, but
something about them gave him pause as he boarded the ship.

"These aren't men." He crossed the deck to where a figure stood at the helm. "They cast no shadows."

"Akhh, I feel safer now, knowing we'll be on a ship full of phantoms," Altair said with an exaggerated smile. He walked up to one of the men and shoved his hand through him, grasping at air. "I can even wring his neck and he wouldn't feel a thing . . . Neither would I, for that matter."

Nasir sighed. The phantom men soundlessly removed the plank and released the moorings. The longer he watched them move about in perfect synchrony, without a gesture or sound of communication, the more it unnerved him.

He looked away. "Stay alert, will you."

For if the Arz was a taste of dark magic and Sharr was evil incarnate, the sea between them would be just as nefarious. He grabbed his bow, but his eyebrows fell when he looked to Altair. "You brought a bow . . . without arrows."

Altair cocked a grin, something calculating in his gaze. "You've got plenty to spare, haven't you?"

Nasir inhaled through his nose, and handed Altair five black-and-silver arrows, indicating how long he expected Altair to last.

He met Nasir's gaze with a startlingly genuine one as he nocked an arrow. "Alert I will be, Sultani."

Ruler and subject once more. He had a feeling Altair knew of Nasir's orders to kill him. Altair clearly knew more than that, judging by the fear on his face that night at the Daama Faris. Why come along if he knew of his impending doom?

But to question was to display weakness, and Nasir was no weakling, no matter how great his curiosity.

"Off we go, children," Altair called, and the ship lurched forward with Nasir's stomach.

Sharr was nowhere to be seen. They had a long journey ahead, but Nasir didn't think it would take as long as when on a normal ship. No, this journey would follow the time of the Silver Witch and the abominable power she held.

It was as if she *wanted* Nasir to find the Hunter. To follow him. To kill him.

The shores of Sultan's Keep became smaller and smaller.

"What have we to fear on this journey, Sultani?" Altair asked.

Nasir had the feeling the general was mocking him, for Altair should know more than he did about the lay of the land—and sea. But as the ship's men continued without so much as a flicker of emotion in their dull eyes, Nasir found himself opening his stupid mouth, recounting names from long-buried tales he should not have unearthed. "There are tales of the bahamut and dandan."

Altair's forehead creased. His head dipped toward his chest and his shoulders pitched forward, shaking. *Seasick.* And so soon after setting sail, the weak bastard. Nasir didn't bother moving from the railing. Heartbeats later, Altair straightened, his face red from exertion.

He wasn't sick. He was laughing uncontrollably.

Nasir scowled.

"Beware, the mighty dandan!" Altair shouted. "I imagine the creature hides in shame because of its own name." He broke off in laughter again. "Dandan? Dandan!"

In answer, the ship jounced. Nasir gripped the railing.

Altair snorted. "Oh, you'll be safe from our dreaded dandan so close to the shore. Sultan's teeth, look at that."

At the shores of Sultan's Keep, a violent crackling filled the air. The Arz was coming back. Trees erupted out of the ground, tossing black pebbles everywhere. The very air began to darken. Trunks rose high, limbs entwining, twisting, spearing. Leaves dripped from branches like dew.

In mere breaths, the Arz had returned, looking as if it had never left.

If the Silver Witch could tame the Arz—rimaal, make it *disappear*—Nasir couldn't begin to imagine the extent of her powers. But it was Sharr that not even she could subdue. It was on Sharr that he could finally meet his demise. After years of expecting death at the hands of his father, he could die on an island, and no one would even know. Not that anyone was left to care.

"You shouldn't have said that about her to the witch." Altair broke through his thoughts, an edge to his voice.

Nasir lifted an eyebrow and propped his onyx-hilted jambiya against the rail to polish. "What?"

"Kulsum."

He paused. "All I said was that she is of no concern to me."

"You use people and discard them. No one is of any concern to you, Nasir," Altair said coolly.

As if he knew. As if he daama knew what Nasir had been through.

Altair and his mouth.

One moment, Nasir was trying to force air through his teeth, the next, he shoved the bigger man against the rail, blade at the smooth column of his throat.

"Let me," Nasir breathed, "tell you a story, General."

Altair's eyes flared. *Good.* It was good to have Altair fear him for once.

"Once, there was a girl in Sultan's Keep. She sang away her nights beneath the stars with my head in her lap and her fingers in my hair. Until she lost what she prized most. Because I loved her. Because *I* was selfish." Nasir spat the last words in his face. "I would have lamented less had she died."

He pulled away. Altair straightened his clothes, the wind toying with the fringe of his turban. Waves crashed, and somewhere, Kulsum was carrying a tray to the sultan.

"You will always be selfish," Altair said, voice strangely level. "Do you know why I stand as an equal beside you, princeling? Because I'm untouchable. Because I'm the man no one has hold over. Not only did you say she is of no concern to you, but in your arrogance, you revealed Kulsum's association with me. You might as well have carried a sign that said *Altair cares for the girl.*"

Nasir stilled. Whether or not Altair actually cared for Kulsum was irrelevant.

Altair saw the understanding on Nasir's face. "Good thing she's of no concern to you, *Sultani.*"

CHAPTER 19

ZAFIRA HAD SEEN SNOW EVERY DAY OF HER SEVENTEEN years. Not once had she left her family for longer than the setting of a sun. And now a ship was about to drag her away. From Lana, Yasmine, her mother. Misk, too. There was a searing through her chest. *Loss.*

Deen squeezed her shoulder. He looked strong and powerful beneath this new sun. Neither was a word she had ever before used to describe him. But today he looked different. Today she felt a fool for not seeing him as she should have.

Funny how eyes worked.

"They'll be safe. I've been to Thalj, remember? The snow is far less and the conditions are better. More food, fewer casualties from the cold. They'll be cared for in the palace," Deen soothed. "It was smart of you to ask for that."

As Demenhur shrank, her heart raced as if she were wading through the Arz. Yasmine and Lana huddled together, Misk behind them. Zafira hadn't spoken to Yasmine after Deen had stepped forward. She had been angry. She should *still* be angry, but she was just numb now.

Movement caught her eye—the camels of the caravan and the soldiers in their uniforms of gray and blue. Dastards. None of them had stepped forward when Deen spoke of loyalty and success.

The caliph was nestled safely among them. The man with a twisted notion that only men could save their kingdom. Now Zafira felt something: a rush of anger, a flicker of defiance.

Her gaze crashed upon Haytham, who risked being charged with treason because of another masquerading girl. No wonder he looked so haunted. Yasmine's words echoed in her mind: *What are you waiting for?*

A thrum started in her chest, traveled to her fingers. *This.* This was what she had waited for, all these years.

It was time to make the Hunter and Zafira one and the same.

She had nothing to fear—the caliph couldn't reach her now. He wasn't *cruel.* She didn't have to worry about her family's safety. She lifted her hands to her hood.

Wind through her fingers.

Cloth against her skin.

Salt heavy on her tongue.

Zafira bint Iskandar dropped her hood. She shook her hair free, and a mane of black tumbled behind her in waves. Deen's breath caught.

Her hair gleamed beneath the heat of the sun. The widow's peak she had inherited from her mother dipped into her forehead. She loosened the clasp, and the cloak she wore to cover her figure fell to the deck.

A small thud of dark cloth, her disguise for years.

Even from her distance, Zafira could see Yasmine's and Lana's broad grins. Misk pumped a fist into the air. Others watched in awe—*daama awe*—and it took everything within her not to hide behind Deen. Relief shook her shoulders, for the news would spread quickly, and a tale was only swayed by its teller. Skies, word could spread as far as Sultan's Keep.

Haytham saluted two fingers off his brow, the ends of his keffiyah fluttering in the breeze. Zafira almost grinned.

But the caliph.

The blanket upon his shoulders barely concealed the rage contorting his features. Zafira had hunted in the Arz for years. She was proof that a woman's actions did not draw out malevolence. Yet there he was, unbelieving. Angry.

If she were standing before him, she would have feared for her life.

The men with him were of mixed emotions. Some of them looked overjoyed. Some of them hooted. Other expressions had darkened, with grim set mouths she could see even from her distance.

But the caliph.

With that one display of emotion, every victory of hers—braving the dark, returning from the Arz, feeding her people—had just been stepped upon and cast aside. Because she was a woman. How could he allow such unfairness to root in his bones?

I will show him what a woman can do. She startled herself with that thought, rough and angry. Because conquering the Arz wasn't enough. Now she was going to Sharr.

She was going to bring her father justice, kings and witches be damned.

And when she returned, magic in her grasp, she would give a calipha her throne. She would give Arawiya magic and make the sultan himself bow before her.

Zafira lifted her chin and met the caliph's gaze in a farewell of defiance, and the Arz sprang back to life.

CHAPTER 20

NASIR WAS SEVENTEEN WHEN HE HAD LEARNED THE sultan's ways and the sultan had learned his. When Ghameq realized pain no longer worked, not when inflicted upon Nasir's body.

For the sultana had ensured that her son's body was strong, unbeatable, withstanding.

It was then that the sultan learned of the compassion Nasir could never shake, no matter how hard he tried. No matter how many times he murmured it, telling himself to believe it, waking up drenched in sweat, adrenaline pumping through him until he made sense of what he woke up repeating.

Compassion kills.

But nothing in Sultan's Keep was easy, least of all death.

The first night after his mother's burial, Nasir had suffered alone, telling himself that this internal, unseeable pain wasn't endless.

The second night, he had sensed someone in the shadows, cursing himself for the hashashin training that made him so aware.

The third night, she had drawn near, the shadows one with her skin, her eyes aglow beneath a dim moon.

The fourth night, she had gathered her beaded skirts and settled beside him on the wall overlooking the desert dunes behind the palace. She, his servant, sitting beside him as an equal. He had been too shocked to say a word, or he would have said something he would still regret.

The fifth night, his lips formed her name. *Kulsum.* And that was when she parted her mouth and gifted him a sound so beautiful, a blackened heart such as his should not have been allowed to hear it. Soon, her lips parted for more than singing.

It continued until his father found them with her fingers in his hair, their lips breaths apart, her voice raw from the eerie tune she had learned from her own mother.

Everything after that, Nasir remembered only in flashes.

The two of them, stumbling down the wall. The two of them, first standing side by side, then one behind the other, master and servant. Dim torches, because his father loathed light. A blade, gold in the fire, poised to strike.

Her mouth parted. Eyes terrified. Body slack. Tears streaming.

Her tongue, in a silver box, gifted to him in the end.

———◆———

The ship swayed as he made his way up the wooden steps. He had barely slept the night, lurching with the sea, tossing and turning, that ornate silver box burning behind his eyelids.

Love was for the weak, compassion for the burdened. If only he could rid himself of his heart and lose this infernal curse. It would make his father happy.

It could make his father love him.

He bent over at the rail, so engrossed by anger that his vision pulsed black. If his father wanted to starve Haytham's son to death, so be it. If his father wanted Altair dead, Nasir himself would cut off his head. If his father wanted the Jawarat, he would find it soon enough, along with the Hunter's corpse.

Nasir's stomach churned with the sea, but he felt calmer. At ease.

The world darkened despite the early sun. The ship, the sea, the very air they breathed swirled with shadow. As Nasir tried to blink it away, the vessel lurched.

Altair shouted over the crash of the waves, and the world righted again, the shadows a figment of Nasir's thoughts. It was rare for the general to rise before Nasir did.

"Oi! Nasir!" On the other side of the ship, Altair readied an arrow.

Nasir rounded the deck. The sea rippled in angry undulations, and his heart sped with a feeling he eagerly recognized: not belittling fear, but excitement.

Bloodlust.

The general didn't know that his mention of Kulsum the day before was what had reminded Nasir of who he was and what he had been trained to do. That compassion would get him nowhere.

Altair studied Nasir before he spoke, and the cadence of his voice said he *did* know. "I think we're meeting your dandan."

A beast rose from the water, twice the height of their ship. It swayed, baring its teeth in a horrible smile.

Nasir smiled back.

CHAPTER 21

WHEN ZAFIRA WAS YOUNGER, THE SKY HAD BEEN BRIGHTER, the snow magical. Baba's stories would envelop her in warmth and wonder. Only now did she see the snow as a hindrance and the sky as a cage.

Even then, his stories were filled with blood and darkness, horrors and terrors. Whenever Umm scolded him with a teasing smile, Baba would say that lies would take his little girl nowhere. That was also what he had said when he put a bow in Zafira's still-baby-soft hands and taught her how to loose an arrow. And so she was given the truth, even in the years when she would look upon everything with a veil of innocence.

He had told her of the Zaramese, who had worshipped the Baransea. They were sailors by trade, and being the brutes that they were, they believed nothing could stand in their way. So when the Arz stole the Baransea, a group of their finest men and women lifted tabars in their mighty fists and stormed the cursed forest. Arawiya laughed at their foolishness, but the Zaramese were determined.

They chopped tree after tree, the darkness thicker than any storm they had faced at sea. Some say the trees of the Arz rose even as the Zaramese felled them. But a will was all it took. They chopped and chopped. Felled and felled. Until they collapsed, triumphant, at the sight of the cerulean waters lapping Zaram's blackened shores.

They never returned. No one knew if the darkness had driven them to despair or if they had dived into the sea out of relief. It was said that any who ventured along the dark path that had carved the Arz in two, intent on reaching the sea, could hear it: the screams and shouts of the Zaramese Fallen, courageous until the end.

Zafira understood, now, where that courage had come from. Had she been given a taste of this freedom, this power, then she, too, would have fought her way through the Arz. There was sea spray on her tongue, wind in her hair, and sun on her skin.

Yet the longer she stared at the swelling waves, the more she thought of Lana and Yasmine, and the harder it became to breathe. Her stomach reeled as it did during her hunts in the Arz, when her distance from her family made her worry for them more than herself. Because if she were with them, they'd be safe. If she were with them, she would *know* what was happening.

That feeling increased tenfold now that the entire Arz separated them.

And it only worsened as night crept into the sky—her first night away from home. So she descended into the ship's belly, growing accustomed to the gentle swaying and sudden lurches that came with the sea. The Silver Witch would take care of her, she knew. Because the woman needed something.

The thought didn't make her feel any safer.

Something told her the witch was trying too hard. There was too much malevolence in the way she held herself, too much for mere redemption. Perhaps the lost Jawarat could deliver magic back to Arawiya, but it was more than that.

Zafira could feel it in her bones.

Which meant she needed to find it and bring it back to the caliph *before* the witch could get her hands on it. On her.

If such a thing were even possible.

———◆▷———

When she woke the next morning, the cabin opposite hers was empty, Deen's strewn dark sheets reminding her of a crimson smile. She made her way to the hold with a sigh, setting her lantern beside her when she sank onto a wooden chest. She unclasped her cloak and held it against her chest, her hair a curtain of darkness, the violence of the Arz's return flickering in her thoughts—the crackling branches and moaning limbs as the forest reached for the skies like sharp-edged spears. What bothered her most was what the return of the Arz had shown her: it was a wall, beyond which stood all her yesterdays. Her voyage would take her to her tomorrows.

Possibly the last of her tomorrows.

If she hadn't boarded the ship, she would have continued to hunt in the Arz, continued to help her people, ignoring that beckoning darkness as she always had. Ignoring the creeping forest until it devoured them, bones and all.

But oh, how everything had changed in the span of a few days.

She straightened when the stairs creaked with the heavy tread of boots.

"You're blaming yourself," Deen said by way of greeting, concern etched on his features.

"I'm supposed to, aren't I?" She struggled to meet his eyes. "If I hadn't stepped on this ship, you wouldn't have."

"If anyone's to blame, it's the witch." He sat beside her.

"I'm afraid of proving him right."

He knew she spoke of the caliph. "You're not expecting to die, are you? The only way you can prove him right is by dying. And you have a penchant for punching death in the face."

She cracked a small smile. "You don't have to tend to me."

"I wouldn't miss it for the world," he said.

That drew a laugh from some part of her. "You are so very banal, Deen."

He shrugged. "The way I see it, phrases become banal because they're overused by everyone else. So I'll say them again and again until you tire of them."

The smile that curved his lips sorrowed his eyes.

She fiddled with the clasp of her cloak, the one little buckle that had separated Zafira from the Hunter for years.

She looked at Deen, at his sloppily wrapped turban, and felt the ridiculous urge to straighten it. He stilled, noticing the change in her thoughts. How was it that he noticed so much about her?

His eyes held hers as he reached for the cloak clenched in her white-knuckled fingers. "I'll rid you of it."

She shook her head, feeling stupidly, ridiculously weak. "I'm going to wear it."

Whatever she had felt upon removing it had disappeared. She was still Zafira. Still just a girl with a bow and a hoard of venison to her name.

He was silent a moment, until he stood. "Very well."

She started plaiting her hair and stopped when warm hands closed over hers.

"Let me?" he asked softly. "I'll even crown it for you."

She nodded. Deen's fingers were deft, for this wasn't the first time he had plaited her hair, but it felt different now, entwined with some form of melancholy. She tipped between lucidity and sleep the longer he wove.

Until she felt it.

Soft, barely there. The brush of lips against the back of her neck.

Zafira stiffened and felt him stiffen, too. She turned and met his eyes.

"No matter how many times, it's always the same," he murmured. "Akin to striking flint beneath the cold skies, striking and striking, until that gratifying spark comes to life. If only you knew."

She didn't know what he spoke of, yet she couldn't find the words to ask him, not when he was looking at her with so *much*.

"If only you knew what it was like to feel the weight of your gaze," he said, half to himself.

Oh. She pursed her mouth. Her neck burned from the touch of his lips, and she was abuzz with warmth like the first sun above the cold horizon.

"I'm sorry," she whispered.

I'm sorry, too, he said in the silence, but Deen Ra'ad never had anything to apologize for. He was too pure. Too perfect. Too *good* for this world basking in darkness.

"I sometimes forget you're no longer that girl I helped from the trees all those years ago. That girl who dirtied herself in the mud and made sure I was just as filthy," Deen said softly.

She sputtered a laugh, and he wove her braid into a crown.

"You're a woman now. The Huntress who will change Arawiya."

Silence lifted his words, echoed them within the dark confines of the ship's belly. How could she summon words knowing she couldn't spin them in half the beauty he could? But he saw her thoughts. He would always see every notion as it clicked into place and he exhaled the smallest of smiles.

The ship lurched to a halt.

We're here. Here. Here. Here.

She pulled her gaze away from his beautiful face and drew on her cloak. Her fingers trembled when she reached for the waning lantern and stood, Huntress once more.

CHAPTER 22

NASIR HAD NEVER SEEN THE DANDAN, ONLY HEARD OF ITS TALES. Before, when he used to listen raptly to the lies that were stories. The creature before them was most certainly a dandan. It was serpentine, something out of myth, trembling as it rose from the sea. Because of the Arz, it was likely that the creature had rested for decades. In unsatiated hunger.

It was twice as wide as Nasir's height, the bulk of its body obscured beneath the waves rocking the ship. Thick scales overlapped, glistening a deep iridescent blue-green beneath the glow of the sun.

Altair whistled. "Shame such a beauty is tied with such a ridiculous name."

The creature's head swayed, two depthless black eyes shifting to and fro. A strange hissing escaped its mouth, gills contracting on either side of its narrowed face.

"I don't think it can see," Nasir murmured. At his voice, the creature's head tipped to the side in an almost innocent gesture.

Altair backed away, footsteps slow and measured, before he drew his bow and leveled for the creature's eyes, or gills, Nasir couldn't tell.

He threw a glance at the oblivious crew still going about their work. They blinked and flashed with the light, solid yet ethereal. The dandan didn't notice them any more than they noticed *it*.

Nasir drew a steady breath and nocked an arrow of his own. "We should—"

The creature released a high-pitched screech, loud enough to ripple sand at the depths of the sea. As soon as the screech ended, with deafening silence and a gust of salted wind, it began again.

The dandan reared back and shot toward them, jaws parted to reveal razor-sharp teeth and a gaping black hole of a mouth. A green tongue lashed within.

Nasir and Altair let loose their arrows.

Both of them were deflected.

Nasir cursed and ducked against the side of the ship.

The dandan's head pierced the mainsail, tearing down the mast as it crashed onto the deck. Altair shouted out. Water slickened the wood and soaked Nasir's clothes as the ship tipped to the side with a terrifying creak.

The dandan whipped its head, hissing and screaming, even bigger than it looked from afar. It passed through the phantom crew as it slid toward Nasir. *Kharra.* He leaped to his feet and darted aside, but the dandan was faster.

Much faster.

He was thrown against the wall of the ship. His bow fell from his hands and skidded across the deck. He struggled for breath, pinned between the creature and the rails, scales like bones digging into his stomach.

A gill parted near him, and the dandan's steaming breath nearly suffocated him. He jerked away when another slit parted and a depthless black hole stared back. *If an eye and gill are this close, then its mouth—*

The creature screamed again. Sound exploded and Nasir shouted in surprise, clamping his hands on his ears while gritting his teeth. Red and black streaked across his vision. The sudden silence that followed the dandan's cry was just as deafening.

The monster lifted its head, swaying the entire time, and twisted to look at him.

It can't see, Nasir reminded himself as his ears continued to ring. He swayed and held steady. But when the creature revealed its teeth, Nasir wasn't so sure of the stories he had heard.

Until someone shouted.

"Oi! Dandan! What was your mother thinking, giving you such a silly name?"

Altair, the fool.

The dandan stilled. It contracted its gills and narrowed its black eyes.

"Dandan, oi! Dandaaan," Altair sang. "Look at you, so green and blue. What a name! What a shame! I pity your mother, and your brother. Oi, dandaaan!"

The creature tossed its head, body undulating, and Altair carried on with more ridiculous singing.

Nasir opened his mouth to stop Altair from shaming his family to oblivion, but the dandan's eyes rolled to the back of its head. It convulsed, green scales falling like loose shingles on a rich man's roof. It croaked a halfhearted cry and slumped, slipping back into the sea with a heavy splash that sent the ship rocking.

Altair grinned at him from the other end of the chaos.

"That, princeling, is how you defeat a dandan."

Nasir looked over the edge, expecting the creature to return with more of its kind.

"It's dead?" he asked, incredulous.

Altair joined him. "Afraid not. I had forgotten, though. The stories, I mean, because we call it a *den*dan. They're maimed by the sound of singing— they could *die* from it."

Nasir wondered whom the "we" entailed. He didn't dare ask. "Because 'dendan' and 'dandan' are so different, you couldn't remember," he mocked instead.

Altair ignored him. "They would swallow whole ships in the dead of night, when no one could see them or know they were near. Until captains learned to hire maidens who sang through the entire voyage, poor souls. But it's been so long since anyone sailed the Baransea that the creature probably abandoned all notion of day and night and attacked the moment it sensed us."

The glaring sun had already dried Nasir's clothes, and now sweat trickled down his spine. The ship rocked.

Their battered, broken ship.

Nasir turned to survey the mess, ears still ringing, but the broken mast had been fixed and the torn sail rippled unharmed in the breeze. Everything gleamed. He strode to the steps leading belowdecks and picked up his bow, hooking it behind him as he studied the undisturbed crew. His skin crawled with the essence of magic, just as it did whenever he neared his father and that wretched medallion.

"Oi! Princeling."

"Call me that one more time, and——" Nasir stopped when he saw what Altair had seen: a jagged swarm of darkness quivering beneath the sun.

Sharr.

ACT II

A LONG WAY FROM HOME

CHAPTER 23

THE SHIP HAD STOPPED, YET WHEN DEEN SAID, "WE'RE dismounting," as if the ship were a steed, Zafira puzzled over the stretch of water between them and the mass of land obscured by the blistering sun.

But Deen's lips at her neck. Those words in her ears.

"We'll have to get there by rowboat," he answered before she could ask, perfectly at ease, as if he hadn't just cracked open his soul and told her things she had never heard before.

She climbed into the little boat, which looked in danger of sinking, and anger soured her thoughts. Anger at him, for saying what he had and remaining wholly unperplexed. She pressed her eyes closed and inhaled before opening them again. This was Deen. Her Deen. She didn't have to feel demure.

The rowboat touched the water and he clutched the oars. After a few odd shuffles that nearly sent them both into the water, he finally deciphered the rhythm and began rowing them forward.

"I thought you'd take us all the way back to Demenhur," she taunted, feeling instantly at ease again.

"Ha, ha," he deadpanned, a laugh teasing his mouth.

Both of them gasped when the sun dipped from view, clearing its harsh glow from their sight.

Sharr.

A towering edifice, jagged like a monster's teeth, reached for the sparse clouds. A wall, she realized, made of hewn stones held together with mortar. It may have once been the tan of limestone, but it was gray now, with veins of black creeping along the pebbled surface. The gaping darkness behind the aging cracks flashed and winked.

She looked away. What was it with the darkness, always coaxing?

Deen continued to row them ashore, the ship shrinking behind them. He was as inexperienced as she when it came to the sea, and water lapped into the little boat. Even the sea begged for her. *Only a touch*, it seemed to call. She leaned closer, and the boat tipped with her.

"Zafira!"

She sat upright at Deen's shout, ducking her head in panic, and she had to remind herself there was no man here to shun her. No za'eem to marry her off.

"I wanted to see what it felt like," she said, grasping her cloak.

"Please don't test your mad notions here."

Her hood obscured most of the withering look she gave him. "Row."

He laughed. "But of course, sayyida."

She realized then what the wall was for: to keep something in. A remnant of the prison fortress that once stood glorious and imposing. A world within itself.

A world Zafira was not sure she would outlive.

By the time they reached the shore, Zafira was soaked in her own sweat. She swayed when she set foot upon the sand. The grains shifted and sank, a living thing beneath her, swallowing all pockets of space.

There's sand beneath my boots, Baba. Something stung in her eyes.

She stumbled forward, slowly understanding how to dance to the tune of the sand. The shift and the sink. Once that hurdle was over, the grains scorched her feet through her soles and her gloves suffocated. She shoved them into her satchel.

"You should remove your cloak, too," Deen said, a hand to his brow as he surveyed the wall. He squinted at her. "This is just the beginning. If my understanding is correct, there's a desert beyond the stone." He handed her a vial with a questionable green tint, and she recognized the bottle from his parents' apothecary trunk. "We're not weathered enough for this sun."

She rubbed the salve on her skin, thinking of Yasmine. Of Lana's parting sob. Of the odd bout of nervousness that came over Haytham yesterday as he stared into the horizon in anxious anticipation. As if he were waiting for something worse than the Arz.

"Zafira." Deen's voice was soft. "Don't start down that path. Not now."

Not now. Not now. Not now.

"I'm trying," she whispered.

The wall imposed in a cold, lifeless way, except for the brushwood sprawling at its base and the few wending palm trees fanning dark leaves against the stone.

"How are we supposed to get past it? We can't scale it like daama ha-shashins," Deen said. Zafira had half a mind to cross her arms and summon the Silver Witch. *If* she could be summoned.

Zafira didn't trust her. Sometimes the most truthful words were merely elaborate lies. And if one was banned from lying, that was all the more reason to learn a new way of stringing words together.

A shadowed alcove cut diagonally against the structure. "There," she said, pointing. "I think those are stairs."

"What if we go up those stairs and find no entrance, Huntress?" Deen asked, looking skeptical. "Akhh, I wish we had a map."

Zafira was the Hunter. She could find deer in absolute darkness and return home despite the odds. She had never needed a compass to find her way, and she certainly wouldn't need a map now. She stomped past him to the foot of the stairs.

Something hummed beneath her skin, rushing alongside the blood of her veins. A boost of energy she couldn't understand. She tamped it down and started up the umber steps, sand crunching beneath her footfalls.

And Deen, loyal as he was, followed.

CHAPTER 24

NASIR HAD NO WAY OF COMMUNICATING WITH THE phantom men as they anchored the ship at least a league from the island, but four of them stood beside a small boat waiting to be lowered to the sea, so he supposed that was where they were to go.

"I hope you can row, princeling," Altair said, climbing in after him.

Nasir settled on the side farthest from the oars, making it clear he would do no such thing.

Altair sat on the other end and matched Nasir's glare. The crew lowered them to the sea, and water lapped inside as the rowboat tipped with the weight of two.

"Oi," Altair said with a huff, and grabbed the oars, shooting Nasir a withering look before he started rowing toward the island.

Nasir was crown prince of Arawiya. He would do no rowing.

The closer they crept, the more desolate Sharr looked. The walls of the fortress were crumbling, and all they seemed to keep out were the sea and its breeze.

"I hope you can climb," Nasir said.

"Do I look like a monkey?" Altair asked.

"That would be a disgrace to the monkey," Nasir answered, and stepped out of the rowboat, ignoring Altair's mock dismay.

When Altair finally followed, he carried one of the oars with him. Water trickled down the pale wood and sizzled on the sand. "You think we should keep this? Could be useful for thwacking our enemies."

Nasir gave him a look. "We will not be *thwacking* our enemies. What are you, a child?"

"Fine. Don't blame me if someone else comes equipped with one," Altair called after him.

Nasir heard the sound of the oar clattering back into the boat. He certainly hoped no one else came. The Hunter would be enough.

"So what's the plan, if it doesn't include thwacking?" Altair asked.

Nasir stalked up the sloping plain of sand, studying the stone structure as he charted his northward path.

"We could just see if there's an entrance," Altair suggested.

"Might as well find us an inn while you're at it, and roasted venison," Nasir said. He wound his turban around his head before his hair could burn off. "We need to get beyond the wall, then head south."

"South?" Altair asked as he followed Nasir, his heavy boots sinking into the sand. "What does the compass say? Is that where you think the Jawarat is?"

Nasir did not trust that compass any more than he trusted the Silver Witch. "No, but that's where the Hunter will be."

But it *would* be a good way to test out the magical compass. Which pointed south.

"And you know this how?"

"Because, you inebriate, Demenhur is south of Sultan's Keep and they would have sailed here along the quickest, and that means straightest, path. Can you not calculate?" Nasir said.

Altair lifted a single brow and pondered this for a moment before he began to climb, more swiftly than Nasir would have expected given his hulking figure.

"Getting right to business, then, aren't we, Sultani?" he called down. A vulture circled the cloudless sky, already awaiting death.

Nasir felt the grit of stone beneath his fingers.

Altair would get his turn soon enough.

CHAPTER 25

ZAFIRA REACHED THE WALL'S TOP WITH A SENSE OF satisfaction. One hurdle down, only a thousand more to go. Or considerably less, if the next hurdle killed her.

Deen made a sound behind her, and she whirled to him. To what he stared upon.

Sharr.

A desert spread before them, its horizon shrouded in a veil of dust. Uneven forms of stone rose in the distance, gnarled by the wind. Dunes the color of dark wheat rose and fell. It was a sea of umber, winking beneath a generous sun. It was sand, it was *dead*, yet Zafira's heart soared at the sight.

Ruins unfolded directly below them. A menagerie of stone with carved arches, and columns with trellised windows. Minarets dotted the landscape. This wasn't a prison—it was a metropolis. Living quarters, the tattered cloth roofing a sooq, wide steps leading to structures that may have once been beautiful.

People had done this. They had defied the sands and defied the suns. All to bring towering edifices of magnificence to life.

The warden hadn't kept them locked in cells—she had given the banished creatures a place to live, to work, to *be*.

"I've never seen anything so illustriously tormented," Deen murmured in awe. A breeze tousled the end of his turban and billowed her cloak. She still felt the echo of his lips against her neck every time she looked at him. "They lived here, Zafira."

She felt the rushing need to quiet him, for she discerned the prickling sense of being watched. The desert was too still; the stone held its breath. Every shadowy slant twisted and beckoned. "I don't think we should stay in one place for long."

"There's no one around for leagues."

"Where do you think the monsters went?"

They may have roamed free on the island, but that didn't mean they were any less evil. And if the whispered tales of her childhood were true, Sharr had been full of them. Ifrit, who could take the shape of anyone. Shadows that killed. Sirens known as naddaha. The bashmu, which put other snakes to shame. And other things she couldn't remember the names of.

The very land was to be feared. It breathed dark magic, for when the Sisters of Old came to defeat the Lion of the Night, they brought magic with them, and Sharr had swallowed them all. Zafira unhooked her bow and nocked an arrow.

"Akhh, I don't even know where to go," Deen said.

She gave him a funny look. "The plan is to head to the center," she said, and steered him toward a path that careened downward and veered in two different directions. That thrumming in her veins smiled at her choice. It was happy she listened to it.

"The center? I don't even know where we came *in* from—the south? The north? And who says the Jawarat is in this center we're *supposedly* heading toward?"

"It's like the Arz; the more you think about it, the madder you'll become. But I have a feeling it will be in the center." She stepped into the shadows, sweat beading above her lip. The world became warmer. Hotter. The shadows warned of danger.

"Zafira," Deen said.

She had to stop and turn because, male that he was, he wouldn't continue until she did. She saw him slide a compass behind his back.

"This is *Sharr*. We don't have a map. We don't know of a way out. Are we really going to head deeper inside this place based on a notion of yours? A feeling?"

"Yes," she said matter-of-factly. His features flattened and she hurried to add, "You can check your compass as we go. Unless you have a better idea."

His face gave way to a rare expression of exasperation. It made her smile.

"No, no, I don't," he said.

———◆———

They had awakened Sharr from its slumber. She knew this from the groan of the stone as they whispered past. From the debris skittering to the shadows and the wall's inhale as they brushed against it, sand coating their parting fingers.

She could only hope it awoke on a more favorable side.

They emerged from the alcove to a barren wilderness. The ruins appeared even more haunted up close, and dust swirled, uncaring of the magnificence it defiled.

But the heat.

It besieged her, laved dryness against her skin in a way she never thought possible. How could someone *feel* such dryness? It was a weight. A sweltering thing, rippling in the distance.

"Only in the desert can you see the heat," Deen said, following her gaze.

"If these weren't ruins, I don't think I would mind," Zafira said, running a hand along the dusty stone. She pulled at her collar. Desolation roamed everywhere.

"No one will judge you." He gestured to her cloak.

She looked away. "Give me time."

He nodded and they pressed onward, climbing over run-down steps and wood that had long since petrified. Zafira stared at the columns they passed. Had magic created this? Or labor? The stories never spoke of Sharr being *lived* upon, just used as a prison.

She heard movement and saw the curl of a scorpion's tail as it scuttled beneath a slab of stone. Zafira's eyes widened as she hurried forward, barely suppressing a shiver.

When she could no longer summon saliva for her parched throat, she spotted a shimmer of blue a stretch from their course and stumbled forward, ignoring the goatskin at her side.

Deen grabbed her arm. "A mirage, Zafira." He nodded to their right. "There's an oasis this way."

"How would you know?" Zafira had only heard of mirages in stories. They were always magical, miraculous. Now it seemed like a taunt. A way to draw the thirsty forward so the sands could devour them.

He pointed to the sky, where a trio of birds circled. Then below, where a date palm curved. "Life."

Zafira was surprised by the greenery when they reached the small pool. Wild ferns and bright shrubs. The water was so clear, it reflected the clouds as pristinely as a mirror. But when Deen cupped his palms and bent down for a drink, Zafira glimpsed black stones glittering beneath the glowing waters, reminding her of the Silver Witch.

"Well, Huntress? What say you?" he teased, letting the water trickle through his fingers.

"I wouldn't drink it," she said, lips twisting back. She handed him the goatskin hanging by her side.

"You know this won't last forever, yes?" he said, limiting himself to a sip.

"Until I'm dying of thirst and hunger, I'll pretend it will," she said, capping the skin.

He twirled his jambiya and looked ahead. "Let's hope it never comes to that."

If there was one thing Zafira didn't do, it was hope. Hope was as much a disease as love was.

They trekked onward in silence, jointly attuned to the desert around them and the eyes that tracked them soundlessly. An ifrit? Worse?

"How does your compass rate our progress?" Zafira teased after a moment.

Deen slipped the disc back into his pocket, looking up at her with a rapid blink of his eyes. "My what? I've no idea what you're blabbering about."

She thwacked him on the side of the head, and he laughed, the sound filling her with remnants of home. She was glad he was here. Glad she wasn't alone in this uncharted place.

Zafira kept her arrow nocked, tensed and ready, but after at least a league of walking in silence, with no way to tell where the sun now hovered, she let her shoulders relax. Perhaps she imagined the eyes following them, because one moment they bored into her from behind and the next they pierced her from the front.

Maybe the tales of Sharr were mere exaggeration. Maybe the extent of the danger was falling prey to a mirage or getting caught in a sandstorm.

Or so she made herself believe, until she heard the sound she had been waiting for. Far off, but near enough to make the hairs on the backs of her arms stand on end.

The sound of someone trying to stay silent.

CHAPTER 26

THE TWO DEMENHUNE DRIFTED TOGETHER LIKE GHOSTS, with ethereal skin and aristocratic features, though much of the Hunter, Nasir noticed, was obscured beneath a heavy cloak and hood. No doubt the fool was suffocating in this heat.

If what Nasir had heard was true, however, the Hunter would sooner become a pool of perspiration than reveal his identity. He just hadn't expected the Hunter to come accompanied—a slip easily remediable.

The Hunter drifted through the ruins soundlessly, and his companion prowled after him. Nasir unhooked his bow.

Altair followed his gaze. "Eyes on the prize?"

Rimaal, this man.

Altair nocked one of Nasir's arrows. "You never know," he explained with a forced grin. "I've heard the Hunter never misses, and I'd hate for my dearest prince to be impaled by one of his fine twigs."

Altair seemed to have heard a lot of things, and since that night at the tavern, Nasir had begun to wonder about the general he had thought oblivious to everything but women and drink. Whom did Altair share his knowledge with—Ghameq? Unlikely.

Altair ducked beneath a weathered archway. Nasir moved aside a clutter of debris, readying an arrow of his own. He exhaled and aligned his aim to the second Demenhune, who stared after the Hunter with a look of . . . *yearning* in his eyes.

The intensity of it gave Nasir pause. This was his chance to stop. To shatter the hold of his father and retain the fragments of humanity he still clutched in some corner of his black heart.

But Nasir had one shot, one arrow before they lost the element of surprise. He breathed. Cleared his mind.

The hashashin bowstring, engineered by the Pelusians of Sultan's Keep, stretched without a sound. He sighted his aim and was about to release the string when he heard it: the sound of another, less silent bowstring being pulled tight. The Hunter and his companion were in front of him, and Altair was to his left, which meant—

Someone else, shrouded from view. His pulse quickened. One of the others Ghameq had warned him of. Or, worse, an ifrit. The dark tip of an arrow peeked between the columns of limestone.

Leveled at Altair.

Nasir set his jaw but did not shift his aim.

If the unknown archer killed Altair, Nasir wouldn't have to see the light fade from the general's twinkling eyes. *Twinkling?* Nasir was no coward. The only reason Altair wasn't yet dead was because Nasir needed him. Altair was *Nasir's* to kill. He didn't want someone else to do his work for him, as tempting as it was.

He heard the archer's bowstring tighten, the aim shaky but true.

He saw Altair, oblivious to the arrow pointed at his heart.

Nasir exhaled.

Three arrows flew at once.

CHAPTER 27

Z AFIRA HEARD THE SNAP OF A BOWSTRING: THRICE. EVERYTHING
happened quickly after that. She saw the arrow, spiraling toward
her.

Then Deen, yelling. Hands on her shoulders, pushing her away. Her own
bow was nocked with an arrow that she let fly, letting her heart lead it
because she couldn't see, couldn't think. A rustle of something else behind
her. The ground, rushing to her face. Sand, gritting against her cheek. Stone,
hard against her bones. Sound, sound, sound, beating against her eardrums.

And then,

silence.

Before everything rushed back with a noise: a choked gasp for air. *No.*

Zafira scrambled to her feet. The greedy desert was already swallowing
up the blood, sand reddening to black. Her vision wavered.

No. No. No.

"You fool. I told you, *I told you.*" She dropped beside him and searched for
the arrow. She dared to hope, to wish, only for a moment.

Only to suffer. For the arrow had struck directly beneath his heart.
Deen. Deen. Deen.

He tried to smile, but it looked like a grimace. His face had paled, hazel eyes dim, skin coated in sweat and a smear of blood. She shook her head. It was too late. Like when Baba had stumbled out of the Arz and she couldn't save him. Like when Umm had pierced his heart and Zafira couldn't save her.

She remembered those nights after Baba had died, those nights after Deen's parents had died, when they had held each other, chasing away fears with simply the other's presence. The years and years of him being everywhere, no matter where she looked.

He struggled, hacking a cough as he dragged something out of his pocket. It blinded in the sun. A gold chain and, at its end, a ring. He held it out in a loose and trembling fist.

"You would never wear one"—he gasped—"on your finger."

The chain trickled like molten gold from his palm, and she picked it up, sand sticking to her damp fingers. The gold band swayed, perfect and unblemished. Nothing like Zafira.

"One moment, you wanted to explore past Arawiya, you wanted marriage, you wanted *me*. Then you turned around and joined this journey. You threw everything aside for—for *this*."

Deen's eyes slowly swept across her face. Zafira thought she would explode. *If only you knew.*

"Why, Deen?" she begged. "Why did you come to this island?"

"For you, a thousand times," he choked, but she knew the rest of those words. Words he had said countless times before. His eyes flickered. *A thousand leagues and a thousand sands. For you, a thousand times I would defy the sun.*

He was always asking for the impossible. Always asking for what she wouldn't give. She brushed her lips against his cheek, and he exhaled. This time, she wasn't hungry for more. She longed for what she had already lost.

And hadn't he told her that, when they embarked on this journey?

"Find the Jawarat, Zafira. Trust . . ."

He reached for her, and she let his fingers trail the side of her face. He dropped his hand and curled his pinkie around hers, his grip already faltering.

"Today was that day," he whispered. He breathed one last time before that small finger fell away from hers. Before that beautiful heart that harmed none and loved too much—stopped.

"Farewell," she whispered, waiting, waiting, waiting for the tears to spill. But they stayed where they were, suffocating her heart.

She thought of Yasmine's tin of cocoa, sitting in her cupboard, the empty vial of honey. Had she known in the vague way the bond of blood worked?

It was Zafira's fault for boarding the ship yesterday, knowing he would do anything, *anything*, for her.

Anger, raw and foolish, quaked through her fingers.

They'll tell stories about us, he had said.

There once was a boy with a future.

Until all he had left was his past.

⟨◆⟩

He looked calm, as if in sleep. But the longer Zafira stared, the more she felt it: loneliness.

It encompassed every limb of her body, weighing her down to the sand beneath her legs. She was far from home, in a place no one could find her. The one man who loved her was dead.

Yaa, Deen. If Yasmine was the sister of her heart, more than a best friend, then Deen *was* her best friend. Deen was her everything, second to Yasmine.

How was such unfairness to the best of souls possible?

He was a body now. Flesh molded into beautiful features that would no longer alight at her voice and smile at her words. Zafira sobbed at last.

Something cracked.

She lifted her head. She didn't care who was out there now. Whoever it was must have wanted *her* dead, not Deen. Surely the archer had another arrow to spare? She croaked a laugh: The witch had lied. Someone else *had* been sent.

There was also that second presence—the rustle she had heard behind her as Deen had jumped in front of the arrow.

The cracking grew more incessant now, a howl accompanying it. She shivered and rose to her knees.

Shadows twisted out of the ground, winding around Deen's limbs and torso. His indigo turban melded with the pooling black, bronze curls darkening. The sands stirred like water beneath a breeze. Black wisps unfurled and draped over him.

Sharr was taking his body.

Zafira leaped to her feet but hesitated. He would have some semblance of a burial this way, or so her addled brain told her. The arrow glinted in the shifting light as the shadows dragged him deeper still, farther into the sand.

The arrow. Zafira crept closer and tried to pull the arrow free from the confines of Deen's chest. It snapped hollowly, and her heart cried out, but the upper half of the ebony shaft with the dark silver fletching tapered to points was what she needed.

She took his jambiya and satchel but couldn't bring herself to take away his beloved tabar.

Zafira stood back as Sharr swallowed the man who had loved her, until not a trace of him was left. Hollowness tugged at her again, weighted her arms and burned in her eyes. She felt nothing and everything at once.

She slipped the chain around her neck, the ring falling at her chest. There were words inside it: "for you, a thousand times." She bit her cheek. She would find the lost Jawarat. But first, she would avenge Deen's death. She held the broken arrow up to the kiss of the sun, and stilled as the world dimmed.

Shadows began to rise, adrift in the wind, at one with the sands. A low groan carried through the thickening air, and panic crept into her bloodstream when she realized what was happening.

Sharr had been fed.

CHAPTER 28

NASIR'S ARROW HAD GONE STRAIGHT THROUGH THE skull of the ifrit. He knew it was an ifrit only because its human form had shifted into something dark before Altair fell with a sickening rasp.

A sound that made something in Nasir rear its head.

Altair was dying.

An arrow had reciprocated from the Hunter, too. It had zoomed into a dark window, but it would have struck Nasir's heart had he not turned at the last moment. The fact was not lost on him that the Hunter had aimed true in the midst of the fray.

The general stared up at him from the shadows of the cramped archway.

Nasir forced words from clenched teeth. "Are you out of your mind? You nearly killed the Hunter."

Altair stretched a horrid smile across his face. "But I didn't, did I?"

They had been *this close* to losing the Hunter, their one ticket to finding the Jawarat—and the bastard was smug?

Nasir grabbed the arrow protruding below the general's shoulder and twisted. Altair heaved upward, teeth gritted in pain, hands trembling.

"Fight," Nasir said, and cursed. He wanted pain. He *needed* pain to help him remember and forget. Had the other Demenhune not intervened, the Hunter would have died. The entire mission compromised.

Altair didn't move.

Nasir growled, reaching for the arrow again. Altair's eyes flashed in the dark, and Nasir felt a spike of satisfaction when the general shoved him to the stone, dust clouding from the impact. The exertion sent blood spurting from Altair's wound, and Nasir jerked his head from the dripping red.

"Don't touch me," Altair snarled, breath warm on Nasir's skin. Flecks of darkness swam in the blue of his eyes.

"Go on," Nasir taunted softly. "Inflict pain the way your heart begs to."

Altair's massive hands closed around Nasir's neck, fingers pulsing against his slick skin, tightening until Nasir felt a prickle of . . . *fear.*

It was a welcome rush, a spike that heightened his senses. He nearly smiled.

But then Altair blinked, remembering something, and fell back onto the stone as if nothing had happened. "I wasn't trying to kill him."

Nasir sat up slowly, confusion dulling his senses again. He eyed the general warily. "That's what happens when you unleash an arrow. Something will die. It's no one's fault you're a terrible shot."

"Kill me," Altair grunted suddenly, pressing the skin around his shoulder with a grimace.

Of everything Nasir had expected from Altair—

Altair breathed a mirthless laugh. "Did you really think I would come here oblivious to your father's plans? I know about the Hunter and what Ghameq thinks he is. I know what he told you to do. Get it over with, Sultani."

He spat the title with vehemence.

"You know nothing," Nasir said, voice low. "You only assume."

Altair pulled the arrow from his shoulder with a hiss, and blood flowed freely. The shaft and fletching were crudely built, as nondescript as the ifrit had been. But why had the creature aimed at Altair and not Nasir? It wasn't as though Ghameq had any control over Sharr.

Altair's mouth twisted into a snarl before he contained himself. "I . . . have eyes . . . everywhere."

He tossed the arrow among the debris and heaved to his side, pulling his satchel closer with his tongue between his teeth. The perspiration on his skin glistened with the light filtering through the small archway.

"You mean to tell me you have a spy," Nasir said.

"Many," the general huffed as he dug through his bag.

Nasir thought back to that morning two days ago, when the sultan had summoned him. When he had knelt on the hard ground of Ghameq's chambers, listening to orders about this trek. When a servant had swept into the room, a fruit tray in her hands. When she had lingered, lighting bakhour and filling the room with its sensuous scent.

When she had been in Nasir's rooms while he was at the Daama Faris with Altair.

Rimaal.

Kharra.

It couldn't be. Disbelief wrapped dark hands around his lungs.

"Kulsum," Nasir rasped. "*She's* your spy?"

Altair watched him. "Did you think she came to you of her own accord? Did you really think someone stolen from her family and enslaved to the likes of you could fall in love with a monster?" He scoffed and tore a strip of fabric using his teeth.

Nasir felt something within him tearing the same way, jagged edges and limp remains.

He knew he was a monster. Acknowledged it, even. But Kulsum . . .

"You're even dumber than your father says you are."

Nasir stared back dully. He liked to think he had taken care of the weakness that was emotion, after all that he had been through and all that he had shunned. But *Kulsum*. Kulsum was different. Kulsum was the one who had pulled him out of that endless despair.

Kulsum had loved him. She had come to him, even after that wretched night when his father had gifted him that silver box.

Or had that, too, been Altair's doing?

Nasir knew that finding a person he could love, who could love him, was near impossible. He knew, yet he had been too blinded by mere affection to see clearly. *Fabricated* affection.

He fisted his hands and tugged at his already-lowered sleeves. Those years lay in the past for a reason. The words on his right arm had been inked for a reason. What mattered was now: He loved none, and none loved him. Love was a fantasy.

Life, this terrible existence, would go on.

"Get up," Nasir said.

Altair had finished dressing his wound and had paled from the loss of blood. For a beat, Nasir thought he should have helped tend to his injury. But the beat—like the panic that had gripped him when Altair was shot, like all else—passed, and he felt nothing again.

The general tossed the remainder of the bloody cloth aside. "Decided you still need me?"

Nasir wouldn't give him the satisfaction of a reaction to his spying. To Kulsum. *What's there to spy about me anyway?* "Still deciding."

Altair stood. He held his right arm rigidly, shirt stained red. "Don't worry about me, Sultani. I heal faster than your unimaginative mind can fathom."

"Right. Because you're some sort of legendary creature."

"You'd be surprised."

"Nothing about you can surprise me."

"He's dead, isn't he? The Demenhune," Altair said. His tone was softened by something like regret.

Nasir's brow furrowed. "You knew him."

Altair answered with a half shrug. Yet another fragment of his mysterious knowledge that seemed to transcend caliphates. "He was"—he paused and shortened his answer—"involved in a rescue mission once. A good man."

"A rescue mission. You." Nasir scoffed. And with a *Demenhune?* The rescue of what? Nasir bit his cheek against the questions.

"I don't kiss and tell, princeling."

Nasir mock-yawned.

"Well," Altair said with forced cheer. "It's just the two of us again, and my, what a couple we make."

Nasir gifted him a look that could wither crops. "Keep up your endless yipping and only one of us will be left."

Altair grinned. "Ah, but I was already dead the moment I set foot on Sharr. Might as well have some fun along the way, laa?"

Neither mentioned the fact that Nasir had saved Altair's life. Or that an ifrit had made an attempt on it.

Nasir didn't know what had spurred him to shift his aim at the very last moment. To save the man whose words were spent belittling him. Who, against all odds, was his only ally in Sharr.

Nasir was tired of talking. Feeling. Thinking.

"The Hunter will be alert now, and we've wasted enough time with your indisposition."

The sun had dimmed and shadows had risen from the sands. Sharr, coming to life. No matter, Nasir's task still stood.

It was time for the Hunter to become the hunted.

CHAPTER 29

ZAFIRA WAS BEING FOLLOWED, BUT ALL SHE COULD THINK OF WAS Sharr. Guzzling Deen's blood and hungering for more, darkening the sands, scaring the sun.

She clambered up stone steps, circled past broken columns, and wended her way through tattered stalls made of eroding wood. She would have taken a moment to contemplate the abandoned sooq of Sharr if she wasn't being daama pursued.

The wind howled, and she could barely see beyond the next five steps. Her cloak wrangled her, a beast in league with the heat. But she didn't want her pursuer to know who she was, and so she stubbornly swiped at the sweat with the back of her hand, cursing the desert.

If you want something to do, go melt Demenhur.

The shadows stirred, laughing.

She stumbled once, twice—her boot caught on a step she couldn't see, and she rolled down an incline of rough stone. She let out a string of curses only Yasmine would use, the words echoing in the ruins until the limestone spat her onto more sand, a handbreadth away from a scorpion spearing a lizard, tearing the breath from her lungs. She scrambled away with a hiss.

And then: a rustle. From *ahead*. Not behind, where her pursuers should have been.

She stood slowly with battered bones, clenching her trembling fingers. She was the daama Hunter—it wasn't like her to be so shaken. Spotting a crevice between two trellised arches, she ducked into the hollow and waited, carefully sliding her jambiya free.

She had killed animals, yes, but never a living, breathing human. Still, if she had to, if the other was a threat, then she was ready. Her father had taught her well.

The sand stirred and she held her breath as a man stepped from the haze of dust, looking back as she had seen him do so many times before, curls shimmering bronze. She thought of his pinkie twined with hers, of his ring at her bosom.

Deen.

She was going mad. She was the daughter of a madwoman, the daughter of a madman. Madness lived in her blood. That was the only explanation for this.

But he looked solid, real, *alive*. She had seen him die, she had stared at his still form as Sharr had taken him away.

No. Sharr hadn't taken him away. Sharr had fixed him and given him back to her.

She stood without a second thought, not bothering with silence. He turned at the sound of her boots.

"Deen," she said.

Maybe it was a trick of the light that made him look strangely still. Maybe it was because she had spent so long staring at his unmoving chest that it seemed so even now. For who ever looked to make sure another was breathing?

He lifted his hand, long fingers uncurling uncertainly. Something about the gesture made her pause, but he noted her hesitation, the way he noticed everything about her, and smiled.

Deen smiled, the kind of smile that could war with the sun, and all was righted.

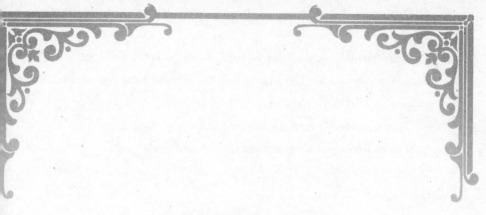

CHAPTER 30

NASIR ALMOST GROWLED ALOUD.

The fool of a Hunter was mad. He witnessed the creature, ugly and dark, and sheathed his jambiya.

Relaxed his defenses.

Stepped closer.

Nasir watched from a dilapidated vestibule, frustration making him jittery.

The ifrit trod with caution. It was a creature of smokeless fire, imprisoned on Sharr by the Sisters. And with the darkening sky, it wasn't just ifrit that would stray from the shadows.

"Do you really think the Hunter sees the ifrit for what it is?" Altair asked, carefully rotating his shoulder.

Nasir didn't care. If he waited any longer, it would kill the Hunter and their only way to the Jawarat would die, too. Why was the man always in danger?

He lifted his bow, the compass heavy in his pocket. He did not tell Altair that since they had climbed Sharr's wall, the compass had changed direction, twice.

That it had led him to the Hunter, twice.

The beginning of a scream scattered Nasir's thoughts.

CHAPTER 31

I T WAS ZAFIRA'S SECOND TIME SEEING DEEN DIE. SURELY SUCH torture had an end.

The arrow struck again below his heart. The same arrow as before, ebony with a tapered silver fletching. A look of rage twisted Deen's features as it happened. A violence she had never before seen on his face.

Yet as he fell, her heart took control of her voice and elicited half a scream before her brain made it stop. It wasn't a sound she ever made.

But.

He was decaying before her eyes. *Changing.* His hair thinned until his head balded, his eyes darkened to depthless black as the body fell into the shadows of the sooq.

She shrank back with a curse. Deen's death had addled her so much that she had lowered her guard and fallen for Sharr's trap. An ifrit. Creatures that fed on despair and grief. Sharr hadn't buried Deen's body, or even eaten it.

It had stolen it.

Something snapped behind her, and Zafira stilled. Another snap—a deliberate sound meant to be heard.

Heavy boots on terraced stone. Whoever had saved her from the ifrit now and had killed Deen earlier. She reached behind for her bow and—

"Freeze."

It was a cold voice, accustomed to giving orders without ever having to repeat itself, despite the low timbre of it. She froze, hand hanging above her head before she slowly curled it into a fist.

"Don't move, Hunter."

At that, she stiffened.

"Your reputation precedes you."

Her eyes fell to the corpse of the ifrit, where the black-and-silver arrow taunted. *Real* silver, which meant it belonged to someone with means. Black and silver, black and silver. She racked her memory. She knew those colors. She knew where people spoke with that soothing lilt.

Her breath halted. *Sarasin.*

"Drop your rida'."

Rida'. Sarasin for hood. Sarasin, like the ones who had ambushed her at the edge of the Arz. Like the sultan himself.

"I said, drop your rida'."

She weighed the odds of the man killing her from behind. A dastardly move, but not one she could discount a Sarasin from doing. He had, after all, nearly killed her before Deen—

No, if she was going to die, she wanted to see who had stolen Deen from Arawiya too soon.

She turned and dropped her hood.

There were two of them. Both young. Smoky kohl framed their eyes, and Zafira dimly thought of how highly Yasmine would approve. The larger was fairer and prettier, with the sun-kissed skin of Arawiya and an amused twist to his mouth. His turban was carefully mussed around his head, stray strands of deep gold peeking out. A patch of blood stained his right shoulder, hastily wrapped cloth marking a fresh injury, and a jewel-studded jambiya sat against one muscled thigh, his sirwal an opulent hue of purple.

The other man was leaner, power rippling from the sharp cut of his shoulders and the set of his jaw. The hair dusting his forehead was as dark as the shadows weaving the island, his skin the deeper olive of the men who had ambushed her. A black-and-gray-checkered keffiyah circled his head, fringe whispering at his neck.

He wore a suit that she hadn't seen the likes of before, surprisingly void of weapons, though that was likely the point of it: to look unsuspecting. A scar slashed the right side of his face, from his forehead to the top of his cheek—it was a surprise his right eye was still intact.

His eyes. They were a tumultuous gray like the dead ashes of a fire, adrift on a cold wind. He was the one with an arrow leveled at her heart, eyebrows lifted in surprise.

It was new, to be assessed by a man when she was a woman. She was so used to people looking at her shadowed figure that she nearly folded into herself. But she felt the ghost of Deen's fingers at her chin, and she straightened, allowing herself a smirk as the Sarasin struggled for words.

"You're a girl."

CHAPTER 32

NASIR DOUBTED HIS FATHER KNEW THE RENOWNED DEMENHUNE Hunter was a girl. He didn't think Ghameq would even care what the Hunter was.

"And you're a murderer," she retorted without missing a beat. Her words were shaped with the rugged lilt of Demenhur. She lifted her chin and met his gaze without a care for the arrow pointed at her.

She was tall and broad-shouldered, both features that would have helped her facade of masculinity. She carried two satchels, her sirwal tucked into supple boots, leather sheaths hoisted on either leg. Her loose qamis was cinched with a sash of black, obscured by her cloak when she dropped her fist.

He had met Demenhune before, but none like her. Everything about her was harsh, from her cheekbones and the cut of her lips to the point of her nose and the starkness of the dark hair crowned in a hurried plait around her head. A profile of angles, a study of ice. Even her gaze was hard to hold, pale blue shards, cold and unfeeling, fringed with lashes that feathered her pale cheeks.

She slid her gaze to Altair and then back to him, raising her slender eyebrows. "Go on."

Even her voice was ice. He lowered the bow, and her eyebrows flew even higher.

"Don't stop now," she said. "You were aiming for me earlier, weren't you? Take your shot, jaban. I won't flinch."

Nasir's grip tightened at the word "coward."

"He changed his mind," Altair announced, striding up to her. Nasir pursed his lips as Altair plastered on the smile that usually melted the women he acquainted. "Altair al-Badawi."

Silence. She slid her gaze to Altair again. It was a careful slide, a cold, deliberate shift. Anger pulsed her jaw, sorrow weighted her features.

"Does that work?" she asked flatly. The wind howled, throwing stray strands of hair across her face.

"Hmm?"

"Stepping too close and pulling that harebrained smile. Does it work?"

Nasir bit down a snort.

But Altair recovered as quickly as always. "Sometimes. But you're one of a kind, aren't you, Huntress?"

She stiffened at the word and stepped back toward the blackened corpse of the ifrit. Nasir wasn't sure an arrow to the chest would kill an ifrit, but he wasn't about to warn her that the creature might still be alive.

Her. The Hunter was a girl.

"Do you want us to bump noses and be the best of friends now? After you killed"—she choked off, unsure how to label the relationship between her and the man who had stared after her with wanting she clearly hadn't reciprocated—"my best friend?"

Lies. She was a terrible liar.

Altair crossed his arms. "I'm afraid there are better places to make friends than on Sharr. We're here to propose an alliance . . . Since my companion and I are heading toward the same thing you are."

"The lost Jawarat," she said.

He nodded.

At her disparaging look, Altair's mouth crooked with the telltale sign of him fighting a grin.

"You come here, try to kill me, murder my friend instead, and now you want to be my . . . ally? You Sarasins are more barbaric than they make you out to be."

"Perhaps." Altair tipped his head and his playful demeanor vanished. "The way I see it, we could kill you and be on our way. But the three of us together might stand a better chance." He nodded at the fallen ifrit, now obscured by the shifting sands. "We did save your life."

The girl had the most open features—Nasir could *see* her thinking the proposal through.

She lifted her eyes to him, those shards of ice discerning the real threat. Nasir's nocked arrow had led her to assume he had killed the Demenhune.

"And when we find the Jawarat?" she asked.

Not if, *when*. There was nothing more respectable and dangerous than a woman of confidence.

This time, it was Nasir who spoke. "We decide then."

CHAPTER 33

FURY BURNED IN ZAFIRA'S VEINS, HARSHER THAN THE BLAZING sands. The Silver Witch had sent Deen *and* daama Sarasins.

Why the allyship? If they could hunt her down in this abyss of stone and sand, they could find the Jawarat themselves. They had no reason for her. Being the Demenhune Hunter held no merit in Sharr. She was no more than a girl from a caliphate where everyone had snow in their brains and smiles on their faces. The taller one didn't even give her a true surname; *al-Badawi* meant "nomad." A common name men used when they wanted to obscure their origins.

She was bait, or a shield.

But it was die now or die later, as with her decision to accept the wretched invitation. If the Sarasins hadn't saved her from the ifrit wearing Deen's face, she would *already* be dead.

Prolonging her death gave her time to think of a way out of this mess. Better yet: a way to avenge Deen.

So she nodded, and the dark-haired one nodded back. It was by no means an oath. Just a fragile deal held together by the inclines of their heads. She chortled, ignoring the funny looks they gave her.

"Now that we're all allied and well, how about you tell us your name?" Altair began, as if he hadn't just threatened to kill her. "I never thought the infamous Hunter would be so pretty."

Zafira rolled her eyes. "Do you always talk so much?"

He scowled, a perfect half circle of downturned lips. "I would think you'd prefer my small talk to the deathly silence of this one."

The dark-haired one studied her, the gray of his eyes now an unflinching steel. That ghastly scar on his face gleamed. He might not speak, but his head was full of words. People like him, Zafira knew, were dangerous.

Altair began leading them, wielding a curved scimitar like an extension of his hand. He held one in the other, too, but the bandage wrapped near his shoulder made clear why he wasn't using it. The muscles in his large arms flexed against the cords strapped around them, and Zafira averted her eyes. How much did he have to eat to hone muscles like that?

"I see you watching me, Huntress. Worry not," Altair said, glancing at his wound. "I'll be good as new in no time." He eyed his companion. "Do you ever wonder why women focus so much on me?"

"Maybe because you resemble a lost, rabid dog," the dark-haired one suggested in perfect seriousness.

Zafira bit down a laugh, and Altair swiveled to her with a comical pout. She was unsure of the relationship between the two Sarasins. They didn't look like brothers, nor did they seem friends, yet they had a mutual respect she doubted either acknowledged. One of them held power over the other, yet she couldn't discern which one.

Murderers, she reminded herself. That was all that mattered. And if the arrows with the silver fletching and fine wood were any indication, they had more means than Zafira could ever dream of.

After a beat of silence, she spoke. "Zafira."

"Who's that?"

"You asked for my name," she said. Sand danced in the distance, sparkling beneath the sun's rays. The world was still a shade darker than when she and Deen had first arrived. She touched the coolness of the ring he had given her and nearly swayed at the reminder of his still chest. Of the tears huddling in her throat.

Altair nodded, oblivious. "Seems your mother was following in the sultana's footsteps when she named you."

She blinked. "Oh?"

"Zafira means 'victorious.'" Altair used the end of his turban to wipe the sweat beading at his brow. The cloth was dark and rimmed in red. It reminded her of a snake, the ones with vibrant colors, poisonous and alluring at once. "So does Nasir, the name of our beloved crown prince. You see, Huntress, I know a thing or two about names."

"He knows a thing or two about too many things," the other one growled.

"Oh, come now, hashashin. Is that jealousy I hear in your voice?"

An assassin. That explained his garb and calculated movements. It would have been easy to assume he had killed Deen, had Altair not threatened to kill *her*.

"I know what the prince's name is," she said.

Altair gave her a funny look, and the hashashin merely looked the other way.

They turned east, through an arching pathway littered with shattered stone and tiny dunes of sand. Altair hacked away dead vines as he went, and as happy as Zafira would have been to leave him to clean the ruins, she had a Jawarat to find.

And an escape to plan.

"We're supposed to head this way," she said, turning north and out of the shadows.

The Sarasins shared a look.

"I have a feeling the Jawarat will be closer to the center," she added.

The hashashin eyed Altair's path. "That's where we're going."

His low, dead voice made her shiver before she replied, "No, that path will take us along the outskirts of the island."

"Is that what your compass says?" Altair asked. "Did you . . . receive one?"

"Receive one?" she repeated, then recalled Deen's compass and her heart cleaved in two as she remembered everything afresh. She shook her head before Altair could see her distress, before the hashashin, with his cold and calculating gaze, could read her.

He approached with a compass of crimson and silver in his gloved palm. It reminded her of the Silver Witch.

Altair looked over his shoulder. "Where does it point?"

"It's broken," he said, and snapped the lid closed.

Liar. She saw the point shifting.

"We don't need a compass," she said. "I know where I'm going. I've always known where I was going."

She just didn't know how. She once attributed it to experience. The way a baker would never measure out his semolina before making his daily batch of harsha. She had never needed a tool to show her where to go. But if a baker was faced with a wild, uncharted maze of a quantity, wouldn't he at least hesitate? Wouldn't he need a tool then?

Zafira hadn't thought twice about which path to take in Sharr's ruins. But that odd frenzy in her blood only settled when she turned in the direction she wanted to go.

"Ah, yes. Come, let's follow the girl who decides her path based on how she feels," Altair said, pulling her from her thoughts.

She rolled her eyes and left them behind. But hadn't Deen said something like that, too?

Her path had gotten him killed.

Just as she paused, she heard the sheathing of scimitars, followed by the drag of boots across the sand-skittered stone. Leading the giant and his growling companion to their deaths wouldn't be so bad.

"I know what you're thinking," Altair said, ever suave.

"No, you don't," the other said.

Zafira wouldn't bother asking for his name.

"Why do you always think I'm talking to you?"

"Does it look like she's listening to you?"

"Why do men think women can't hear them unless we're looking at them?" Zafira snapped.

Moments later, she heard nothing at all and swiveled to see them right at her heels, deathly silent. So the earlier shuffling *was* a ruse. The mystery of why they needed her set her on edge.

Zafira touched Baba's jambiya at her thigh. "Well? Out with it."

"With what? Would you like me to sing to pass the time?" Altair asked.

"The results of your apparent mind-reading," she deadpanned.

"Ah, it's just that I can see you plotting our murders leagues away," Altair said. There was an edge to his voice when he added, "A little thing to remember, Huntress: your face thinks before you do."

"My brain, unlike yours, works before the rest of me does," Zafira retorted. She knew her face spoke before she did. Everyone knew. But Deen knew it best of all.

Altair laughed. "It would be uncharacteristic of me to disagree."

As they continued away from the cover of the stone structures, she was fully aware of every weighted glance the two young men shared when they thought she wouldn't notice. She was even more aware of the way the dark-haired one watched her.

The longer Zafira alternated between sand and relentless stone, the harder it became to breathe. Her hood became a cage, and her eyes burned as sweat seeped between her eyelids. The world tipped more than once; the horizon rippled.

She ran her tongue along her chapped lips.

Water. Everywhere she looked, there was water.

A mirage, Zafira. It's a mirage.

"Huntress?" Altair paused by her side when she grasped a trellis to hold herself upright. She gave him an impatient wave, and he carried on with a shrug, shuffling sand in his wake.

Breathe. Remove your wretched cloak. What was the point of it anymore? They knew she was a girl. She lifted her fingers to the cool clasp of her cloak and . . . *no.* She wouldn't be bested by a cloak. She could endure a little heat.

A shadow fell to her side, and Zafira glanced sharply at the dark-haired hashashin. Something shifted in his features, just barely, when she met his eyes. A mix of surprise, and a stir of anger. There was a vulnerability in the way his dark lashes brushed his skin when he blinked.

"Take off your cloak," he said.

Her throat closed and her head spun. Spurts of sand struck her skin.

"What do you want with me?" she whispered as her breathing grew shallow.

He murmured a reply, but all she heard was that silvery lilt before the sun winked away and she tipped into darkness.

—◄●►—

Zafira finally understood why Arawiyans celebrated the moon. Why the sight made people weep.

It was the desert. The sweltering heat that drained them to their core until the sun sank into the horizon and the moon swept across the dark expanse of sky, gifting them her cold touch. It was a beauty they didn't appreciate in Demenhur, because of the shy sun.

She had never been happier to see that majestic sphere of white.

Moss was cool beneath her back. A figure was bent over her, silhouetted against the moon. He brushed a damp cloth across her forehead and pursed his lips when he saw that she was awake. The dark-haired hashashin. Altair was nowhere to be seen.

Skies. She had blacked out. She had blacked out in the middle of an uncharted island with two Sarasin men. Panic tightened her chest and she scrambled back, boot heels digging into the dirt, moss sticking to her palms.

A pool of water glittered darkly beneath the moon, surrounded by lush plants. Beyond the small oasis, sand dunes stretched for as far as she could see. Her cloak was folded to the side. Her satchels were there, too, untouched.

The moon cast the hashashin in shadow, sharpening the hollows of his face. "You passed out because of the heat, and you would have cracked your skull if I hadn't caught you. Altair carried you here. I removed your cloak." He turned his head and lifted a hand to his neck. "Nothing else."

His voice looped with the darkness, near silent. As if the very idea of speaking disgraced him.

"Who are you?" she asked him. She folded her arms across herself, ignoring the cloth in his extended hand.

He dropped it to his side. "Depends on the slant of light."

Desolation laced his words.

"What do you want with me?" she asked again in a whisper. *Why did you try to kill me? Why did you care for me?*

His lips parted.

"Ah, the sayyida blesses us with her presence, as pale as the moon herself!" Altair called as he emerged from the shadows, bathed in blue light. Zafira nearly sputtered at the sight of his bare chest. Golden, sculpted— *skies.* He grinned, the shameless man. "About time, too. We need to get moving."

"We're staying here for the night. She needs rest," the hashashin said.

Now Zafira glanced at him in surprise. Judging by the sound Altair made, it was clear the hashashin rarely paid heed to anyone's needs but his own.

"I'll keep watch," he continued.

Altair toweled his body. "But of course, sul—"

The hashashin cut him off with a growl, and Zafira lifted her eyebrows. Altair let out an exaggerated sigh and responded with a two-fingered salute.

For Sarasins, at times they seemed oddly . . . normal. As Zafira struggled to avert her gaze, Altair wrapped a fresh bandage around his wound. He threw on his clothes before unfurling his bedroll, an intricately woven carpet of blue and green fringed in beige. Then he lay back, crossing his arms behind his head with a wince. Kharra. Zafira hadn't brought a bedroll of her own.

Altair grinned wickedly, noticing the same. "We can share."

"Ah, no, shukrun," she said quickly, tempering the flare within her as she slipped back into her cloak. Deen would have offered his bedroll and slept on the sand if he had to. She grabbed Deen's satchel and set it against an eroding stone. Deen. Deen. Deen. All that was left of him were the things he had touched. A tin of cocoa and a vial of honey, both as empty as the world without him. She closed her eyes.

No. She wouldn't close her eyes amid the enemy again. She had a mission. She needed to stay alive.

A chill wove across the night, and she wrapped her arms around her knees. Funny how the same desert that had given her a heatstroke such a short time ago now made her shiver.

Altair turned to her, something like earnestness on his face. "I'm sorry." He glanced at Deen's satchel. "About your friend."

Ahead, the hashashin cleared a short boulder and sat with his back to her. She drew her hood over her head, letting it fall over her eyes. That was how much Sarasins valued life. Kill and apologize. Make up for a felled soul with a word.

Whatever fatigue she felt was soon overtaken by numbing grief. She slipped her finger inside the ring, rubbing her skin against the inscription. "For you, a thousand times." She felt Altair's gaze on her, yet she doubted he had ever known loss. She stared at the back of the hashashin's head and guessed he hadn't experienced it, either.

Sarasins truly were heartless.

Eventually, Altair's breathing slowed, and she fought a losing battle to stay alert. She fought harder, unsure if she was even awake when the rustle of clothes knifed the night. She watched with hooded eyes as the hashashin turned away from the oasis.

By the glint in his eyes, Zafira could tell he was focused on Altair. A long moment later, his gaze drifted to her and she stiffened, but he didn't seem to notice.

After what felt like years, he sighed, heavy and resigned, and faced the night again.

Zafira pondered that oddly human sound before sleep dragged her away.

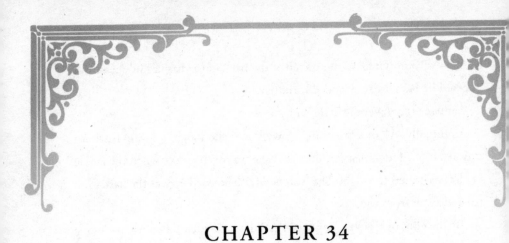

CHAPTER 34

THE GIRL SPOKE IN HER SLEEP.

Rimaal, a girl. The Huntress. She murmured strings of words dotted with curses that would make Altair hoot with laughter; the words "not now"; and a name, over and over and over. If Nasir were to guess, Deen was the Demenhune Altair had killed, and he doubted this Deen had been merely a friend.

She murmured for a sibling, too. Two of them. Sisters whose names made a whisper of a smile twitch at the corners of her mouth. What was it like to have a brother or a sister born from the same mother? Every relationship Nasir had experienced was either fabricated or lived a short life.

He stood over Altair, whose features were blunted by sleep, and stared at the smooth column of his neck, where the qutn fabric of his turban had shifted. It would be easy. A clean cut, painless.

It would make his father proud.

That last thought was what made Nasir nudge Altair's bare bicep with the toe of his boot. Altair's right eye popped open instantly and Nasir clenched his jaw—he should have known.

"For a moment, I thought you might do it," Altair said.

"Do what?" the girl asked. She yawned as she brushed her teeth with a siwak.

Altair's mouth curled into a grin. "Kiss me."

Nasir kicked him, and Altair's laughter only increased.

"We're leaving now," Nasir said.

She met his eyes again, and his step faltered. Aside from his father and his dead mother, there were only two people who ever looked him directly in the eye: Altair and Kulsum, but she, too, only briefly.

As if holding his gaze was as painful as spying on a monster like him.

He shut down that line of thought and holstered his bow. The sun was still making its way past the horizon, so the air was cool. He untied the keffiyah from his neck and wove it into a turban around his head.

Altair extended a share of his pita and a trio of sukkary dates to the girl, who eyed them with suspicion.

"It's perfectly safe," he said.

"As is my own food," she replied, digging through her satchel for darker safawi dates.

"You know it won't last forever, yes?" Altair said, extending the food to Nasir, who ignored it. Altair shrugged and stuffed some pita into his mouth, dusting crumbs from his close-trimmed beard.

"Until I'm dying of hunger, I'll pretend it will." She bit her lip, as if speaking those words inflicted pain. Her eyes fell closed, nostrils flaring.

Altair raised his eyebrows.

"If you're done napping," Nasir said, adjusting his gauntlet blades, "we need to reach higher ground and chart our course."

"Yes," she snapped, eyes flying open, twin scythes of blue fire.

He flinched; he was not proud of it.

Steel hissed as Altair drew his scimitars without a care for quiet. *Both of his scimitars*, Nasir noted in surprise. *Healed so soon.*

He led them, Altair on his heels, the girl trailing behind noisily, still addled by her exchange with Altair. Nasir gritted his teeth against the urge to snap at her to keep up, but she didn't need a man to tell her what to do. That much he knew.

Almost in response to his thoughts, he heard her readying one of her white arrows, her footsteps lightening until he barely heard the whisper of her presence—in moments becoming the Hunter everyone in Arawiya knew of. The *Huntress* very few knew.

All Demenhune looked like ghosts, but the Huntress moved like one, too.

Nasir wondered what it was like to live without the endless and ever-shifting sands beneath one's feet. Without the sun deepening one's skin and rooting in one's soul. Without the push and pull as the heat of the sun drenched and the cold of the moon caressed.

He glanced back to find her watching him, for once, unreadable. Her lips were pursed.

Why did the compass lead me to you? he wanted to ask.

He looked away first.

CHAPTER 35

Z AFIRA WOULD BE AN IDIOT IF SHE WORE HER CLOAK AND FAINTED again, so she tucked it away with great reluctance. She straight-ened the sleeves of her tunic and rewrapped her scarf before adjusting the folds of her sash. She felt bare. Light. Different.

But the world was changing, and she needed to adapt. It *continued* to change. Ever since Sharr had devoured Deen, the island had been darker, and the farther they ventured, the more it darkened still.

Today's plan was to reach the small town Altair had spotted from the oasis, where they would survey the terrain from one of the minarets. Zafira studied the Sarasins as she trailed them, slipping between debris and gliding over rubble. The dark-haired one noted far too much—she caught him watching her several times, once to assess her clothes, and she wasn't sure what to make of it.

She didn't think either of them realized how synchronized they were, or they wouldn't bicker as much as they did. Or maybe Altair knew, and the other just had a blatant dislike for anything and everything but himself.

But his touch had been gentle last night, his words almost kind.

When the time came, she would need to avenge Deen's death. She wasn't sure which of them had killed him, but Deen couldn't have been the target—he had jumped in front of the dark arrow whizzing for *her* heart. And now that the Sarasins had the chance to kill her, they weren't taking it. They had even *saved* her yesterday.

The hashashin threw an arm across her stomach, sending a shock of heat through her before he pulled away with a sharp intake of air, as if he hadn't realized what he had done until he'd done it. Once more, that oddly human sound gave her pause.

Before she realized why he had stopped her.

She gripped the wall nearest her and scrambled back, heart pounding. They had reached the town, it seemed. Climbed the minaret, too, while she was lost in thought.

She teetered at the edge of the tower where the ledge had crumbled, an entire portion chipped away by the wind. One more step and she would have plummeted to her death. Her heart had crammed into her throat, thrummed at her fingertips.

"First, I learn you're a woman. Then you faint. Now you're trying to pitch yourself off a tower," Altair said with a laugh. "The fun never stops."

Zafira saw red. It flared in her vision and flashed behind her eyelids. Murdering Deen wasn't enough? Now he was laughing because she had nearly fallen to her death?

She nocked an arrow and turned to them, seething.

Dust swirled in the blue sky, playing to the whistle of the wind. Altair raised his hands with a smirk. The dark-haired hashashin merely lifted his eyebrows a fraction. The stone wall behind him stood intact, shading them from the sun.

"Tell me who you are," she said to him, her voice surprisingly smooth, "or I will put an arrow through your throat."

"I thought you knew," he said, canting his head.

"Don't think," she snapped.

Something shattered in his unfeeling eyes before they slid to the arrow, then back to her.

"If I told you my name, would you bow?" His voice was soft. A melancholy caress. He lifted his chin when understanding dawned on her face. "Or would you flee?"

The arrow trembled in her grip.

Hashashin. The silver fletching. The authority in his voice. His *name*.

Crown Prince Nasir Ghameq. The Prince of Death. The end of his turban fluttered in the breeze.

Sweet snow below.

She loosed the arrow. It caught his turban, pinning him to the stone behind, giving her the moment she needed to dart past him to the stairwell. Each stone step jarred her teeth until she lost her footing and skidded down a trio before hoisting herself against the sandy railing, nearly invisible in the shadowed corridor. *Breathe.* She doubled over, sweat burning her skin. The shadows curled around her arms and she jerked away from them.

The daama crown prince. Half safin, half human. No wonder he ordered her about as he pleased.

It was said that he tallied his kills on his body, that he had begun with his arms but ran out of room far too soon, for he never left a job unfinished. His body was as black as his heart.

"Kharra, kharra, kharra," she cursed, taking off again.

Rough hands grabbed her by her middle and pushed her against the stairwell wall.

Altair *al-Badawi*.

General al-Badawi: the son of none with no lineage to his name. He could very well be the commander of the army that had slain Yasmine and Deen's parents.

Both of the men she'd been traveling with were cold-blooded murderers.

"Once you leave the stairwell, he will shoot you down," Altair warned, releasing her.

"Will he? Or will you?" she seethed.

He stiffened. "I'm not so handy with a bow."

"And now you're concerned for my safety?"

"I've always been concerned for your safety," he murmured, and looked up the stairs. "Hurry up, Sultani!"

Sultani. Zafira bit back a sob. Not only had the Silver Witch sent Sarasins here to Sharr, she had sent the two worst Sarasins in all of Arawiya. The sultan's prized general. The sultan's own daama son.

"The Silver Witch lied to me. She said she didn't want the sultan to know," she whispered.

"The silver woman cannot lie, Huntress. She would have worded that a little differently."

"Why? Why did she send you?" She needed to make sense of what was happening.

"She didn't." Altair shrugged as the prince came into view. *Skies.* The prince. Prince Nasir Ghameq, whose name shared the same meaning as hers. Whose hands were stained red.

Whose touch on her forehead had been gentle.

He met her eyes with the ashes of his own. The end of his turban was torn, but she couldn't summon satisfaction at the sight.

Altair nudged her forward, and she stomped down the steps again.

She would not bow. She wouldn't treat them any differently than if they were her servants. She turned back to him. To the daama prince. "If the Silver Witch didn't send you, who did?"

"The sultan," he said matter-of-factly. "He learned of your quest, and because no one trusts witches, he sent me."

Zafira had trusted the witch. Not entirely, but enough to board her daama ship. Before she could ask *For what?* Altair interrupted, "And me.

So the next time you think of killing him, just know you're supposed to get rid of the less important one first."

"How did you cross the Arz?"

The prince tipped his head. "Ghameq counted on her knowing. She helped us cross the Arz and gifted us with a ship, much like she did for you, I assume."

"But that doesn't make sense," she said. Why would the Silver Witch favor the crown prince if she wanted to keep the journey from the sultan? Zafira doubted quite a bit when it came to the Silver Witch, but there was no reason to stay clear of the sultan and then aid his son in the same breath.

No, whatever her reason, it had to do with the prince and Altair themselves.

"No one asked you to make sense of it," he said in that same monotone, and Altair pushed her down the stairs again.

"Where are we going?"

"To the next oasis," the prince said with a sardonic twist to his mouth.

"And then?" she asked.

"And then we'll find the Jawarat."

"And then?" *Will you kill me?*

Mirth touched his voice. "Fate only knows."

"Are you always this insufferable?" she fumed, straightening her scarf.

"He's twice as bad when hungry," Altair offered.

Zafira bit back a snarl. They were both insufferable children. With death counts.

CHAPTER 36

MURDER BURNED IN THE HUNTRESS'S GAZE, BUT she turned and continued with graceful prowess, allowing Nasir to breathe. It was proving difficult to think when she looked at him.

Laa, *more* of him decided to think.

She was right to be confused. The sultan had sent him and Altair because he didn't trust the Silver Witch, but then the witch herself had turned and aided *them*. Not only with the Arz and the ship, but with the compass in his pocket. Those parting words.

He was missing something. Something important.

When they left the confines of the minaret, the Huntress rounded the tower and slipped past the ruined quarters surrounding it. Her movements were always precise, calculated without calculations. Her entire form knew where to move before she did, and she waded the sands as if she had lived her entire life within them.

"If you stare too hard, she might disappear," Altair mock-whispered in his ear.

"If you talk too much, you might disappear, too," Nasir retorted, pleased with how quickly he thought of that one, and he left Altair behind to catch up to her.

She pursed her lips when he neared, and he didn't know why he opened his mouth.

"Being an eminent killer doesn't make me the only one."

"You're the worst there is," she said with a wheeze.

Nasir felt the sting of something he didn't welcome.

"You killed Deen."

He didn't deny it. *Intentions are akin to action.*

"You led those Sarasins to their deaths," he countered. Surprise widened her eyes. "Not even one week past."

"That was an act of defense, not deliberation." *Ah, there it is.* The fissure he expected, the break in her voice before she collected herself. "I don't go murdering people on a whim."

"Neither do I. Hashashins don't uphold the brutality of murder. We are poets of the kill, working from the shadows. A mark rarely knows his fate until he falls." There had once been respect in the hashashin's creed. A level of esteem.

Unlike the Zaramese, who reveled in torture and torment. In their caliphate, they hosted tournaments where contestants were pitted in an arena, the crowds full of cheering people, even young children.

Still, he supposed he deserved the disgust she directed at him and the detest in her voice when she said, "No. Death is death, Sultani."

Never had he loathed princedom more.

"Do you hear that?" Altair called before the wind rose to a sudden howl.

Sand whipped across Nasir's vision, and he rewrapped his turban cowl-like around his neck and head. He would have thought it odd that a storm had appeared without warning, but this was Sharr. And then, through the rain of umber, he saw them.

Five silhouettes prowled with the calculation of men. Nasir squinted. No, worse than men—gold rings glinted from their elongated ears. Safin.

"What happened to their shirts?" the Huntress asked, shrinking back.

"They aren't wearing any," Altair explained candidly.

"I can see that," she sputtered, and threw Nasir a sharp glance when he drew his sword. "What are you doing? They're human."

"Safin," Nasir corrected with a cant of his head. "And I can assure you, they are not the friendly type."

Altair flexed his arms. "Safin won't live here willingly, and the only unwilling reason to be here is if they were locked in cells, which I would bet a pot of qahwa they were. So grab an arrow, Huntress."

Only Altair valued bitter coffee so much.

"Safin," she murmured with a touch of awe. "Maybe they just want to go free. We don't have to kill them."

Was she really so cloistered?

"Kill or be killed," Nasir contended. "There are three of us and five of them. Whether you help or not, they will die. I'm merely giving you a choice of involvement, and no one would be surprised if you stepped aside." He allowed himself a smirk when he added, "Safin can be very scary."

She unleashed a string of curses, damning him to the Wastes.

The laugh that crept up his throat terrified him.

"I could have you killed for that," he murmured.

She looked stricken for no more than a heartbeat. "I've defied the odds long enough to know I won't die for blaspheming a prince."

Then she nocked an arrow and breathed down its shaft, utterly uncaring. It almost made him smile.

The five safin stopped before them, scimitars studded with the copper of rust.

Altair spoke first, his voice cutting the tense air. "You don't happen to know where the nearest inn is, do you?"

"And here I thought you had come to save us," the one in the center said. Though he spoke with the signature mocking tone of his people, his words lacked Alderamin's annoyingly slow lilt.

"You were imprisoned here for a reason," Nasir said, though he didn't know the reason itself.

The safi to his right laughed, dry and mad. "Must a sin cost an eternity? Is that justice?"

"We're sorry," the Huntress said.

Nasir lifted his eyebrows as she lowered her bow. He was not sorry.

"Come with us," she continued, "and when we find what we seek, we will help you."

Nasir and Altair stilled when the safi stepped closer to her. She stopped breathing altogether, struggling to avert her gaze from his shirtless state.

"We do not take aid from mortals," he rasped.

Then he lunged.

The Huntress was faster. She ducked beneath his grasp and darted out of reach, elevating her bow as the other four spurred into action. Nasir hurled a knife at one of them, then gripped his scimitar with both hands and swung at another, sure that his blade would rend the rusted one in two.

It did not.

Steel clashed and the safi growled, less elegant than safin normally were. Nasir leaped back, using the flat of his blade to parry the safi's quick blows. The breeze picked up, tossing sand across his vision, and he ducked his mouth beneath the folds of his turban. The signature swoops and clangs of Altair's twin swords echoed in the ruins.

The safin were weathered and hardy. Worthy foe, had they been equally matched.

As if in answer to Nasir's thoughts, another figure leaped into the fray, a red sash at her hip. She twirled a spear in her hands, the gold tip gleaming in the fractured sunlight.

Human. Judging by her dark skin, red attire, and shorn head: Pelusian.

"Sultan's teeth. One of the Nine Elite," Altair shouted, his voice muffled by the wind. "You're a long way from home, lady."

"Aren't we all?" she shouted back.

Nasir caught Altair grinning at her quick tongue.

"So lonely, too," the general said.

She snapped her spear to her side, chin low as she sized up her opponent. "I like to travel light."

Metal swung for Nasir's head, and he focused on his attacker again, his reciprocating strike barely scuffing the safi's bare arm. However one of the Pelusian calipha's own elite warriors had gotten here, it seemed she would be an ally in this battle. To his right, the Huntress pulled back her bowstring, breathing down the shaft of a white-tipped arrow, the bottom half of her face tucked beneath her scarf.

Her aim was low, unfatal. Rimaal, this girl.

"Ogle later, princeling," Altair shouted in his ear.

Nasir hurled another blade and then caught sight of the Huntress, who was—

Running?

Nasir swerved from the safi's blade. *She is going to get herself killed.* He gritted his teeth and lunged. Swift, precise. He plunged his scimitar through the safi's chest with a sickening crunch of bone and shoved him to the ground. The immortal choked, sputtered, and then breathed no more.

One down.

Nasir darted past the twin hisses of Altair's scimitars and found the Pelusian locked in a losing battle.

"You should have stuck to your books, human," the safi snarled at her.

The spear in her grip faltered, the safi's scimitar bearing down on her as she gritted her teeth and pushed back. An angry gash on her left arm dripped blood. She was lithe, but the safi was brawny.

And the Huntress was going to save her. She raised her nocked arrow, aiming for the safi's back.

She fired.

The arrow struck his shoulder, buying enough time for the Pelusian to break free. As the safi cursed in the ancient tongue, the Pelusian paused to give the Huntress a small nod of thanks, barely concealing her surprise.

These people were Nasir's enemy. He had come here to slay them.

Air compressed behind him and he whirled, clashing steel with another safi. *Why won't they die?* He clenched his jaw and twisted his blade free, and when he dared to look away, he saw the Huntress.

On the sand, her long body pinned beneath the safi who had first spoken, his rusted scimitar raised to strike.

CHAPTER 37

ZAFIRA COULD BARELY BREATHE. THE PRINCE HAD SPOKEN OF death as if he were weighing the sweetness of dates. And now she was being squashed like one.

This was not how she had hoped to meet an Alder safi for the first time. She had never expected to meet one so *bare*, either. His torso, copper from the sun, glistened with sweat. Her face burned, and she wondered if this was the pathetic moment when she would finally blush, as Yasmine had proclaimed she would at a time that felt like eons ago.

He struggled to hold her down, but she refused to die in such an ungraceful way. *Death by suffocation. Because a half-naked safi sat on me.* She shoved, managing to break his hold on his scimitar. It sliced through the sands by her head.

He snarled and weighed her down as she jabbed her knees against his stone-hard body. His eyes narrowed between the folds of his filthy turban. Funny how his face was obscured when the rest of him wasn't.

Sweet snow, she was *hot*. She craned her head to the hands around her neck and lashed out with her teeth, connecting with weathered skin.

The safi pulled away with an ugly snarl. "I will gut you and feast upon your flesh."

Her eyes widened at the words. Safin weren't supposed to be vicious. They were collected, smart, vain, and elegant. These safin were monstrous. She jabbed her knees up again, this time connecting with his unsuspecting limbs. He howled and rolled to the sands.

This time, she pinned *him* down. He would send her flying the moment he recovered, but she would have her moment. No one, safi or otherwise, would feast on her tonight.

He swiped with his nails. She was more disgusted than afraid now. She threw a fist at him, wondering where she ever learned to inflict pain. She was the Hunter. She killed rabbits and deer with the least amount of agony possible.

Shouts and curses rang out in the distance, and she blearily registered Altair's voice. The Pelusian woman who had appeared out of thin air was fighting, too. Blood roared in Zafira's ears. The prince was likely leaning against a broken column, waiting for everything to sort itself out.

"Suffer as I have, Demenhune. Perish here, as I will," the safi rasped as he reached for his fallen sword.

Zafira unsheathed her jambiya, but a dagger was no match for a scimitar. He kicked her off, tearing the air from her lungs. She fell upon stone, bones jarring, teeth clacking. He swung the sword at her, the sharpened end slicing straight for her neck.

Terror tore through her.

Kill or be killed. The Prince of Death's toneless voice rang through her ears.

She wasn't going to be torn apart by a rogue safi while the prince looked on in boredom.

Zafira rolled, once to the right, then to her left as the safi brought his scimitar down, again and again, tossing sand and shards of loose stone with his every strike. There was a crazed look in his eyes.

She kicked at his feet, and he stumbled, righting quickly. His blade arced down again.

I have

to get out of

the way.

But there was nowhere to go. Stones hemmed in on either side, pressed at her back. Panic clawed at her skin. The darkness taunted from where light refused to go, the shadows churning in a frenzy. *Fight him. Do what you must.*

Zafira pulled him down with a twine of her legs. She gasped for air. Jabbed her blade up. Twisted her hands out of instinct.

"You—" The safi choked, garbling on something liquid-like.

Baba. Baba. I'm sorry.

Stickiness spread through her fingers, and heaviness settled in her bones, weighting her atop the debris. She saw red. Her thoughts flickered, blanked. The safi fell, as surprised as she was.

Dead.

By Zafira's hand.

She was used to blood dripping from her fingers, seeping beneath her nails, but not the blood of sentients. Of a death from violence.

She dropped her jambiya and croaked. She wanted to scream. *I did this.* What did it mean, now that her soul had darkened? *Kill or be killed.* She was a fool for listening to the prince, for not remembering that there was always a compromise. She could have maimed the safi, she could have—

The sands yawned open, but she was too numb to react as the island swallowed the dead safi. Sharr was pleased with her. The wind thanked her with its howl.

Zafira could only watch as the island ate its fill, certain the prince's soul was the darkest of them all.

CHAPTER 38

N ASIR EXHALED. IT WAS NOT LENGTHIER THAN USUAL.
It was certainly not a sigh of relief because the Huntress was
alive and seemingly unharmed. He watched as she shrank
into herself, like a girl lost among the many stalls of a sooq.

"Akhh, I thought she'd be a little more useful in battle," Altair said.

Nasir cut him a glare. "I need her more than I need you."

"I am going to pretend you didn't just insult me."

Nasir shifted some sand with the toe of his boot, but the five slain safin
and their rusted scimitars were gone, all five consumed by the island.

"Sultan's teeth, did Sharr eat the woman, too?" Altair asked, looking
about.

The Pelusian was nowhere to be seen. Had Altair not mentioned her,
Nasir would have thought Sharr had conjured her, playing tricks on his
depraved mind. Sharr, which was always watching. While the Huntress
displayed her weaknesses for the island to revel in.

"Huntress," Nasir said, but she only closed her eyes and tilted her head to the skies. He could have sworn the temperature rose without her cold gaze. His eyes fell to the smooth column of her neck, unblemished except for a small speck of darkness above her right collarbone. A birthmark.

He forced himself to look at her face.

"Odd spot for safin to hide," Altair commented, kicking something to the shadows, where it clattered noisily.

"Sheltered, secluded from ifrit. Near enough to an oasis for water and game. Not odd—prime. They never had hopes of leaving, or they wouldn't have been so violent," Nasir said.

The Huntress reached for her satchel but dropped her hands and closed her eyes again when she saw their bloodied state. Rimaal. They needed to get moving.

Nasir stalked to her. "Stop feeling sorry for yourself."

Her eyes flew open and she shot to her feet, her lips raw and red. "Oh, laa. I'm not here to be ordered around. I am daama tired of you and your beloved general telling me what to do, where to go, when to move. Your threats mean nothing to me."

She stepped closer and he pulled back, regretting it instantly.

"If you want me obedient, Prince, kill me and carry my corpse."

Her voice echoed in the silence. Her mouth was crooked in rage, her eyes ablaze in a fire of ice. Nasir should have turned away.

He should not have given in to the sensations of how she looked. Of how, in one fell swoop, she had thrown the Prince of Death to the ground and trampled his existence with her words.

But he did. So his traitor of a chest made him laugh.

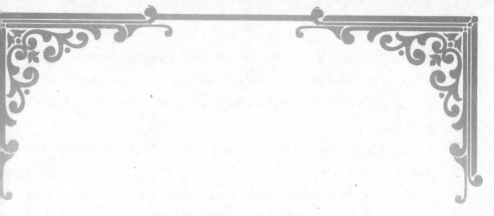

CHAPTER 39

ZAFIRA HAD TENSED FOR A FIGHT. FOR THE PRINCE TO SHOVE her to the ground and chop off her head the way the dead safi had wanted to do. She hadn't expected him to laugh in her face.

It was a raspy sound tinged with surprise, as if his throat weren't used to laughing, as if he had forgotten what it meant to laugh. Then his heart chastised the absurd thing his mind had allowed him to do, and he stopped.

If he had a heart, that was.

But the laugh still glittered in his dark eyes when Altair capped his goatskin and smacked his lips. The prince—no, *Nasir*; calling him "the prince" in her head was too much to bear—looked at Altair's goatskin before uncapping his own and extending it to her.

"There's blood on my hands," she said softly.

He held her gaze and splayed his long, clean fingers. Gloveless. "Mine, too."

The Prince of Death. She would have thought it a reminder, if a chasm hadn't opened in his eyes. He was adept at keeping his features clear of emotion, but those stone eyes had betrayed him more than once.

"Are you immortal?" she asked out of nowhere. "Like full-blooded safin are?"

"There's only one way to find out, isn't there?" he said in that voice that looped with the wind.

He tipped the goatskin over for her, and when the last of the red stains left her fingers, she tucked her stark hands away. If she felt like an anomaly in Demenhur, where *everyone* was pale, she felt even worse here, among the umber sands and darker skin of the Sarasins.

Altair held out her cleaned jambiya. "Congratulations, Huntress. You're officially a murderer. Welcome to the club."

Nasir looked at him coldly. She almost didn't take the blade back. Baba's blade.

I've killed a man. An immortal safi. His crimes didn't matter—he was another person who had breathed like she did, who might have once had a family and dreams of his own.

"We shouldn't have met them armed. They could be alive now," she said, momentarily forgetting that these two Sarasins were as much her enemies as the safin were.

"They attacked first. Kill or be killed, remember?" Altair said.

"What, you're his mouthpiece?"

The general gave her a sly grin. "Are we talking about talking? Or other mouth adventures? Because—"

"No one wants to know about your mouth adventures," Nasir interrupted.

Altair sighed and sauntered away. "Another time, then. Maybe when the grump's asleep."

Zafira found it odd how easily Altair insulted the crown prince. He might be the general, but the prince wasn't known to have friends. Or admirers. No one liked him, and he liked no one, khalas—the end. And considering how quick he was on the draw, it was surprising Altair had survived this long.

Poets of the kill. The ring against her chest was a reminder: She was never safe.

"Ah, princeling?" Altair called, and Nasir's features tightened. "As much as I loathe to admit it, I seem to have lost count." Zafira turned to where Altair stood amid the safin camp. "How many safin did we kill?"

"Five?" Zafira offered, and then she saw what he was seeing.

The safin had created a home for themselves in the ruins. Smoothed-out stones served as beds, tarnished goblets and platters lay to the side. Everything numbered seven. *Seven?*

Nasir gripped his sword as footfalls sounded ahead of them, where the winds still stirred sand. Zafira tensed, but she could barely summon the will to grab her bow. How many more lives would she end before this was over? She had come here fearing for *her* life. This was infinitely worse.

The two remaining safin sped toward them, and it was the first time Zafira noticed how agile they were—far faster than she had ever seen humans move.

Altair drew his scimitars from the twin scabbards at his back, but both safin froze mere paces before him, panic widening their eyes.

With twin croaks, they crumpled to the sand, like puppets whose strings had been cut.

Foam trickled from their open mouths.

Death stole their last breaths.

Tendrils of blue glittered in their wake. *What sorcery—*

Two figures emerged from the dust. The Pelusian from before, her gold-tipped spear gripped at her side. The other was weaponless, elegance marking his steps, a broad grin on his face.

"Well, here I am. What were your other two wishes?"

CHAPTER 40

NIGHT FEATHERED THE HORIZON, PAINTING THE skies a blend of charcoal and winterberries, while a smattering of stars winked and danced in shy greeting. It was an odd sky—light enough to discern color, dark enough to host stars. A desert sky.

Amid the tense silence, Zafira was struck with how little control she had. In the face of spears, swords, double scimitars, and . . . *sorcery*, she was nothing. She was a blade of grass to be trampled.

Or, worse, cut down.

Where were these people coming from? First a warrior from Pelusia, and now a man dressed in finery that looked awkward among Sharr's ruination.

Before Zafira could move, Nasir clamped down on her arm and pulled her deeper into the shadows of the ruins. She pulled free with a hiss. "What are you doing?"

"Getting away," he said simply.

"From what? What about your friend?"

"Friend?" he asked, appearing perplexed at the idea of having such a thing.

She gestured wildly to Altair, who was grinning madly at the newcomer. Nasir stilled, giving her the sense that he was unaware of this acquaintance.

Altair clasped the newcomer on the shoulder. His tone was endearing. "Any longer and you would have found my corpse."

"A thousand and one apologies. Old age, as you know," the newcomer replied, though he looked no older than Altair. His voice was lilting and smooth, decadent like that chocolate drink she, Yasmine, Deen, and Lana had drunk on one of Demenhur's warmer nights beneath endless skies.

"Who is he?" Zafira whispered.

Nasir looked at her. "If I knew, did you think I would tell you?"

So he didn't know. "Altair knows him. I imagined you would, too. You're the prince."

Something in his eyes caught in the moonlight. "I'm afraid that's all I am." Then he tightened his mouth, angry at himself for saying as much. "We need to go."

The shadows behind them stirred. "And where exactly are you planning to go now that we've saved your sorry lives?"

The Pelusian. She spoke so quickly it was a marvel she found time to breathe. Nasir extended his gauntlet blade, but the woman merely stared at Zafira, unfazed. Not a woman—a girl. Likely a year or so older than she was.

"Why did you save me? You don't know who I am," the Pelusian asked, her shorn head aglow. A length of gold cuffed her upper arm.

There were three sectors in Pelusia: the farmers, the erudites who consisted of inventors and scholars, and the warriors. The crossed-spears emblem on her cuff marked her as a warrior of the calipha's Nine Elite. Yet one of her arms—from shoulder to fingertip—was inked in the old tongue, the mark of an erudite, for only they valued the knowledge of the ancients enough to stain their bodies with it. Had she switched when her calling did?

"Are you my enemy?" Zafira asked, and Nasir released an exasperated growl.

A smirk played on the Pelusian's full lips. "I never did like the idea of the Demenhune Hunter, and I could spear you to the ground before our prince even moved his arm, so if those are what it means to be your enemy, then I suppose I am."

Zafira struggled to uphold her composure.

"Well? Why did you do it?"

Zafira opened her mouth, but only a whisper of a sound escaped. She shook her head, feeling Nasir's gaze heavy on her. "Because it was the right thing to do."

Something flickered across the Pelusian's face. "Honor is dead, girl."

"Is gratitude dead, too, where you're from?" Zafira snapped.

For a moment, she thought the Pelusian might shove that spear through her foot, but she only barked a laugh and clasped that feral rod with both hands before lowering her head. "Kifah Darwish, sworn of Nine to the great Calipha Ghada bint Jund of Pelusia, south of the realm." She jerked her head toward Altair and the newcomer several paces away, and her amity vanished as quickly as it had come. "Now move."

Nasir set his jaw and stalked forward without a sound. Zafira turned to ask Kifah where she had come from and how and why, but the girl was busy poking a threaded needle into the flesh of her bloodied arm without so much a flinch. Zafira's eyes widened.

What have I gotten myself into?

"Ah, you've decided to join us," the newcomer said to Nasir. He moved with the feline grace Zafira had only ever attributed to the people of Baba's stories. His checkered keffiyah was held in place with an ornate circlet of black ore, face accented by a dark beard cut against his skin, much like Nasir's but with far more sculpted styling. His golden skin shone in the moonlight, too fair to be Pelusian. A tattoo curved around his left eye, the ink a dull gold, nearly bronze.

"Who are you?" Zafira asked.

His kohled eyes fell on her, and he smiled, teeth gleaming.

It was a smile that made her feel safe. A smile that made her question everything.

"My name is Benyamin Haadi," he said.

Then the man who had helped them kill the rogue safin lifted the ends of his keffiyah to wrap turban-like around his head, unveiling two gold rings glittering from the top of one ear.

An elongated ear. *A safi.*

CHAPTER 41

BENYAMIN HAADI WAS NO WISH-GRANTING JINN. HE WAS VAIN, immortal, and from Alderamin—a safi. He also happened to be Nasir's cousin and son of the Alder calipha. Though Nasir knew of the sultana's sister's son, the double barrier of the Arz between Sultan's Keep and Alderamin meant the two of them had never met.

As all haughty safin were, Benyamin was quicker, faster, and wiser than humans. If only more of that safin blood had carried on to Nasir.

What was his connection to Altair? Moreover, how had he *gotten* here? The Silver Witch wouldn't convene with safin any more than safin would lower themselves to convene with the sultan.

"And so, here we are, in an oasis of shadows, readying to maul one another as if we were but animals in a pit."

"I thought your overuse of words was a side effect of seasickness. If I had known you'd talk so much, I wouldn't have come along," Kifah groaned.

Benyamin seemed to ponder that. "If one has been gifted with eloquent speech, why ever not make use of it?"

"Perhaps because not everyone loves the sound of your voice as much as you do?" the Huntress replied flatly.

He scowled.

"I sort of like the sound of his voice. Nothing like a nice accent," Altair mused. "What do you think, princeling?"

"I think," Nasir said with a grit of his teeth, "you need to stop asking for my opinion."

Altair sighed. "And you thought traveling with a prattler was difficult?" He looked at Kifah with a hint of respect. "Who might you be, One of Nine?"

"I never asked for your name," she said, giving him a look. She couldn't seem to stand still for more than two beats, a restless energy pulsing through her limbs.

"Which is why I'm being the gentleman," he said pointedly. "I am—"

She rolled her eyes. "Kifah Darwish, and I don't care."

Benyamin sauntered around, one hand on the pouch belted across his middle. He was pathetic and weaponless. Kifah stayed close to his side, even when he stopped in front of Altair and canted his head, something passing between them in the silence. Nasir narrowed his eyes.

The Huntress murmured something beneath her breath and angrily yanked an arrow into her bow. The others turned to face her.

"Akhh, time for another interrogation," Altair said cheerily. "I think—"

"Don't think," she snapped.

Nasir flinched at the words that had been directed at him countless times before.

Altair lifted two fingers to his brow with a wicked grin. She shifted her aim across the four of them.

"Who sent you." Her voice was a staid monotone, not a question. There was courage in the slight lift of her chin. Confidence in the press of her mouth.

Benyamin gave a slight shake of his head. "No one did."

"Then how did you get here?"

"On a ship," Kifah said smugly as she wound fabric around her arm. Benyamin smirked.

Nasir could see the Huntress's patience wearing thin, but there was only one way to deal with safin: by challenging their pride.

And it seemed the Huntress had come to that realization herself: "Did you crawl through the Arz on your hands and knees, then?"

Appall flashed across Benyamin's features, and Altair smothered a laugh. Nasir lowered his head to hide the crack of a smile.

"Caravans make their way through the Wastes every so often. I joined one of them and stopped in Pelusia to ask their calipha for aid from one of her esteemed Nine. Together, Kifah and I journeyed to Zaram, tracked down a willing sailor, and crossed the path of the Zaramese Fallen. We arrived in time to save your lives, and now I stand before you, perfection incarnate."

"The last part is debatable," Kifah said.

"Ah, but not downright negatable."

So he hadn't received the same favors Nasir and the Huntress had. No disappearing Arz, no phantom ship. His cousin had gone through terrible lengths to get here, which meant he had good reason to.

And by recruiting the help of a Pelusian and a Zaramese crew, he had ensured that all five caliphates would become entwined with this island.

"You ventured this far to save us from two rogue safin," Nasir said flatly.

Benyamin's demeanor turned cold. "An added bonus, depending on how you view it."

"Very few know of the mission," Nasir pressed. "News couldn't have reached Alderamin in time for you to have crossed the Wastes, Pelusia, *and* Zaram."

"Befriend enough spiders, and one will garner enough gossamer," Benyamin mused.

The words slapped Nasir with sense.

Altair.

Altair was one of Benyamin's spiders. Altair, whose every action was painstakingly deliberate. Nasir remembered the server girl and the scrap of papyrus—Altair didn't even step into a tavern for the sole purpose of a drink. How much of Arawiya spun in a direction the sultan did not order?

He should kill them. Kill them and take the Huntress. It was the right thing to do—in the sultan's eyes.

Nasir hadn't looked through his own eyes in a very long time.

Benyamin watched him closely, and Nasir noted a shift in the safi's umber gaze. Something had softened in them.

"At ease, Prince. I'm afraid we have a lot to talk about."

CHAPTER 42

Zafira held her distance as Benyamin led them past an outcropping, all jagged points like a crown. She kept expecting Nasir to do away with the safi, but the hashashin seemed docile for once.

An expanse of stone widened in a circle, the soft gray vaguely familiar and equally out of place among Sharr's many shades of brown.

"A jumu'a?" Altair asked.

That was where she had seen it before. It was nearly identical to the one on which Yasmine's wedding had taken place. Zafira didn't know the Sisters had laid jumu'a stones on Sharr, too.

"Indeed. We passed it on our way to save you," Benyamin said.

"Don't get too conceited, safi," Nasir said. "We could have handled two more of your kind."

"Semantics," Benyamin replied with a quirk of his mouth.

Zafira froze when the ground shook—so fiercely, she felt its tremor in her jaw. The carvings along the stone deepened and undulated.

"Kharra," Nasir murmured, throwing a sharp glance at Benyamin, who shook his head quickly, denying all blame.

Zafira never imagined the collected prince would curse, but she supposed even he had his limits.

Altair chuckled under his breath. "You're getting worse, Sultani. Next—"

The gray stone flooded in darkness. *Shadows.* Wind battled with her clothes, tugged at her hair, and a scream cut the quiet. Zafira ducked as the night became impossibly black.

A creature hurtled across the skies, long wings shifting like the waves of the Baransea, power rippling across razor-edged feathers dark as a falcon's. A beak in the hues of sunset shaped at its mouth. Altair whistled.

"A rukh," Zafira marveled as it screamed again and lifted to the clouds.

"It doesn't need a name besides 'gigantic bird with daggered claws,'" Altair said.

"It helps to know what you're facing," she countered, referring to more than just the bird as she leveled him with a look.

"She's right," Kifah said as the skies cleared. In moments, the rukh was barely a speck in the horizon, a black star in the dark sky. "But let's hope we won't be facing that thing anytime soon. I didn't leave the calipha only to become fodder."

"The stories always described them as large and strong enough to grab an elephant in its talons. I never knew it was *that* big," Zafira continued.

"The stories also say elephants tromp in a mythical isle far east, but only you would find any of this interesting, Huntress," Altair said with a yawn.

They spent the rest of that night on the jumu'a. Zafira reclined against the surrounding outcrop, trying to stay awake while her eyes drifted closed. Benyamin claimed to be tired from his journey and slept right in the middle of the stone without a care for the murder blazing in the prince's eyes.

She had so many questions that needed answering. *Too* many questions. A safi wouldn't come all this way based on a cacophony of rumors.

Regardless, both Benyamin *and* Nasir were more capable than she was, so why had the Silver Witch sent her? The more she tried to make sense of it, the more her head spun.

She would get her answers, even if she had to hold her jambiya to the safi's perfect neck. *Someone's getting violent*, Yasmine sang in her head.

She must have dozed off at some point, because soon, light was skittering through the sparse clouds, the early sun's miserly heat sending a warm shiver through her.

It reminded her of chilly mornings in Demenhur, when Lana would place steaming harsha in her hands, buttery and grainy, the cake melting in her mouth as she readied for another day of hunting. She missed food that wasn't dried dates and bread hard enough to knock a man senseless. She missed her sleepy village.

The Prince of daama Death leaned against the outcrop on the other end, one leg folded, arms crossed. His head was tipped to the sky, eyes closed. He hadn't attempted to kill anyone overnight, which likely meant he was scheming. He could easily slip into the ruins beyond and vanish, but more than once she caught him on full alert, scanning the jumu'a until he settled on her and his stance grew lazy again.

Why would the Prince of Death seek her out if not to kill her?

She rolled her shoulders and downed a trickle of water before climbing the stone. She pressed the cool metal of Deen's ring to her lips and surveyed the terrain, quelling the grief bubbling up her throat.

The ruins were scattered throughout the distance. Whole sections had been covered entirely by sand, dunes rising and falling in waves. She spotted the large oasis they had seen from the minaret yesterday, a patch of green and blue rippling beneath the sun.

"Spy anything of interest?" Benyamin asked.

She leaped down and dusted off her hands. Sand stuck to her palms.

She still could not believe she had met safin—and killed one, she recalled like a fist to her stomach. He smiled at her scrutiny. To call him handsome would have been a lie, for he was utterly beautiful, with sculpted features and flawless golden skin accented by an artistic beard. The kohl surrounding his umber eyes was pristine, and the two golden rings piercing the top of his right ear winked. Skies, the Alder probably spent entire mornings in front of a looking glass.

"There's an oasis not too far from here," she said, averting her eyes.

"We'll head there next," he said with a nod, and tilted his head at her. "I never thought the Demenhune Hunter was a Huntress."

She slanted her mouth. "Must have been hard trying to get a spider close enough."

"Oh, I had a spider on you, Huntress. I merely underestimated the loyalty of those around you."

Her throat constricted—there was only one newcomer to her circle in Demenhur. Only one who could have learned of her identity, had the sister of her heart shared the knowledge. Had Deen shared the secret with his new friend.

Misk.

She wouldn't let Benyamin see her come undone. "Did you truly cross the path of the Zaramese Fallen?"

"Indeed," he said, regarding her. "I was lucky to have Kifah with me."

Her eyes strayed to his tattoo, the bronzed ink shimmering in the early light. It was Safaitic, she realized. A simple word of two letters, the curvature of the *ha* framing his eye while the *qaf* rounded off smoothly, its two i'jam like birds in flight.

Haqq. Old tongue for "truth."

With his umber eyes and utter grace, the safi reminded her of a large cat. He slunk away before she could ask any more, cloak molding to his slender frame.

He gestured for everyone to draw near, and Zafira's eyes flared when

Nasir stalked to them, confident in his stride, lithe in his step. Altair inclined his head toward him, whispering before sliding a furtive glance at her.

Well, then.

They were stronger than she was, the girl who hunted in the dark for rabbits and deer. Even the dead safin had been better fighters.

But she had a mission. She had her bow and her jambiya and a chance. She would make it count.

CHAPTER 43

NASIR UNDERSTOOD NOW WHY THE SULTAN WANTED ALTAIR dead. He was Benyamin's spider, but he'd spun his own web of secrets in Sultan's Keep. Just how many secrets, Nasir did not know. He knew only that General al-Badawi had arrived here on Sharr with more than the knowledge of being Nasir's next kill.

He had thought, more than once, that the Huntress would flee. Her eyes would dart to the stone outcropping, the upper half of her body angling toward the jagged tops, her body at war with itself. She would take one side of her lower lip into her mouth, deep in thought.

She would toy with the ring around her neck and slip it over her pale finger, once, twice, icy eyes pinched in torment.

"I see you ogling," Altair had sung beneath his breath yesterday.

Nasir had ignored him. It was his job to notice such things.

He told himself he watched to ensure she wouldn't escape. But even when instinct told him she wouldn't, he still found himself looking for her, studying her. The Huntress.

The proud curve of her shoulders, daring him. The cut of her mouth, lips dark from her constant chewing on them.

As if hearing his thoughts, she glanced up, eyes drifting past Kifah's gold-tipped spear, past Altair's bare arms, and alighting on him. She lifted her chin, barely, and it took a moment for Nasir to place the slight tilt for what it was: a show of courage.

He knew, then, why he favored Altair's company. Why his gaze sought her. Because neither of them looked at him through a veil of fear that deemed him a monster the way everyone else in Arawiya did.

"All right, zumra—"

A scream in the distance cut off Benyamin's words. It wasn't one of despair, or anguish. It was a roar of rage, promising vengeance. A reminder of the island—its vastness, its *other*ness. And that here on Sharr, Nasir was prey, not threat. The hairs on the back of his neck stood on end. "Very few of the desert creatures we know remain on Sharr."

Altair made a sound. "Here I thought the growling prince was terrifying."

Nasir ignored him, and Kifah asked, "Zumra?"

"It's old tongue for *gang*," Nasir said.

"I can handle schoolroom Safaitic, shukrun," she bit out.

As he slid on his gloves, Nasir wondered, for the umpteenth time, why he ever bothered speaking.

"I'm not joining any gang," the Huntress said. "I work alone, and I will continue to—"

"Trust, Huntress," Benyamin said softly.

Something shattered in her gaze. Remembrance. A memory. Her fingers drifted to the ring, and Nasir looked away.

"We've all arrived on different counts," the safi went on. "You, with a silver letter; the prince and the general, each with their orders; Kifah and I, with the notion of setting all accords right. You were told to hunt down the lost Jawarat, and here you are, like moths hunting a flame, blindly reaching for a mirage to break the decades-long curse over our lands."

Nasir pressed his lips together. Kifah folded her arms and tapped her foot.

Benyamin looked between Nasir and the Huntress. "Both of you met the liar who cannot lie. Neither of you received the full truth. Yet you fell prey to the allure of her words."

The Huntress drew a sharp breath, and Nasir felt the weight of her gaze, slowly dismantling him.

He had received his orders from the sultan, who had counted on the Silver Witch to aid him. Had he fallen prey to her words? To the compass she had pressed into his palm?

It still pointed to the Huntress no matter how hard he shook it.

"Do you know where magic went that fateful day?" Benyamin asked as the sun lifted higher into the sky, the beat of its rays quickening.

"It disappeared," the Huntress said.

"You'd need magic to make something disappear," Kifah pointed out.

"Akhh, I love conundrums," Altair said.

"If you want us to hear the end of your story, safi, we need to leave, or only our crisp corpses will hear the last of your words," Nasir said. He *did* want to hear the rest of the story. He wanted to understand before he continued on his father's orders. But he would slit his own throat before he admitted that.

Kifah chortled. "Who knew the crown prince had a sense of humor?"

"Oh, he's even funnier after he's had a proper breakfast," Altair offered.

Something played at the corners of the Huntress's lips before she looked at Benyamin. "We can get to the shelter of the oasis. Then I expect to know everything."

The safi flourished a bow. "But of course, sayyida."

CHAPTER 44

Beneath the draping shadows of the palm trees, Zafira refilled her goatskin after Kifah reassured her that the water was safe. Sand drifted into her boots and pooled in the folds of her sash. She tasted its bland weight on her tongue and felt the grit of it against her cheeks. It was *everywhere*.

A breeze whistled through the trees, and she reached for her hood before she remembered that her cloak was in her bag. Deen's fingers ghosted her chin before she could fold into herself.

Altair found a lone peach tree, where he gathered a slew of the fuzzy fruit and distributed it among the five of them.

Kifah drummed a rhythm with her spear, and Zafira steered clear of the Pelusian, watching as she tugged a small black blade from one of the several sheaths along her arm. *A lightning blade*, Zafira realized. Forged by nature's wrath, with balance matched by none. Blood sharpened it; age strengthened it. The blades were rare, for blacksmiths had to lie in wait until lightning struck a mountain before rushing to collect the black ore beneath the roar of thunder and pelting rain.

There were benefits to being one of the calipha's Nine Elite, it seemed.

Benyamin pulled a fold of cloth from his bag. Zafira knew safin were vain, but enough to bring a rug to Sharr? He carefully smoothed out the creases and gently brushed aside a beetle before sitting cross-legged in the center of the red weave, trickling sand from his fists as he waited for everyone. Nasir crossed his arms and leaned against a jutting stone, making it clear he wasn't going to be a happy participant.

"Magic did not disappear, zumra. It was relocated," Benyamin started, skipping a peach pit across the blue waters. He called them "zumra" as if they were a horde of children, not a number of mismatched people wielding weapons against his thin, unarmed self.

"When the warden of Sharr called for aid during the second battle against the Lion of the Night, the Sisters brought magic here. And with their demise, magic did not disappear, but it fell to Sharr, which happily bore the burden.

"It swallowed the creatures of the prison—humans, safin, ifrit, bashmu—everything that stood in its path, and still, the island's hunger could not be sated. It tainted the Baransea, it birthed the Arz. And the longer Sharr remains in control of magic, the farther the Arz will grow, and the worse our lands will become."

"For what?" Zafira asked. "What does Sharr want?"

There was a glint in Benyamin's eyes. "You, Huntress, are too smart for your own good."

She shrank back and nearly missed the look Altair and Benyamin shared.

"If magic exists on Sharr," Altair started, and Zafira had the distinct feeling he was hurrying to mask something, "then we should be able to wield it."

"Through dum sihr at least," Kifah said.

"No!" Benyamin looked as if someone had slit his palm and forced him to use it. "Blood magic is forbidden. *Strictly* forbidden. There's no reprieve for the one who commands it. The price is always great."

"Is that why it's only done in Safai—"

"Superstition. Blood magic is forbidden because it's uncontrollable. The price is a sampling of blood, nothing more," Nasir said boredly.

"We are not going to discuss blood magic any further," Benyamin said harshly before turning to Zafira.

By the look in his eyes, she suspected there was something more to Benyamin's fear of dum sihr. Something personal.

"Altair was referring to the affinities we were born with," the safi continued tranquilly, though Zafira heard the slight undercurrent of unrest. "Particularly the specialty you were born with, dearest Demenhune."

Zafira narrowed her eyes. Nasir stiffened.

"I have magic," she said. Her words were hesitant. Unbelieving.

"You have an *affinity*," Benyamin corrected with a tilt of his head. "Much like everyone else. Without fuel from the magic that once lit the royal minarets, our affinities fell dormant. Constantly hungering.

"That's what makes the Arz so alluring—it's an extension of Sharr. The very same island that contains the magic Arawiya once did. When we near the Arz, our affinities claw their way out, spurring us into the cursed forest. Many succumbed to its whispers, stepping within for the chance to unleash the affinities we've pent up for so long. They may have wielded power. They may have called fire and summoned water, but the Arz is such that they could never return. On the contrary, you, Huntress: Your affinity itself is what allowed you to return time and time again."

You will always find your way. The Silver Witch's words during their first meeting. She had come to see if Zafira really did return from the Arz in one piece.

A breeze fanned the leaves of the palm tree, cooling her skin, and a bird took to the skies with a sweep of its wings.

Benyamin looked at the others. "Here on Sharr, free from the entrapment of the Arz, we can *all* wield our powers. The Huntress's only disparity is that she has been in control of her affinity for years."

Thanks to the Arz. *Skies.* That cursed forest was a land humming with magic. A place she had ventured within for *years.*

"What's my affinity?" she asked. It was becoming harder to breathe.

Benyamin considered her, brown eyes intent. "You could ask our prince here. He and Altair had the right idea."

Neither Sarasin was even the slightest bit surprised. She looked wildly between them and scrambled to her feet, nearly stumbling in the sand. She dropped her eyes to Benyamin, who sat calmly on his gold-fringed rug.

"Tell me," she breathed. "What am I?"

"A da'ira."

"A what?" she said softly, feeling the edges of her sanity coming undone.

"You are the compass in the storm, the guide in the dark. You will always find your way, Zafira bint Iskandar."

His words became a drum in her head.

No—she was a gazelle in the desert, vulnerable before a horde of lions. She shrank away, eyes darting to the prince and his general. Then to Kifah and Benyamin.

And she did what a gazelle does best. She ran.

CHAPTER 45

Z AFIRA RAN ACROSS THE VERDURE OF THE OASIS, IGNORING THEIR calls, ignoring the way Arawiya's crown prince regarded her with unflinching eyes, scorching her blood.

"Let her go," he said softly, and she paused. "She needs time."

Zafira didn't wait to hear what Altair said to that. She tucked herself between a host of date palms, pressing her back against a prickly trunk as she caught her breath. The trees welcomed her, whispering as they cocooned. *Stay a while. Rest.*

The shadows mimicked her distress. The date palms wilted when she sank to her knees.

She blinked, and they righted again.

A da'ira. She turned the old Safaitic word over her tongue. A *compass*.

That was why she'd never thought twice about how to find the Jawarat on this forsaken island. Because her affinity had always been leading her somewhere. It had been leading her for *years*.

Her sense of direction wasn't a feeling or a wild notion. She hunted in the Arz, void of sight, because of it. She stepped free of the Arz because of it.

Baba.

Skies, every time Baba had gone into the Arz, he had been with her. Guiding her aim, sighting their kills, following her lead. Until his very last one. The venture that had driven him mad, twisted his ideals.

If only she had known.

"Oh, sweet snow below," she breathed, recalling that frenzied hum in her bloodstream as it steered her on the right path.

Of everything she could have wielded from the tips of her fingers— fire, darkness, illusions—she had been gifted with *direction*. She hadn't even known that direction *was* an affinity.

A hysterical laugh echoed from the trees and Zafira had her bow drawn before she realized the laugh had clawed its way out of her own broken self. A sob slipped past her lips. This weakness wasn't her. It disoriented as it tugged at the pieces of her heart.

Everything suddenly made sense. Why the Sarasins had tried to kidnap her in Demenhur. Why Altair and the prince had "allied" with her: so they could use her to find the Jawarat. She shivered as she remembered Nasir's gray eyes tracking her every moment. She understood now why he watched her, why he had saved her from the ifrit.

He had been protecting an asset.

He had known all along, which meant the sultan knew, too. Or, at least, the sultan had an assumption and the power to act upon it.

They were all loyal to the same kingdom, yet the Silver Witch and the sultan seemed to be at odds with each other. There were two sides, here. A hostility Zafira didn't understand. She couldn't even understand why the prince and general had tried to kill her.

Perhaps neither side favored her.

She didn't top the Silver Witch's list of hunters—she *was* the list. The only known hunter who could find the Jawarat, and if she had never set foot in the Arz, if she had never made her accomplishments known, the Silver Witch would never have known. The sultan would be unaware. The Jawarat would remain lost until some other da'ira exposed their affinity. If more existed.

Skies. Affinities, powers. Magic that had ceased to exist.

She needed to lie down. What was she, an old man? She didn't need to lie down.

Glorious slants of gold shone on the green foliage ahead of her, where a path unfurled in the stillness. Colorful flowers spread petals, coaxing her near with soft chimes. *Be free, Huntress.*

She didn't need the others, the shadows reminded her. She could make her own way from oasis to oasis, ruin to ruin, and find that wretched book. She could single-handedly restore magic to Arawiya without worrying about who had allied with whom and which of the others were plotting her death.

But.

She remembered the gentle stroke of that cloth on her skin. The sorrow in the prince's eyes. Altair's laugh. Benyamin's persistence. The shadow haunting Kifah's dark eyes.

She needed answers. Answers that Benyamin had.

She turned back, hoping this wasn't a decision she would come to regret.

CHAPTER 46

NASIR STARED INTO THE TREES, WAITING—*HOPING*—FOR her to return. A rare thing, for him. Hope.

As much as it was Benyamin's fault, Nasir had . . . learned something from their little chat. The safi had given him answers to questions he could never bring himself to ask.

"All this tension is making me old," Altair said, flexing his arms, blades in hand. It was alarming how jovial and deadly he could be at once.

"Age typically leads to wisdom," Kifah pointed out, the look on her face suggesting Altair was anything but wise.

"Says the girl who tagged along with a chattering safi. Why'd you come, anyway?" Altair asked, turning to her. She didn't flinch from his extended blades.

Kifah studied him a moment and then shrugged. "Magic. Revenge. The usual."

Altair laughed, and Nasir tried to stop his own lips from quirking up.

Rimaal. He'd never had to stifle so many smiles before. Benyamin paced along the oasis, brow furrowed.

At last, the Huntress emerged, looking upon everything with an eerie stillness. Unease stirred in Nasir's stomach. Her shoulders curled forward before she came aware of it and straightened, lifting her chin.

Benyamin leaped to attention, relief casting his eyes in burnished gold. "I wanted to offer an apology," he said to her slowly. "Safin tend to overlook human sentiment. I should have ruminated before depositing such a hefty revelation upon you."

It was easy to forget that Benyamin wasn't human. Like the Silver Witch. Like half of Nasir's self.

"I'm no hashashin, but in my humble observations, it seems you can't take your eyes off her," Altair drawled in Nasir's ear.

"Jealous?" Nasir asked. The torn end of his turban flickered in the gentle breeze, the cloth soft against his neck.

"I would be, if I didn't know you stare at me just as much."

Nasir's brows flattened. "I need her."

"Which is what every man says when it comes to—"

"Close your mouth or put it to use elsewhere," Nasir growled. He marveled at why he even bothered talking to the oaf.

Altair mimed sealing his lips shut, but his silence lasted no longer than a dying insect. "Oi, whatever you were thinking, I wasn't."

"Shut up," the Huntress snapped when she drew near.

Altair flinched, to Nasir's satisfaction.

"I came back only because I know you'll follow me otherwise, and I'm tired of the two of you breathing down my neck."

"Do you even know what it feels like to have a man breathing down your neck?" Nasir asked. *What did you just say, idiot?* He was spending too much time with Altair.

Even the general looked surprised. Kifah snorted, and Benyamin prayed to the skies for patience.

The Huntress paused, and Nasir saw the exact moment when she recalled a memory. How hard was life when your very thoughts played out on your face? Her fingers drifted to the ring, telling him the rest.

Realizing her mistake, she met his eyes defiantly. "Don't look at me like that."

"Like what?" he asked, lifting an eyebrow.

"With your stupid mockery of pity."

He laughed, a dry sound. "Did you think yourself in love with him?"

She didn't answer, and her silence made him push harder, for the others watched. For he was his father's son.

He stepped closer. "Let me tell you a secret, Huntress: The dead man loved you, but you did not."

"Bleeding Guljul, leave her be," Kifah said, hand against her bald head.

"Death is the one thing certain in human life. Why does it still come as a surprise when it happens?" he asked.

"You know nothing of love or loss," the Huntress hissed, and Nasir flinched from her gaze, so cold it burned. "You're likely among the privileged who tumble a different woman every night, only to kill her by sunrise."

Nasir donned a wolfish smile. "Fancy yourself Shahrazad, then?"

The strangest look crossed her face before she spun to Altair. "Give me that."

"Me? What?" Altair bumbled, eyes wide. She stalked to him and reached for one of his scimitars. He was taller, but she was tall enough. She stood on her toes and pulled his blade free with a slow hiss, nicking his shoulder.

Kifah lifted an eyebrow at Altair's bewilderment. "This will be interesting."

The Huntress leveled her stance. Something in her gaze gave Nasir pause. Something more convoluted than anger, for anger he knew how to defeat.

Something feral.

He dropped his hand to his sword, body humming, blood racing, grateful for the challenge. Benyamin rushed between them, stirring sand, but Nasir had settled into a fighting calm, and he wasn't about to stop.

"Step aside, Alder. She's a woman, not a decrepit old man. She doesn't need your protection."

Benyamin canted his head. "What makes you think *she* needs protecting?"

CHAPTER 47

ZAFIRA HADN'T THE FAINTEST CLUE HOW TO USE A SCIMITAR. But how hard could it be? It was just double the length of her jambiya.

All right. Maybe triple.

It winked like spun gold with the reflection of the sand. She had sparred with Deen often enough to know she was good with a blade. She just hoped the wretched prince wouldn't call her bluff, despite the better half of her brain saying he would. But if her heart led to her hunt in the Arz, couldn't she charm a blade into his heart?

She blinked at her dark thoughts. Emotion was a terrible thing to act upon. But he had insulted Deen. Worse, he had been *right*: She had never loved Deen the way Deen had wanted her to.

When Benyamin stepped away, concern wrought on his brow, Zafira knew her notions were his, too. She tossed her satchels to the sand and held the scimitar a little higher.

"Are we sure this is a good idea?" Altair asked no one in particular.

"I don't know what's a good idea anymore," Kifah said dryly. "I'm on *Sharr.*"

Nasir drew his sword with a flourish, the hilt dancing across his knuckles as it pivoted in the air. A look that claimed Zafira was purely ridiculous flashed across his face. For a prince who preferred secrecy and shadows when she first met him, he seemed to be enjoying the attention now.

Fear spiked through her, churning with a thrill she welcomed. She knew the stories. She knew exactly how deft the Prince of Death was with a blade.

He stepped closer.

And everything

moved

quickly.

She threw up her blade and he did the same, black hilt melding into his gloves. The air was a blur of flashing steel until metal clanged against metal, jarring her teeth, her brain, her idiocy, and—skies, what a fool she was.

But he wouldn't kill her. He needed her. They all did. *She* didn't need them.

The one person she needed was dead because of him.

She put all her weight behind the clashed swords and pushed. Nasir was stronger, taller, broader, but he slid back a hairbreadth. He was the greatest assassin unused to his kills fighting back.

She pushed again with renewed fervor.

"How endearing." He pulled free with a whispered laugh.

She stumbled, pushing a hand against the rough stone to regain her footing. She growled and lifted her arm before he clashed against her scimitar again, the force rattling her teeth. *He isn't holding back.*

Didn't he need her?

Zafira feinted left, but he didn't react. Then she feinted right, and he raised an amused eyebrow, anticipating her move before she even perceived it. Altair chuckled. Her neck burned.

They clashed blades again, and he leaned close.

"You know who I am. Give up, Huntress," he murmured, his dark voice rumbling straight through her.

She saw her opportunity the moment he prepared for another strike. For she was the Demenhune Hunter. Quick. Precise. Untrained. She could rival a trained, methodical assassin.

She darted forward and ducked beneath his arms. His breath swooshed past her skin and she hooked her boot around his leg and pulled. He pitched backward, nostrils flaring. He saw her triumph and growled, locking her legs between his in one last fight before he fell on his back with a muffled thud.

And she atop him, the breath yanked from her lungs.

She threw one of her hands on his shoulder to stop her fall, but their legs were a tangle of limbs, sand sinking beneath them. Her torso brushed his, the traitorous ring settling on his heart, rising and falling with his heavy breathing. Their faces were mere breaths apart. Without the shelter of her cloak, every brush of him against her felt as if she were wholly bare. Heartbeats galloped in Zafira's chest.

"Any closer and I'd have to close my eyes," Altair remarked in a loud whisper.

And the prince had the nerve to grin.

A lie, said her stuttering mind, for that gaping unhappiness was reflected in his eyes, the color of dead flames and lifeless stone.

"Go on, end my misery," he said, voice soft. The cool words caressed her skin. Murderous hashashin weren't supposed to be gentle.

Only then did she realize she had the scimitar pressed against his throat, the same way she held her jambiya to the throats of her kills when she hunted.

Zafira pressed the blade farther into the skin of his neck, watching the smooth column of his throat bob. Goose bumps skittered along his golden skin, and she had the insane urge to smooth her finger down them. To touch her mouth to them.

She swallowed her gasp and gritted her teeth. Deen's throat would never bob again. Because of him. Because of this murderer beneath her.

The trees of the oasis waited with bated breath. But Zafira's entire focus honed on the gleaming metal against his throat.

Don't be an equal to the ones who hurt. Deen's words, when Zafira had taken it upon herself to challenge the yellow-toothed boy who had broken Deen's nose during a game of kura years and years ago.

Zafira stared into those gray eyes, and the ashes inside them scattered beneath her stare. She lifted the blade.

Not a flicker of surprise shone on his scarred face. Zafira swallowed her scream with a growl.

"Three things. Wahid, don't touch me. Ithnayn, don't look at me. Thalatha, don't even think about me." Zafira stood, relishing his hiss of pain as she dug her knees into his legs just for good measure.

He rose and mock-saluted her with two fingers across his brow. "As you wish."

She ran her gaze across the others before pinning him with a look of ice. "If wishes came true, you'd be dead."

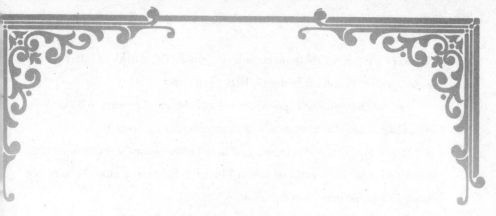

CHAPTER 48

NASIR STILL FELT THE COOL KISS OF METAL AGAINST HIS neck, like the phantom of a burn.

The last time a woman, or anyone for that matter, held a blade against his neck, Nasir had been in training. After that, after his mother ensured he was no more than a whisper in the dark, no one could get close. But the Huntress had no training. That wildness took hold of her, jarring his calm, and she tripped him like they were children in a daama schoolyard.

His neck might have still felt the kiss of metal, but the rest of him felt the heat of shame.

"Akhh, I love when a good sparring session ends with . . . other things." Altair grinned when the Huntress handed his scimitar back without a word.

"What now?" Kifah asked. The hilt of a knife danced across her knuckles, and her gold cuff shone like a beacon in the sun. "Shall the rest of us begin dueling to our deaths?"

"No more dueling." Benyamin sighed like an exasperated mother. His gaze kept darting to their surroundings, where the world had darkened a shade further, despite it being no later than noon.

"Yes, listen to our beloved safi. If we kill one another now, who will we use as bait when the ifrit come knocking?" Altair exclaimed.

"You, maybe?" the Huntress asked as she straightened her clothes. Nasir wondered if he imagined the barest hint of color on her face. "You're big enough to keep them busy for a while."

Altair adjusted his turban, a gleam in his eyes. "I'm big enough to keep anyone busy for a while."

Nasir gagged and Kifah sputtered. The Huntress merely looked confused at their reactions. *Cloistered.*

Benyamin gave Altair a look but let the remark slide. "We need to start moving."

"We're not going anywhere, safi," the Huntress said, steel in her voice.

He turned to her. "You say it like I'm vermin."

"Maybe you are." She shrugged and Kifah barked a laugh.

He looked incredulous. "Your people would be bowing before me."

"My people also have snow for brains. What of it?" she retorted. "We're not leaving until I have answers."

Benyamin nodded. "Soon, dearest Demenhune. The trees bend close, and the shadows have a master. We will converse when the time is right."

She shivered at his words, and the others fell silent. Sharr seemed to grow even more ominous.

Somehow, Nasir knew this master was not the Silver Witch, and it certainly was not Ghameq, for his father's reach could not extend this far. This master had created fear on Altair's face that night in the tavern.

This master made Sharr into the monster that it was.

The Huntress disappeared into the palm trees after a murmur from Benyamin, who stepped after her, beckoning with a quick "Yalla, zumra." *Let's go, gang.*

Nasir held back. A hashashin's strength lay in stealth and solitude.

Nothing was going as planned: His cousin had shown up, Altair breathed, the Huntress was a girl—*laa, woman.*

If there was anything other than shame he had felt when she fell upon him, it was that she was wholly woman. Nasir loosed a very slow breath.

And now Benyamin was warning of a greater threat.

Altair looked back at Nasir when they were alone for the first time since Benyamin and Kifah had arrived. "Well?"

Nasir tipped his head. "I'll take care of the Pelusian—"

Altair snarled and shoved him into the trees. Sunlight vanished behind the dark boughs. Nasir shot to his feet and turned with clenched teeth. His vision burned black as he drew his scimitar.

Anger blazed in Altair's eyes. "Change of plan? Going to kill me first, is that it? This is no longer about finding the Jawarat and traipsing back to your beloved father, you fool."

Nasir struggled to control his breathing, but the darkness had amplified, and he could barely see beyond the surrounding trees. Trepidation pulsed against his heart.

"Call for help, spider," Nasir said, voice low.

"Are you jealous I whisper in someone else's ear? I told you—whatever I do, I do for the good of the kingdom."

Nasir didn't care. "I could slit your throat before you even lift an arm."

Altair lifted his hands, livid. "By all means."

In his mind's eye, Nasir saw himself raising his sword, hefting it back, swinging it forward. He saw a horizon of red across Altair's neck and those eyes of azure fading. The ripple as his soul fled free. He saw it, he did. Along with the Huntress's corpse.

But his blade was too heavy now.

It pulsed in his hands, and perspiration trickled down his spine. Benyamin nearly tripped on his rush back to them, dread tugging his lips when he came into view. The Huntress and Kifah shadowed him.

WE HUNT THE FLAME

"Your mother's son is still in there, Prince," Benyamin said cautiously, as if Nasir were an animal he was afraid to startle.

Had it been anyone else, Nasir would have cut him down, but Benyamin had a claim to the sultana. Nasir held Altair's gaze and slowly sheathed his scimitar.

"Let him take a look around. Let him see that we are allies by circumstance, not enemies, and let him give murder a rest. Let him open his heart to trust. Perhaps there is more to your quest than what you came for."

The strange string of the safi's words reminded Nasir of the crimson compass.

Something rustled in the bushes, sand shifting beneath feet. Nasir froze, and the others slowly turned to the browned palm trees. The unmistakable scuttle of eyes pebbled Nasir's skin as the *swoosh* of something rushed past.

And shadows swarmed from the trees.

CHAPTER 49

ZAFIRA HAD COME TO EXPECT A LOT FROM SHARR. BUT she had never expected to see Yasmine drifting toward her in all her ethereal beauty, sand beneath her bare feet.

A strangled sound escaped her throat. Not Yasmine, too.

Benyamin touched the skin of her wrist and Zafira wished for her cloak, her gloves. His voice was garbled by her ear.

"Huntress, look at me."

Zafira blinked and saw Deen, pierced by an arrow. Baba, crawling from the trees on hands and knees. Dirty. Bloody.

Dead.

Benyamin shook her. "Huntress. *Look. At. Me.*"

She hated the sympathy in his eyes, the way he spoke to her as if she were a child.

"That's it. Breathe, slowly. That's not who you think it is. Do you re-member? Are you listening?"

Yasmine. Yasmine. Yasmine.

"It's not him," he continued gently.

Him? No, this was a her. This was sweet Yasmine. Foul-mouthed Yasmine. Married Yasmine.

"Breathe, Huntress. Easy now. It's not real."

Only then did she notice there wasn't just *one* Yasmine. There were many. And as Zafira's gaze darted from one to another, eerie against the fat trees, she saw the faces shift.

"Ifrit," she whispered. Sweet relief buckled her knees, and she gripped the nearest trunk as the world spun back into focus.

Benyamin held her up with a hand around her shoulders. "I need you alert."

"Tamim?" Kifah's voice cracked. Was she seeing a lover? A brother? A friend?

The ifrit continued to shift, slowly surrounding them. Lana, Deen, Umm, Haytham, Baba. At the one that looked like Baba, Benyamin stiffened.

"Do you see him, too?" she asked, willing the tremble from her fingers. She could no longer see the end of the oasis. The sun seemed to have disappeared altogether.

"I see someone, but not the same person you are seeing," Benyamin choked.

It was an obscene thing, reaching into a soul to pull out the face of a loved one. One ifrit could portray a hundred faces at once—it was all in the eye of the beholder. Unless the victim was strong enough to see past the tricks. Then one would see nothing at all.

"We're surrounded." Nasir's soft murmur came from a little ways behind her.

Zafira knew what it was like to be engulfed by the darkness, but that didn't stop trepidation from creeping into her heart. The *tick, tick, tick* going a little faster, a fever she couldn't contain. *An excitement.*

She could survive the darkness; she always did.

But could the others?

They need you, a voice in her head said. They didn't *care* for her. And there was a good chance that when she found the blasted Jawarat, they might all line up to kill her.

She could easily slip through the trees and escape into the desert.

Yet when she blinked, she saw a blade through Altair's still chest. She saw Kifah's unblinking eyes and Benyamin's stomach ripped to shreds. She saw the prince's sad gray eyes, colder in death. She couldn't leave them, even if they might never repay the favor.

With one swift maneuver, she lifted an arrow and nocked it in her bow, familiarity settling between her shoulders as she pulled it back.

"Back to back," Altair murmured, and Zafira wondered if the general had to bite his tongue to hold back further commands.

One of the ifrit hissed. Another one shouted, words garbled by the old tongue.

"In case you didn't notice, there are more of us than you and your prince," Kifah said, a crest to her voice, her restlessness thwarted by the adrenaline of a skirmish.

The five of them rearranged themselves in a ring, backs to one another. Zafira tried to ease into the calm of her hunts, but her thoughts wouldn't settle. The world buzzed and she couldn't think straight. More shadows slipped into the small clearing. Even Zafira found it difficult to see.

Still, she counted twelve ifrit against the five of them.

The one nearest her wore Umm's face as it tilted its head, streaks of white in her hair, almost as if listening to an order. *Not real, not real, not real.*

Then the world became fire.

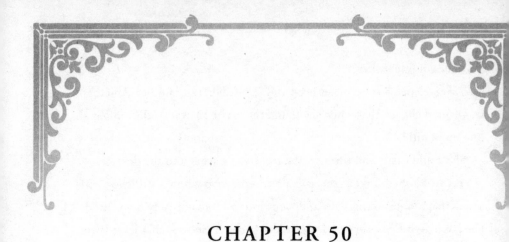

CHAPTER 50

THE WORLD BURNED, BUT AT LEAST NASIR COULD SEE. HIS LIP curled at his optimism. Spending time with Benyamin was doing him no good.

He blinked against the remnants of the weighted darkness and took in the scene as it flashed in flares of orange. The creatures of smokeless fire appeared unarmed at first, until Nasir realized *they* were weapons. They darted between the palm trees and glided over the sands as if they were ethereal. Staves of fire appeared in their hands, flickering in the darkness. Heat sweltered and made it difficult to breathe.

From their reactions, it was clear the others saw the ifrit as people they knew, but Nasir saw them as they were: faceless beings, always disappearing from view. Just when he thought he saw one, his vision wavered. They were *there*, always there, but never in full sight. It was the gift of having a heart as dark and closed off as his.

Altair made a sound. Anguish.

"Do you see someone?" Kifah asked him softly. Her dark eyes glowed in the sudden flares.

"My mother, before she was murdered by the man I hate."

Nasir didn't know anything about Altair's parents or the people he disliked other than Nasir. The general released a breath and fired his first arrow, which whizzed into the shadows. One day, Altair would learn he simply couldn't be an archer.

Nasir twirled his sword as a howling wail pierced the sudden darkness. He calmed his thoughts and everything blurred, the others forgotten. A hashashin worked alone. A hashashin didn't pay heed to anyone but himself. A hashashin put the mission before anything else.

A stave of fire came swooping toward him, and he ducked, knee brushing the sharp leaves littering the ground before he swung his scimitar up and to the left. It hissed through the air, the ifrit out of reach.

He darted forward, but the ifrit had disappeared. The heat of another stave kissed Nasir's neck, and he turned, but only darkness blinked back. He caught a glimpse of gleaming hair, double scimitars raised to strike. Altair. But the general disappeared from his vision between one breath and the next.

A chill settled in Nasir's spine, despite the heat and the burning air.

The ifrit weren't only using their weapons to attack; they were using them to blind.

———◄●►———

Zafira knew the game the ifrit were playing. Every time her eyes adjusted to the darkness, they flared their weapons of fire, attacked, and began the cycle anew.

They meant to intimidate, but she was the Demenhune Hunter. She knew the bleeding black.

She inhaled slowly. Baba's voice was by her ear. She may have been the one to find her way in and out, but he had helped her become one with the darkness. *Let it in, abal. Become what the heart asks of you.*

In the chaos surrounding her—the shouts, the flickering flames, the stench of sweat and fear—Zafira found that vein of stillness where the shadows beckoned and whispered. Zafira breathed the darkness.

She *was* the darkness.

Marhaba, darkness, my daama friend.

She felt a swell of elation, despite the battle surrounding her. With each careful inhale, the world pulsed into focus, until Zafira made out the ifrit surrounding them.

Not two paces away, an ifrit swung a stave at Nasir, which he avoided in one fluid movement as if he were made of the darkness himself. Zafira shifted her focus to another ifrit, this one brandishing a stave. She had two, maybe three shots before they noted her ability to see, and she would make the most of it.

For a startling moment, she didn't see the face of anyone she loved— she saw nothing. A faceless face. It turned to Kifah, whose skin glistened with sweat as her spear danced in her hands.

Before the ifrit could flash its stave, Zafira released her arrow, which struck the creature between the eyes. Its dying howl shattered the chaos.

Everything, and everyone, paused.

Steady now. She noted the pulsing ebb and flow of the darkness. Tendrils of black curled around her arms, nuzzled her skin.

She loosed another arrow, striking an ifrit dangerously close to Altair. That did it: the ifrit turned to her.

The others caught on. Benyamin pulled vials from the belt at his hip. He wound strips of something around needle-pointed knives before tossing them effortlessly. So *that* was how the slender safi fought without a fighter's build. Banes. Poison.

He raised his head and flashed her a smile, which was notably directed too far to her left, tattoo ablaze in the firelight. Zafira bit back a grin. Despite his feline grace, he certainly couldn't see as well as a cat.

On her other side, someone roared, likely Altair, and Zafira heard the quick swoops of a single scimitar that could only be Nasir. Out of the corner of her eye, she saw Kifah drop to a fighter's stance, twirling her spear fast enough to create a moving shield.

Zafira reminded herself that they only needed her to find the Jawarat, and that no one was helping her because they cared. But she was grateful for them then, for the creatures' focus had shifted away from her.

She nocked another arrow and fired.

———◄●►———

Nasir knew the Huntress was skilled. He had seen her aim when she was in the midst of falling, when her Demenhune companion had taken an arrow for her. She was agile, lithe in war. But seeing it again: her rapid stream of arrows—each one finding its mark—made him feel . . . he didn't like how it made him feel.

They were down to four ifrit when the creatures doubled their weapons to a stave per hand and even the Huntress began to grow tired. Nasir tore his scimitar through an ifrit and shoved Benyamin away from another's oncoming stave.

It occurred to him that he was helping them. This was worse than not killing them.

Nasir swung his scimitar, locking with another of the fiery weapons. The ifrit brought its face close, meaning to intimidate, but Nasir saw nothing.

His will wavered when the heat licked at his hands like dogs starved of hydration.

And then his grip

began

to falter.

Laa. The word echoed deep inside that ever-moving dark mass he called a heart. He couldn't have come this far only to lose his grip on his own sword.

He threw his weight behind the blade, and the sounds of battle rushed from around him as he lost focus. A roar, a hiss. The clang of metal. The rustle of movement, scuffles. Dark laughter, trickling into his ears.

And then, nothing.

He stumbled forward, the ifrit gone. No, not gone.

Twitching at his feet with a pristine white arrow through the head, as graceful as its owner. Kharra.

A blood debt.

Nasir released a breath. *Kill or be killed.*

Save and be saved.

Sweat trickled down Nasir's neck. He sought her out, and despite barely being able to see, he felt their gazes lock amid the fray. And before his pride returned, he acknowledged her with a small tip of his head.

The Huntress nodded back.

CHAPTER 51

THE MOMENT ZAFIRA FELLED THE LAST IFRIT, ALTAIR WENT over them for one final cut across their unmoving throats. The air reeked of burnt flesh. At Zafira's questioning look, Benyamin leaned back on his heels and said, "Only safin steel keeps them dead."

Still, they hurried out of the oasis as soon as the task was complete.

"Sharr is upset we killed its kin," Kifah said, looking at the sky. Zafira would have thought that Sharr should be happy it had more to feast upon, but Kifah's dark eyes were void of mirth.

Swells of sand marched into the distance, the umber now a shade forlorn because of the gray sky. Aside from nicks and scratches and more than a few burns, everyone had made it out alive, if a bit weary. Altair shared strips of dried goat meat with them, and even Nasir begrudgingly accepted.

"Well, dearest Demenhune? Which way do we proceed?" Benyamin asked carefully. His voice slid eerily in the silence of death.

Zafira shook her head. She was tired of not knowing what was happening. "I need answe—"

"And you will get them," he said before she could finish. "When we stop for the night."

She opened her mouth to protest but remembered safin couldn't lie. So she hooked her bow and relaxed her limbs, listing her head as she sifted past the chime of sand and the whisper of shadows.

There. A thread humming in her bloodstream, a murmur slithering through her veins. A frenzy drawing her forward. So many years of relishing that insisting hum in her bloodstream, and now she knew. *This* was magic.

She couldn't summon excitement at the thought. Ever since welcoming the darkness during the attack, she had been feeling . . . a little less afraid but also a little less *whole*. As if the space she occupied was now shared with something else. Some*one* else. She exhaled and started toward the ruins fanning out to their right, and the others fell into step behind her.

"And now we're off again, tagging along with the Demenhune Hunter and the Prince of Death," Kifah said, giving the prince a long look. "A murderer."

"I find 'murderer' to be a relative term. How many bugs have you killed with your feet?" Altair asked.

Kifah snorted, and Zafira heard the rhythmic *thump* of her spear against her leg. Nasir was silent. Zafira didn't turn to see his face, but she wondered if it hurt, being called a murderer. It wasn't as if it were a lie.

Her thoughts seized when something screeched in the shadows.

"I think I prefer a murderer on two legs than one I don't know about," Zafira said.

"At last, a voice of reason!" Benyamin exclaimed, ignoring a salacious comment Altair made about legs.

As they moved, the stillness of Sharr *did* feel like an accusation for killing so many of its own. She did not like to consider what would happen if they further wronged the umber sands and haunting ruins. She did not want to think of why the ifrit had ambushed them, either.

Yet . . . it hadn't felt like an attack. It had been more of a test. One the darkness had watched from the confines of itself. One she had *passed*.

The shadows steepened when they reached the crumbling slabs of stone.

"We're stopping here for the night," Nasir said, and all sounds ceased. He didn't implore, didn't request, didn't ask. His voice was an order, and no one questioned him as they began readying the camp.

———◄●►———

They set up camp in the alcoves of the stone ruins beneath the moon, and Zafira wanted to climb to the highest point and curl beneath her glow. To make sense of the way the shadows called to her.

The others would likely follow her, worried their compass was going astray, so she settled before the fire with a sigh and rubbed her hands. The chill was nothing compared to Demenhur's weather, but she found it odd how cold the relentless desert could become.

Weariness tugged on her bones, and she looked forward to resting— once she had her answers.

The others unfurled bedrolls around the fire. Kifah hunted down a trio of cape hares after eyeing Zafira, who didn't make a move when Kifah asked who would hunt.

"I'm impressed, One of Nine," Altair said, inspecting the hares. "Nothing can outrun these critters."

"I'm not nothing, am I?" Kifah asked as she cleaned her spear. She barely looked out of breath for someone who had snared hares only a cheetah could outrun.

Altair skinned her catch, and Kifah roasted them to mouthwatering perfection. There was a certain thrum of excitement as Kifah cooked, and Zafira found it charming that the warrior whose restlessness was only thwarted in battle could be so happy while handling cuisine.

Kifah had even brought her own spices from Pelusia—a blend of cumin, sumac, cardamom, and other things Zafira couldn't differentiate—which she rationed begrudgingly. The aroma carried Zafira away to Yasmine's wedding, to Deen's pinkie curling around hers.

It felt so far away now. A different life.

Altair had unraveled his turban and wrapped part of it around his neck against the chill. Oddly, Zafira had yet to see him without a turban at all, not even on that night when he had returned from the waters of the oasis without a shirt. He sat cross-legged beside her and gave his portion of hare a lick.

"I'm going to pretend this is a mighty leg of lamb, roasted with garlic and harissa," he said wistfully as he tore the roasted skin with his teeth.

"What's wrong with my spices?" Kifah asked with a scowl.

Altair looked like a startled deer. "They are most delectable. Slip of the tongue, not the fault of my brain."

Kifah hmmed. "Which you seem to have misplaced."

"Dearest Kifah Darwish, I find your many retorts endearing."

Kifah appraised the general as if she were seeing him for the first time. "You remember my name."

Zafira scrunched her nose. "I'll have mine without the garlic."

"You don't like garlic?" Altair asked, eyebrows raised. "At least we know for sure you aren't an ifrit."

"Ifrit like garlic? What, you asked one?"

"Ifrit like everything that reeks," Altair said matter-of-factly.

Zafira's brows flattened. "So you acknowledge that it smells wretched, yet you crave it anyway."

"I eat the food, not inhale it. It's all about the flavor. Right, One of Nine?"

Kifah nodded as if this were a conversation of utmost importance, and Zafira turned away in exaggerated disgust. Benyamin leaned against a wall, one leg propped, a leatherbound book in his hand. Only a safi would find time to read on Sharr. The crackle of the fire shrouded the silence, and after a moment Altair continued with a list of what he would devour had he been in Sultan's Keep.

"There's this one dessert I'd kill every single one of you in a heartbeat for. It's a pastry made of cheese and soaked in syrup and—"

"I know what kanafah is. We western village Demenhune might be poor, but we've had the sultan's delicacies," Zafira said.

"Oh, good. You looked forlorn there for a moment," Altair said with a grin.

Zafira tossed a rock at him. "I don't know if I'd kill for it, but I guess that's how barbarians work."

"You wound me, Huntress," he mocked, a hand on his broad chest. Then he frowned and rubbed his arm where the rock had struck.

Zafira knew she shouldn't speak to him. She knew he was cunning and would slowly glean information from her as well as she knew she was drawn to him. But when he spoke, teasing and heedless, Zafira gravitated toward him. The darkness stepped back, and his charming grins lifted a weight off her chest.

He reminded her of Yasmine.

She was beginning to forget that he was not her friend. This was not her zumra. They were allies by circumstance, nothing more.

Zafira suspected that Altair's demeanor was what kept the prince glued to his side. Despite his growling and cool indifference, Nasir likely tolerated Altair's taunts not because he couldn't do a thing about it, but because he *craved* them.

For the thousandth time since that afternoon, she questioned her split-breath decision to save the prince from the ifrit. What had he done in return? Nodded. *What had you expected, a kiss?*

He sat on a fallen column a little ways away, eating slowly, lost in some dark thought. Zafira barely made out his silhouette in the flickering light, but the gleam of his gaze was clear enough as it drifted among them. She felt it snag on her, too, and something raced beneath her skin in response.

Her mind conjured the moment she'd felled him during their own fight earlier in the day. His body beneath hers without the barrier of her cloak between them. His lips close to her skin. His depthless eyes dark and knowing. The way he had seized up, the way his breathing had quickened. Something crackled in her chest.

He's a murderer.

And she was starting to forget that he was.

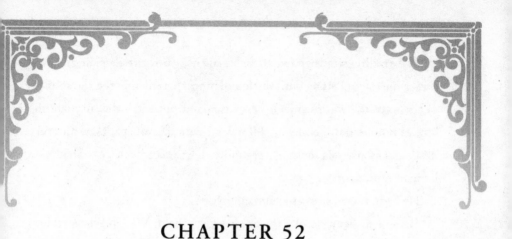

CHAPTER 52

NASIR WATCHED THE OTHERS ENJOYING THEMSELVES. IT was only a trio of hares, meager meat for five famished. Yet they ate and spoke as if they were enjoying a grand feast. As if death weren't lurking in the too-heavy darkness.

He had gathered his peasant-size share and taken it away from the small fire, seating himself in the shadows while Benyamin's zumra clung to every word Altair uttered. The general started with food but drifted off to other things: journeys he had taken, sights he had seen, and battles he had won. He teased them, enraptured them.

Nasir watched as the Huntress laughed at Altair's words, the harsh lines of her face softening. He watched as the general's eyes dropped to her lips and followed the curve of her smile. How did Altair feel, knowing he was the first to coax a genuine smile across her cold-hard features after the death of her companion?

She had molded too much of herself into cool marble, and he did not want her to shatter.

She withdrew into her own thoughts and her gaze drifted up, meandering across the slabs of stone until she found him. He remembered the softness of her body, the way she met his eyes as no one but Altair did, dismantling him as no one did. Fearlessly. Effortlessly. As if, perhaps, beneath every death and monstrous act he had committed, he was only flesh and bone—a human, nothing more.

He hadn't been seen as a human in years.

He looked away, despite the fire between them. Why did she seek him out? Did she regret her decision to save him?

No matter. For now, she and the others could enjoy themselves. Soon enough, he would get back to the task of killing them off.

But a voice whispered a tendril of a word in his ear, the same voice that had made his credence waver when he had leveled his scimitar at Altair.

Liar, it said.

—◆►—

After the meal, Zafira turned to Benyamin and opened her mouth, but he only held up his hand, silencing her before he moved his stupid red rug closer. Altair stretched himself upon his bedroll, bare arms crossed beneath his head, ever shameless.

"I thought we weren't going to talk," Kifah said, rubbing a salve on the still-healing gash across her arm. "Whatever happened to 'the shadows have a master'?"

Benyamin released a lengthy breath. "That was the plan, but Sharr has shown its hand. I see no reason for caution now."

An uneasy silence weighed upon them. Beneath a sudden gust of dry air, the fire crackled like footsteps on the sand-studded stone.

"What a poetic way of saying one of us is going to die," Kifah said.

"Are all Pelusians so bitter?" Altair asked, voice strained as he looked to the open skies above them.

"I'm not bitter. I'm realistic, and I see no reason for unnecessary optimism."

"Akhh, Nasir might have finally found his soulmate," Altair drawled.

Was the prince listening to their conversation? Was he plotting his next kill? Was he watching her? *Zafira, you vain oaf.*

"Where should I begin?" Benyamin asked, tucking his book aside.

"With you." Zafira stretched, trying to will away her exhaustion and the ache in her back from their endless walking.

"I was born on—"

"I don't think anyone wants to know about you, safi," said Altair, and Kifah mumbled her agreement.

Benyamin sighed and straightened his keffiyah. "One day, my person will find esteem and all of Arawiya will desire my humble history. They will scribe poetry in my name and sing ballads of my triumphs. Mark my words, dear friends."

Altair snorted, but Zafira couldn't help but smile.

"I'm here," Benyamin went on, "because, though she may not be able to lie, the Silver Witch can't be trusted."

"You came a long way to say something I already know," Zafira said.

His lips quirked. "Oh, but I came a long way to tell you something *no one* knows."

"Go on," Kifah said.

That surprised her. Zafira had thought the Pelusian warrior knew everything. But it seemed she, too, had joined the quest with minimal knowledge.

"Have you ever wondered why the Silver Witch wields magic on a land where there is none?" he asked. "Have you ever wondered why the sultan keeps her close?"

"You sound like a merchant trying to sell trash," Altair groaned, a hand over his face.

Benyamin held Zafira's gaze. The fire crackled and the darkness settled in, waiting for his response as intently as she was. "Think, Huntress. There were only six beings who wielded magic from within. Who were vessels of magic as much as wielders."

Six beings. Vessels of magic who imbued the five royal minarets with their limitless power. Only five minarets, because one of those beings had been here on Sharr, guarding the prison she created with her own power, born from the good of her own pure heart.

Zafira broke away from his gaze. Her heart was a drum.

No one can be that pure.

"Then—that means only five Sisters perished that day," she whispered.

He nodded. She thought of Sukkar and Lemun, frozen solid. She thought of the Arz disappearing, and the phantom men aboard that unnatural ship. Magic when no magic should exist. Powerful magic.

Skies.

"The Silver Witch—*she* was Sharr's warden. She's . . . she's the sixth Sister."

Benyamin's silence was the only confirmation she needed.

For a long moment, no one spoke. Altair's shaky laugh broke the heavy quiet, mimicking how Zafira felt.

"I've dropped many revelations in my day, but that, safi, tops all," he said, but he sounded far off, as if this revelation struck him deeper than it did the rest of them.

"It is truth," Benyamin said, spreading his hands.

"So the greatest of the Sisters turned evil," Kifah said with a sigh. "Why am I not surprised? The best are always the worst."

Zafira sensed years of resentment behind that line.

The Silver Witch was dark, powerful, *something else.* But Zafira didn't know if she was evil.

When she said as much, Kifah gave her a look. "I don't know what rock you live beneath in Demenhur, but the witch convenes with the sultan far too much not to be influential. Look what's become of him, Huntress."

There was an edge to Benyamin's voice when he responded. "We are all flesh and blood, soul and heart. Capable of malevolence, just as much as benevolence. One wrong does not make evil."

It *could*, though. Zafira was wholly aware that Benyamin didn't answer Kifah's implication. She supposed every creature that could not lie was adept at doling half-truths. Answering questions with more questions.

He had given them only a slice of the entire truth. Barely a page of a hefty tome stored in the library of his thoughts.

"If she isn't evil, and she was here when it happened, why won't she get the Jawarat herself?" Zafira asked. "She said she was trying to make things right. Why isn't she helping us?"

"Sharr contains magic only because it drained the Sisters of theirs during the battle with the Lion of the Night. If she sets foot upon these sands, she will share the fate of the other Sisters. She escaped the first instance only because her power exceeded theirs, allowing her time." Benyamin canted his head. "Then again, if she knew where the Jawarat was, she could merely materialize for a trifle, grab it, and disappear. But I don't believe that is how the Jawarat works."

Zafira blinked.

"That is where you come in, dearest Demenhune, and the rest of us. We are stronger as one, more likely to succeed as one. As a zumra. You might have already perished had I left you to your own accord."

"Shukrun for your vote of confidence," Kifah said dryly.

"So once magic is free from Sharr, the Arz will fall?" Zafira asked.

Benyamin nodded.

Zafira continued, "Then chaos will break out across the kingdom. Only a few know of the quest."

"Once the curse lifts and the Arz disappears, my runners will take to the streets, sending notice to the caliphs and their wazirs. Order will remain. See, I like to plan ahead," Benyamin said with a smug smile, and Altair shot him a look.

Zafira was too impressed not to show it.

Altair interrupted. "Tell me something, One of Nine. How do *you* know of the silver woman?"

Zafira had wondered the same. She hadn't known of the Silver Witch's existence until the woman materialized before her.

"It's not common knowledge, but I'm one of the Pelusian calipha's trusted Nine Elite, no?" Kifah answered.

Zafira's eyes strayed to the trees, where she swore she was being watched. *Come, come, come,* the trees seemed to chant, the call curling around her cheeks. It was as if the darkness had reached a frenzy when it heard of the Silver Witch's identity. When it learned the woman who had controlled them still lived.

Or maybe it was magic. Zafira didn't know. The island was rife with magic and darkness, entwined.

Skies, Zafira had met one of the Six Sisters of Old.

Somehow, the revelation allowed her to breathe a little easier. She had more questions, and she still didn't know how or why Benyamin had come, but she felt her purpose had been reinstated somehow. That the Jawarat had been made more real.

The others dispersed into their own corners of the ruins. Altair hummed some ridiculous ballad, and Kifah dusted off her bedroll. Zafira remained by the fire, breathing in the soft rustles of the night and something else . . . water? The faint trickle of it sang in her ears, but because no one else pointed it out, she judged it to be farther away. She had been eating with hands smudged in dirt for days now. Getting clean would be nice.

A shadow slanted over her, obscuring the moonlight. Kifah. Her turban had been tied around her neck, and the solemn plains of her face glowed in the embers. She carried three velvet bags that Zafira had seen Altair eating from earlier: one full of dates, another of dried goat meat, and the third with candy-coated almonds in pastel hues that didn't belong in Sharr.

The Pelusian asked something around a mouthful of food, and Zafira raised her eyebrows, mindlessly tossing grains of sand into the fire, irritating it. Benyamin and Altair discussed something tiredly.

Kifah swallowed and held out her velvet bags. "Would you like some?"

Zafira eyed the pouches. One blue, one red, one green. Deep, dark colors, probably made with cloth spun in Demenhur. Every caliphate needed the other, yet they still wielded their differences like swords, their bitterness like walls.

"Why?" Zafira asked.

Kifah blinked. "Why what?"

"Why are you offering me your food?"

She shrugged. "You look like you could use some."

"That's not what I meant," Zafira said, and Kifah knew it. *She* had been the one eager to spear Zafira to the ground.

The flames reached fists of fury to the sky, trapped as they were on an island they couldn't comprehend. Zafira could tell Kifah was carefully stringing words together in the silence.

"I always thought the Demenhune Hunter was a fabrication. Not because I doubted you could venture and return, but because you had no name. You claimed no glory, no fame. People aren't like that anymore," Kifah said. "Then you saved my life. Honor meant something in this world once." The fire drew her attention for a long moment, and Zafira had the sense that Kifah was elsewhere.

"Is that why you came with Benyamin?" Zafira asked. "For honor?"

"The Darwishes are born to be erudites. To sit with folds of papyrus and dole out brilliant ideas as cows dole out milk. I like words all right, but I prefer the power of the blade. Even when they shoved a reed pen into my fist, I wanted that pen to be a spear. I wanted the power that came with knowing I stand between someone and death.

"My father's a high inventor, and he hates nothing more than he hates magic. But I'm a close second, because he wanted all his children to be little copies of himself, and I refused. He made my siblings loathe me the way he did, but Tamim was different." The warrior's voice cracked at the name. "Had my brother not saved me from my own father in my own bleeding bedroom, I would have ended my life. My father punished him. He sent my beloved brother to the Arz. I followed, thinking I could save him, but they knew I'd come. They'd slit his throat first, the cowards."

Kifah laughed. A soft, bitter laugh. "My scholarly brother bled out in my arms, and I screamed. And in answer to my anger, the trees disappeared, if only for a little bit."

Zafira looked at her sharply.

"Tamim called it love, just before he died. Its own form of magic. Now I know it was the Arz, letting me change those trees to leaves because I'm a bleeding miragi."

A miragi. An illusionist who could take one thing and make it something else entirely. That was how Kifah had hunted the cape hares. She didn't need to outrun them; she only needed to illusion a trap.

Kifah shook her head. "His body wasn't even cold before I took a razor to my hair and used his cuff to fashion the head of my spear. They say no one joins the school of the Nine Elite so late in her years. Yet here I am, wicked world."

The fire curled and the moon held still as Kifah spoke her bladed words.

"I buried myself with Tamim that day. There is freedom in knowing you're dead. When you're a specter no one can touch." Her smile was a knife. "The calipha refused Benyamin's call for aid, because 'Sharr is a gamble.' But the dead are bound to no one, laa? I took my leave and joined the prattling safi. Not for honor, but because there's no revenge sweeter than bringing back what my father loathes most: magic." Kifah met Zafira's eyes. "Do you see now, why I believed honor to be dead? When a woman who founded our kingdom cannot be trusted? When a father can't even be trusted with his own daughter?"

Zafira didn't know what to say. She knew the world was cruel, but she had never tried to perceive the limits of its cruelty.

"Did he— Did your father—" She couldn't finish her question.

Kifah's answer was a break in her stare, a parting of her mouth before she clenched her jaw and steeled her gaze once more.

It was answer enough.

"You and I are strangers, Huntress. Allies by circumstance. We may leave Sharr and never think of each other again. But in this moment, we are two souls, marooned beneath the moon, hungry and alone, adrift in the current of what we do not understand. We hunt the flame, the light in the darkness, the *good* this world deserves. You are like Tamim. You remind me that hope is not lost."

She fell silent when something moaned in the shadows. A gleam shone in Kifah's eyes when she continued. "Together, we will raise dunes from the earth and rain death from the sky. Together, we are capable of anything."

Zafira didn't think it was the fire that warmed a crevice in her chest.

Kifah Darwish lifted her lips into a smile, and it felt like the beginning of something Zafira never hoped for.

"So would you like some?"

Zafira stared at Kifah's outstretched hands and took the blue pouch.

Candy-coated almonds it was.

CHAPTER 53

ZAFIRA REMAINED ALERT LONG AFTER ALTAIR HAD drifted off to sleep. Benyamin had tucked himself so far into his book, she might as well have called him asleep, too. Kifah slept on her back, red sash beneath her head, spear across her body, a fierce maiden at rest.

In this moment, we are two souls, marooned.

That was life, wasn't it? A collection of moments, a menagerie of people. Everyone stranded everywhere, always.

Zafira rose and swept her gaze over the ruins. She couldn't see the prince, which was for the best.

She snatched a fresh tunic and dug out a bar of her favorite soap from her bag. She pulled her cloak over her shoulders, the weight familiar and foreign at once. Almost like a barrier, almost like a cherished blanket.

She jerked away from scuttling beetles and hoisted herself to the highest point of the ruins, holding her breath when rubble crunched beneath her feet, and looked out. A small fold of trees dotted the landscape not too far from where she stood. If there was a stream, she intended to use it.

The sands held their breath as she stole between the fallen stones and stepped upon the shifting ground. *Marhaba, darkness, my daama friend.*

Marhaba, Huntress, our old friend, the sands whispered as they danced from dune to dune. The gibbous moon cast them in a tint of blue and black, a haze of shadow dulling her shine, steepening her cold to draw a shiver from Zafira's bones. Ripples appeared across the dunes, deepening shadows that slithered like snakes. The wind moaned, cried, begged to be free.

What are you?

To define is to limit.

Zafira released a slow exhale. First she thought the darkness was calling to her, and now the sands were speaking, too? She paused to look back: The fire was a glowing pinprick between the slabs of stone, but the stillness promised her presence wouldn't be missed.

She quickened her steps until she passed one palm, two, and then entered a glade of several. She brushed aside brittle vines, gliding between meandering roots and rogue stone.

Tall grass settled to a shorter cover of plants. The stream was small, but it rushed from west to east, dusky blue beneath the still-heavy moon. Zafira grinned, never so happy to get clean.

Until she heard it.

Steel knifing the night. She breathed a string of curses and slipped back into the shadows.

There. The glint of a curved blade, a little ways to her left.

Against the moonlight, his profile gave him away: lithe and still. Uncovered, disheveled hair. Sharp nose. Barely parted lips. She imagined his bleak eyes churning a storm. He tipped his head up, and the length of his scar flashed.

Nasir. Something simmered in her stomach.

The prince lowered his head and leveled the scimitar ahead of him in slow movements. Zafira peered to her right but couldn't see an opponent. *He's alone.* She drew her eyebrows together as he shifted the scimitar ever so slowly, blade glinting in the moonlight, before it cut across the air in swooping crescents.

He paused with his scimitar extended, and she followed the glister of the blade to his arm as he drifted elegantly through the grass. She had heard of the hashashins and their training, but she had never guessed their drill could be anything less than violent brutality.

This wasn't violent or brutal. This was a dance, graceful and lithe. A performance of finesse. He moved as if he were made of the water beside him, with a stillness in his shoulders and the length of his back. She could only imagine how much smoother his motions would be if he were gliding through sand, rather than the uneven grass of the oasis.

Lightning quick, he leaped, turning a full circle before slashing the scimitar down in a swooping arc. He finished with the flat of it against his other arm and exhaled.

He lowered the blade, setting himself in a new angle. Her eyes flared at the sight of his bare chest, slight ridges along his stomach casting shadows on his skin. Lean muscles coiled and flexed in time with his breathing. A pair of dark sirwal billowed, low on his hips.

When he turned to the water, her breath caught and her stomach heaved.

Leeches covered his back. Fat lumps of black in neat rows, almost as if arranged. They started at his shoulder blades and continued down, stopping at the waistband of his trousers. He disappeared into the stream, which had to be larger than a stream if he could vanish within. Perhaps it was a river. How would she know? Zafira lived in Demenhur. They had only snow, snow, and more snow.

She thumped her head against the nearest tree. She could almost feel Yasmine's presence beside her, theories dripping from her friend's lips like rose water at a wedding. A prince with leeches on his back, for what? Bad blood? Poison? Illness? He seemed healthy enough.

For the fun of it?

A muted splash interrupted her thoughts. Nasir emerged from the water, dark hair plastered to his skull, sirwal clinging to his legs and . . . She pinched her lips together and made a sound as her pulse quickened. Her neck warmed. *But the leeches,* Yasmine said in her head. *You're looking at him because of the leeches.* Zafira added a touch of slyness to her friend's voice for good measure.

She raised her gaze as he ran a towel across his body, movements slow. He rubbed it along his back without a care and turned, his back to the moonlight.

Shadows glinted and deepened.

Sweet snow below. They weren't leeches or lumps. They were scars. Charred and blackened.

Zafira hissed a breath through her teeth.

Nasir stilled.

She did not move. She did not breathe.

He tilted his head.

She cursed, turned, fled. Skies. What was she doing, spying on the Prince of Death? She wasn't sure if he would catch her, but she couldn't leave the shelter of the oasis. She cursed the hindrance of her cloak when it snagged on the fringe of a palm, and she tugged it free before barreling forward. At the edge, she stopped and tucked herself into the trees, trying to catch her breath while she listened.

Silence, except for the pounding of her heart. Not a single sound of pursuit.

Until air compressed behind her.

A hand on her shoulder, and she was thrown against the tree. Long fingers pressed against her chest. Her hood fell back and she bit her tongue against a cry of surprise.

"*You,*" Nasir exhaled, his voice a tangled chord of chaos. Surprise flickered across his face. Water glistened in his hair, dripping onto a white linen qamis snug across his shoulders, sleeves rolled to the middle of his forearms. Every nerve ending crackled and simmered low in her belly. He looked younger, dressed the way he was, without his hashashin's garb. Almost innocent.

It wasn't just the clothes that had changed the prince but also the look on his face. The walls that had fallen, showing fear, surprise, that gaping unhappiness, and so many emotions Zafira couldn't make sense of in the dark. His eyes swept across her face, snagging on her mouth, and her neck warmed again.

"Yes, me," Zafira breathed.

That was all it took. Her voice, two words, and the walls returned, his mask firmly lifted back into place.

She looked down at his hand against her chest, foreign in its bareness without that dark glove enclosing it. He had long, elegant fingers. What would he have become, if it hadn't been for the dark calling in his blood? Her gaze snared on the inside of his arm. *Ink.* His breath hitched and he snatched his hand away. Zafira licked her dry lips, ignoring a flare of disappointment.

"Hunting, Huntress?"

There was that voice. The soft one, still and apathetic as it looped with the darkness. She knew it was deliberate. She knew he felt things but hid them.

"Or spying?"

Her heart wouldn't slow. *Murderer. Murderer. Murderer.* It seemed to pound. His pitted scars flashed in her mind. What senseless torture was that? The word "murderer" faltered and fractured in two, giving room to doubt and . . . something else.

Change.

Her insides burned. A sweet sort of weakness trembled in her legs.

"I was heading to take a bath, but it looks like you beat me to it." If he was looking for proof that she had seen him, she wasn't going to make matters difficult.

His expression flattened at her self-satisfied grin, and he made a low noise in his throat.

There's the growling prince.

"There are rules, Huntress," he said, stepping closer.

Zafira stopped breathing.

"Wahid: Never sneak up on an assassin, unless you want to get caught."

And closer. Her heart climbed up to her throat.

"Ithnayn: Never wander near a murderer, unless you want to be next."

He slipped even closer, and she had to tip her head up, slightly. She could smell him now, a hint of amber and a touch of myrrh. His breath was warm on her skin. She only needed to lean closer and—

"Thalatha: Never watch a man undress, unless you want him to get the wrong impression."

Oh.

He pulled back, mouth pressed into a thin line. He backed away farther, mouth shifting, scar gleaming. *Is he . . .* Zafira's breath seized. He was daama grinning. This wasn't the hashashin prince she was coming to know. This was a boy she knew nothing about.

Oh no. She wasn't going to leave without a last word. But everything had slowed when he stepped so daama close, and everything she had built in her mind scattered like snow in a storm.

She pushed away from the tree and dusted off her hands, ignoring the ricochet of her pulse.

"Watching you undress would be a bore. I got there after," she said. Then she leaned closer and lowered her voice. "For the good stuff."

His eyes dropped to her lips again, and Zafira knew he felt the same pull she did. It darkened his gray eyes. Trembled on his exhale. She thought she would explode—never had anything felt more thrilling. For the first time in her life, she wished she hadn't worn her cloak. He lifted a hand.

And let it drop by his side.

"Run away, Huntress." He sounded tired. "The dark is no den for a fair gazelle."

CHAPTER 54

NASIR HAD BEEN FOOLISH. MINDLESS. HE HAD BEEN the mutt his father always called him.

Now he had a blood debt, someone had seen his scars, and he had been seen without his mask. He knew she had seen him, because she was a daama open book herself.

He had never cared about how those scars made him look until last night. He had never *felt* as much as he had last night. That soap still plagued his senses. Heady, sharp, stirred with a touch of femininity that sent his pulse racing. Sandalwood, dark oud, smoky rose. Rimaal. He cursed the portion of his mother's training that had forced him to learn every scent there was.

He didn't know which was worse—the encounter with the Huntress or Benyamin's smirk when Nasir had returned to the camp before she did, fresh from a bath.

The river he had bathed in rippled beside them now, the sun beaming above. Nasir never thought he could miss the unwavering sun until Sharr. They may have a bleak future in Sultan's Keep, but sun against sand was what made them who they were. Not this haze of shadow that obscured everything, darkening the world. *Sentiments are for the weak.*

This journey was changing him.

Kifah used a glass instrument to concentrate enough sunlight to start a fire. When she saw him watching, she shrugged. "My father made it. It works best when I imagine I'm lighting him on fire."

Nasir quirked an eyebrow.

He knelt by the small fire and sharpened his scimitar, and after a moment she left him to taunt Altair, who was refilling their goatskins. Benyamin washed clothes, and the Huntress helped wring them. Nasir tightened his jaw at their camaraderie.

It would be foolish to kill them off now when he could avail himself of the benefits of the zumra, particularly the comfort of knowing that the others had his back if ifrit—or worse—ambushed them again.

"Careful, or you'll murder the blade," a voice said. He stopped his grinding and glanced at the worn brown boots that had stopped beside him. Smoky rose soothed his thoughts. *Soothed?*

"What do you want?" he asked.

The Huntress crouched beside him, sand dipping beneath her boots. "Iced cream. My best friend. A vial of honey. My sister's smile. Don't ask if you can't provide."

It took him a moment to realize she was teasing. And by the time he did, she had moved on.

"What's on your arm?"

Nasir paused. She had seen it *and* had the audacity to be curious. He felt a flood of shame because she didn't fear him and a crackle of comfort because she didn't fear him. What were these warring sentiments? The hissing of steel filled the silence as he resumed his grinding.

"Cloth. Or a gauntlet and its blade. Teeth marks from an old lover since I tumble one every night. Depends on which part of my arm you're asking about."

"Arrogance will get you nowhere," she said.

Her ring twinkled in the sunlight, blinding him even with his gaze pointedly down. *Did you love him, fair gazelle?*

He had been so sure of so much, but now he wasn't certain of anything anymore. He paused and met her eyes. If a poet were to describe them, he would say to look into her eyes was to see the sea's first glimpse of the sun, drinking its reflection with endless ripples. Or something like that. Nasir was no poet. And though she held his gaze unflinchingly, some part of her had retreated. Did his scars repulse her? Did *he* repulse her?

"I'm here, aren't I?" he said.

"This would be my definition of nowhere."

Her slow drawl was accompanied by a look of amusement. A breeze wound through the grass and she shivered, reaching for her hood before her eyes tightened in the realization that she wasn't wearing her cloak. Her fingers brushed her ring, and her lips parted ever so slightly. He watched, transfixed, wondering how those small, mindless motions always drew his attention.

Something had shifted between them last night. *Want* pulsed at the pads of his fingers.

He swallowed. "This doesn't look like nowhere to me."

This was as peaceful as their journey would be. The waters undulated a brilliant cobalt beneath the teasing wind. Rare, clear skies cupped the sun. It was softer, fighting the growing darkness, barely lifting the small hairs on the back of his neck, but it was more than he had seen in a while. And if he were feline like Benyamin, he would be curled beneath it, relishing in its warmth. But he was no stray, nor was he one to sit idly and relish anything in life.

It wasn't peaceful, he decided. It was a moment between moments. The calm before a storm.

"Looks can be deceiving," she replied.

Beneath the beat of the sun, all he saw was the starkness of her skin and the sharp cut of her lips. But last night, beneath the glow of the moon, that skin had coaxed and those lips had beckoned.

They still do. Nasir twisted his mouth and resumed his sharpening. The hiss of a blade knifed the sway of the tall grass, and a hand extended toward him bearing a jambiya, the point facing away. He took the dagger and studied the simple leather hilt, worn from age and the exchange of palms. Her father's or mother's, he assumed, and likely the only blade that felt comfortable in her hand.

Murderer, she had said that first day. It was no small deed, handing over a trusted weapon to an enemy.

He set his sword down and started grinding her blade. "It's Safaitic."

"What is?" she asked, watching him.

"The ink. My arm. It's Safaitic. I don't expect you to know how to read it." Kharra. He should have phrased the words as a question.

She only pressed her lips together and neither denied nor agreed. "Then there's no harm in showing me, is there?"

"Define 'harm,' Huntress." He ran his fingers along the edge of her blade, and it snagged on the leather of his glove—sharp, but it could be sharper.

She glanced to the others. Altair made Kifah laugh as she tossed her lightning blades at a tree. Benyamin had climbed up the same tree and was lazily flipping through his book.

"Physical pain," she said.

He gave a dry laugh, her dagger wheezing under his ministrations. "Then you've never experienced real pain before."

"Emotions are an inconvenience." But her tone suggested she didn't believe the words. She was saying them for his benefit, to study his reaction with those sharp eyes.

"Until they broach into the level of pain," he said softly. He stood and passed her jambiya back. His fingers brushed hers and despite the barrier of his glove, he drew in a sharp breath, every part of him alert.

She slid the dagger back into its sheath. How could a hunter be so delicate? Not even a speck of dirt marred the skin beneath her nails. She started to leave but stopped, head half turned as if to say, *This is your last chance.*

He felt he had reached some sort of . . . understanding with her. A bond, fragile and bleak. Perhaps it was pity, for what she had seen the night before. A protest stirred in his chest, begging him to *shatter, shatter, shatter.*

Bonds held no place in his life.

He hesitated for a beat of his heart before unstrapping his gauntlet and lifting his sleeve. He averted his eyes from the twisted calligraphy as she drew close a little too quickly. It was one thing to know what had been written on his arm; it was another to see it, to be reminded of the day he had it pierced into his skin. To be reminded of his mother.

The Huntress's breath caressed his arm as she leaned in, warm despite her iciness. Her shoulder brushed his. Her ring tapped his elbow in a steadily falling beat. Sensations clashed and he wanted—no. She reached out, and he saw the path her fingers were about to take, the words she wanted to trace.

"What happened to no touching?" he asked.

She pulled away with a sharp inhale.

He tugged his sleeve down and strapped the leather back in place. He cursed the rasp in his voice, the falter. She had seen enough. She had seen too much.

———◆———

Zafira watched him leave, his shoulders stiff, the sun casting his dark hair in a gleam of light.

He couldn't have known that she knew Safaitic. Baba had tried to teach her, and it was rusty at best, but she was able to read the words on his arm. The swirling black, shaped like a teardrop on his golden skin.

I once loved.

She had heard those words elsewhere, but they seemed forever ago now. He was a mess of scars like the sky was a mess of stars. From the one stretched down his face, to the craters on his back, to the ink on his arm. For that was what scars were, weren't they? A remembrance of moments dark.

There was more to the prince than she'd first thought.

"Bonding moment khalas?" someone asked.

Altair. Yes, their bonding moment certainly *was* over. There was a weight in the general's eyes now, likely a product of learning that the Silver Witch was one of the daama Sisters.

She took the replenished goatskin from his hands, wiping the stray drop-lets with the edge of her tunic. Altair and Nasir were so different, it was a marvel they hailed from the same caliphate. Nasir was the dark to Altair's light. The night to his day.

"We were just getting to the good stuff," she said dryly.

Altair laughed. "Sounds like Nasir. Trust him to leave when things are getting good."

"You say it fondly."

He made a choking sound, and a laugh bubbled to her lips. She still puzzled over their relationship. They were well acquainted, that was cer-tain, but how Altair could be a ruthless general was beyond her.

Her smile slipped and her thoughts stumbled to a halt. A ruthless general. A coldhearted murderer. How could she have forgotten?

Altair turned to her, blue eyes bright with whatever he wanted to say. They were the same hue as the stream, a thought she stabbed quiet. But he took in her expression, the stiff set of her shoulders. The distrust she should never have neglected.

He looked away without a word, and the curve of his shoulders col-lapsed.

When they reached the others, Benyamin smiled, but whatever peace she had felt before had disappeared, and all she could do was stare back.

Kifah pursed her lips before deciding against whatever she was about to say. "We should head up the stream. Avoid the sun," she remarked instead.

"The sun has been a coward ever since the ifrit attack," Nasir said, glancing to the dull skies.

Altair was still quiet, and the conversation felt forlorn without his commentary.

"There's no point following a trail that won't lead us where we need to go," Zafira said, and Benyamin *hmm*ed in agreement. "We're supposed to head that way."

They followed her outstretched hand to a point in the horizon where the skies deepened to angry black and the sands swelled in waves of copper.

"If I were less realistic and more pessimistic, I would say we're going to die," Kifah drawled in the silence.

Nasir sheathed his scimitar and stalked forward.

"Best not keep death waiting, then."

CHAPTER 55

WEARINESS AND WARINESS BECAME A COMMON exchange, the sun weighing them down despite its gloomy glow. They trekked and tracked for five whole days without incident, taking short rests and eating dates to maintain energy.

No, not tracking. Zafira was no tracker; she was a hunter. She *hunted*. But hunters tracked, and trackers hunted, didn't they? *Where are you going with this?* Zafira tilted her head and imagined her thoughts shifting into a box she closed tight. If only it were that easy.

An idle mind is the devil's playground, she told herself, but the words felt like shadows against her lips.

As they shuffled through the sands, Zafira listened for sounds of life. Birds, the hiss of sand critters, a predator cry—only the silence ever shouted back. Sometimes their surroundings mimicked her thoughts, wilting and wavering before she blinked and everything righted.

The darkness was always happy to see her.

Zafira could *feel* its happiness whenever the sun dimmed further or they traversed an outcropping or another passage of ruins where the shadows lived. They bent and shifted in a dance of elation. Tendrils drifted beneath the folds of her tunic, curled around her arms, nipped at her ears, a lover she could not see. Did no one else feel what she did?

Benyamin glanced sideways at her. "Trouble, Huntress?"

The genuine concern in his voice nearly undid her. She blinked and refocused on the stone ahead. A set of columns had toppled, one against the other, creating a bridge for creatures to hop across.

"No," she said softly.

Nearly everything dragged her mind to grief—Yasmine, and how Zafira would tell her of her brother's death. Deen, dying for her. Lana, caring for their mother. Umm, and the five years Zafira had spent avoiding her. Nasir, and the way her body had begun to react whenever he was near. Why had Arawiya's lethal hashashin succumbed to a needle and inscribe the word "love," in any form or tense, on his skin?

"Why is there a flower in your turban, you bumbling fool?" Benyamin asked.

Zafira threw a glance at Altair, whose red-rimmed turban housed a blood lily.

Altair frowned. "What are you talking about? My fashion tastes are too exquisite for flowers."

"Says the flower on your head," Nasir pointed out.

Kifah, not one to miss out on a quip when it came to the Sarasin general, was unusually silent.

"Akhh," Altair grumbled, and Zafira heard the shuffle of him pulling something from his turban. "You call this a flower?"

The vibrant flower on Altair's head was now a dead leaf in his hand, curling into itself. Zafira darted a glance at Kifah, who winked. The miragi's work.

"It's the island, alerting you to your terrible taste," Nasir said.

Kifah snickered at Altair's wide-eyed bewilderment, and the general tossed the leaf to the sand and stomped on it for good measure.

They passed dunes, dunes, and more dunes. Sometimes Zafira would catch Altair leaning close to Kifah, making a tender smile bloom across the warrior's lips. Other times, she would catch the general and Benyamin in conversation, eyes forlorn, voices low. Nasir watched them all, mouth pursed, ever weary.

To a darting glance, the prince was cool indifference. To someone who watched him, his focus was intent and inquisitive. The mark of someone born with a curious mind, but forced to use it elsewhere: In calculating death. His gaze slid to Zafira, and she quickly looked away, neck warming.

"Are you sure we're going the right way?" Kifah asked as the desert darkened once more. It wasn't a cover of clouds that obscured the sun. It was the sky itself. Caging them away from the orb of light.

"No," Zafira said, eyeing the knife twirling in Kifah's hand. How could she explain the song the darkness sang? The frenzy in her bloodstream that only settled when she led them in the direction it wanted? "But if you have a better idea, by all means."

Kifah grumbled something beneath her breath.

"Couldn't you have brought a few camels on that ship of yours?" Altair groused.

"You should have sent me a letter asking for one or ten," said Benyamin.

Kifah gave Altair a sidelong glance. "Or you could ask him to carry you. Put some of that safin strength to good use."

Zafira wasn't sure Benyamin could carry Altair, safin strength or not.

"Such an imaginative mind, One of Nine," Altair said.

After what felt to be hours, Altair complained that his stomach was eating itself, so they stopped to rest and the shadows swallowed the sky, their only indication of nightfall. There wasn't a single star in the dark expanse, despite the tales Zafira had heard of the stars leading bedouins through unremarkable sands.

"Who will be assuming the role of watchman tonight? For it will not be me," announced Benyamin.

"Do you think I like it when you stare at my perfection?" Altair asked.

Zafira crossed her arms. "He probably can't sleep unless a woman's looking at him."

"Kifah looks at me," Altair said, grinning at the Pelusian.

Kifah scowled. "Only because I'm wondering how best to chop off your head with your own sword."

Altair turned to Zafira. "Do you volunteer? Because I—"

Nasir cut him off with a growl. "I'll take the first watch."

"Such generosity, princeling," Altair exclaimed, clapping him on the shoulder. "No one else would oblige so readily, you see. Akhh, I'm not worried about my well-being in the slightest. But I think I'll take the second watch. Just to be safe."

No one objected, and after another meal of roasted hare, Zafira settled into her makeshift bed. Kifah spoke to Benyamin in low murmurs, Altair piping his opinion every so often. Like friends. They spoke to one another because they wanted to, not because they *needed* to.

They spoke to Zafira to ask which way to go or which path to take. She was a daama tour guide.

And she was alone, as always.

She sighed and turned to her side, looking to where the prince was keeping watch against the mottled stone. Only, he wasn't facing the desert. He leaned against the oddly shaped thing.

Watching her.

She looked away, and it was a long time before sleep claimed her soul.

———◄ ● ►———

Nasir knew how she felt, when she turned to him, something bleak yawning in those scythes of blue fire. She had changed since he had first aimed an arrow at her Demenhune's heart.

She tipped her shoulders less. Every morning since her heatstroke, she would take her cloak from her satchel and silently debate donning it. But that had ceased, too, after their . . . run-in at the river. It was as if she had been born to a skin she did not fit within, and only now, in the desolation of the desert, was she allowing herself to take command of it. To mold herself to it.

She stretched her long limbs and slid her gaze to him. He did not think she could rest, for night was when the demons awoke. Memories no one wanted to remember. Ghosts no one wanted to see. Nasir's demons tended to join his slumber, too.

Good night, he wanted to whisper.

But he was the Prince of Death, *Amir al-Maut*, as his mother had once called him in the old tongue, and good night always felt like goodbye.

CHAPTER 56

N ASIR SHOOK THE HUNTRESS'S SHOULDER AGAIN. Rimaal, she slept like the dead.

If not for the rise and fall of her chest, he would have believed her dead. Just as his sleep had conjured her last night. First with her lip between his teeth. Then with her eyes glassy, red dripping from his blade.

"Yalla, yalla." His hand trembled. A hashashin never wavered.

Her eyes flew open and locked with his, panic fleeting across her features. He shrank back from the fear in her open gaze. Fear was his constant. It was in every gaze that turned his way, so why did seeing it in one more pair of eyes make him feel as though hands were tightening around his throat?

He swallowed and her startled eyes dropped to his throat. Kharra, this woman. "You sleep like the dead."

"You must have been hoping I was."

No, but what a distraction to be free of. "Lower your voice," he said, trying to ignore her sleepy rasp.

"Now's not the time, habibi," Altair murmured.

Indeed. They had bigger things to worry about than Altair calling him *beloved.*

Like the line of growling creatures surrounding them in the crumbling ruins.

"What are they?" the Huntress whispered. "Wolves?" She rose, lifting her bow and nocking an arrow in one fluid movement.

Altair's response was a low murmur. "Meet your newest adversary: the kaftar."

They were larger than wolves. Their agile bodies were coated in sparse fur, mottled in a darker brown than their coats. Long tongues lolled out of mouths cut in perpetually wicked grins, some bearing rows of sharp teeth.

"Hyenas?" she asked. One of the seven creatures growled and yipped.

Benyamin laughed his soft laugh. "Somewhat. Though in comparison, a hyena and a kaftar are like a stream and a stormy sea."

Another growl.

And one of the sleek storms leaped.

Powerful muscles undulated, and its depthless dark eyes flashed. Its brethren fanned out, stalking closer.

Nasir breathed down the shaft of his arrow, but before he could loosen the bowstring, a metallic arc cut through the air, catching the meager light. The moment the liquid gold touched the creature, time seemed to still.

The kaftar shifted into a man and landed on his feet.

Nasir heard the hitch in the Huntress's breath. The hyena-turned-man shook his head like a wet dog, pinning Benyamin with glowing eyes like qahwa not steeped long. He looked like a typical Arawiyan: dark hair, dark beard, light brown skin, except for that unnatural gaze glittering with anciency.

"Alder," the kaftar said to Benyamin in a garbled voice. Did he see Benyamin's pointed ears through his keffiyah, or could he sniff the safi?

To his either side, the other kaftar slowly shifted into men as the remnants of Benyamin's gold substance touched them. They were dressed in thobes, ankle-length and white, with ratty hair emerging from dark turbans. How they had attained such pristine white thobes during their shape-shift was beyond Nasir.

Benyamin tipped his head. "Kaftar."

The kaftar bared his teeth in a smile, and Nasir thought he saw a snout and pointed teeth. Then he blinked, and the creature appeared as a man once more.

"How long since you've stood a man?" Benyamin asked, calm and collected, as if the kaftar were wholly human and nothing else. *How long before one of you leaps and rips out someone's throat?* was what Nasir would have asked.

The kaftar stretched his neck with a sigh. This time, his voice was smooth when he answered. A hot knife through butter, a keen blade through flesh. "One hundred and four years."

Benyamin noticeably stiffened. Nasir's grip tightened around his drawn bow.

"One hundred and four years since we've eaten a meal cooked to perfection. One hundred and four years since I've lain in a warm bed and held a woman in my arms. Kaftar must shift at sunset and at sunrise, but it has been one hundred and four years, Alder"—the man's eyes burned murderous as he stalked closer—"since your kind cursed me and my brethren to the bodies of beasts, imprisoning us upon this island."

"Not a step closer, creature," Nasir said, voice low.

Surprise flickered in the murky pools of the kaftar's eyes. "A Sarasin, defending an Alder? Arawiya must truly lie in ruin." He lifted a hand to his beard.

Nasir held his breath as the kaftar's fingernails lengthened and sharpened into claws. One move, and both sides would clash.

The kaftar set his gaze on Altair. "I smell a sweetness in his blood, Alder, and I wonder—"

"*Enough!*" Cold alarm crossed Benyamin's face. The Huntress jumped. Kifah looked at Benyamin sharply. Very little ever fazed the safi, and they all took note.

"I can change you back into the monsters you were cursed to be and let them run you through with their weapons," Benyamin continued, gesturing to the others, "or you may leave us and remain in human form."

The tension crackled.

The hairs on the back of Nasir's neck stood on end.

"Why have you come?" the kaftar asked.

"A shadow stirs," Benyamin ceded. "Arawiya darkens."

"You panic, Alder." The kaftar stepped forward. His eyes glowed with barely contained savagery.

"The Jawarat will not remain lost much longer."

This time alarm befell the kaftar, and Nasir felt a cold grip in his chest at the reminder: whatever tome this Jawarat was, it was more than an answer to the disappearance of magic. The kaftar stared longingly at Altair, inhaling deep, and Nasir nearly stepped between them, but Kifah moved first, crossing her arms.

After a long moment, the kaftar stepped back, and his brethren mimicked his movements.

"Take your leave, Alder. Whistle, and my pack might assist." His gaze drifted to Kifah before it settled on the Huntress, roving across her form. Nasir wanted to cut him down where he stood. "But the cursed take no oaths and make no promises."

CHAPTER 57

NASIR TURNED HIS BACK ON THE KAFTAR WITH HEAVY reluctance. He never left a threat breathing. He hardly left the *innocent* breathing. His blood still boiled from the way the lead kaftar had nearly undressed the Huntress with his wandering gaze.

Which was why, the moment they had distanced themselves from the wily creatures, something in Nasir's calm snapped. He shoved Altair aside and flung Benyamin against a remnant of a wall, a plume of dust showering them from above.

Everyone froze.

Altair laughed. "I was waiting for this. Habibi Kifah, you owe me that spear."

"The only way you'll ever touch my spear is when I shove it through your throat," Kifah snapped.

"Charming. Then you owe me that gold cuff."

"Go sink yourself."

Nasir brought his face close to Benyamin's, who stared back without a hint of emotion. "First you convince everyone to traipse behind you, and then you befriend the foe of Sharr? Next you'll be holding hands with ifrit."

Benyamin didn't answer.

"Ten paces down this very desert, the kaftar could be waiting to kill us for your kindness."

The safi's face turned mocking. "Like you? You know, I keep wondering when you'll do the same, yet you continue following me around." He worried his lip. "Laa, you just keep *traipsing* behind me."

Nasir growled. "I'm not following you. No one is following you. Thanks to your big mouth, everyone is following the Demenhune."

A small click of metal punctuated his words, and Altair yanked Nasir back, easing the gauntlet blade back down.

"Come now, Nasir. You're ruining his keffiyah."

Nasir shrugged him off but kept his distance with narrowed eyes.

"Why are you really here, safi?" Nasir said, voice low. "Your lot has evolved past magic. You can live perfectly fine without it."

"I could ask the same of you. What need does Sultan Ghameq have for the Jawarat when the *Demenhune* intends to use it to return magic to the same kingdom he governs?"

Nasir gritted his teeth in the sudden silence. His neck burned.

Because he did not know.

He never knew. He was no more than his father's errand boy. A prince kept in the dark. A pawn who moved without question. *A jaban.*

He did not know why the sultan wanted the Jawarat. He did not know why the Silver Witch—Sister of Old and warden of Sharr—wanted the Jawarat. He knew only that the Huntress bore no evil, not the way he did.

"Tell us, Crown Prince Nasir. What does Ghameq want with the lost Jawarat?" Benyamin repeated.

He didn't think Benyamin bore evil, either, despite the knife of his words, cutting into Nasir's chest.

Never had his father's hate and disrespect mattered as much as they did now, here, with people from nearly every caliphate watching him. Never had the words *I don't know* felt so damning. The ruins darkened, or maybe it was his vision.

One thing was certain: Control was only slipping further from his grasp.

Altair watched him, and he had the acute sense that the general was sifting through his thoughts. For once, Nasir didn't know if his mask was in place, or if Altair could simply see past it.

You are weak. A mutt.

A lapdog.

"He doesn't know," Altair said.

To Nasir's surprise, there was no mock or amusement in his tone. Only steel and the harsh edge of protectiveness. Shame penetrated Nasir's every bone.

Benyamin laughed without mirth and adjusted his keffiyah. "Do you truly expect me to believe the prince isn't privy to his sultan? Knowledge without action is vanity, but action without knowledge is insanity."

Altair stared. "If you were son to the Sultan of Arawiya, safi, believe me, you wouldn't be privy to anything. Laa, you'd be a husk, begging to be tossed to the rats."

Nasir's exhale trembled along with the tips of his fingers. *Weakness.* Cursed emotion. He clenched his fists, willing his control to return. He could feel the Huntress studying him and wished, for once, that he could vanish.

Altair sliced the heavy silence with the draw of his scimitars. He swooped them through the air and disappeared into the trees. When no one followed, his bored voice floated back, "Yalla, Huntress. Everyone moves only when you do."

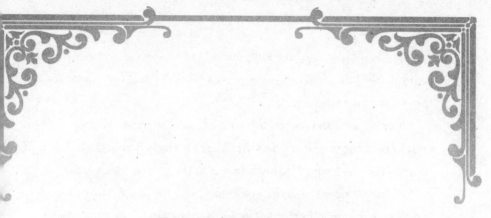

CHAPTER 58

Z AFIRA HURRIED AFTER ALTAIR, STEPS ECHOING ALONG THE
stone of the ruins. She couldn't stomach standing with them any
longer, where the air was rife with awkward tension. It was pride.
Pride had sparked that ridiculous conflict no one had needed.

"You defended him," she said, trying to understand.

Altair grunted, as grumpy as Nasir, and kicked at a pile of debris before
barreling forward. They were in a hall of sorts, a maze of rooms where stone
walls had collapsed. Zafira looked back, where the others were starting to
follow. Altair was right: Everyone moved when she did.

"Why?" she asked.

"Why what?"

"Why did you defend him?"

"Am I not allowed to defend anyone?" he asked with mock innocence.

Zafira scowled and followed him up a short run of crumbling stairs.
"Why did you defend Nasir?"

"Why are you so adamant?"

"I just want to know," she said, ducking beneath a dangerously unstable archway. She heard a hiss in the silence, a reminder that this was Sharr and they were never safe.

Altair stopped and pinned her with a look of anger she'd never seen on him. Was he angry he had defended Nasir? Or angry Benyamin had pushed Nasir to the point where Zafira saw fear in the prince's dead gaze?

"If I hadn't intervened, he could have wet his pants. Do you see any streams we can get him cleaned up in? Neither can I."

Men can be such beautiful trash, Yasmine said in her head with a sigh.

"You care for him," Zafira said, pushing for a reaction.

He raised an eyebrow and studied her before stomping ahead. Wasn't she supposed to lead?

"I do not," he said matter-of-factly when she caught up. There was an undertone of warning to his voice. "But careful, Huntress—I'm beginning to think you do."

The others reached them before she could protest his choice of words.

Benyamin yawned loudly and stretched like a cat, ignoring the prince as if he hadn't torn him apart. As if hyenas hadn't shifted into men before their eyes.

"When I'm back in Alderamin, I'm going to say hello to my beloved and maybe my sister, and then I'll take a very, very long nap. The longest one Arawiya has ever seen," the safi proclaimed.

"Say hello for me, too," Altair said. "To the calipha-to-be, not your beloved."

"My sister does not want your hello," Benyamin said with a scowl.

"I'm going to visit my father and gloat," Kifah said, and Zafira knew she hadn't imagined the bitterness in her tone. "Then I'll celebrate with the biggest lamb the calipha's kitchens can find."

Altair hummed in agreement. "Akhh, have that lamb marinated to perfection with ras el-hanout. Roasted potatoes garnished with basil. Qahwa in the evening with date biscuits."

"What's ras el-hanout?" Zafira asked.

"The mother of all spice mixes. It hails from Pelusia," Kifah replied, "but the Sarasin bastards stole it."

"You can't steal something that grows out of the ground. That's like saying we stole sand," Altair retorted.

Kifah shrugged.

"I'm going to take my falcon on a hunt. Poor thing probably misses me." The general looked at Zafira. "What about you, Huntress? What will you do back in Demenhur? Without the Arz, you can finally stop hunting."

Her step faltered. She hadn't made that connection, that simple realization. Taking down the Arz that killed her father meant there would no longer be the Arz that made her *her*.

Skies.

She would no longer be the Demenhune Hunter. She wouldn't be *anyone*. Something clawed up her chest. What was Zafira bint Iskandar, if not the Hunter?

Benyamin touched her sleeve.

"This is your chance for the Hunter and Zafira to become one," he said softly. Her cloak weighed heavily in her bag. "Meld them. Become yourself. The Huntress. The girl who freed magic from the darkness and so freed herself."

The Huntress. She bit her lip.

But the safi did not understand that freedom was sometimes a burden of its own.

———◄●►———

The others settled into the silence of reminiscence. No one asked Nasir what he planned to do when he returned, making him realize he had never thought beyond this journey. He had no naps or rich meals to look forward to. When he returned to his father, he could not gloat.

He would only await his next summons.

He lived for his orders. For the mistake he made in not heeding them.

No, there was nothing for Nasir after Sharr. Nothing but tears and corpses and the next bleak sunrise.

CHAPTER 59

Z AFIRA WOKE TO THE GROUND SWAYING BENEATH HER and birds screeching in the distance. Sunlight burned her eyelids and a breeze brushed her skin.

Frowning, she opened her eyes and nearly scrambled off a plank. Her bare hands snagged on splintering wood. *Breathe, Zafira. Then assess.*

She was on a fishing boat. A dhow. The sails billowed in a breeze that teased her tongue with salt, a blood-red diamond centered on the beige cloth.

Ululations broke the hush of the azure waves, and Zafira swiveled to a fisherman reeling in a net full of thrashing fish. They slipped and slid, their slaps atop the polished wood a soundless scream for salvation. She had never seen live fish before, but she pitied them, for their suffering ended with suffocation rather than a hunter's clean cut.

There were five shirtless men on board, plummy brown skin glistening with sweat, heads bound with sienna turbans. What was it with Arawiyan men and their shirts? They wore rough-cloth sirwal, muscled arms ten times larger than hers; they'd even put Altair to shame.

None of them looked at her—one stepped over the plank she sat on without a glance her way. It reminded her of the Silver Witch's phantom sailors, and an icy finger trailed her spine.

"Yaa, land!" a fisherman cried. The others echoed his jubilation.

The land they'd sighted drew closer with every beat of her heart. Until it was there. Here. Before her.

And her heart clenched at the magnificence of it all.

Faceted domes gleamed in a gold that warred with the sun; diamond-tipped spires and minarets speared the cloud-dusted sky. The domes nestled buildings of creamy stone, doors welcoming, windows open. Some were connected with ropes in bursts of color, clothes left to dry upon them wrinkled and stiff. Date trees dotted the landscape, reddish clusters of fruit tucked amid the fanning leaves.

People roamed the streets, dressed in an array of colorful gowns and thobes, some with tunics atop sirwal, turbans or scarves embellishing their heads. Some guided grinning camels carrying rolls of cloth. There were people of every shade—the deep brown of Pelusia, the pale of Demenhur, the copper and olive of Sarasin—though the majority were shades of the desert, gleaming with the heat of the sun.

This was nothing like the sands of Sharr, which whispered of ruin and sorrow. This sand sprawled over the ground the way snow did in Demenhur. It churned with the feet wading through it. It clung to the alabaster walls. It was everywhere.

Where am I?

"I was beginning to think you would never ask."

Zafira's vision faltered before she could turn toward the voice. When it righted, she was no longer on the dhow but on land.

She turned a full circle, noting the people who shuffled along, some hurrying, others moving slowly and leisurely. No one acknowledged her existence.

It was almost as if she didn't exist at all.

A camel chewing on a reed sauntered past, and Zafira searched for a flash of silver among the crowd, a cloak that hooded bone-white hair and a crimson smile, but her searching brought her to a different pair of eyes, umber, feline, and lazy. Half a fig in his hand.

Benyamin leaned against a date palm, dappled sunlight splotching his skin. He was overdressed as always: a black robe decked with gold over a white thobe, a checkered keffiyah on his head, calfskin sandals on his feet.

"You can read minds," she said.

He tilted his head and licked the remains of the fig from his fingers. "That would be a silly affinity, laa? And quite a pain, if you really pondered upon it. Alas, you asked the question aloud, Huntress."

Had she? She couldn't recall. "Just tell me where I am."

Benyamin carefully tugged at the keffiyah, adjusting it beneath a black circlet before he pushed away from the tree and sauntered toward her with sinuous grace. She found it surprising he didn't have a tail to curl around his feet.

"This is the Arawiya of old. Before the snows blanketed Demenhur, before the sands of Sarasin darkened and Zaram was cut off from the sea. Before the ever-fertile lands of Pelusia were sickened, dulling their great minds."

"This?" she whispered. It was a desert, it was almost exactly like Sharr, but it *throbbed* with life. The people were exuberant, the architecture astounding, and the climate warmed every fiber of her being. This Arawiya was *alive*. This was true Arawiya, before the Sisters' final battle with the Lion of the Night swept aberration across the kingdom like a plague. "I'm in the past?"

He shook his head, avoiding her gaze. "Quite current, I'm afraid. This is Alderamin."

She sniffed. "So you brought me here to shove your privilege in my face?"

He tilted his head again, this time meeting her eyes. "Aren't you going to ask how you *got* to Alderamin?"

"That was my next question," she snapped, suddenly annoyed.

She had merely momentarily forgotten. Because she was in Alderamin, the caliphate of dreams. Of everything everywhere else was not.

His question settled on her shoulders. Laa, it slapped her in the face, and her breath froze. "How did I get to Alderamin?"

Triumph glowed in his gaze. "Now *that* is the reaction I was hoping for."

Zafira huffed. Him and his extra words.

"You're not *in* Alderamin," he said. He gestured to their surroundings, where people bustled and the dry wind wove between the creamy buildings.

Somewhere in the distance, a bird cried. Zafira couldn't breathe past the delight expanding in her chest.

Benyamin twirled his finger, and Zafira's sight shimmered and settled again. She hadn't moved—there hadn't even been a stir in the air—but now they were on a balcony. Bereft, she reached for the cool, burnished railing and peered into the curtained room behind her, glimpsing a massive dining hall. Ornate chandeliers were lit with flames, the light amplified by mirrors. Engineering done by the Pelusians. Aesthetics by the artistic eye of the Demenhune. A majlis with cushions of deep red was flush with the floor, arranged around a gold rug, where a fancy-spouted dallah and cups sat on a tray.

She turned back to Benyamin.

"Then where—" She stopped. From their height, a scene from an artist's canvas unfolded beyond the railing.

The sands glittered far below. Farther ahead, the sea—the Baransea, she realized with a start—lapped the shore with lazy waves. To her left sprawled a masterpiece of stone, a mosaic of blue pieced together to create domes that rivaled the clear skies. Slender spires ended in the diamonds she had seen throughout the landscape. One tower stood out from the rest, its stained-glass windows at the very top dark and forlorn without magic. *The royal minaret.*

"This is Almas, our capital," Benyamin said wryly beside her.

Fitting that the Alder safin had branded their capital with a name that meant "diamond."

"And this magnificence behind us is the calipha's palace. Who happens to be my mother." It was no wonder he carried himself in such a princely way. He leaned against the railing and tapped a finger to his head. "I cannot read minds, but what I can do *is* related to the mind."

"Will you please stop baiting me?"

"Sabar, sabar," he soothed, asking for patience. A breeze lifted her hair, the first time her surroundings reacted with her. "Not counting anomalies, you do know our affinities are generally classified into two groups, yes?"

She shook her head. She knew very little of magic, let alone the classifications of them.

"There are the Jismi, whose affinities pertain to the body and mind—seers, healers, miragis. Then there are the Ensuri, whose affinities pertain to the elements—firehearts, aquifers, blacksmiths. The wielders of light and shadow. Jismi use magic to pull from themselves, Ensuri use magic to pull from the environment. Like you, I am among the Jismi. I'm a dreamwalker."

"A dreamwalker," she echoed.

He nodded. "This is a memory, a fragment reconstructed in my mind with two additions: you and me. Minus the Arz. Seeing Alderamin tainted by those trees shatters my soul every time."

That would explain why no one in the city was looking at her. "Sounds like a lot of mind work."

He lifted a shoulder in a shrug. "Being able to find your way seems like a lot of mind work, too." There was a gleam in his eyes when he leaned close. "That's why it's called magic." He sighed happily. "I haven't been able to session a dreamwalk in years."

319

A bird soared across Zafira's vision, feathers a dappled brown. *A falcon.* She had never seen a falcon before. She had never experienced true Arawiya at all, khalas. Yet here she was, in awe of a memory. The bird dipped behind a date palm, and her heart swooped with it.

She turned to Benyamin. "You said *years.* That means the last time you dreamwalked was when magic existed." She stopped, eyes wide. "How old are you?"

"A little older than you?" he chanced, and shrugged when Zafira glared. "Twenty-three."

She lifted an eyebrow.

"Plus, ah, one hundred."

She stared. He twisted his lips and rubbed a hand across his stubble before growing serious again.

"You lived in a world where magic existed. You lived under the rule of the Sisters," she murmured. That was more than ninety years ago.

"I was there for the Lion's reign of darkness, too." He lifted a shoulder. "It's been so long, I sometimes wonder if magic was a dream."

Zafira could not imagine how life once was, if this was life in Alderamin now. "Why 'truth'?"

"What?" He blinked.

"Haqq," she said, gesturing to his bronze tattoo. There had to be a reason why an immortal would ink his own face, knowing full well he'd live with the inscription for eternity. "What's it for?"

He brushed a hand across the word with a soft smile, followed by a flash of pain he quickly masked. "Each of the safin in my circle have a similar tattoo, a word for what we value most. For me, it is truth followed closely by trust—separate vines of value entwined at the root."

He had a fondness for zumras, it seemed. Though she didn't think the one he was trying to form on Sharr could compare to the majesty of a zumra of elegant safin.

A murmur carried from the balcony, the voice rising and falling ever so gently. *Singing.* It reminded Zafira of laughter beneath a bright sun. Of tears before a still soul. It was beautiful, despondent.

"Who is that?" she asked, repressing a shiver.

Benyamin turned to face the balcony, a rueful smile on his face. "My wife."

"I didn't know you were married."

"I would have invited you to our wedding, but you weren't alive at the time," he teased.

The tune changed. The words were rife with sorrow and Benyamin's shoulders bunched. Zafira heard a rattling before he shook, and she realized he was crying.

She did not think vain safin could cry. It didn't seem right.

"Don't cry," she said quietly, and it sounded like a stupid thing to say, but she didn't know what else to do. "This is your dream, your memory. Your first dreamwalk in years."

"There's no greater curse than memory," he said finally. He closed his eyes and tried to recollect himself, the tattoo on his face mourning with him. "Tragedies happen once, memories relive them eternally. You understand that, don't you? You have floundered in loss."

She had. She didn't think she would ever stop seeing Baba's face. His last word before he lunged at her. His final breath gasping from his lungs as he looked at the woman who killed him—and smiled.

"We get to choose which memories to relive. You brought me here to Alderamin without the Arz. You chose to relive a memory without its tainted trees," she said. "Memories aren't always bad."

He shook his head. "My wife is the most beautiful safin Alderamin will ever behold, second only to one other." She almost laughed at his certainty, but he was wholly serious. "My son. Did you know that until him, I had never seen a coffin so small?"

Zafira froze.

"Safin are immortal, Huntress; we heal quickly and never fear old age.

We can die, of course, and though such a thing is rare, I have buried my fair share of safin—battle-hardened safin, fallen in war.

"But never a child—until my son. Whose hands were too small to carry a sword, whose teeth were too small to taste the sweetness of an apple. Whose laugh was the smallest I have witnessed, but the most bountiful sound—" Benyamin choked off.

She had seen small coffins in Demenhur. Umm would always say that no parent should have to bury their child.

"I'm sorry," she whispered, and it felt cruel, saying those words.

"I am, too," he murmured, because he understood.

The Baransea churned in the silence, and the gossamer curtains behind them billowed in the breeze. Birds called to the sun, and the din of the people below filled her lungs. Benyamin's wife continued to sing for her dead son. It was melancholy. It was sad, but also not.

Benyamin inhaled and turned away, though rivulets of pain still shone in his umber eyes. "You were never intended to make the journey to Sharr alone, Huntress. The Silver Witch guards her words for reasons you do not understand. We may not trust one another completely, but it is important we carry on as a zumra. It is important to remember that everything and everyone has the capacity for both evil and benevolence."

Zafira scoffed. "Don't tell me you believe the prince has the capacity for good."

He held her gaze. "Everyone has a turning point. A breaking point, too."

Those black scars flashed in Zafira's mind.

"You know him well," she said, softer this time.

"My knowledge comes from a mutual acquaintance."

Altair. She doubted there was anyone else so close to the prince. Not by the way they acted around each other.

"In that vein," Benyamin continued, "Alderamin is no better than the Sarasins in Sultan's Keep. Neither sends delegations or attempts alliances.

It isn't merely the Arz that keeps us apart. Alderamin views the rest of
Arawiya as a disease, so we've quarantined ourselves. Sarasin sees the world
through the eyes of a vulture, as a feast of land to be had."

"Ah, but vultures feast on the dead for a reason," Zafira pointed out with
a twist of her lips. "Sarasin has the greatest army in Arawiya. I wouldn't
call them vultures."

He nodded. "And now all of Sarasin's strength lies in the hands of the
sultan. A teetering shift in the balance of power."

Zafira studied him. "You know why this is happening. Why a supposedly
good sultan is now going mad, controlling a caliphate he shouldn't be able
to touch."

"Indeed. I also know the caliphate with the second-greatest army is
next on his list. Or was. I've been gone far too long to know," he said cal-
lously.

Demenhur. Zafira's pulse quickened. Yasmine, Lana, Umm, Misk. *Skies.
Bakdash*, even. She was struck again with that terrible feeling she'd had on
the witch's ship, when the Arz had erupted between her and Demenhur.
A wall keeping her out. A wall keeping them in.

A bird's cry broke the hushed churning of the waves.

Benyamin studied her, brown eyes softening. "It is futile to worry. A
shadow stirs, sinking its claws into every hold of power, one of which is
the sultan. The Jawarat is the only way to bring this madness to an end."

Futile to worry? She almost laughed. Or sobbed. She felt like the very
heart of her was being torn from her chest. She forced herself to breathe.

"What shadow? Is it the master of Sharr?" she asked, struggling against
her closing throat.

"The master of Sharr," Benyamin repeated in a murmur, as if speaking
aloud in even a dream would wake the monster he feared. "He is the reason
for the Silver Witch's obscurity. The reason I came to the island. The reason *you* came as well."

Zafira ran a shaky finger across the railing.

"We can strengthen our bodies and fortify our minds, but the heart is a monster of its own. The Silver Witch was free of ill intent, once. Pure of heart—"

Zafira snapped her eyes to his. *No one can be that pure.* The Silver Witch had been puzzled, then. As if the very idea of doing something for nothing was unseemly.

"What is it?" Benyamin asked, studying her.

She shook her head. "What happened to her?" she asked. "What happened to her pure heart?"

"The Lion of the Night happened," he said. "I always thought it strange he showed his hand so boldly when he had vied for the throne, all but allowing the Sisters to cut him down so effortlessly. But he did nothing without a plan—he *wanted* to be sent to Sharr, where he could rally the creatures of the island to his side. He was a maestro of words, and he preyed on the Silver Witch. He told her the Sisters stationed her on Sharr because they feared her immense power. He spun lies of love and loneliness, feeding on the insecurities she had not even revealed to herself.

"He wiled her into loving him. Into believing he reciprocated her love. Together, they drew the Sisters to Sharr and trapped them. Drained them of their magic. And by the time she realized her mistake—"

"Mistake?" Zafira scoffed. Any sympathy she held for the witch vanished. "She's just as monstrous as I thought."

Along with her anger, she felt a sense of relief, for she had always known that the Sisters hadn't stolen magic. Now she had confirmation—they had protected Arawiya with the final beats of their hearts, despite how the Caliph of Demenhur had twisted it.

Benyamin continued holding her gaze. "I was there when she returned from Sharr. She was not a monster."

"Does living past a century dull your head?" Zafira was beyond keeping her voice level now. "She's a witch. She's one of the Sisters of Old. If she can't fake a look of remorse, skies, then I don't know how she managed to keep an entire metropolis in order. If she escaped from Sharr all those years ago, then what has she been doing all this time? Sleeping?"

"Some secrets are not mine to give."

"And until I hear of these secrets or see the amends you think she seeks to make, I won't believe her."

"She sowed enough seeds to ensure I would know to follow you. To assist you. Sharr is a dangerous place for a mortal to venture alone."

"Are you trying to give me reasons to doubt you, too?"

He shook his head. "I want you to trust me. Allow me to assist you."

This was the trust Deen had spoken of. Had he known Zafira would face this choice?

She ran her gaze over the word curling around his eye. Truth. One of the two values he treasured most. He had given her enough of the truth to gain her trust, hadn't he? And she did trust him, she realized. Enough to turn her back on him without fear of a blade through her heart, a tremendous feat on a place like Sharr.

She supposed that would have to be enough.

CHAPTER 60

Z AFIRA THOUGHT OF THE DREAMWALK AS THEY CONTINUED
onward the next morning. She thought of Alderamin and quelled
the hope that rose when she pictured Demenhur the same way—
alive, free from the Arz and endless snow. Yet every step solidified another realization: finding magic meant losing herself. She would need to
bury a part of herself in Sharr before she left. *If* she left.

It wasn't as easy as Benyamin had put it. What purpose would she have,
if she was no longer the cloaked figure who fed her people the magic of
the Arz?

The more she thought about it, the further she unraveled.

The darkness no longer simply called to her; it had opened a void inside
her, gaping and hungry. Everywhere she glimpsed, she saw the kaftar's
roving eyes and the ifrit's fiery staves. The glimmer of a silver cloak and the
curve of a crimson smile. Zafira fought a shiver.

Is it wrong to seek redemption as any mortal might? The words could be taken a hundred ways. Everything the witch had said had been carefully worded, her emotions deliberately enacted.

Zafira did not trust her, she realized. But she did not distrust her.

"Are you all right?" Nasir asked.

He was likely concerned about his compass going astray. The hum she was beginning to associate with his presence started up again.

"I'm fine," she said as she tried to make sense of their route.

"You don't look fine."

She turned to him angrily. His dark hair had fallen over his forehead. A smear of blood stained his cheek. What did he know about how "fine" looked? About how *she* looked?

"Then stop looking," she snapped.

She had journeyed to Sharr with one purpose: to find the Jawarat. Now a thousand different paths had unfurled like intricately woven Pelusian rugs, and she wasn't certain what she was doing anymore.

The idiot prince didn't leave her side. Not even when she sidestepped a length of brushwood and changed direction. Still, she kept pace with him, because . . . because she didn't *want* him to leave her side.

"Will there ever come a time when you won't see me as a monster?" he asked suddenly.

She stopped at the softness of his tone, so unlike the unfeeling prince she had come to know. Some part of her wanted to reach for him, to smooth away the unhappiness creasing his face, to touch the scars that made him *him*.

"Monsters cannot become men," she whispered instead, and the darkness hummed its agreement.

He exhaled through parted lips, and his unhappiness only increased. "Of course. That was selfish of me."

That does not mean I cannot love a monster.

Where did that come from? *I can't very well say "like," can I? Doesn't have the same ring to it.*

Zafira closed her eyes and dipped so far into her thoughts that when he spoke again, she almost jumped.

"You feel it, don't you?" he asked.

He was standing so daama close, she could feel the heat of his body.

"The darkness. Luring."

She pursed her lips against her surprise. *He feels it, too?*

"My mother once said that just as our eyes tailor to the darkness, so do our souls."

This time, she couldn't hold back her surprise. He was the last person she expected such a thing from.

He read her face and looked away, and her eyes traced the knotted skin of his scar. She knew that tone. The way he said "mother." It was how she spoke of Baba. It was how they spoke of one who was but never again will be. His tone was rife with unspent love.

"You miss her," she said, feeling guilty for thinking he was incapable of the sentiment. Was his mother the reason for the ink on his arm?

He didn't answer, and she didn't think he would, until some moments later, when he spoke.

"Sometimes," he said quietly. "Most times."

She couldn't stop her smile.

His eyes dipped to her mouth, and the gray of his eyes turned liquid black. Like a fool, Zafira ran her tongue across her lips. Their gazes crashed, and she drew in a sharp breath, for there he was, a boy again, unmasked.

Still every bit a murderer as he always was. But. *But what?* Zafira didn't know, except that a "but" had begun to slip into every thought related to the Prince of Death.

She couldn't muster more than a whisper. "Who killed Deen?"

Nasir lifted his mask back into place. "A monster. For a monster will always be enslaved to a master."

CHAPTER 61

CONTROL WAS SLIPPING BETWEEN NASIR'S FINGERS LIKE THE sands of Sharr. He was aware he'd had very little control since arriving on Sharr, but it only worsened with each passing day.

He had come with a simple plan: kill the others, find the Hunter, retrieve the Jawarat, and return to Sultan's Keep. Now everything was in shambles, including himself. When she met his eyes and flashed her smile and spoke in her lilting accent, he wasn't heir of Arawiya, hashashin, and Prince of Death.

He was a boy.

"We'll stop here for the night," Benyamin said when they followed a trickle of a stream to a glade of dying palm trees. Here, the structure was still intact, the pointed archways like mouths waiting to devour them.

Altair frowned up at the starless sky. "Not that there's a difference between night and day anymore."

"Do you ever not provide your opinion?" Kifah asked, picking up a scorpion's molt and studying it.

Altair bowed. "I like to think I'm lightening the mood, shifting focus away from our impending dooms. You're welcome."

"I never thanked you."

"I know. I'm saving you the extra breath. You're welcome for that, too."

Dread had settled across Nasir's shoulders. If his calculations were correct, it was their tenth night on Sharr.

Which meant his time was up.

Altair made a face when Kifah returned from the shadows with hares in hand. "Once I'm out of Sharr, I will never eat hare again."

"Be thankful you've got hare to eat," the Huntress said as Altair crouched to skin and clean the animals.

"I'll catch you a fox next time. Just try chewing on that," Kifah said. She marinated the hares with her blend of spices before setting the meat on a makeshift pit. The fire crackled and the aroma of sizzling meat filled the air, permeating Nasir's senses. It smelled good, he supposed.

He didn't miss Altair deliberately pressing his leg against Kifah's when he stoked the fire, nor did he miss the surprised smile she sent his way, dark eyes soft. *Well, then.*

Beside them, the Huntress fashioned arrows from wood she had gathered, painstakingly stripping them down just so the shaft would gleam white.

"You really believe we'll go home," he heard Kifah say, ever optimistic.

"The first step to getting anywhere is believing you can," Benyamin said darkly.

Kifah was silent as she turned over the roasting hare in the spit.

Nasir wasn't so sure of that—he believed in very little, but he got around. Ignoring the way his mouth watered at the hare, he had begun sharpening his scimitar when a shadow fell over him. He raised an eyebrow at Altair.

"So. You and the Huntress?" asked Altair.

Nasir wanted to run him through with his blade. He growled, "What level of daft are you?"

"I wanted to remind you of what happened to the last woman you loved."

Nasir stilled, blade glinting in the firelight. "Which moment are you referring to? The time when she lost her tongue? Or when I learned it was all a lie?"

Altair's face stretched in a wolfish smile. "Both should suffice."

"You seem to have grown just as attached."

"This is about *you*. Before this game is finished, you will need to end lives, not grow attached to them."

Nasir rose, stone crumbling beneath his boots. He tolerated a great deal when it came to Altair, but interfering with his work wasn't one of them.

His voice dropped. "I don't need you to tell me what to do. Unlike you, I remember my place."

"You couldn't resist pulling that card, could you?" Altair asked, laughing softly. His face hardened into a cool mask before he bowed. "Forgive me, Sultani."

Altair returned to the others. An iris unfurled in his turban while Kifah looked on with a small smile. Oblivious, he murmured something in her ear and she barked a laugh before turning the meat again. Nasir pursed his lips.

Me and the Huntress.

——◆——

Here we go again, Nasir thought as he leaned against the tree.

"Murderers are murderers. I know what I saw that day," Kifah was saying, about an incident back in Pelusia's capital of Guljul. She glared at him, but Nasir kept his gaze pointedly elsewhere. "Hashashin or not."

"No hashashin will kill a man in his sleep," Benyamin insisted. "There's nothing more cowardly."

"How do you know it was a hashashin? Maybe it was a drunkard prancing around in that ridiculous garb. I wouldn't know the difference," Altair said.

The Huntress flitted her gaze to Nasir.

Benyamin sighed. "You're all being children—"

"Compared to you, my grandmother is a child," Kifah drawled.

Altair snorted water, choking until the Huntress thwacked him on the back.

"Enough," Benyamin said, smoothing out his bedroll. "Kifah, you're keeping watch."

"Your wish is my insomnia," the warrior said with a salute.

They took their time falling asleep. As if this were a trip of leisure, where they could rise when they desired and enjoy the world around them. But Nasir, unlike his father, was patient. Being a hashashin required it.

He waited until Kifah turned before he wove his way through the bedrolls, pausing longer than necessary in front of Altair. His eyes dropped to the general's neck again, the exposed skin calling to his practiced ease in swiping across flesh and tendons. Altair's every exhale beckoned.

But a hashashin never killed a prone figure. Even Benyamin knew that.

Nasir carefully stepped over him and tossed more wood into the fire, watching the light dance across the Huntress's pale features. The widow's peak of her dark hair dipped into her forehead like the head of an arrow. Her hair—still plaited and coiled—looked like a crown, and she a queen.

You will need to end lives. In his mind, he saw the slender column of her neck drenched in red as the light in her eyes dimmed to nothingness. He saw her skin ashen with death. His breath caught.

Her hand moved, closing around the ring at her chest, murmurs shaping her lips.

Kifah turned.

Nasir pursed his mouth and darted for the ruins, pockets leaden with misfortune.

He moved without a sound, the shadows setting his heart ablaze. It didn't take him long to find a vestibule away from the camp, secluded with a window facing the other side. He shoved a plank of wood aside and entered. His footsteps echoed, and something skittered away.

He wanted this to be quick, done before it began. But hope was for the desolate, so he cleared his mind and began his work. He gathered brushwood and scraps of wooden debris, piling them inside the shadows of the stone chamber. The cool breeze from the yawning window snatched his attempts to light the little hoard aflame. It wound its way around his neck, kissed his throat, and whispered in his ear.

Nasir swallowed, ears burning against the sensations, and tried again, exhaling only after the satisfying hiss of the fire inhaling its first breath broke the silence. The chamber was soon awash in a dance of orange and gold.

He pulled the cursed leather sleeve from his pocket. Inside were three strips of papyrus. Three, in case he lost one. In case he lost the second one, too, being the mutt that he was. Thoughts of his father stirred memories of his mother. Her dark hair, her quick laugh. Her razor smile when she bested him with her ebony scimitar in the training grounds. The words that calmed him, a balm in the dark when she worked Alderamin's quick-healing black resin into his burns.

No one truly treasured a mother's touch until they could no longer feel it. No one missed a mother's love until the well was depleted.

The flames mocked him.

He gritted his teeth and choked on his breath. This was the curse of memory. Of a wound ripped open. His eyes burned, and he knew they were rimmed in red.

The world wavered, and in the desolation of Sharr, Nasir Ghameq slowly came undone. He saw the hurt in the Huntress's eyes. Felt the anger burning in Altair's gaze. Heard the lash of Benyamin's words. Tasted the blood of the hundreds he had slain. Smelled the burning of his own flesh when the poker touched his skin.

Again and again and again.

He fell to his knees and grabbed fistfuls of sand. The grit bit his palms and the darkness amplified, nearly swallowing the flames whole. He had people to kill and a book to find and orders to follow. He had an endless life to continue.

He threw his head back and screamed a soundless scream to the sky. Only the stone ceiling stared back.

Like a tomb.

Dread spread through his limbs and numbed everything else. He climbed to his feet and gripped the wall with a steadying breath.

He pulled one strip from the leather sleeve and tossed it into the fire, ignoring the words inscribed in blood. The Silver Witch's blood, because only her blood rushed with magic, both vessel and wielder. The greedy fire crackled, devouring his gift.

Jaw clenched, Nasir murmured the words and took a step back, waiting for the Sultan of Arawiya to arrive.

The monster awaiting his master.

CHAPTER 62

ZAFIRA WOKE DRENCHED IN SWEAT. DESPITE HERSELF, SHE looked to the ledge where Nasir was resting, but the growling prince was nowhere to be seen.

The glint of metal caught her eye—Kifah, twirling one of her black lightning blades. The fire had dwindled to embers, and the camp glowed with the waning moon that peeked between the laced leaves.

She froze when the crackle and hiss of a new fire whispered in her ear. Then she was off without a second thought.

She slipped between the bedrolls and into the maze of stone, taking in the alleys of a run-down sooq as she stole past. She felt her way past the ruins, ancient stone crumbling at her touch as she followed the crackling of the other fire. She should have made sure Altair was asleep before she left. The last thing she needed was to cross paths with an undressed general. Again.

It didn't take long to spot the dark stone painted in the brilliance of firelight.

She recognized the unkempt hair, the still stance that barely concealed silent strength. Had she been anyone less attuned to the world and accustomed to silence, he would have noticed. Zafira did not doubt the stories of the hashashin prince.

She did not doubt her own stealth, either.

He was in a small chamber, barely as wide as a bedroll was long. She slipped beneath a pointed arch and through the length of a hall, stopping in the shadows of the crumbling threshold. He faced the fire stiff-backed, and that was how Zafira knew something was amiss. For even in battle, she knew, he was always relaxed.

The fire howled eerily. It grew, bursting and roaring toward the ceiling, unnaturally tall. Zafira swallowed.

The gigantic flames shimmered and hissed, shifting to the same shade of plum that permeated Demenhur's skies in the earliest hours of the day. She heard Nasir draw in a quick breath.

As a man rose from the fire.

Sweet snow below. What dark magic was this? The prince wasn't surprised in the slightest, which meant he was familiar with the occurrence. Zafira's eyes were wide, burning from refraining to blink. Though the man seemed to exist before her, she had the sense he wasn't really here.

Then where was he? *Who* was he?

He wore a turban, though his fiery form obscured the color of the cloth. He towered a full head over Nasir, and his thobe stretched across his broad shoulders. Power rippled from him.

"Well?" the man asked Nasir by way of greeting. The cool tone of his voice was almost like Nasir's. Zafira could barely make out the prince's features, but he seemed to have changed.

Weakened. Shrunk.

Her confusion amplified, and so did the fear ricocheting in her chest. She shivered, and if she hadn't been so focused on the scene before her, she would have heard the footsteps behind her. But when the barely perceptible crunch of sand sounded directly behind her, it was too late.

A hand clamped around her mouth. She struggled as silently as she could, trying to part her mouth and use her teeth.

"Shh," a voice whispered, warm breath on her ear. "I'm going to let go, and you're going to keep silent. Understood?"

Altair. Oh, this kept getting better and better. She nodded, and after a beat his hand fell away.

He stepped to her left, face grim.

"Ten days have passed," Nasir said to the fire, voice flat. Dead.

The fire figure shimmered. "Do you think me inane like you, boy? I know how long it's been."

Zafira flinched at the man's discourteous tone. "Discourteous" was describing it mildly. He had the same gray eyes as Nasir but an even colder version of them. The rest of the man's features looked vaguely familiar, too. *Is that . . . ?*

"Who is that?" she whispered, dread settling in her stomach.

Altair set his mouth at an angle. "Your king. The Sultan of Arawiya."

The man who had murdered Sarasin's caliph. The man who had sent two men after her. The man who made the Prince of Death, feared across Arawiya, cower before a fire.

Nasir cleared his throat. "You wanted me to summon you."

"I know what I told you to do."

With that, the sultan turned away, leaving Nasir clenching his fists and staring at the back of his father's head. His daama father.

"What is the sultan doing here?" Zafira asked slowly.

"Not here. He's in Sultan's Keep—Nasir summoned him using dum sihr," Altair said, frowning. "Likely with blood from the Silver Witch, because there's no other way to perform such a spell in Arawiya."

"He looks as grumpy as Nasir," she said, then nudged Altair forward with her shoulder, whispering, "Say hi."

He cut her a look of disgust. "This isn't funny."

She nearly laughed at the look on his face. "I didn't say it was. I'm so used to you cracking all the jokes. I missed them."

Zafira paused. Altair stilled. "Did you—" he started, just as she said, "Actually—"

Did I really just say I missed something about him? No, she told herself. She missed his easy banter, because she missed Yasmine's. She missed Yasmine, khalas.

"Why would Nasir summon him?" Zafira asked, breaking the uncomfortable silence. She refused to believe Nasir would do whatever the Sultan of Arawiya ordered. He was a prince. He was deadly. He was privileged. He—

"He follows orders."

"But *why*? Is he afraid of the sultan?" She recalled the scars on his back. The rows and rows of black. "He's afraid of being hurt."

Altair scoffed. "Nasir? He doesn't fear pain. Not anymore."

Not anymore.

The chamber brightened with a shift in the fire, and Nasir took a step back. Altair grabbed her hand and they froze, though they were safe in the shadows.

"Have you retrieved the book?" the sultan asked, turning to Nasir again.

"No." Even that simple word made him shrink further into himself.

"I should not have expected better."

Nasir flinched and Zafira bristled. What kind of father belittled his son with every breath?

"Have you disposed of the others?"

Disposed. As if they were trash in a bin. Nasir's pause was answer enough.

"You are failing, unsurprisingly. Altair?"

Another pause, and the sultan scoffed. Altair tightened his grip.

"I merely need more time," Nasir said in that dead voice of his.

It angered her. Why couldn't he stand up to the man?

"What of the Hunter?"

Nasir stiffened.

Zafira drew in a sharp breath, and Altair held her still, fingers pressing in silent admonishment.

"The Demenhune Hunter is a girl—a woman." There was a crack in Nasir's careful voice.

The sultan didn't react. "And?"

Silence. Zafira craned forward, desperate for Nasir's answer.

The sultan laughed, a mocking sound that boiled her blood. "So you thought to spare her. Did you think this was your chance for redemption? Silly boy, darkness is your destiny. You were born for hell."

Nasir's shoulders dipped, barely. If Zafira hadn't been so focused on him, she wouldn't have noticed. She doubted Nasir even noticed what he had done.

Skies.

The Prince of Death was trying to earn his father's approval.

"Kill them and bring me the book. Do not return until you do, or her tongue won't be all she loses."

Kill them. So that's what he was sent here to do. Her exhale shivered. Beside her, Altair muttered a curse.

She waited for Nasir to speak. To stand up against the man.

"Did you hear me?" the sultan asked.

Silence steeped between them, and she sensed the sultan's impatience. Every part of her awaited his answer. Awaited his protest—

"Yes, Sultani."

—which failed to arrive.

Zafira shook her head, his acceptance bombarding her calmness. *Laa, laa, laa.* She pulled free from Altair's grasp and took a step back without thinking.

Something snapped beneath her boots. The Nasir she knew came back to life, tossing something into the fire, ending it without a spark before he turned to the shadows.

To where she and Altair stood.

She drew a sharp breath.

Altair grabbed her hand and they were off. She didn't look back because she knew she wouldn't be able to see or hear the prince. Hashashins defied senses.

At the camp, Altair threw her a glare that said it was all her fault before he hastily settled into his bedroll and she into her makeshift bed, Kifah nowhere to be seen. Not two breaths later, Nasir crashed into the camp.

His face was flushed, hair standing on end. His mask was gone—in its place, despair and red-rimmed eyes. He scrambled among the bedrolls, and Zafira closed her eyes, slowed her breathing.

Or tried to. Failing, she held it instead, her wild heartbeat a drum in the night.

The prince didn't even pause on her.

———◄●►———

Nasir didn't bother with sleep. He climbed to the remnants of the minaret and sat upon the crumbling stone. Dunes disappeared into the dark horizon. He was angry with himself and the things he allowed himself to feel.

Kill. Kill. Kill. How had his father known of Benyamin and Kifah? The sultan had been uncertain during his briefing in Sultan's Keep.

A shadow fell over him as Benyamin sauntered into view, settling beside him with his legs crossed. One push and the immortal safi would career to his death.

Death. Did he think of nothing else? He almost laughed.

"Your father was meritorious, once," Benyamin said, but Nasir could only think of Benyamin's harsh words after the kaftar ambush, stripping him bare.

"He's my father. I know what he was and what he is," Nasir said wearily.

Now get out, he wanted to add, but he was tired of fighting. He was tired of everything.

"His love still lives," Benyamin insisted.

Any more and Nasir would give the safi the fatal push he was begging for. He kept his eyes on the deep sky and said, "And let me guess: you know what ails him."

"The very thing that sank its claws in Sharr. With each day that comes to pass, Ghameq loses more of himself to what festers within him. Before long, the Sultan of Arawiya will be a puppet to an ancient evil."

He was nearly there. There was no other reason for him to seize Sarasin. For him to gas Demenhur. Nasir just couldn't understand *what* this evil wanted.

"I'm not wrong, am I? You've seen it. Glimpses of the man he once was," Benyamin said.

Nasir saw it that day beside the gossamer curtains of his father's bed. His curiosity opened his mouth. "What is it? What grows in him?"

"The moon wanes, but the night waxes, steeped in a desperate black from which most of us will never emerge. I would tell you of what stirs in the shadows, but we need your strength."

Nasir met the safi's eyes, but Benyamin wasn't finished.

"For if he were to learn of it, not even the Prince of Death could summon the courage to go on."

CHAPTER 63

Z AFIRA WOKE EARLY. OR MERELY DECIDED TO RISE EARLY. SHE
had barely slept, tossing and turning, plagued by the image of a
haunted Nasir and the Sultan of Arawiya.

How long would it be before the prince succumbed to his father's
demands and ran her through with his glinting scimitar? Zafira had thought
he was changing, that he was becoming an . . . ally. Or something more.
But it was clear she was a means to an end.

She tugged on her chain, loosening its cutting hold on her neck, and
sat up.

The crown prince stood before her. Scimitar in hand.

She looked to his blade and then slowly latched her gaze on his with a
lift of her chin.

He breathed a soft laugh. "I knew it was you."

She didn't like when this Nasir arrived. The one who let his mask slip,
who could venture to laugh, to look at her with something other than that
stoic coolness. It made her uneasy. Uncertain.

It lit her aflame.

"Get it over with," she challenged before she could stop herself. But every part of her hoped there was another reason for him to be standing there.

He blinked. Looked to his scimitar. "I wasn't—I wasn't going to kill you," he said, then grimaced, scar undulating, as if he had swallowed something bitter when he said the word "kill."

"I was completing another drill." He twirled his scimitar, considering it before he frowned. "It helps me think."

Mimicking the act of killing helped him think. Zafira almost laughed.

The sleeves of his coat had been tugged up his forearms, lean muscles flexing with his movements. She glimpsed his tattoo, and when he saw that she did, he sheathed the scimitar and tugged his sleeves back down.

"It's only a matter of when you'll do as you promised," she said, her voice tremoring in anger. She wanted to add *like the coward that you are,* but he'd had enough insults from his father to last a lifetime.

She pitied him. The silence he kept. The power at his fingertips, useless because of his tether to the sultan. She did not think he had ever gone against his father.

"The longer you delay, the harder it will be," she said softly, surprising herself with how much she meant the words. He took a small step closer, and she wanted him to take another. And another. And another.

"In what way?" he breathed. As if, maybe, he was trying to make sense of this just as she was.

"I don't know."

Someone yawned, and she heard the rustle of clothes as someone else stretched. She heard the timbre of the sultan's voice again.

"You're *not* afraid of him," she realized aloud.

He stiffened.

"You're afraid of . . ." She paused, brow creased. "What did he mean when he said 'her tongue won't be all she loses'?"

He closed his eyes. Lines wrinkled his forehead, and she noticed that his beard had been trimmed. When did men have the time for such things?

"I am afraid," he said simply, avoiding her question, and when he opened his eyes, the Prince of Death had come, slashed with a scar, his irises dead ashes in a grim wind. "I am the coward you wanted to call me."

———◀ ◆ ▶———

They set off early to avoid the sun Benyamin did not think would arrive. The night he had warned of was settling in, the gloom deepening despite the morning hour.

Nasir blinked away the fatigue that had taken shelter behind his eyes. He thought to the night before, when two pairs of feet dashed across the stone. The lighter pair, he knew now, was the Huntress. The heavier pair could only have belonged to one man, and Nasir hoped Altair was pleased with all the belittling he'd heard.

The Huntress led them without a word, brushing the loose strands of her dark hair back with a sweep of her fingers. When she had risen that morning, her eyes twin scythes of blue lifting to his without fear or mask, Nasir had felt oddly, inexplicably saddened.

He was always sad, he knew. But there was a difference between a perpetual state of unhappiness and a sudden gust of it, leaving him cold and helpless. Floundering with no sight of an end.

His exhale was slow.

Altair had been right. Sometime between pledging to kill the Demenhune Hunter and now, Nasir had come to feel something for her. He had grown attached. Feelings had transpired without permission, conspired without his brain, working with what was left of his heart.

It really was only a matter of when. He couldn't go against his father, the notorious sultan of the entire kingdom.

But you are the Prince of Death.

Shut up, darkness, Nasir hissed in his head. The darkness chuckled, and Nasir paused, thinking through the idiocy of that before the Huntress collapsed.

She fell

to her

knees.

He felt the impact like a blow to his stomach. He pushed past Kifah and Altair and dropped down beside her. She trembled. Her head tilted to the skies.

She stilled when he neared.

"Is it the darkness?" he murmured before the others were within earshot.

Benyamin approached her next. "Are you well, Huntress?"

"What is——" Kifah began, before the Huntress silenced them all.

"Look around us," she said. Her voice was haunted. Raw.

Nasir's eyes roved the brushwood, the crumbling limestone, the dunes of sand. The same patch of saltbush blooming with the same white flowers he had seen yesterday.

"Kharra," Kifah murmured, dropping her spear.

"Do you think the Silver Witch considered what would happen when her compass failed?" The Huntress's voice was a knife. She rose, fury igniting her features. Fury directed at him. "You should have killed me." She was close enough to touch. To smooth, with his lips, the harsh lines of anger marring her skin.

The last thought seized him.

When had he ever wished to kiss anyone? Even Kulsum had been the one to kiss him first, to . . . *use* him. Tribulation weighed him down. It matched the look in the Huntress's eyes.

"What use am I now, Prince? All you have is a broken compass."

Use. The word cut deep.

Altair broke the silence first.

"You aren't broken." He rested a gentle hand on her shoulder.

But she wasn't looking at the general. She looked to Nasir, waiting to hear what he would say. He was skilled in many things, but not words. He couldn't speak as those shards of ice begged him to.

"This is your fault," Nasir said suddenly, eyes flicking to Benyamin. The safi jerked at the accusation. "If you hadn't told her what she was, this would not have happened."

Kifah seethed. "Of every self-centered thing you could say—"

"Laa, I think the prince is right," Altair interrupted. "You aren't broken, Zafira."

Nasir flinched at the sound of her name from Altair's mouth. He could scarcely refer to her by name in his head because he felt . . . he felt he did not deserve to.

"You've always followed the direction of your heart," Altair continued. "It was a subconscious effort you trusted without a doubt. But now that you know what you are, you've begun to use your head. That has led you astray."

"So now we're stranded?" Kifah asked. Her words were followed by another layer of black, bleeding into the sky.

Benyamin clenched his jaw as he studied the unfolding shadows. "The night stirs," he murmured.

Nasir did not know what to say to that.

There was something bittersweet about a day long awaited. She heard them speaking. But they were like voices singing a song, one she no longer heard.

She had reached the destination she always feared she would. And now that she was here, she felt it had been inevitable from the very beginning: She had always been on a steady journey toward finding herself lost.

It had only worsened the night before, when the Sultan of Arawiya had reminded Nasir of what he was sent to do. When Benyamin had reminded her she was a means to an end in the witch's game.

Unlike the darkness, which had only ever looked out for her. It was her constant. It cared.

Now it whispered a welcome once more. Perhaps being lost gave her a sense of freedom. Untethered her from her obligations.

For Zafira bint Iskandar embraced the darkness.

And the darkness embraced her back.

ACT III

THE LIES WE EAT

CHAPTER 64

Z AFIRA WAS ELSEWHERE, AND IT WASN'T THE SHARR SHE HAD come to know and dread.

The subdued light made her think of dark rooms and the rustle of clothes. Hushed whispers and stolen smiles. This place certainly was no desert. Or ruin. Or *outside*.

The ceiling arched high. Walls of dark wood and stone were cut in the most intricate trellises, so fine that they looked to have taken years to complete. A glow came from behind them, throwing a kaleidoscope of shadow and light across the copper ground. It was a place of extravagance.

A majlis sprawled to her right in rich hues, cushions a deep shade of purple. A darker corridor yawned to her left. Something stretched in its shadows, low whispers crawling from its depths. She averted her eyes with a shudder.

There were no windows allowing her to glimpse the outside and guess at where she was. There were, instead, swaths of art with bold strokes of color, everything abstract. She could sometimes make out words of Safaitic, but wasn't the point of abstract to make one see what they wanted?

"Peace unto you, Huntress."

The voice was smooth and rich. Velvet and dark. Hearing it was like returning to someone long lost. She had no fear in her heart, no worry in her chest. She felt . . . at ease. Zafira turned toward the owner of the voice.

The man stood in the shadows of the archway. He lifted his lips into a smile of welcome, cool eyes of dark amber assessing her as she assessed him. There was a scar across his temple, disappearing beneath his dark turban. He was young, but not dreadfully so, perhaps a little older than Nasir. His thobe, a mauve so deep it was nearly black, was fitted to his lean frame, silver buttons winking.

He was beautiful. A terrible sort of beautiful.

Zafira smiled back.

"Where am I?" she asked, glad her voice held no quiver.

"Home," he said in a way that insisted she should have known.

"And who are you?"

"The Shadow."

Wariness lifted its head. "That isn't a name."

"When you've lived a length of isolation as long as I have, the purpose of a name eludes you until the name itself disappears."

How long must one live before one ceased to remember their own name? Zafira thought of the Silver Witch. Both ancient and young at once. *Immortal.*

He stepped into the golden light, and Zafira's breath faltered at the sight of a bronze tattoo, curling around his left eye. *'Ilm.* She traced the letters with her gaze, piecing together the old Safaitic in her head. *Knowledge.*

Benyamin had—

The Shadow smiled again, and Zafira was struck with a catastrophe of emotions at once, forgetting what she had been thinking. The zumra was nowhere to be seen. She was in a dark place, alone with a man. Not with a boy who would fear repercussions, but a man whose smile was a wicked, knowing curl of his lips.

Perhaps she shouldn't have listened to Yasmine's tales, which made her overthink. The tales Yasmine swore would make her blush but instead only heated her blood, for Demenhune didn't blush.

The Shadow extended his arm toward the majlis, long fingers unfurling. "Sit."

She was painfully aware of him as she placed one foot before the other. Painfully aware of her uncleanliness in the face of this extravagance. At the edge of the rug, she slipped out of her boots and set her foot on the plush fabric. She sat on the cushion, tucking her feet beneath her thighs.

He sat across from her. There was an ornate dallah on the round cushion between them, steam rising from its crescent-shaped spout. Small, handleless cups were stacked beside it, and a bowl of pomegranate seeds glittered enticingly. The Shadow began to pour, darkness trickling into the cups. The mellowed scent of rich coffee, mixed with cardamom, cloves, saffron, and other spices, permeated the air.

If Zafira had thought being seated would calm her racing pulse, she was wrong.

"Where are we, truly?" she asked.

He nudged a cup toward her with the back of his hand. The steam that rose from the cup looked black.

"The strongest qahwa you will ever sip," he insisted in that dark voice.

Zafira lifted her eyebrows, barely, and a corner of his lips quirked upward.

"You are in my home."

She had yet to understand where the boundaries were with this strange man who had arrived from nowhere. But she was well acquainted with darkness. How different could a shadow be?

"On Sharr." He smiled. "But your friends—laa, exploiters—cannot find you."

"They aren't my exploiters." Her brow furrowed. *Nor are they friends.*

He tipped his head. "Are they not? Each one of them is the very definition of an exploiter: one who uses another to gain a selfish end."

That was how it had seemed. But somewhere between the first time she set eyes on Nasir and the moment she had gotten lost, leading the zumra astray, Zafira's feelings had altered, and she still hadn't sorted the disarray of her emotions.

She steered the conversation back to the Shadow's invisible house. "A tracker could find this place. It isn't exactly discreet."

He almost laughed. He set his cup on the ottoman and leaned back, lacing his fingers around his upright leg. One crepe-thin end of his black turban peeked out of the layered folds. It curved around his right ear. Such a tiny, mundane thing to capture her attention. She almost didn't notice the elongated points of his ears, marking him as immortal.

"Do you not trust me to care for you, azizi?" he asked in that voice of velvet.

She pressed her lips together at the nickname "my darling."

"You are not a captive. You may leave whensoever you desire."

"How can you speak of trust when I don't even know you?"

The Shadow's amber eyes turned liquid with hurt. He took another sip of his qahwa, and Zafira watched the shift of his throat and saw his tongue sweep his lips. Yasmine's stories returned to her head.

"Ana Zalaam. Ana Zill."

I am Darkness. I am Shadow.

She shivered. "I don't understand."

"You should not." The words were punctuated with barely concealed intensity.

Again, she was struck with that strange feeling of familiarity. As if she had known this strange, beautiful man all her life.

He spoke. "I was your succor in the Arz. Your soother on Sharr. The one who kept you company, always and always."

Zafira's pulse fluttered.

"The darkness," she said slowly, trying to comprehend. Piecing together the years of shadow and black and welcoming night. The voices. The shadows shifting in elation, kissing her, caressing her. The answer when she greeted the benighted trees, here on Sharr and at home in the Arz. "It was you."

How did the darkness that encompassed all become a man? Why was he on Sharr?

"You believe me to be wicked, azizi," he mused. "Darkness is the absence of light, the mere reason light exists. Without darkness, light would have no confines. Laa, it would be a curse." He straightened the cups and pressed a single pomegranate seed to his tongue. His fingers were long, aristocratic, but when she blinked, they looked almost clawed. "Everything that exists does so to repress its opposite."

She clamped her lips against a slew of thoughts. The Shadow studied her, seeing her conflict.

"I am as you see me now, and when the need arises, I am zalaam. I am zill."

A man who could shift into darkness. Wonderful.

He rose and extended his hand. His tattoo winked. She stared at his outstretched fingers and curled her tongue. If she refused, he might not speak so readily anymore. If she accepted, he could take advantage of her easy trust.

His hand held steady, even as she wavered.

She accepted.

He pulled her to her feet. Only, he didn't pull her upward. He pulled her *toward* him, and she threw out her hand to stop from toppling them both. He looked down at her fingers splayed across his chest, and Zafira froze at the wicked twist of his lips when he gripped her wrist.

"Why am I here?" she breathed, eyes wide.

"We have known each other a very long time, azizi." He spoke just as softly as before, and Zafira's pulse quickened. "I thought it was time we met."

He was too close. She was too close.

"Aren't you pleased to have met me?" he asked. His lips brushed her ear, and she nearly came undone.

She couldn't think straight. She knew she should pull her hand away, but the warmth of his skin through the linen of his thobe held her in place. Until another realization chilled her blood.

He had no heartbeat.

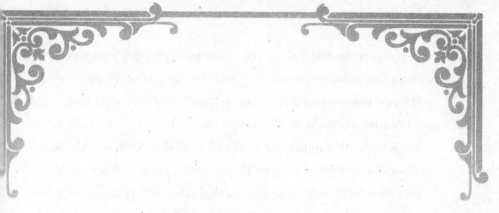

CHAPTER 65

S HE WAS GONE. *GONE.* NASIR TREKKED AHEAD BUT didn't see the flash of the Huntress's snowy skin or the glint of her ring. Not that he needed to.

He felt her absence in the depths of his bones.

When he returned to the others, he paused at the expression on their faces: expectancy. Nasir had never been the recipient of that before, and he shook his head, destroying their hope in breaths. *That's more like it.*

"She was right there," Kifah said, using the tip of her spear to shift the sands. "There isn't a trace."

The shadows deepened and sand spun. A storm was coming. Benyamin's dismay was wrought on his face. "We're too late. We're too late. She's—"

"Don't make me slap you, safi," Altair snapped, an edge to his voice.

Kifah climbed the outcropping to search.

Laughter rose in Nasir's throat. They were lost. They were without a compass to help them find their compass. *The compass.* He locked gazes with Altair's knowing look, and he wondered how long Altair had known that

WE HUNT THE FLAME

it had always pointed to the Huntress. Nasir pulled the disc from his pocket, loosing a breath when the whizzing settled on a point northeast.

"I know where to find her," he said, not bothering to explain. How could he explain what he didn't understand?

Kifah leaped down from the rock and studied his compass. She didn't question him. "There's a drop up ahead, though I can't tell how steep."

He nodded. He could leave them as they were. If they died, that would save Nasir from having to watch the life leave their now-familiar faces.

He slid his scimitar from its sheath and inhaled, briefly meeting Altair's eyes. Benyamin gave him a firm nod.

He had a Huntress to hunt.

CHAPTER 66

Zafira took her time lacing her boots, staring at the swoops on the elegant tiles as she tried to rein in her quick breathing. She straightened. He stood close. Very close.

"You are continuously searching for an escape, azizi."

She didn't deny it. "It won't be long before they find me. Exploiters don't let go of their assets so quickly."

"You mean your lover," he said softly, with a slight tilt of his head.

"My lover." The idea was so preposterous, she nearly laughed.

"The crown prince. After all, he is the only one capable of tracking well."

Zafira shrank back. "He is not my lover."

There was a cruel slant to the Shadow's mouth. "Oh, but he wishes he were. I've lost count of how many times he has imagined his hands trailing your thighs, his mouth against yours, his teeth at your lip—"

"Stop," she whispered as the words whittled at her core and lit her slowly aflame. There was only one explanation for how the Shadow had preyed on Nasir's thoughts: The prince was further into the clutches of darkness than she was.

"Such a naughty boy," the Shadow scolded with a *tsk*. But his amber eyes took in her every motion; he was as much a hunter as she was.

"That isn't love," she said.

"Indeed. There is a grand difference between love and a lover. I would say the latter is much more pleasurable. A pity you crave the former."

"Love is for children." *It preys on the weak, on the ones born with too much hope.*

His eyebrows drew together. "Is that so? Because I've made a few discoveries."

He lifted a hand and slowly began closing his splayed fingers. "To win the love of your father, you picked up a bow and carved yourself into the Huntress he wished you to become."

His voice of velvet dug beneath her skin.

"To win the love of your people, you braved the Arz. You fed them. You parted with those beautiful skins. You confined yourself to a life of mystery. Though you owed them nothing."

That wasn't the reason.

It wasn't.

No.

Could she have been so adamantly against love that she'd inadvertently become a slave to it?

"More recently, to win the love of your caliph, despite knowing your hand would not have been forced, despite knowing you could very well perish on this island, you joined this journey."

"I have never needed to win the love of anyone. Not my father when he lived, not my people, and never my caliph."

"Oh? Then why did you do what you did?"

The Shadow leaned against the dark wall and lifted one corner of his lips. His eyes were a touch. His smile was a whisper at her neck. She felt things she had never felt before, burning inside her.

"I would say, Huntress, that you very much believe in love. Your every action as you aged and matured came from the need to be seen. To be loved. You have always wanted it." He leaned so close that his next words brushed her lips. "You crave it."

She swayed back with a sharp inhale. Every nerve ending snapped to attention when his golden eyes dropped to her mouth.

"There is nothing wrong with love, azizi. Indeed, love is a strength, as much as a curse."

She had never craved love. If she had, she would have leaped into Deen's arms the moment he proposed. She hunted for her people because they would starve otherwise. She boarded that ship because they would die otherwise. She did everything with the knowledge that *she* could very well die.

Every musing of her mind unraveled, spun off course. He began leading her toward the dark corridor. The one the voices had been trying to crawl from.

She was still armed, she realized. Her jambiya at her hip, her bow at her back, arrows, too. But when she inhaled, the richness of the qahwa lathered her senses, and her mind turned sluggish.

The Shadow was not a threat.

He had shown her so much. He had helped her sort her life into what she had always wanted: love. He had brought her into his home and treated her like a guest.

He studied her with parted lips. "I have lost count of the years as I have lost the letters of my name. You may take much from a man, but you can never take away his desires, his passion, his revenge."

Zafira's heart stuttered at the word "revenge."

"As such, I am in need of a partner."

"A partner," she said, rolling the word as they neared the corridor. Something told her it was not a place for her.

"You search for the Jawarat," he said carefully. "I require it as well."

What had he called the others? Exploiters. He was one, too.

"Is that why you're on Sharr?"

His mouth slanted, and he seemed to be considering how much he should unveil. "Some would say so."

They paused beneath a pointed archway. The dark wood was cut in tumultuous patterns; the beauty of its intricacy grasped her breath.

"The Jawarat," he started once more.

Zafira almost bared her teeth. It was as if her very presence was now synonymous with the book she was coming to dread.

"I have come to learn that only you are able to find it."

"So I've learned as well."

The corners of his mouth twitched. "I'd like to propose a deal. I will assist you in your search, and when the Jawarat is uncovered, you will return it to me."

She met his eyes, wanting to demand if he was daft. "Which part of the deal is for me, then?"

If she hadn't been watching so closely, she wouldn't have noticed the barely perceptible lift of his dark eyebrows. Had he not considered that she would be adamant?

"I have need of it only for a moment. It will be entirely yours after that."

"I see," she said, not seeing. "I have an evil sultan who wants the Jawarat. And an entire kingdom whose people need the Jawarat. Now *you* need the Jawarat?"

The silence stretched thin until he released a weary sigh.

"If it weren't for me, azizi, you and your zumra would already have perished."

Zafira froze. At last, the tone she had always expected of darkness. Of zill and zalaam. Of a man who lived on Sharr with barely concealed malevolence. Chaos and madness in the hush of the night. Power that hummed in the silence.

He smiled that smile, one she now recognized as equal parts terrible and beautiful. She did not doubt his claim. She remembered the ifrit listening to a silent order. She remembered the shadows, shielding her, welcoming her.

Who *was* he?

At the entrance to the corridor, the Shadow paused. Only then did Zafira realize that her bow, her arrows, her jambiya—she still had them because they were pointless. Nothing could protect her from him.

He searched her face, but he did not find what he wanted.

His lips curled into that secret smile. He leaned close and brushed his lips at her brow. She shivered, barely holding herself back.

His voice was low. "Should your lover come, azizi, I will tear the flesh from his limbs. I will cut him to pieces and feed him to the flames."

Zafira could not breathe.

"Chain her up," he said to the shadows, and became one himself.

CHAPTER 67

NASIR WAS GETTING CLOSER. HE COULD FEEL IT.
At least, that was what he told himself to keep going. The shadows lengthened and shrank with his breathing. It was too early for night, but the starless sky was heavy with black.

And it was too late to turn back. Even if he could recall the way, the others would have moved. Only the Huntress could find them now.

Zafira.

Only Zafira could find them. He had to stop walking when he voiced her name in his head for the first time.

He continued on the erratic path his compass pointed out until he heard the unmistakable shift in the air, alerting him to another presence.

Nasir held still. His fingers melded to the leather hilt of his scimitar.

A silhouette stood against the outcrop.

He didn't need her to come into the light for him to recognize that swaying gait. The billowing of her dress. Her skin shone in the slender shafts of light, as beautiful as the deepest of sunsets.

"Kulsum," Nasir breathed.

She tipped her head. Nasir's brow furrowed and his pulse trembled a warning, but he lowered his blade. Sheathed it. It felt as if a storm had run rampant in his mind, scattering the dunes of his thoughts.

"My prince," she said in that voice of silk, the one that had freed him on countless nights.

Nasir was suddenly in a hundred places at once, none as terrifying as this simmering storm.

"The Huntress is not worth it."

Nasir spoke slowly. "I need her if I am to find the Jawarat."

"And when she finds it and attempts to take your life—what then?"

"She wouldn't." He did not doubt that.

A smile flitted across her face and something ached inside him. "She is no longer the guileless girl who set foot on this island." Kulsum gestured to the dunes. "Sharr changes people. Like you. You have begun to love her."

He closed his eyes but made no attempt to deny her words.

She continued, softer now. "Have you forgotten me?"

"No, Kulsum," he said. "I did not forget. I *never* forget."

He stepped closer, wanting to touch her. Hold her.

One last time.

"Even if I wanted to," he murmured, "I could never forget that you did not love me."

He stared at her beauty, into the dark chasms of her eyes. His last words were a rasp, because it was his fault.

"And that you have no tongue."

He leaped, toppling her to the ground, tearing a sound from her mouth. The ifrit that she was emerged, and he dipped his gauntlet blade into the creature's flesh. Safin steel, to ensure it would never rise again.

He had known it wasn't her the moment she spoke in a voice he would never again hear, but he had still wasted valuable time. Longing had made him selfishly draw out the conversation. Longing to understand, to finally close that open wound.

It was the first time an ifrit had shown him a face, but there was no time to ponder that. As he stood with a shaky exhale, something slick wrapped around his ankle and pulled him toward the steep drop, his shouts drowned out by the shadows.

CHAPTER 68

Z AFIRA CAME TO IN DARKNESS.

Her back was to a cool wall. Circlets of metal encased her wrists and chafed her bones. Her arms were stretched and pinned on either side of her. The same had been done to her legs: pinned too far apart for comfort. When she tried to roll her shoulders, she heard the protest of chains.

Pain reigned over her emotions. The angle of her arms pulled at her chest, her throat, her skin. The stretch of her legs wrenched at the insides of her thighs.

The familiar jab of her bow was gone, and the weight of her jambiya at her waist was a cruel joke when her hands had been rendered useless.

A stale breeze feathered her skin before the *scritch* of a match broke the silence. Zafira locked her gaze on the tiny flame as it moved, the tang of sulfur tainting the air.

A wary light allowed Zafira to drink in the rectangular room in which she hung. She was in the center of a longer side. Opposite her was a chair grand enough to be a throne, with gleaming black wood and adornments in tarnished silver. It was empty.

A rush of air, laa—her heart stuttered—*darkness* whispered past and gathered before her in a swirl of ink, transforming into a man before the throne. A king, crowned in shadows.

He sat, amber eyes appraising.

"Had a change of heart?" Zafira rasped. "Ya laa, I forgot you don't have one." The only creatures she knew of without heartbeats were ifrit. But ifrit needed to be commanded. They were not so sharp. So ancient.

"So bitter," the Shadow mused in a slow drawl.

She raised one eyebrow, proud of herself for not shrinking back from his assessing gaze. "I'm not in a position I'd consider sweet."

Amusement shifted his features. "Fair enough. Are you thirsty, azizi?"

A girl materialized to his right. She was the picture of Arawiyan beauty— dark skin, dark eyes, the soft curve of crimson lips. She wore robes of blue, an orange scarf around her slender neck. She gripped a misty pitcher of water in one hand and an empty glass in the other. Zafira failed to mask her surprise.

"Relax. She is ifrit," he soothed. "I couldn't stand them shifting their faces every few minutes, so I had them"—he looked to the girl—"alter their ways."

"What do you want with me?" Zafira croaked, drawing his attention away from the girl. Ifrit. Whatever she was.

"I told you what I wanted," he said, tilting his head.

"So you decided to chain me before I could accept your deal?" She hoped the others wouldn't come for her. She hoped Nasir wouldn't come.

"Oh, you already refused. Now you are in no position to negotiate."

He took the glass from the girl. "You were like this glass once—icy, empty, a vessel of eagerness waiting to be brimmed." He gestured for the girl to fill the glass. "Once I learned of what you are, I called to you from the Arz. Whispered to your father. I honed you into the bladed compass you became. I created something from nothing.

"But I am a patient man, and darkness is eternal. If you cannot do what

I ask, after all I have done for you, azizi," he paused and ran his tongue along his lips, "it is of no loss for me."

He dropped the glass.

Zafira flinched as it shattered, scattering shards and bolts of water across the copper ground.

Like the shards of her heart, dispersed into the shadows.

⊰●⊱

Later, much later, the Shadow returned. Zafira felt his fingers grasp her chin, gentle and cool, before she opened her eyes. Every part of her became aware of the five points of his fingers, and her traitorous pulse raced when he swept his thumb across the side of her jaw.

The strain from her arms and legs was blurring her mind. She would do anything for a moment's relief. She wanted the others to find her. *No.* She didn't want to watch them be skinned alive.

But they *couldn't* find her. Without her, they were blind folk in a cage of wolves.

"Let me go," she murmured.

"You've had the entire night to think. Will you bring me the Jawarat?" His voice was as gentle as his touch, and she wondered how someone so beautiful could be so cruel.

She almost said yes. "I will kill you."

His soft laugh was lazy. "Death is for fools, azizi. Darkness is indestructible, eternal, unconfined to human limitations. Your weapons cannot harm me."

To define is to limit.

"You've been planning this for years," she said as she realized it. "Ever since I returned from the Arz for the very first time."

For as long as the sultana had been dead. Before Baba had died. Before Umm went mad.

Who was this man?

"The Silver Witch," she rasped. How did she factor into all of this?

"A most beautiful woman, no?" he said, sinking into his chair. "She was adamant in her quest, but she was bereft of love, alone in her work. I placed my traps and spun my words, and soon enough, my patience was rewarded. The sultan of Arawiya, on the other hand, once he was gifted the medallion he adores more than his own son, the rest was quite simple."

Bereft of love. Realization pulsed in her blood.

She posed her next question. "Why—why do you need the Jawarat when you command an entire island?"

"Sharr burgeons out of control. Do you think I *desire* the Arz devouring Arawiya?" He slumped back in his chair. His tattoo shimmered.

He was lying. Sharr was land; it had no need to threaten them with an army of trees.

"I am not fool enough to desire destruction, azizi. I merely wish for order in all things, and great sacrifices must be made to achieve great feats."

"So you're just like any other criminal—you use dum sihr to get Sharr to do your bidding."

He tilted his head, and something flashed in the amber of his eyes. "Did you not read of me in your texts? Of the one who commands magic without the use of blood? Tether yourself to the vessel, and it is yours without the price. I grow tired of borrowing, of the limits of one affinity, even if I may touch upon others. Why remain the wielder when you can be the vessel?"

Did you not read of me in your texts? Of the man who lay control to magic as no other had. Of the man who surpassed dum sihr, almost as powerful as the Sisters themselves.

Zafira knew who the Shadow was.

She knew why he had no heartbeat, why the sharp points of safin ears crept above the folds of his turban. Half ifrit, half safin.

The Lion of the Night.

CHAPTER 69

EVENTUALLY, THE THING PULLING NASIR STOPPED, but he had lost track of everything: time, location, the Huntress. If he doubted it before, he was well and truly lost now.

The vine around his leg slithered back into the shadows. Laa—this was darkness absolute. Fear clouded his vision.

He stood, straightening his clothing. He tried not to think of the ifrit wearing Kulsum's face. He tried not to think of how Sharr was changing him. Weakening him.

She is no longer the guileless girl who set foot on this island.

"We feast upon lies when our hearts are ravenous."

Nasir stilled at the solemn voice. What level of monster could live in such benighted grounds?

"Those who have hearts, perhaps," he said, turning slowly. "Show yourself, creature."

"You fear me, Prince," the voice said again, edges steeped in amusement. It was decidedly feminine.

Nasir pulled back. "I fear nothing."

It laughed, a wheezing, dying sound.

"What are you?" he asked.

"One of many trapped on this island," the voice rasped. "Not all as wicked as you."

Nasir did not refute his wickedness.

He felt the slither of the thing that had wrapped around his ankle and realized there were more than one of them. Tentacles? Before he could demand again, there was a scuttle to his right, and the heave of stone made him turn.

The dust settled and gray light poured from the world outside. A palace sprawled before him, a massive creation of shadow and stone. Domes of black glittered beneath a shrouded moon.

"Shift the imbalance. Bring us light. Destroy us so we may rest in peace."

He stepped onto the stone pathway and slipped the compass back into his pocket. He turned back, slightly, and found he could now say a word more easily than before.

"Shukrun."

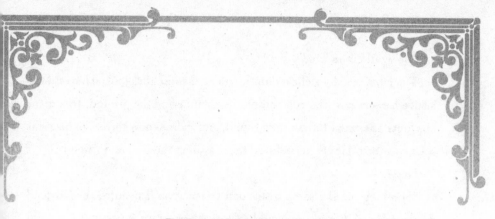

CHAPTER 70

"YOU'RE THE LION OF THE NIGHT," ZAFIRA BREATHED, HER will coming undone. She could no longer find the strength to hold herself and slumped, chains rattling.

He smiled, his amber eyes cool. The eyes of a lion, she realized.

This was the master Benyamin had been too cowardly to reveal. *This* was the creature to whom Sharr answered. *This* was the reason for the sultan's change. Why wasn't he dead?

Breathe. Assess.

If, by some miracle, she escaped the Shadow's—the *Lion's*—clutches, she had nowhere to go. If she found the Jawarat, he would take it from her. If she deliberately failed, he could send someone for her family.

If Zafira died, no one would miss her. No one would be able to find the Jawarat, either. Her death would be a sacrifice.

"You never could keep your thoughts to yourself." The Lion of the Night breathed a laugh. "Azizi, *I* would miss you."

She spat at his feet.

"*He* would miss you."

The latch of a door clicked in the silence, and Zafira looked beyond the lattice screen, past the rug and pillows blanketing the ground, to a man. His footsteps swept the copper ground, and Zafira knew the toe of his right sock was torn. He set his beloved tabar against the wall and smiled.

Deen.

"Showing me the same dead man twice? You'll need to try harder," Zafira drawled, hoping he wouldn't notice her erratic pulse.

"Zafira?"

That voice. Ifrit couldn't borrow voices.

She could feel the brush of the frigid Demenhur air, the steady comfort of her cloak, the warmth of his smile, the thrill of Yasmine's laugh. The sun in his curls and the reassurance of a pinkie around hers.

"Why can't you stay dead?" she whispered.

"I'm not deaf, you know," he—*it*—pointed out. Her resolve was being skinned from her body.

"You're not real, either."

She stared at the Lion, unable to muster the strength to look away as he read her face. As he saw how close she was to losing her sanity, despite her bold words.

"We will see how real he is."

———◆———

A wrought-iron door with a pointed arch marked the palace entrance. Nasir ducked behind the underbrush to the structure's side and scanned the area. Though he saw no guards, he heard the unmistakable sweep of sandals—patrols making the rounds.

On the base floor were several large windows, all latched. He lifted his gaze—*there*. A window was open on the second floor, another on the third, gossamer curtains of crimson rippling in the dry breeze.

He swept past the foliage and crossed the paved ground, pausing before the dark wall of the palace. The scent of bakhour carried on the slight breeze, heady and sensuous. He set his jaw and scanned the wall, eyes snagging on the stones that jutted and dipped, noting where his footing was likely to slip.

A scratch of sandals broke his thoughts as a guard turned the corner.

Alarm crossed the guard's eyes before Nasir slashed his gauntlet blade across his neck. He croaked and slumped to the ground, blackened blood oozing. Not a him. An *ifrit*.

Nasir hooked his arms beneath the ifrit's and began dragging the corpse to the underbrush, but a scream stopped him. Knifed his chest.

Her scream.

Kharra. Nasir left the body where it was—stealth be damned—and rushed to the wall. His foot slipped twice as he scaled the old stone. He barely breathed as he pulled himself to the window ledge and vaulted into the black hole of the second story. Fear prickled his insides.

A palatial rug sank beneath his boots, the air intoxicating with alluring oud, saffron, and sandalwood. *A bedroom.* Though he saw nothing, the combination made him think of the rustle of clothes and hushed murmurs. It heated his neck.

The Huntress—*Zafira*—screamed again.

He followed the sound of her whimpers through the room. Whatever was compelling her to make such a sound was no easy overpowerment, for she was not weak.

He eased the door open and entered a balcony overlooking a foyer void of life. A majlis sprawled in shades of crimson and violet. Two qahwa cups sat on its center ottoman, one littered with rinds, the other full and long since cooled.

The staircase leading from the balcony ended at the majlis, which was in direct view of a darkened corridor where the screams and whimpers crawled from. *That way's moot.* With a quick inhale, Nasir leaped off the balcony railing and landed in a crouch beside the corridor entrance, the impact a bolt of force against his jaw.

He paused before the shadowed entrance. His exhale quivered.

A cry spurred him forward, boxing him in, a slip of nightmares. His fear was instant. Hushed whispers bombarded his senses, and he gritted his teeth against their pleas. They were the very whispers he'd heard when he once touched the medallion around Ghameq's neck. The ones that called to him from the crevices of Sharr.

Rimaal. Were they connected?

He was going to meet the master of Sharr. The one Benyamin claimed controlled his father.

Nasir extended his gauntlet blade with a soft click. Perspiration dampened the back of his neck, his scalp, the facets of his resolve.

Silly boy, you fear the dark.

What do you fear? Kulsum had once asked him, days after his mother's death. He had no answer then. He didn't even fear his father, who had taken everything but the life Nasir never valued: his own.

He feared the dark, for he could not see. For here, the ever-alert hashashin was blind to his surroundings, and fear stifled his other senses in turn.

Her sobs and the wan light at the end of the hall drew him onward, until he stood at the entrance of a room shrouded by whispers and shadows.

He saw her first. *Zafira.*

Her long body was chained to the gray wall. She stared at an ifrit at her feet and yanked at her chains, pleading to stop. *Qif, qif, qif.*

His eyes locked on her face. Torn and helpless. He knew the weight of anguish that could drown a city in sand. He knew that look, that feeling. To watch a loved one suffer. To know one could have done so much but can now do nothing at all.

It was the feeling that made him stop feeling.

Every rational thought vanished. Rage rippled through him, pulsed at his fingers. Rage that she was suffering as he had. Rage that she was in pain.

"Leave her be," the Prince of Death said, a single level above a whisper, and the room froze.

She lifted her head, eyes darting in and out of focus. Gone was her iciness, her resolve. That wild gleam he had come to love. A sound—a shout—emanated from him and out of him at once.

His vision darkened as shadows swarmed around him.

Laa. As the shadows swarmed *from* him.

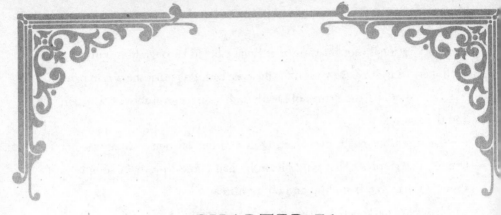

CHAPTER 71

A SLOW CLAP SHATTERED THE SILENCE.

Nasir choked a breath and the shadows receded, the world spinning back into focus.

"Ah, Prince. Fitting for the boy accustomed to the darkness, no?" the man before him said.

His face spoke of aristocratic beauty and youth, but his eyes were ancient—and oddly familiar.

Nasir did not understand a word he'd said.

"What have you done?" he rasped. He was on his knees like a common peasant.

"I've done nothing."

Nasir stared at his hands, at the wisps of black swirling out of and into his palms. Like the ones he knew existed around his benighted heart. Something rushed beneath his skin, surged through his veins. He quelled it.

He had been quelling it ever since he set foot on Sharr. He had just been too cowardly to admit it.

"Nasir!" Zafira shouted.

He lifted his head. Her first time addressing him by name and she wasn't even looking at him.

Shackles of steel clamped around his wrists. He was lifted as if he were no more than a sack. Something told him he should struggle. Fight. Try to break free. But the darkness, the shadows. The very thing he feared.

He

had

become it.

This was his affinity. The reason for his vision darkening every time he lost control of himself. He could wield the dark as if it belonged to him. His arms were wrenched upward. The click of a lock echoed in his ears, and then he was hanging on the wall beside her, shadows dripping from him.

Darkness is my destiny. His father was right.

It leaked like smoke from his fingers, from his lips when he exhaled, from *him.*

His eyes fell to the ifrit on the ground, stunned he could see a face, a form. Almost as if the creature were wholly human. It was the Demenhune. *Deen.* His torso was riddled with her white arrows, and black blood oozed from the wounds, the only sign he was an ifrit. Nasir knew blood and torture as well as his own name, but as Zafira pulled at her chains and begged them to stop, he felt a helplessness bordering on insanity.

"There's been a change of plan," the man said as he studied Nasir. He gestured to the bloodied ifrit. "Clean him up. I may still have need of him."

Against the backdrop of her screams and the creature's moans, two other ifrit pulled him—it—away.

"Fear becomes you, Prince," the man said.

Nasir stared numbly. He had failed. Failed like the mutt that he was. Failed like the brainless boy his father claimed him to be. His father, who might be controlled by the man before him but was right about many things.

Her dark crown was coming undone, a snake coiling around her. Her arms were chafed in red, and the ring swayed with her labored breathing.

"Huntress," he said, and something cracked in that pit where his heart should be. "It's not real."

She only wheezed. He made sense of the word she chanted over and over and over. *Deen. Deen. Deen.*

"Zafira," he said gently, unable to savor this moment of whispering her name aloud for the first time.

She stilled and looked at him. Twin scythes of weeping ice.

"It's not real," he repeated, the words faltering on his tongue. The spirals of black escaping him were very, very real.

"Who are you to claim what is real and what is not?" the man asked. Nasir dragged his gaze to him. He was cloaked in darkness. His very words dripped with it. Darkness incarnate. "When your own mother holds enough secrets to bring you to your knees?"

Nasir only understood half of what the man said. The other half was obscured by the black bleeding from him.

Some semblance of the Huntress returned when she groaned, "Stop with the riddles, Lion."

"For you, azizi," he simpered.

Nasir went very, very still. The man shifted his amber eyes to him.

He's alive. That was his first thought. *He's been alive all this time.* He remembered Benyamin's claim of a darkness festering in Ghameq, and Nasir understood the familiarity in those eyes.

He had looked into them every time he looked at his father.

No wonder Ghameq knew of Benyamin and Kifah.

"Bring me a knife," the Lion of the Night murmured. But when he studied Nasir's unflinching gaze, he smiled, and the shadows stirred in excitement. "Laa, bring me the poker. The Huntress must know I am not lax with my promises."

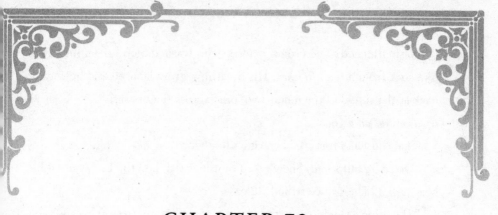

CHAPTER 72

A S MUCH AS SHE HAD WISHED HE WOULDN'T COME, ZAFIRA couldn't quell a small echo of elation when the prince arrived. She was a little less alone now, a little less lost. Even if he was strung up beside her. Exhaling shadows.

"Will you bring me the Jawarat, azizi?" the Lion asked her in his soft murmur.

She clenched her jaw, and he read her clearly enough.

An ifrit brought him the poker, the steel rod black and unassuming. The Lion gripped it in his palm and set his cool gaze on Nasir.

And Zafira watched as the aloof prince came undone. Fissures in his wide gray eyes, a tremor across his parted lips. The shadows wept from his form, and a sound tore from his mouth.

A cry.

A cry.

She didn't understand. Not even when the Lion pressed the poker into the fire and drawled a word. "Pathetic."

Nasir flinched. The crown prince, who washed blood from his hands like soot from a fire, *flinched*. His breathing grew labored and he shrank back at the sound of the metal swooping across the dry air.

The scars on his back.

That senseless torture. The ridiculing word.

"Don't," Zafira said. She choked on the word, and the Lion canted his head at her. The prince stilled. "Please."

"Touching," the Lion purred. "Did you expect me to stop because you were polite?"

She felt the heat of the poker as he drew close, Nasir's ragged breathing harsh in her ears. Her desperation burned, and she gave in. "I'll bring you the Jawarat."

Anything to make the prince stop shaking.

"Ah, but I would be loath to place my trust in a mortal. Let me propose something else: Until you bring me the Jawarat, I will keep him here. Continuing the rows of scars his father placed for him." He furrowed his brow, looking at the prince. "Or was it I who did that? Pity, I've lost track."

He was cruel. He was—

"Some villain you are, toying with the shackled," Zafira said, gritting her teeth.

The Lion laughed softly, raising a hand to trail down her cheek, searing her calm when he swept his thumb across her skin. Nasir watched, stiff beside her. "What a mouth you've developed, azizi. Let me teach you to tame it."

And then the Lion of the Night pulled aside the collar of Nasir's robes and pressed the poker to his skin.

◄●►

Nasir
fell apart
at the seams.

He gritted his teeth against a cry, the sound clambering up his throat from a time that existed years ago in a palace far beyond.

Shock became pain became anguish. Pain was nothing. A reaction to an incursion, an emotion instinct begged him to act upon.

But he was the Prince of Death.

Pain, for him, was always confined to the enclosures of his heart. In memory, and what each infliction uncovered. *Forty-eight times.*

Today marked forty-nine.

And then he could take it no more—he wept.

He clenched his teeth and bit his tongue until copper crimson spilled from his mouth, twining with the salt dripping from his chin and welling in his eyes. Melding into the darkness spilling from him.

As he remembered and remembered and remembered. *Forty-eight times.*

"Stop!" she cried out. Kulsum. His mother. The Huntress. *Zafira.*

Her chains rattled as she begged. But it was done, wasn't it? The poker was discarded, glowing in the firelight. Just as it had been discarded forty-eight times before.

Smoke rose from his skin, the stench of burnt flesh besieged him, reminding him. Fitting, since he had run out of room on his back.

Nasir slumped in his chains. Skeins of black bled from his form, as if he were fading into shadow himself.

The Lion only laughed. The Lion of the Night, who still lived.

Nasir fought to remain lucid. *Pain is nothing. Pain is a reaction.* He thought of the medallion around the sultan's neck. The Lion, staring back at him every time his father ridiculed him. Hurt him.

That poker had touched his back again and again and again. He had screamed, at first. He had bit his tongue until it bled, next. He would have taken each press until his body was covered in black, but his mother had interfered.

Only once, a black teardrop on the skin of her arm that Nasir would never forgive himself for.

His mother. Whose grief had overtaken her. Whose love had turned around and plunged a dagger through her beating heart.

And then Nasir had killed. Bloodied horizons across innocent throats. Final exhales that sighed across his knuckles as he tore his blade from left to right. Endless feathers tipped in red. A woman when she was nursing her child. A man as he was saddling his camel. Owais when he was scribing on papyrus. The Caliph of Sarasin when he was dining with his wazir.

Death upon death upon death.

The smile he had carefully folded into his memories rose behind his closed eyes. His father, before the Lion laid claim to his mind, body, and soul, making him a monster.

Making Nasir a monster.

The Lion *tsk*ed, studying him. "No one to protect you now, is there? Worry not, it's almost time for our family reunion."

Nasir's every heavy inhale shook, every exhale trembled. He could not turn his face to look at her. Zafira. To see her pity. *You are weak.*

His vision wavered as he stared back at the Lion with as much indifference as he could muster. He had the Lion to thank for the mask he donned. "My father has suffered enough in your hands."

"Ghameq?" the Lion mused. "Laa, laa. I was referring to your brother."

Nasir only gritted his teeth, tasting copper on his tongue. "I have no brother."

"I seem to recall you do."

He was tired of being toyed with. Tired of being the mouse between the lion's jaws.

"Eat your lies, Lion. Ghameq had only one son." Nasir knew this for a fact, as certain as the wisps of darkness that spun from his fingers. As certain as the burn beneath his collarbone.

He was darkness. He was adrift in the desert, lost to himself.

"Perhaps." The Lion tilted his head, enjoying this. "But your mother had two."

Three forms stepped from the corridor. Two ifrit, one man. Blood oozed from the man's lip. His muscled arms glistened with sweat, and his golden hair stood out like a blaze. Hair Nasir had never seen without a turban.

A turban that had obscured the elongated points of his ears.

He lifted a feeble smile, and Nasir's heart faltered once more.

"Peace unto you, little brother," said Altair.

CHAPTER 73

ZAFIRA KNEW THE PRINCE WAS A KILLER. A MURDERER. ARAWIYA'S greatest hashashin.

She did not know he could cry.

She wanted to tear the Lion apart with her bare hands, but all she could do was beg. Promise him the Jawarat. Curse the shackles holding her in place.

And then it was done. The lapels of Nasir's robes hung open, revealing his copper skin and a new scar across the expanse of his soul. Zafira stared at the wound, the blistering flesh. Her eyes burned with the wrath of a thousand storms.

Nasir lifted his head and spoke as he always did. But she saw the difference. In the crack of his voice, the tremble of his mouth, and the shatter of his gray gaze.

Altair looked from the Lion to the poker to Nasir's open collar. Cold rage crossed his features, and she saw Arawiya's prized general for the first time. Nasir's brother. She had never thought they could share blood.

The Lion regarded Altair with an expression she couldn't read. "Kill him."
Nasir's reaction was a wheeze. Zafira choked.

"Come now, Lion. We've only just met. Aren't you going to offer me
some torture, too?" Altair drawled, and Zafira wondered if this was how
he dealt with emotion. The ifrit near him actually paused, bewildered, and
the Lion gave a weary sigh.

Altair smiled. "I'm here for my damsel in distress. I'm not dying yet."

"I am not your damsel and I am not in distress," Zafira hissed.

She was surprised to feel a pang of emotion when he looked at her. She
had *missed* him.

"Who said *you're* my damsel?" he asked, tossing a wink at Nasir. Anger
still crooked his mouth.

The prince didn't react, but his eyes brightened and the corners of his
lips twitched.

"Even more of a clown in person," the Lion mused. "Yalla. Kill him."

If the Lion really wanted Altair dead, he needed only to flick his wrist.
Wrap him in shadows and suffocate him. Confusion riddled Zafira's aching
arms.

The two ifrit gripping Altair released him to draw swords. Altair threw
his arms behind him, and as he unsheathed his scimitars, the sound of steel
against steel was a song to her ears. The ifrit lunged.

Altair never faltered as he fought both ifrit at once, and Zafira wondered
who was the better fighter: Nasir or Altair. She wondered who had killed
Deen: Nasir or Altair. The general roared and an ifrit howled.

The Lion's fingers shifted at odd angles.

"Altair!" Nasir shouted hoarsely, coming alert when the Lion launched
a volley of darkness. No, *darts* of darkness, spiraled and sharp, smoke
trailing in their wake.

Altair ducked, and three of the shadow darts pinned an ifrit to the wall,
the others embedding around the dead creature with whizzes and thuds.
Altair fought the remaining ifrit, and even through her pain, Zafira could

tell he was purposely delaying the creature's death. The Lion made no move to attack again, still observing with a far-off look.

"He's stalling," Nasir murmured.

Two more figures darted through the dark corridor: Kifah and Benyamin, grim-faced and armed. Zafira sputtered a mix of a laugh and a cry.

Benyamin's immaculate keffiyah was wrapped as a turban on his head. He tossed a vial into the center of the room and the glass shattered, releasing a haze of green mist that triggered rounds of coughing. She heard the safi's voice, low and urgent, followed by the Lion's soft laugh. Zafira's vision blurred and her mind slowed.

The shackles holding her in place loosened. The prince's bare fingers brushed hers as he undid the chains at her wrists.

"How—"

"Hashashin. One chain or ten, we train for this specifically," he said quietly.

She felt his hands slide to her waist and she swallowed. The clash of Altair's scimitars, the whistle of Kifah's spear, the Lion's shouts—everything drowned away at his touch. His fingers trembled as he lifted her down. She felt the warmth of his skin, the pads of his thumbs below her stomach. The *thump, thump, thump* of her own chest. The drop of his eyes to the birthmark on her skin, and his anguish as he struggled against a wave of pain.

He crouched to remove the circlets from her ankles.

Everything rushed back.

"Yalla, Huntress!" Kifah shouted.

Zafira dragged her right leg toward her left, limbs stiff from the angle she had been stretched. A wave of dizziness rolled over her, and she gritted her teeth.

An ifrit approached from her left, and Nasir slashed his arm across the creature's neck, a line of black painting its throat before it fell. He slid the blade back into his gauntlet.

"Can you walk?" he asked her, not unkindly. He sounded distant.

She started to nod, started to follow, but stumbled instead. Nasir swerved to catch her, hands sliding up her arms, ragged breath at the curve of her ear. His face was close and her brain was a blur. She didn't know if it was the pain that caused her vision to darken.

Laa. The *room* was darkening, and Nasir glanced at his hands in alarm.

The Lion's eyes fell upon her, and she thought of the poker as a very different sort of darkness folded her into its embrace.

————◄●►————

Nasir had no black resin to heal him. He had no mother to tend to him. He was alone, but he finally understood why this curse of darkness was only now displaying itself. It had tried to, during the rare times when his control slipped, but it had never gone this far.

He had trekked across Sharr for days, and not once had his affinity slipped past his iron defenses.

Until her. This pale demon. She had done this to him.

She had cursed his life with her presence. She had whittled at his caged heart and made him remember what it was like to feel. It was how the ifrit knew to show him Kulsum. How these dark wisps knew to unveil themselves.

The darkness showed itself when he felt, perceived, listened to sentiment. Like now. Shouts clamored as everyone turned blind in the sudden black that *he* caused.

The familiar suffocating fear returned, pelting him as his vision and perception disappeared, because he could no longer see. Fitting that his power—*kharra, his power*—was associated with the thing he feared most.

She fell and Nasir caught her. Held her. Feared her. Wished like a fool.

And then—

In the absolute darkness, a veil lifted and Nasir, despite his pain, could finally see.

CHAPTER 74

WHEN ZAFIRA CAME TO, HER HEART SEIZED AT
once—the Lion, his dark corridor, the chains. The poker
touching the prince's skin. Panic clawed its way up her chest
until the familiar basalt scent of Sharr's sands calmed her.

She was free from the jaws of the Lion's den.

An outcrop of stone towered before her. A stream trickled to her left,
small plants dipping into its waters, and Sharr's dry breeze was a welcome
touch on her skin.

Her throat was parched, and when she sat up, every part of her ached.
A strap rested on her lap; only one of her satchels had made it out of the
Lion's lair.

The prince lounged in front of her, his back to the stone. His robes hung
open, tan skin shadowed by the dark layers, still held partially in place by
the wrap around his waist.

He was watching her, something distant in his gaze. Something broken.

"The Lion. The ifrit. Where are the others?" she asked carefully.

"Far enough that I don't have to carry you anymore." There was a crack in his voice. He didn't meet her eyes, and she had the acute sense that he was nervous. She studied the shell of his ear, the smooth curve of it marking him as human, despite his half-safin blood. "You're heavy."

Of all the things he could say. "Are you expecting an apology?" she asked.

His handed her his goatskin. Darkness swallowed the gray of his irises. "No."

She drank, swiped her sleeve across her mouth, and refilled the skin. When she turned back, he was staring at the flowing water. "I buried my mother by a stream. Or her coffin, at least. I never saw her dead body."

The sultana. He was the prince—he lived and breathed in a different world than she did. Extravagance at his every glance, people at his beck and call. Zafira had never wished for more than she had, but she wondered, now, how life was for someone like him.

He clenched his jaw and pulled back his shoulder, a tiny reaction to something that had to be very painful. How much pain did one have to endure before a burn became as bearable as a nicked thumb?

She could help him, she realized. She dug through her satchel, finding the tin of resin, running her finger over the lid as she watched him. She was nowhere near as skilled as Lana when it came to healing, but Umm had taught her enough.

He stared back without a word, the gray of his eyes fractured. If she could catch a wish-granting jinn, all three of her wishes would be spent in mending his heart, for not even Umm would know how to treat such sorrow.

"It needs to be treated," she said before she could stop herself, and pulled the tin out of her bag. He dropped his gaze to the silver can but didn't object.

She pulled out more from her kit—a clean cloth, liniments, a salve made of honey, a small canister of copper salts, and a vial of tannic acid.

Then she washed her hands and wiped them down before crawling toward him.

A vein flickered in his jaw as he watched, and her pulse raced.

"Does it hurt?" she asked softly.

"Not right now," he said truthfully.

He stilled when she neared. His exhale trembled when she lifted her leg to his other side, pinning him between her thighs. His hands twitched, as if he were holding himself back. *Skies.* She hadn't thought this through, or she would have waited for the others to come. And now her legs were threatening to give way beneath her and his mouth was so close, all she needed was to tip his head up and—

"Do I disgust you?"

The words were so soft, she wouldn't have heard them if she wasn't this close. She wouldn't have heard the strangled chaos beneath the simple question.

She pursed her lips and thought of her cloak. "I would be the last person to judge based on appearance."

His response was half of a broken laugh. "And character?"

It took her a moment to realize the Prince of Death had cracked some semblance of a joke, but there was too much in his steel eyes for it to be funny. Too many questions and too little distance between them.

She could feel the heat of his skin this close, and she blamed the quiver in her fingers upon the fatigue in her bones as she reached for the folds of his robes. She pulled the cloth aside, casting the wound in Sharr's wan light. Her knuckles swept his collarbone and she heard the hitch in his breath, felt the quicken of her own.

What was she doing so close? Sweet snow below, she should have asked him to lie down. Then she wouldn't have had to climb all over him. Yasmine waggled her eyebrows in her head.

"I wasn't going to come after you," he said as she soaked the cloth in cool water. "The last person I tried to save lasted two days before I buried her with my own hands. Before I learned killing was easier."

"But you did come," she said, wanting to ask *who*. She pressed the cloth to his skin. He flinched, and she gripped his shoulder to hold him in place.

Something had changed when he was shackled beside her. Something had broken after the poker touched his flesh and the shadows erupted from his fingertips. He wielded the darkness as if it were his.

"I didn't want to lose my compass."

There was something about his voice that stopped her from snarling. He stared at her, his eyes tracing her face with a look she couldn't decipher. She didn't realize she was starting to fold into herself until he spoke.

"I couldn't find your cloak," he said softly.

Her gaze crashed into his, expecting to find something mocking in the gray, for no one mourned the loss of fabric. But he was solemn.

"I don't need it anymore, I suppose," she conceded. It had been her companion as much as the darkness had. But she had wandered Sharr without her cloak, slowly becoming one from it. She picked up the honey salve.

"No, I suppose you don't," he agreed with something akin to a smile. She wanted to pause this moment and capture his smile, however faint.

She kept one hand on his shoulder and brought the other to his skin.

"Don't move," she whispered. He froze at her words, at her touch. He didn't even breathe, though she could feel his thunderous pulse beneath her fingers as she rubbed the ointment across the ruined flesh. The distance made her drunk and she swayed closer, pulling back with a clench of her jaw. *Distract yourself.* "My mother was a healer."

"Was?" he breathed. She tasted sukkary dates in his exhale.

"She's sick now," she said shortly with a sad laugh. "The irony is not lost on me. She and Deen's mother were two of the best healers in western Demenhur. Now one is dead; the other is very near it herself."

She swallowed the sudden swell in her throat. Blinked away the burn in her eyes.

"Who killed Deen?" she asked softly, and leaned back to look at him. She needed to know. To expose that wound to the air before it festered even further.

He drew a sharp breath, and a window closed behind his eyes. "Why do you keep asking that? It doesn't matter which of us killed him; the other had every intention to."

"If he were here now, would you kill him?"

A piece of her fractured when he lowered his head, a fraction that would have been insignificant on anyone else but was an earth-shattering display of defeat for him. For unlike that moment with the poker, he was now in full control of his emotions.

"A monster will always be enslaved to a master. Even if that master has a master of its own," he said.

"But a monster has *power*," she insisted. Anguish drew lines on his face. "The power to break free of his bonds. You are not your father, nor are you the Lion that took his soul. You are not the sum of his disparagement."

He stilled at her words, and all she wanted was for this broken boy to understand.

His slow, weighted words were a harsh whisper. "Then who am I?"

Zafira knew of his scars. His fear. He was just like anyone else: flesh that could be flayed. A human who could be punished and beaten. Used and discarded.

"Nasir bin Ghameq bin Talib min Sarasin," she said instead. "Crown prince to a kingdom begging for someone to stand up to a tyrannical ruler."

An empty laugh escaped him, and Zafira's heart cleaved in two.

A dark tendril unfurled from his fingers and he clenched his fist, killing the dark flame. "I stood up once."

Zafira didn't breathe. He watched her hands as she uncapped another tin.

"I refused to kill. My resistance lasted however long I could withstand the pain. You saw all of my disgusting scars. They're a tally of my kills—only I was tallied *before* each kill, with the poker, by my father's hand." He exhaled a heavy breath. "By the Lion's hand.

"But the destruction to my body was nothing"—his voice cracked. The Prince of Death's voice cracked and Zafira's eyes burned—"compared to what I felt when I saw my mother crying as she watched.

"She was the one who trained me, employing the kingdom's best hashashins. What was the point? Why does a prince need to be an assassin? Eventually, I could withstand the pain for as long as the sultan would press that poker to my flesh. As long as my body was being brutalized, someone did not have to die by my hand. But then he turned to my mother." His breath shook. That was why the pain meant so little to him—he had learned to ignore it. "I had to choose between watching her suffer or killing another innocent person. And by the time I decided I would stop fighting, that I would do as he asked, it was too late."

Kill or be killed.

A rim of red ringed his eyes. He looked at the streaks of shadow trailing up his fingers, blackening his skin, and then beyond her shoulder, to where the Lion's palace loomed. The master of Sharr, maestro of words. Alive for the past nine decades while the people of Arawiya believed him to be dead.

She smoothed the paste onto Nasir's skin, and he made a sound before he could stop himself.

"I should be relieved my father didn't become a monster of his own accord. But . . . the villainy that took him whittled away at me, too. There's no Lion controlling me. I became this."

"There's nothing wrong with being a poet of the kill," Zafira said softly, using his words. "Remain in the shadows and serve the light. Your father may never have control over his will again. *You* still do."

His only response was the twist of his lips, as if what he had already said was enough to suffice a lifetime.

She changed the subject. "The others—"

"Will join us here." He left no room for doubt.

He trusts Altair to stay alive. His brother. A safi who hid his identity. *For what?*

And why, when he had the chance to kill Altair, had the Lion held back?

"Why did you come to Sharr?"

She opened her mouth and he stopped her, a gleam in his eyes. "If you say 'honor,' I will draw my sword and you will fight me."

Her eyes widened and something raced beneath her skin. She was fully aware of the way she was pressed against him. The way the insides of her thighs held him in place. The way his eyes roved her, as heavy as a touch. "What's wrong with honor?"

"Nothing, except that an act done for honor is done for honor alone. Nothing else."

"I don't do what I do for anything else. What do you know of honor, anyway?"

The corners of his lips twitched upward. Almost sadly. "A true hashashin follows a creed. I'm nothing but a loyal lapdog. You, on the other hand, you may do what you do for the good of your people, but that's not the only reason, is it?"

Zafira bit down on her tongue. She thought of the Arz, the moments before her hunts. When she stood in the face of death and uncertainty and rushed into it. When the darkness beckoned.

"The first time I visited the Arz, it was because we were starving," she said. "I know I could have stolen a goat or lamb, but 'thief' doesn't have the same ring as 'hunter,' does it?"

He shook his head quickly when he realized she was waiting for a response.

"After that, I went because I couldn't stop. When you live a life of endless winter, where the snow drifts the same, where the trees stand the same, where your mother—where 'methodical' becomes a daama *disease*, you . . . gravitate. It gave me purpose. Because a life without purpose is no life at all."

"And?" he said, leaning closer. His legs shifted beneath her.

She shook her head, stopping him. Thinking of the Lion folding his fingers as he listed his proof. She couldn't be doing everything for the mere purpose of being loved. She couldn't.

"I've never seen a face more open," he said with a soft laugh before growing intent, stealing her breath. "You do it for them. For them to love you."

She opened her mouth to protest, but he cut her off.

"We're so quick to dismiss the sentiment as weak, but hearts *beat* for love, don't they? A life without purpose may be no life, but a life without love is nothing but an existence."

She rubbed the backs of her knuckles across the ache in her chest. Something loosened, helping her breathe. He was right. The Lion was right, too. Nasir held her gaze, a strange look on his face.

Almost as if he had come to the same realization as she.

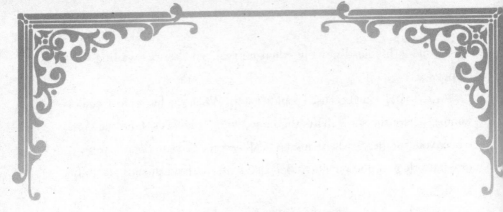

CHAPTER 75

*Z*AFIRA SMOOTHED THE RESIN OVER HIS WOUND. IT WAS NOWHERE near as potent as the black resin of Alderamin, but it would heal in its own time, without turning the skin black.

He must have sensed she was finished, because he grew still. "Huntress."

"Back to titles, Prince?" Her whisper shook.

His voice was soft. "What are titles if not names, *Zafira?*"

Sweet snow, the sound of her name from his mouth. Something wicked darkened his irises, and it was so unlike the growling, grumpy, sad prince Zafira had come to know that her heart very nearly stopped.

He made a sound and lifted his palms to her thighs, and she couldn't stop her gasp. She felt the heat of his hands so acutely that she nearly swayed. She drew her lower lip into her mouth, and something flickered in his hooded eyes as they swept her face.

"Fair gazelle," he whispered. His touch seared her, and she relished the delicious chafe of her legs against his as she slid closer.

The imposing outcrop held its breath, the *hush hush* of the stream the only sound. She looked at him, oh so close. Near enough to touch. To run her finger down his scar, across the bow of his lips.

He swallowed. Looked away. His body thrummed beneath hers. His throat undulated, and she wondered how it would feel to press her lips to that pulse at his neck. Her heart pounded as fiercely as if she were running for her life. As if part of her wanted to get as far away as possible, while the other wanted him closer, *closer*.

Skies.

He clenched his jaw with a look of anguish and murmured something that sounded like *that wretched splotch* before lowering his head to her right collarbone, the one marred by her birthmark. His temple brushed the crook of her shoulder. The hiss of his breath branded her neck.

She felt the feather of his lips on her skin.

His breath rasped. Hers echoed.

She was the reason the stoic prince could hardly breathe. She was the reason his gray eyes glowed liquid black. Her chest crackled with embers when he lifted his tilted head and she leaned closer, sliding her palms beneath his parted robe and—

Someone cleared their throat.

Nasir pulled back with a growl, tearing his hands from her legs, and disappointment pinched Zafira's skin. *Deen, Deen, Deen*, pulsed a reminder, but the rest of her was scorched by the fire in her belly.

The others had returned.

"Thank you, dear Huntress, for ensuring my prince was well cared for," Altair wheezed.

He leaned against the outcrop and mopped sweat from his brow. There was a bloody gash on his forehead and a limp to his step as he tossed Zafira's bow and quiver to her. His elongated ears stood out like a blossom in snow, and Zafira was struck with just how little she knew of him.

She moved away and tucked the salves, tins, and kit back into her satchel, trying to stop the quiver in her hands. Her neck was aflame as she rose to her feet, Nasir doing the same before closing his robes.

"Perhaps a little *too* well cared for?" Kifah asked, holding her right arm gingerly. She gripped her spear in the other, fierce as always.

Benyamin had merely lost his perfection: turban a mess, clothes rumpled, face smudged in soot—which for vain safin, Zafira supposed, was akin to losing an eye.

"We seem to have arrived at a most inopportune time," Benyamin mused, and the sound of his voice made something in her snap.

She pushed past Nasir and grabbed the safi's thobe, shoving him against the outcrop with a force that jarred her own teeth. She felt a flicker of remorse at his bewilderment, but she squashed it down at the sight of his tattoo. Almost identical to the Lion's in style, except for the word itself.

"Trust, trust, trust," she snarled. "So much spiel about trust, and you couldn't tell us the daama Lion of the Night was alive? That he, of all creatures, was part of your circle of friends?"

"Is that you talking, Huntress? Or the darkness?" he murmured, feline eyes assessing.

"I ran away from the darkness. Did you not see?"

"No one can escape zill and zalaam," he said softly. "Least of all the ones he loves."

"But she's right, safi," Kifah interrupted, oddly calm. "You had more than one opportunity to tell us. Why didn't you?"

Altair grasped Zafira's shoulders and pulled her back. "I'm sure he has a sound reason."

"Just as you have a reason for hiding the fact that you're safin?" Zafira snapped, rounding on him.

"What I am has no relevance to this quest." There was an edge to Altair's voice. Nasir watched him closely. "What I am has never had any relevance."

Kifah steered them back to Benyamin. "Well?"

Altair angrily dabbed at his bleeding lip, strangely bitter.

Benyamin straightened his turban and released a shaky exhale. He clenched his jaw, and Zafira saw a waver in his pride before he collected himself. "It is not only my people's cruelty that must be blamed for the Lion's dark rise, but my own kindness, too. After he was shunned, ridiculed, and treated like filth, I brought him into my fold. I had sway. There were no caliphs and caliphas at the time, but my family's eminence existed then, too. I gave the Lion a place in my circle of friends, taught him Safaitic, gave him access to texts few else had. Knowledge. There is nothing he loves more.

"My kindness arrived too late, for the damage was already done. Once he received what he required of me, he left, leaving two of my closest companions dead."

Guilt swirled in his umber gaze. This was why Benyamin was here. He, too, wanted to rectify a wrong. But Zafira couldn't bring herself to sympathize—even if she understood, now, why he had been unwilling to trust them. His reluctance was what had led them here, to this moment in time when everything seemed to be falling apart.

"Had you known your foe was the Lion of the Night, where would you have summoned the courage to go on?"

Kifah's look of disgust mimicked how Zafira felt. She jabbed her spear into the sand. "Did you really have so little faith in us, Benyamin? You're no better than he is."

Benyamin looked away.

Altair drew his scimitars with a sigh. "There are better uses for our energy than fighting amongst ourselves. We need to rest and decide on our next course of action. We know the Lion won't kill the Huntress, but he won't be so discreet in his intent anymore."

After Kifah murmured her agreement, Nasir led them to a gathering of trees farther ahead, where the stream continued. Altair brushed past him. Neither Sarasin acknowledged their newfound relationship. Zafira couldn't blame them—*she* certainly didn't want to acknowledge the way her blood raced beneath the prince's touch. *He's a prince*, she reminded herself. *You're nothing but a peasant with a bow.*

The trees cast eerie shadows, and Zafira glimpsed amber eyes in every slant of the golden sunset. She still had no sense of direction, she realized. Her trip to the Lion's lair had shaken her as much as Nasir's lips at her collarbone, and the compass of her heart whizzed without end.

Benyamin was right. Her courage waned with the dim sunlight. If not even the Silver Witch could be free of the Lion, what chance did the zumra have in stopping him?

CHAPTER 76

NASIR WAS IN NO MOOD FOR RESTING, AND IT SEEMED no one else was, either. How could he, when he still felt the weight of her limbs and the buzz of her skin? The featherlight brush of her hair. It felt as though every emotion he had ever quelled over the years had decided now was the time to explode. Or implode.

First it was the black that bled from his fingers. Then the Lion of the Night. The poker. Altair.

And then it was her. That pale demon. His fair gazelle. *His?*

"You knew."

The venom was so unlike Altair, Nasir looked at the general sharply.

"It was not my secret to tell," Benyamin said carefully.

"Ah, yes," Altair spat. "We certainly had a heart-to-heart before you arrived, safi."

They stared at each other, Altair exhaling in angry huffs before he softened at the remorse on Benyamin's face. Nasir did not understand a word they shared, but he was too tired to ask. He'd had enough revelations for one day—rimaal, enough for a lifetime.

When silence fell, he looked up again. Benyamin stared into the trees in contrition. Kifah massaged a balm onto her arm, foot tapping a beat against the stone. Zafira had folded into herself, knees to her chest, and all he could think of was her touch as she tended to his burn.

This was the zumra. The zumra he belonged to.

He was no longer here to kill the Huntress and take back that old tome. He was here to help her and the others. It was no longer about the book and magic—they needed to vanquish those amber eyes for good.

Free magic. Free Arawiya. Free his father.

A pained hiss broke him out of his thoughts. He turned to see Altair had rolled up the fabric of his pant leg, blood streaking his shin from a wound inflicted by the Lion's ifrit. The general was struggling for his bag, opening his goatskin with bloody fingers.

His elongated ears stood foreign against his dark hair.

Nasir drew in a breath and cautiously made his way closer. He clenched his jaw and crouched beside Altair, the black of his coat settling behind him.

A monster couldn't be free of his master if he never tried.

Altair choked and coughed at the same time. "I'm shocked, princeling."

Nasir was, too.

"I was about to ask the Huntress for help. She seems to know her stuff." Altair waggled his eyebrows, anger forgotten. Nasir glared and wordlessly took the goatskin from his bloody hands to refill by the stream.

Altair gritted his teeth as Nasir cleaned the wound and carefully wound the bandage around his leg, reciting three words to himself over and over again: *He's my brother.*

Altair tilted his head as he regarded him, and it was the most insulting thing the man had ever done: dismantling the apathetic mask Nasir had taken years to perfect.

"You're my brother," Nasir said suddenly, and as Benyamin shifted his focus to them, he realized he was beyond phrasing his questions as assertions. "All this time and you didn't think to say anything?"

"Half brother," Altair said with a groan. "So half the time, I *did* think of saying something. The other half"—he seemed to ponder his next words—"I very much wanted to kill you. You *are* the reason our mother is gone."

The words were a knife to Nasir's stomach. A noose of letters around his throat. His pulse fluttered when a wisp of black unfurled from his fingers, and he bit his tongue, reining it in. Every day he breathed was a reminder of his mother's death, but hearing the words from Altair was different. Worse.

He recalled Altair's hands around his neck after Deen had died. "You had your chance to kill me."

"I made an oath, or I would have killed you years ago," Altair murmured, and Nasir did not doubt it.

"An oath," Nasir repeated. He tightened the bandage, and Altair hissed again.

"Allegiance is my undoing, it seems. If Ghameq could keep an oath to her, I figured I could, too. He was a good man. Treated me like his own and never went back on his promise. Not once was I harmed. Until he sent me here with his son, who had orders to kill me. That, princeling, was the moment I knew Ghameq no longer lived inside the body of Arawiya's sultan."

Until the Lion. But Ghameq *did* live. Nasir had seen hints of the man he once was, even if fewer and fewer as the days progressed. When he had mentioned the sultana that day. When the palace cook made her favorite mahshi with an extra squeeze of lemon over the stuffed squash, just as she liked it. "What of your own fathe—"

"You're my brother," Altair said calmly, flexing his leg, "not my secret diary."

Kifah looked between them, spear in hand. "I'm going to find us something to eat."

WE HUNT THE FLAME

Altair nodded at Nasir's wound when she left. His voice was kinder than Nasir had ever heard. "Does it hurt?"

"Any more than the rest of them? No," Nasir said, looking away. His gaze strayed to Zafira, lost in thought, ring clutched in her fist. "Do I need your secret diary to learn why you killed the Demenhune?"

Altair clenched his jaw and looked away.

"You didn't mean to kill him, did you?" Nasir cast him a pitying look. Altair remained silent, and Nasir scoffed softly. "You weren't even trying to kill Zafira."

Altair's lips twitched at the sound of Nasir saying her name before they dipped into a frown, his eyes downcast. "There was a second ifrit that day, during our little skirmish. The one you killed to save me? It had been trailing us since we set foot on Sharr. The second one was trailing the Demenhune. It was . . . near her then, when I shot that arrow."

Nasir never thought a ruthless general could be so pained over a single death.

"Then Deen leaped," Altair continued, "and it was too late. He was a friend. His brother-in-law was, too."

"So you decided *that* was the right moment to attack the ifrit?" Benyamin asked, finally asserting himself.

Altair slanted his mouth. "I was hoping to save them both. Kill two birds with one stone—get rid of the ifrit and, in the process, create enough chaos so that both of the Demenhune could escape, saving *you*, little brother, from another deathmark on your soul." His tone softened. "Instead, I killed one and broke the other."

A sob followed his words, and Nasir looked up sharply.

Zafira. He would have slain a thousand men to remove the raw anguish weeping in her eyes.

"He died because you can't command an arrow," she whispered to Altair. "Because you—" She bit her knuckles against another sob. "He died because of an *accident*."

Her labored breathing was a boulder on Nasir's shoulders. Altair couldn't hide his own shattered face.

"If I could go back and put myself in his place, Huntress, I would," Altair said finally. "If I could sell my arm to make him breathe again, I would. He did not deserve such a death."

Nasir waited for her response. For her angry lash. The bite of her words. Anything beyond silence and the burn in her eyes as she looked between them.

She only turned away.

———◀◆▶———

She needed time, Benyamin had said, and neither Nasir nor Altair went close. Selfish as he was, Nasir wondered what Deen had done to be loved so much.

Kifah returned and Altair, despite his wounded leg, leaped to help, grateful when the Pelusian didn't ask what had transpired in her absence. Benyamin retreated into his book, guilt weighing his features.

Nasir strayed to the stream, climbing the stones that overlooked Sharr's ruins. He kept his gaze pointedly away from the Lion's den far to their right. Everywhere he looked, the dunes glittered beneath the blanket of darkness, shrouding them, pressing closer and closer.

He could see, now, as clear as day. His affinity was very much like the Lion's, he realized. Maybe even the same. He was one with the shadows, like the wisps that curled from his fingers.

At once, he knew he wasn't alone.

A flash of silver caught his eye and he leaped from the stone and drew his scimitar, the outcropping cutting him off from the others.

The Silver Witch.

The only living Sister of Old, warden of Sharr. Her bone-white hair gleamed in the darkness, and he felt the weight of her compass in his pocket.

"Your blades can't hurt me," she said. She sounded tired, almost sad.

"Run away, witch," he said, unafraid. "Or was that another lie and Sharr won't drain you of your magic?"

"It is the truth—it drains me now. I only want to speak."

"About what? About how much you enjoyed watching my father disappear into himself every day you roamed the palace halls?" He stopped and reined in his anger. What had she come to speak of, knowing full well the risks?

"About you," she said, and she seemed to be struggling for words.

An act. It has to be.

"This is not the time nor place, but Arawiya worsens and I may never again have the chance."

"For what?" He did not sheathe his sword. He might be powerless against her, but with a blade, he had some semblance of control.

She dropped her gaze to the dark water. "Did you bury the sultana by a stream that night?"

Nasir narrowed his eyes. "That's an odd thing to bring up."

"I'm merely curious," she said, a hint of remorse simmering her tone. "I wanted to know who you buried and who you mourned, given that your mother is still very much alive."

"My mother was the Sultana of Arawiya. If she were alive, you would know it."

"I do know it, Nasir," she said.

He paused at the way she said his name. It reminded him of another time, another place.

"I know how the people bowed to her, not out of fear but out of respect. How her son smiled at her, not out of duty but out of love. I remember the way he fit into the crook of her arm as a babe, and the ferocity of his eyes when he bested her on the training grounds. I remember the way he mourned me, as no son should have to mourn his mother."

She wavered before him like a mirage. There was a clawing in his throat that he thought he had long ago trounced.

"I remember everything and more. Because *I* am the Sultana of Arawiya. Warden of Sharr. Sister of Old. But before all else, hayati, I am your mother."

CHAPTER 77

BEFORE THE FLICKER OF THE FIRE, KIFAH'S DARK skin glowed as she gave Zafira a share of the roasted meat. Nasir was nowhere to be seen. Benyamin had drifted off to sleep. He had been a ghost of himself ever since she had put him on the spot. She didn't know how to make amends. She was too tired to even think.

Altair was in a similar state, eating in silence, glancing furtively at her every so often. The camp was despondent without his quips. She believed him, but she couldn't bring herself to speak to him. Nothing he said would ever bring Deen back. Nothing anyone said or did would bring him back.

But she didn't want to lose another friend.

Kifah settled down beside her. The cuff on her arm winked.

"Are you all right?"

Zafira had many, many words to say to that but settled with "I am."

"He said he'd wait for us in the pockets of zill and zalaam. Everywhere I look, I see him," Kifah said, and nudged her shoulder. "Not that he's hard on the eyes."

Zafira gave her a shadow of a smile. It sounded like something Yasmine would say. Yasmine felt everything so fiercely, she would have swooned at his feet. Just as she would cry when she heard of Deen's death. Unlike Zafira, who had merely blinked when he had bled to death at her feet.

Kifah was watching, and Zafira wondered if she could read her face as the others could. "I'm glad you're finally free of that cloak. I've heard of your caliph's bias, and it's about bleeding time someone showed that old fool what a woman can do."

This time, Zafira's smile was real. "If I get off this island, I intend to do just that."

"You will, Huntress," Kifah said, sinking her teeth into her food. "You will."

"I thought you weren't one for optimism."

Kifah grinned. "I pick my battles."

The whisper of a sound curled Zafira's toes, and her mind blanked. She was in that corridor again, with those crawling, weeping shadows. The lilt of a voice crept through the dry trees. Laa. Not one voice—*many*. The air stilled and the shadows held their breath.

She latched her fingers around Kifah's arm. "Do you hear that?"

"The sound of my own breathing? Yes," Kifah said, giving her an odd look before gently pulling away.

No. Whispers.

Whispers in an ancient tongue, words crawling from the depths of someplace unseen. She slowly made sense of the words. *Safaitic*. A multitude of voices, begging, calling, reaching. They tugged at her hair, at her arms, her fingers.

She stood as a chill settled in her bones, worse than any the cursed Demenhune snow could cause.

The voices called to her. Nothing like the Lion and his welcoming. This was a plea for help. A cry of ruination.

"Huntress?"

A tremor in Kifah's voice heightened Zafira's pulse. Her blood reveled in the sound of the Pelusian's trepidation.

"Zafira?"

Come. Free us.

Zafira took a slow step toward the voices.

"Where are you going?" Kifah hissed, rising to her feet.

Home. She was going home.

"Let her have a moment," she heard Altair say.

"She's not— Oi! Huntress!"

Zafira stepped into the trees, where a path unfolded before her and closed behind her, the wood of the trees crackling and moaning, swallowing Kifah's frantic calls. The light of the fire disappeared. Zafira crept onward, cautious but unafraid. Blackened branches wove away, entwining above in meticulous, pointed arches.

Marhaba, marhaba, marhaba, the air pulsed. The debris littering the ground smoothed into the glister of marble, forbidding beneath her boots.

There was no light here. But she knew what it was like to hunt without sight. To hear and know all. She picked up words of Safaitic in the whispers, pulsating against her eardrums, thrumming against her heart.

We are the past.

We are the future.

We are history.

We are destruction.

Free us.

"I'm coming," she whispered to them, elated when they smiled back.

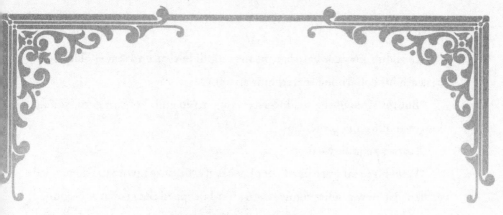

CHAPTER 78

Hayati. *MY LIFE*. ONE STEP ABOVE LOVE. ONE WORD whispered in his ear when he had cried his nights to sleep.

Liar, Nasir wanted to yell as the Silver Witch morphed into someone else, hair deepening to that familiar shade of gold, so dark it bordered black. Eyes softening. Ears sharpening.

Into someone who existed for years and years without end.

"Don't." He could barely enunciate the word past the hands closing around his throat. She shifted back into the witch. "Don't lie to me."

"What need do I have to lie?" she asked softly.

"I don't know, and I do not care." Perhaps the Lion sent her, to toy with his head. "Why are you telling me this now? You've had *years*."

"I might die in this fight. I might never have the chance to tell you."

"You can flee Sharr now, exactly as you did all those years ago."

Her face shattered. It didn't matter which face she wore—he saw his mother either way.

"It was not in my interests that I fled Sharr."

He didn't know what that meant. He didn't care to know. The burn beneath his collarbone seared him afresh.

"But my time in the shadows has come to an end. You are here; you no longer require my protection."

"I never required—"

"I told him you were born out of necessity, because my wazirs demanded an heir. He never believed me, even after I dropped the crown and donned this cloak. He sent you and Altair here, a reminder that he held the upper hand, lest I do something in which the Huntress might go against him. He knew I would interfere before you left Sultan's Keep, and I did. I aided you, I gave you the compass with which you could aid the Huntress, but I could not show my hand."

Nasir understood only half of what she said. He drew in a breath and knew the words he was about to utter would set him on a path that would not end well. "Prove to me that you are the sultana." *My mother.*

She shook her head, and he noted the pieces of his mother that had shifted into the Silver Witch. Or the pieces of the Silver Witch that once lived within his mother.

"Show me proof, or take your leave."

"Once my Sisters . . . perished, I knew the people would turn to the safin for leadership first. The last person I murdered was the safi whose name I claimed: the then-calipha—Benyamin's aunt. I slit her throat and buried her in the grounds of the palace, becoming her in both action and appearance. They appointed me, surprised the Gilded Throne accepted, for no one but that chair knew I was a Sister. I birthed Altair in secret, keeping him hidden in case the Lion escaped Sharr. Alone, I ruled as the safin sultana for decades. Until Ghameq—"

He didn't want to hear the rest. "I don't want your tales."

She knew what he wanted.

She knew, because he saw the havoc in her dark eyes as she lifted her hand to her left sleeve and drew up the silver cloth, unveiling a burn. A teardrop of black marring the skin near her elbow, from the first time she'd stepped between Nasir and the poker.

"I could wear a thousand faces and don a hundred names," she said, her voice soft, "but scars are eternal."

Nasir breathed past open lips. The baba he loved had become a monster. The woman he loved had used him, spied on him. Everyone else shied away, fear in their eyes, hate in their hearts. He had endured it all, every fabricated instance of love and respect and emotion.

Because no matter what, his mother's love had always been real.

"You were all I had," he said. "Everything else could fall to ruin, but you—even *dead* you were mine." He tried to make sense of the way his fingers could not stay still. His voice rose in a way that it never had before. "But you didn't even *exist*."

"The face I wore changes nothing."

Nasir gave a hollow laugh. The Arawiyans believed their beloved sultana had been safin. He had believed *he* was half safin.

Yet another lie.

"I had never known true love until I met your father. I had never felt true adoration until I birthed you. I gave him that medallion, hayati. My one last relic of Sharr. And through it, the Lion found his way to him, and when the Huntress set foot in the forest, the Lion knew the Jawarat could finally be sought. He had found me, and it wouldn't have been long before he reached *her*. A sultana cannot leave her place, and you were in no position to lead. I granted Ghameq the crown. I fabricated my own death."

"Oh, you did far worse," he said. He was crumbling inside. His tone was cruel. "You made me into the greatest hashashin alive and left me in his hands. You made me into a monster and handed him the leash."

She shook her head. "That was not my intent."

His head was tight. His vision burned dark, and only when he lifted his hand did he see the shadows rippling from his skin. "I know you immortals think long and far. Why did you do it, then? Why make your son a monster?"

He didn't think she would answer at first. She looked away, her silver cloak shadowed by the night. He wanted to grab her shoulders and demand an answer at swordpoint.

But he heard a whisper then, despite their distance. A murmur in his head.

Because the only way to end a creature who sees everything is with that which he cannot see.

By the time the full force of her words struck him, she was already retreating into the night, pain wrought in her features.

She had been grooming him to take down the Lion from the moment of his birth.

"I am sorry, my sons," she whispered. "Forgive me."

Nasir swiveled to where Altair watched from the shadows, silhouetted in gold against the firelight of the camp. When he turned back, the Silver Witch, the Sultana of Arawiya, was gone.

CHAPTER 79

ZAFIRA WENDED HER WAY ON THE PATH, LISTENING TO THE whispers. In the benighted terrain, thoughts and memories rose to life. Baba and Umm. Lana and her books. Yasmine and Misk. Deen and his ring. The Lion and his promises.

His words. About how she was merely a creature craving love.

It didn't matter in the end. She was Zafira bint Iskandar, with magic in her veins and a book of whispers calling her name, begging her to free them.

She would do as they asked. For her people.

But something warred within her, and when it raised its head, it said, *Laa.*

She would do it for herself. For the voices.

For zill and zalaam.

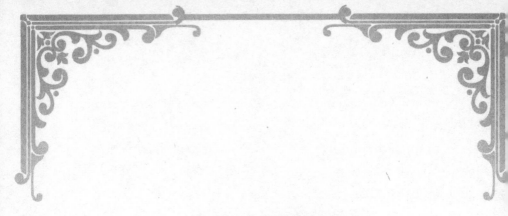

CHAPTER 80

S HE WANTED NASIR TO KILL THE LION. *HIS MOTHER*
wanted him to kill the Lion. She *believed* he could kill the Lion.

Altair studied him, surprisingly void of emotion.

Nasir fisted his trembling hands. "You knew."

He nodded. "Sharr is full of revelations."

Nasir did not want to react to that, or he would tear Altair's hair from
his head.

"I don't know how to put this lightly," Altair started, and his mock-
cheerful tone made Nasir decide maybe he *should* tear the hair from his
perfect head, "but our compass is missing."

"Zafira," Nasir corrected before he registered the rest of what Altair
said. He snapped his gaze to him. "Missing?"

Nasir shoved past Altair and rushed into the camp, where Benyamin
was pacing back and forth and Kifah was rubbing her arms, gold cuff
glinting.

He whirled back to Altair, who held up his hands and started with "Kifah—"

Nasir had Kifah against the tree in a heartbeat. His voice was crisp. "Where is she?"

Distantly, he heard Altair mumble, "What is it with Nasir and shoving people against things?"

Anger flared Kifah's nostrils, but Nasir didn't care.

"Start talking," he said, voice low, "or I'll knock out your teeth and you can use your blood to write your answers."

"Get your hands off me," she seethed, but this time a flicker of fear touched her bold face.

Panic struck him. He released her.

She straightened her sleeveless blouse and hoisted her spear, a sheen on her black skin and bald head. "Next time you touch me, Prince, you'll be without a hand."

"We have a more pressing matter, One of Nine," Altair drawled.

Kifah growled. "She heard whispers when there wasn't a bleeding sound. And then she just started walking away as if I weren't even there."

"Cut the gibberish, woman," Nasir snapped.

"All truth. Then she started whispering to the trees and said she was coming—and the bleeding trees *moved*, almost like a door was closing behind her."

Nasir turned to Benyamin, whose golden skin had lost its pallor. "The Lion?"

The safi shook his head. "He isn't strong enough. Not yet."

Not yet. "What does that mean?"

Benyamin started going through the vials at his waist. "It means the lost Jawarat won't be lost for long."

"Reassuring," Altair said.

"Can you walk?" Nasir looked to Altair's leg.

"Planning on carrying me, too?"

Nasir sighed.

"Worry not, princeling. Thanks to your tender care and my mighty strength, I'm good to go."

Mighty strength indeed. His blood flowed with that of the Sisters, too. Altair met his gaze, teasing eyes now staid, and Nasir knew what his half brother's next words would be. They curdled in his stomach.

"Will you kill her?"

Nasir wouldn't allow himself to consider that just yet. "I'm afraid she'll kill us."

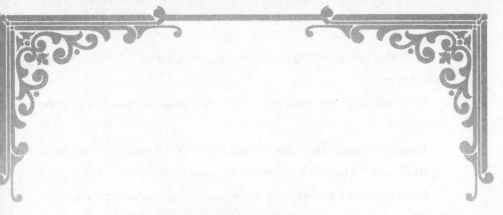

CHAPTER 81

NASIR'S IMPATIENCE HAD WORN THREADBARE BY THE TIME
they uncovered some semblance of a path. Zafira's light tread
was barely traceable until they reached a set of imposing doors.
Odd that they hadn't seen this structure before, a looming mass of marble
whose only entrance was a set of heavy green doors, brilliant in the night.

"The trail ends here," Kifah said with a frown.

Flickering torchlight cast eerie shadows across the zumra's solemn faces.
Darkness was creeping up the green surface.

"How did she get past these doors?" Altair asked after pushing and
pulling to no avail. He even pounded upon them for good measure until
Benyamin asked him to stop.

"If Altair can't get them open, we're all doomed," Kifah said, using the
tip of her spear to try to pry them open.

"There must be a way around," Nasir murmured.

Kifah brushed her hands across an inscription on the stone beside the doors. "I don't think so. There are words here. Safaitic? I don't even know half of them."

Altair hurried to the inscription while Nasir tried to make sense of the writing.

The color drained from Benyamin's face. "There's only one way in."

"Dum sihr," Kifah said, a note of eagerness in her tone.

Benyamin shook his head, the whites of his eyes bright in the darkness. "I told you, the price of dum sihr is always great. I can't do this."

"We have no choice," Altair said, and Nasir envied how easily he forgave the safi. "This isn't a test of conscience."

"The last time I used dum sihr," Benyamin started softly, "I killed my son. No good can come from such an act."

Nasir hadn't known Benyamin once had a son. He knew little about the safi who knew everything. Who wasn't even truly his cousin.

"I do not have the strength to do this again," Benyamin murmured, staring at the inscription.

Altair gripped his shoulders. "Strength doesn't come, brother." He touched his forehead to Benyamin's. Nasir watched their gazes crash, and he didn't know how long they had known each other. Loved each other. "It must be seized."

Benyamin's sage eyes flickered closed as he took a steadying breath.

Kifah nudged him. "Just imagine the tales they'll tell."

He lifted a corner of his mouth in a smile and held out his hand for her lightning blade.

——◆——

The doors yawned open with an echoing groan, welcoming them to a gaping pit of black.

"You don't think you can do more of that dum sihr to shed some light on the place, can you?" Kifah asked, spinning her spear.

Benyamin shot her a glare as he wound a strip of cloth around his slit palm. Altair remained silent.

"The darkness speaks to those who listen," Nasir murmured. "Those who listen are those who've accepted the darkness."

Nasir had accepted the darkness. After the ill of his deeds that led to his mother's supposed death, after the loss of Kulsum's tongue, after the threats against the others in the zumra of whom he had grown unwittingly fond. Darkness was his destiny, his father had said, and now, with the black that crept up his arms, he believed it.

"Darkness is my destiny," he whispered. The words cracked as they fell, winding around the marble walls, around his heart. He didn't need a torch or a light of dum sihr to see.

He would not fear the darkness. He *was* the darkness. A razor-edged smile cut across his face. He stepped into the void, footsteps sounding in the silence.

He felt her presence, just as he felt her loss when she had disappeared to the Lion's den. Perhaps it was the acceptance of the darkness that connected them. Perhaps he was imagining it.

But he saw her. She straightened like a gazelle at the sound of their approach, dark hair gleaming in the torchlight. Nasir had the absurd desire to reach out and run his fingers through the strands.

Then she bolted.

He flicked his gaze to the others and took off after her, Altair's warning echoing in his ears.

You will need to end lives.

CHAPTER 82

Zafira knew the people who were following her, despite the shroud growing in her mind.

A part of her recalled their laughs and smiles. The camaraderie in conflict. One's lingering looks that lit her aflame. The rest of her remembered what they were: the enemy. Her exploiters.

She darted between the wisps of shadow, feet silent, breathing hushed. A single pair of boots pounded behind her, not bothering with stealth.

Only one other could see and follow with such clarity through the darkness.

Only one other was arrogant enough to follow her.

Her ring struck against her chest, a silent reminder. *Murderer. Murderer. Murderer.*

Yet another voice whispered: *savior.*

◆

Nasir followed without a word, making his presence known, but she would not slow.

Just as our eyes tailor to the darkness, so do our souls.

The ground gleamed of polished marble, a soft light rising to an arched ceiling. The place reeked of magic, old and weary. Columns rose up ahead, a wall of shadow growing beyond them.

"Qif!" he finally shouted. Nothing. Only the whisper of her movements and a wheeze as her breathing grew winded. He couldn't bring himself to say her name.

He saw his moment.

He cursed beneath his breath. And leaped.

———◆———

Someone collided with her, knocking her to the ground.

She jolted when the warmth of him entwined with the ice of her. It awakened something. Her senses. Her mind. It cleared the mugginess that had clawed her when she'd stepped upon this whisper-ravaged path.

"Sorry," said a voice that had likely never said the word before. He carefully held himself above her.

His arms encircled her, the fringe of the keffiyah around his neck brushing her shoulders. His gray eyes shone in the dull light feathering above them, darkening as they roved her face, riffling something inside her.

She wanted to trace the length of his scar with her hand. She wanted to run a finger across his lips. She wanted—

Skies, he was beautiful.

Her brow creased. She'd never thought him beautiful before, not even when she had straddled his legs and seen his broken gaze. She had never *allowed* herself to think in such a way before. She had certainly never lay beneath him, his entire body pressed against hers.

Delicious heat spread through her limbs, up her neck, across her nose and cheeks. She was grateful for the dim light, for the shadows obscuring her skin's betrayal. The whispers hummed, and she silenced them as a very different hum stirred from the depths of her stomach.

"I've heard Demenhune never blush." His voice was rough; his words brushed her lips.

She had forgotten that he could see, that he was now as much of the darkness as the darkness was of him.

A sudden snap seized their breathing as one, and Nasir drew her to her feet, sheltering them between the columns. Her legs quivered, and she reached for the cool stone.

He scanned their surroundings, but his exhale told her they were alone.

She wasn't sure if what she felt was relief or panic.

———◆———

Nasir was abuzz.

Every fiber of his being was at war with itself. She was in his arms, pressed against the stone. She was supposed to be at arm's length, leading him to the Jawarat.

She was supposed to be beneath his blade.

But before she had recognized him, the look on her face had scared him. It had instantly cleared the mugginess that fogged his mind when he stepped upon this path. It was a look he knew very well. A look he didn't like.

Murder.

The darkness was taking hold of her, and worse, she was *allowing* it to sink its teeth into her heart. *Why do you care, boy? You're the same.* He clenched his teeth at the echo of Ghameq's voice in his head. The Lion's voice.

The sultan. He was the sultan, regardless of whether his father or the Lion stared back.

Her eyes fell to his mouth and he knew what to do. He knew how to make her forget the darkness. To bring her back to herself.

———◆———

The dangerous charge in the air lifted the hairs on Zafira's neck. She was aware of every subtle thing. Like his shallow breathing and the distance between them. Like the shift that brought him closer.

"Zafira."

His voice was a caress. It lilted across the length of her name, tasting it. Teasing it. She wanted him to say it again. And again and again. She wanted him to do to her what he had done to her name.

Everything inside her stumbled to a crash at that thought. But he was watching. Waiting. Those dark eyes intent, her insides aflame. She said something but didn't know what. Her voice was a distant thing, intoxicated with whatever crackled between them.

"What are you doing to me," he said more than asked. His voice was a rasp. The sharp sounds and throaty underscores of the language from his lips made her shiver. "Am I too close?"

"No." He was too far.

He skimmed his knuckles up the length of her arms, fabric snagging between them. Her heart stopped. Her breath shook, and his echoed.

She felt his strangled emotions in his every exhale against her skin, in the heat of his gaze. The hum of their bodies. He stepped impossibly closer and dipped his head. "And now?"

She shook her head, barely. Yet he paused at every motion that brought him nearer and nearer, waiting for her to pull away and end this madness.

His lips touched her ear.

She lost all sensation when he grazed the sensitive skin, slowly sliding his lips up. Down. Up. Blinding her. Killing her. This was nothing like the moment when he had touched her collarbone. She swallowed audibly and he chuckled beneath his breath.

She swept her trembling fingers down the hard ridges of his stomach, the heat of his skin making her heart race. An almost imperceptible groan escaped his mouth and she bit back her triumph. But he saw it, and she felt the answering curve of his smile at the shell of her ear.

Zafira shivered at the scrape of his jaw. He slipped one hand behind her head and tangled it in her hair. Tilted her head just so. The other fell to her waist, and he searched her gaze, eyes black beneath his hooded lids, dark lashes brushing the tops of his amber cheeks.

Their lips touched.

Once, barely.

Twice, scarcely.

And

her world

disappeared.

She had never expected a hashashin's lips to be so soft. So gentle. Like the first snow across the jumu'a, melting at mere embrace. But Zafira had befriended the darkness. She had slain safin and ifrit. She was the Huntress. She was magic.

Zafira bint Iskandar did not want gentle from the Prince of Death. She wanted *more*.

He pulled back and read her face. She traced his scar with one trembling finger, and he murmured a curse as something wild gripped her.

She knotted her hands in his hair—pausing at the softness between her fingers, the feel of him against her—before she pulled him closer. Closer.

He shifted his hips against hers.

Zafira gasped. A low growl escaped his throat.

Her lips crashed on his. Kissing, nipping, teeth flashing as he drew her lower lip into his mouth, swallowing her soft exhale. He was everywhere and nowhere at once, both of them taking, giving, taking, giving. His tongue slid between her lips and her breath hitched, and she almost pulled back from the foreignness of it all, surrendering with a sigh. The taste of him—dates and spice—combined deliciously with the myrrh of his skin, dizzying her. He pulled her harder against him, and Zafira grabbed fistfuls of his hair.

If this was what it felt like to be lost to the darkness, she never wanted to be found again.

He pulled away and she froze at the emotion feathering his jaw.

As if he had just remembered something he shouldn't have forgotten.

She swayed, bereft, and her hands fell to her sides when he averted his gaze. An emptiness yawned inside her. The shards of her heart that had been soaring settled back into her chest.

"The others await."

She clutched the rarity of his voice, broken and hoarse. Her only proof that he had felt what she had.

At least a sliver of it.

CHAPTER 83

NASIR COULD NOT. HE COULD NOT THINK OR COMPREHEND. He was supposed to give *her* a distraction, a momentary lapse to jog her mind, to clear her intent of destruction. Not to be destroyed himself.

He hadn't wanted to take it that far. He hadn't expected something to stir within him. *Filthy liar.*

She stared with glassy eyes, her lips bruised a brilliant shade of red, her pale skin a glorious display of color. In that moment, he appreciated his affinity for allowing him to see with such startling clarity in the dark.

He wanted to brush the backs of his fingers across the smooth plane of her cheek, the sharp cut of her cheekbone. He wanted to touch his tongue to the splotch of black above her collarbone and relish her exhale. He wanted to savor this image for eternity.

He wanted. And wanting was a weakness.

"This means nothing," he said abruptly, and immediately hated himself. Could he not loosen the sultan's hold on him? His voice was a broken rasp. He still startled when her eyes met his.

It was her boldness that had set him on a path to destroy himself.

Her eyes dimmed. "Did you think I expected you to marry me after a kiss, Sultani?"

Her voice was torn, satisfying him before her words registered.

"The last man who proposed to me didn't even *get* to kiss me."

Deen. *Sultani.* Nasir felt the sting of her words in his rib cage. He stepped back, wanting to take the words back with him.

She was still close. Still a beautiful mess. But he turned away, because as soon as she said the word "kiss" with those lips, he ached to shove her back against the stone and dip his head to hers and—

The cool tip of a blade touched his neck.

Nasir laughed, low and humorless. He faced her slowly. Her jambiya was at his neck, arm steady. A marvel, considering how upended he was.

"Do you intend to kill me?" he asked. The sadness returned, pulling at his heart. Was there no one who truly loved him?

"Let me go," she said.

"No," he whispered.

"Look at you, coward," she said.

He gritted his teeth.

"You came here for the Jawarat, intending to kill me as soon as I found it, and now you're just an errand boy. Did Benyamin ask you to fetch me? Was kissing me his idea? How sickening it must have been to you."

Nasir flinched, each word a physical blow. Pain struck his chest. Surely she had felt at least a sliver of what he had? Was this what the ifrit wearing Kulsum's face had warned him of?

"We both know you won't last a minute in a battle against me," he said finally. The words were ones the Prince of Death would use—because as Nasir, all he wanted was to drop to his knees and weep.

She smiled, a cruel twist of those lips that had been between his teeth moments ago. "No, Prince. We don't."

And in this place, surrounded by a darkness she had welcomed, he agreed.

He truly did not.

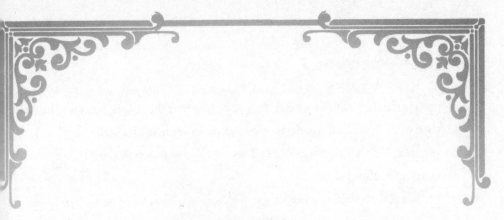

CHAPTER 84

ZAFIRA WOULD NOT GIVE IN TO THE WHIMS OF A man. She saw the war waging in him—the angle of his hand, trying to unsheathe his gauntlet blade. The pleading in his eyes.

She still felt the roughness of his jaw, the whisper of his lips at her ear. Somehow, she had gone from hating his existence to this inconceivable wanting. To thinking him beautiful.

This means nothing. The words stung more than they should have. It meant nothing to her, too. She had no expectations of men. Daama skies. She wanted to bash her head against the nearest slab of stone.

He watched her warily.

But he let her go.

She fled beyond the maze of stone columns. His absence was a cold emptiness that spiked her awareness: she was very much alone. The voices flooded her once more.

We are the past.

We are the future.

We are history.

We are destruction.

The farther Zafira trekked, the more insistent the voices became. Until they were a garble of words she couldn't make sense of. She jerked her head, shook it, but they only increased. They clouded her thoughts until she could think of nothing else.

She stopped before a line of aged trees, odd within the structure of stone and marble. They were unyielding, like bars of a cage. Keeping out intruders. *Or a coffer holding something in.*

Zafira tried to think, but the moment she latched onto one thought, something else appeared in its place, images and ideas she had never conceived before. Slowly, she imagined the faces of her people, reunited with magic, and Zafira knew she was on the right path. She would loan the Jawarat to the Lion and then return to Demenhur, as victorious as her mother had asked her to be. *No, that isn't right.*

"You let her go?" someone growled a distance away. Light flickered behind her. "The Lion will toy with her mind."

The others were catching up.

"I'm here," she told the trees, gritting her teeth as she tried to pry two trunks apart. "Let. Me. In." She darted along the border of trunks, hands searching the gaps between them for an opening.

Sharp slivers of bark snared her palm, tearing open a gash. She hissed and wiped the blood on her tunic, trembling against a wave of anguish. "Please open."

"Where did she go, you fool?" someone snarled.

Altair. They were nearer now.

"Stay calm," soothed Benyamin's voice.

A sudden hiss silenced her emotions. Another hiss—her blood dripped to the cursed leaves. A tendril of white steam lifted, eerie in the darkness. It curled in the shape of a rose. White and wild.

Peace unto you, bint Iskandar. Pure of heart. Dark of intent.

Bint Iskandar. Daughter of Iskandar.

The guarding trees parted, unlocked by her blood. Dull light illuminated a circular jumu'a of black stone. The trees crackled and shifted, curving upward to form a dome of twisting branches, vines, and jewel-like foliage. It wasn't a row of trees—there were five of them, their wide trunks lined with age, branches entwining to form an enclosure.

Protecting something.

Cradling her wounded hand against her chest, Zafira walked across a bed of leaves and stepped upon the stone. She felt a steady pulse beneath her boots. A breeze skittered across her skin, almost as if it were . . . sealing the jumu'a around her.

There it was. The lost Jawarat.

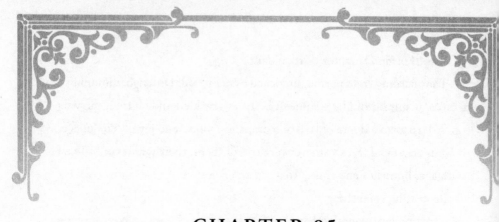

CHAPTER 85

NASIR SENSED THE IFRIT TOO LATE.

Had he not been busy berating himself for the thousandth time, he would have sensed them long ago, but he hadn't until one's stave came swinging straight for his head. He ducked, scanning the stone pillars as he drew his scimitar.

Nasir should not have let her go. *You only ever regret, mutt.*

"We're being attacked," Benyamin announced.

"Barely a handful. We can take care of them," Kifah said, spear twirling.

"Akhh, what else is new?" Altair asked flatly. The hiss of his twin scimitars punctuated his words.

"That, perhaps?" Benyamin asked, pointing in the distance.

"Bleeding Guljul," said Kifah.

Not ten paces away, Zafira stood on a jumu'a of peculiar dark stone, a writhing black mass before her. Massive trees suddenly surrounded them, ancient limbs curling beyond a ceiling they could no longer see. It defied logic, existing within this endless hall of marble.

"Nasir? Tell me I'm dreaming," Altair called.

"You don't have the brains to dream, Altair," Nasir replied, dodging a stave of fire as he swung his scimitar at the oncoming ifrit.

"Charming as always, brother dearest."

Benyamin and Altair stood back to back, felling ifrit with the slash of sword and the shatter of glass. Kifah pivoted her spear beside Nasir. He felt a lick of heat by his ear, followed by a shriek when she pinned an ifrit to his right, while he cut another down to her left. They exchanged a nod amid the chaos, Kifah responding with a two-fingered salute across her brow.

"Oi, the kaftar," Altair reminded them.

Nasir was about to say they could handle the few ifrit themselves when the ground trembled.

A horde of shadow crested the horizon, where the glistening marble met the dark night, slowly giving shape to countless ifrit. Benyamin wasted no time whistling, and Nasir hoped the kaftar wouldn't be one more foe for them to fight.

His heart seized. One more foe, indeed.

At the front of the horde was the Lion of the Night, astride a stallion of shadows, silver armor glinting against the shrouded moon.

———◈———

Chaos surrounded Zafira, the kind the darkness thrived upon. Elation built in her chest and spilt from her in the curve of a smile.

Stone hands atop a pedestal reached upward as if in everlasting prayer. The palms of mottled gray clasped a journal with pages of yellowed papyrus, bound in green calfskin and wrapped in a cord of braided black silk.

The lost Jawarat.

All of this for a book withering in the shadows. She reached for it with careful fingers.

"Huntress."

Benyamin stood at the edge of the stone, weariness weighing down his features. Benyamin, who kept secrets from her. Benyamin, who cried over the small coffin of his son. Ifrit spilled into their surroundings, shrieking and writhing with the shadows. Shouts rang out. The kaftar arrived, summoned by someone's whistle.

"The Lion is near," he implored, "and that stone is your only protection."

She felt detached from herself. Distant to everything but focused on *this*. This book. The darkness continued to ravage her mind as the whispers swarmed around the tome.

Benyamin's next words were cut off by a shout. He fell to his knees, and Zafira blinked as the always poised safi fought for his life.

"Fate brings us together once more, Haadi," said a voice of velvet. The Lion. He sighed boredly. "There is nothing I loathe more than safin. If it were up to them, you would be their slaves. I disrupted their balance, showed them their place. And Arawiya repaid me by trapping me on this island."

Benyamin choked against the vise of shadow coiling around his neck. "Whatever . . . you do . . . Huntress . . . do not . . . step . . . from that stone."

The Lion turned to her with a mocking laugh. His trim robes were deep mauve. Silver armor adorned his shoulders, filigreed at his cuffs. "A heart so pure, zill and zalaam never before had a vessel so eager to plenish. Impart it to me, azizi."

Look to us, bint Iskandar, came another voice.

The Jawarat.

Zafira stepped closer to the book, last touched by the Sisters of Old. There was a silhouette of a lion imprinted upon the pebbled leather, its mane a blaze of fire.

She felt no fear as she closed her hands around the tome.

And the world came undone.

Arawiya unfolded in her mind. As it once was, a beacon of light flourishing beneath a golden reign. She saw six women, rare si'lah who loved one another fiercely, appointing their strongest, Anadil, as the warden of the most impenetrable metropolis of a prison. Zafira saw wars that were waged. Darkness rushing toward gilded palaces and screaming Arawiyans. Caused by a man with amber eyes and ebony hair, vengeance in his blood.

The Sisters locked him within the hold of Sharr's prison after his dark attempts failed. The warden was a miragi, like Kifah, except the limits of her illusions, her *power*, did not exist. She reigned with an iron fist, swayed by nothing, until he seduced her with fabricated love, slowly but surely loosening her hold on good.

As the Lion had said: *A heart so pure of intent, zill and zalaam never before had a vessel so eager to plenish.*

She was Zafira, once.

Anadil, lost to herself, summoned her Sisters to Sharr and drained them of their magic upon the Lion's urging. By the time she realized the truth of what she had done, it was too late: the Sisters had fallen upon marble and stone. With the last of their power and the dregs of their lives, they trapped the Lion on the island with them and created the Jawarat, sealing the truth of that fateful day within its pages.

It was not magic incarnate. It was a book of memories. *Their* memories. And as the Jawarat lay lost upon Sharr, it became a being of its own, gleaning more memories, knowledge, and words: the Lion's.

It was the last remnant of the Sisters, but it had become something darker during its time on Sharr. Every fragment of knowledge the Lion held, every piece of history the Sisters knew—it was the Jawarat's. It was *hers*.

The Silver Witch and the Lion were wrong. They had never needed a da'ira to find the book. Zafira had merely needed to pass its tests, to defeat the ifrit, to escape the Lion in mind and body. And then *it* showed itself to her. *Pure of heart. Dark of intent.*

A searing exploded in her chest, her lungs, her heart. Distantly, she heard the shatter of glass, Benyamin going free. The howl of the wind. The roar of a creature that had lived far too long. *A reign of darkness.*

The Jawarat fell from her hands with a muted thud and a plume of dust. She collapsed to her knees, the stone cruel beneath her bones. She could only stare at the smear of red across the green leather with the knowledge that she had done something very, very wrong.

She had forgotten about the gash in her palm.

The Lion growled. "What have you done?"

Benyamin rose on shaky legs. "Her blood. The book bound itself to her."

I am you, and you are me. The words were a whisper in her heart.

A handful of ifrit surrounded the jumu'a. A stave twirled in her peripheral vision, reminding her that the ifrit didn't need to step upon the stone to kill her. But they wouldn't. Not now.

The book's words spilled from her lips. "Harm me, and the Jawarat will die. What you need will perish."

The Lion paused. Sharr held its breath.

"Stand back," he commanded, and the staves vanished.

Triumph sizzled in her veins.

But the Lion was not finished. "Did you expect to retrieve the Jawarat and leave, azizi? You came here upon the witch's ships, and they are now gone; you will not take your leave that way. Give me the book."

Illusioned ships. She was trapped.

The Jawarat pulsed beneath her fingers. *Fear not, bint Iskandar. We are unstoppable.* She remembered then: Benyamin's ship, the one the Silver Witch ensured he would bring.

As if summoned by Zafira's thoughts, a woman stepped from the shadows. A cloak of silver sat upon her shoulders, crimson lips curved in a smile. Memories collected in Zafira's mind as the Jawarat showed her the past once more.

The Silver Witch had come.

"You should not have come, Anadil," the Lion said.

Which side did the witch belong to now? For whom did she fight?

The Silver Witch dipped her chin and strode toward the Lion. As she moved, her billowing cloak shortened. A crimson sash knotted at her hip. Armor glinted at her shoulders. She flicked her arms to either side of her, twin blades extending in her hands. "Only the lonesome fear the lion."

The lonesome. She was here for them. With them. The Lion realized it then, too, and he quickly halted her in her tracks. Not with a blade to her heart or a vise around her neck.

He merely looked to Nasir and curled two fingers.

Altair shouted as Nasir flew into the air with a wrangled breath, choking as he clawed at invisible hands around his throat. Panic flared in his eyes.

The Lion's words still soothed, his whisper still raised the hairs on Zafira's neck when he directed his command at her. "Give it here, azizi. You know how little his life means to me."

"D-don't," Nasir gritted out.

He wasn't losing breath if he could speak. He couldn't die from that height if he fell. A terrible suspicion weighted her shoulders.

The Silver Witch threw out her hand, but the Lion shoved her to the ground with a flick of his other wrist. She fell to her knees, a black dagger impaling the hollow beneath her shoulder. She yanked it free with a hiss, but she was slow, and Zafira realized her magic was already depleting into Sharr. For a witch who had calculated so much for so many years, her decision to show her hand so quickly made no sense.

The Lion laughed. "I never did like your second son."

Zafira gasped. *The sultana.* The Silver Witch was the Sultana of Arawiya.

No wonder she was acting recklessly. No wonder she had interfered with the sultan's orders and aided them. Nasir and Altair were her *sons.*

A stave of black materialized in the Lion's hand, sharp points extending on either side. Metal, shadow, darkness—he threw it.

Straight

for

Nasir's heart.

"Nasir!" Altair roared.

The Silver Witch watched, powerless. Kifah struggled against a horde of ifrit.

Zafira lost all reason. She ran from the stone, tucking her nose beneath the scarf around her neck, but even in her crazed state she knew she wouldn't reach him in time. As always, she was too late. Too late to save her parents. Too late to save the one who had loved her.

This means nothing.

Still, she ran.

But she should not have stepped from the stone.

A blur of black billowed toward her, veins of black bleeding in its wake. *The Lion.* She cried out from the impact and fell to the burning sand.

And the lost Jawarat, now found, tumbled from her grip.

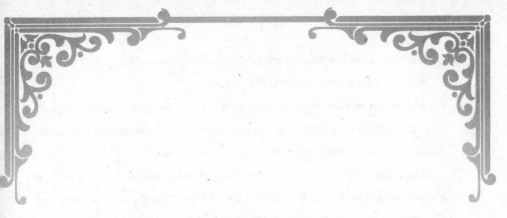

CHAPTER 86

NASIR HAD PICTURED HIS DEATH A THOUSAND AND one times.

Never had he pictured it upon Sharr, a stave of shadow hurtling toward his heart while he hung suspended with no control of his limbs. Distantly, he heard the Lion's drawl directed at Zafira.

"You and that pathetic prince will never understand the consequence of loving the useless."

He was done being called pathetic. He was a hashashin. He was the Prince of Death. He was crown prince to a kingdom waiting for someone to make a stand. And the people this creature threatened were . . .

Rimaal. They were his companions. Friends. Somewhere along the way, he had grown the attachments he had feared and, for once, he didn't feel the heat of shame. *Love gives purpose.*

He clawed at his neck. He thought of Zafira, with the Jawarat. He thought of his father, who once loved him. His mother, whose love had destroyed her.

He thought of his dark heart, finally coming to a halt.

A volley of darkness unfurled from his fingers.

The world exploded in shadows that rivaled the Lion's. Ifrit shrieked in confusion. Altair barreled toward Nasir, double scimitars poised to deflect the Lion's stave, still hurtling for Nasir's heart.

The Silver Witch rose to her feet with the last of her strength. Someone else shoved her to the sands—Benyamin. He was running with the speed of the safin. Leaping. Putting himself between Nasir and the Lion of the Night.

Between Nasir and that dark stave.

Nasir heard a grim shatter of bone before it pierced Benyamin's heart. But the safi made no sound.

The invisible claws loosened from his neck and Nasir fell on his knees. *No, no, no.* He gasped for air as he clambered toward Benyamin, sand burning beneath his hands as the chaos continued around them.

Benyamin remained still for one long, silent moment before he fell on his back, graceful even in agony.

Nasir was numb. Lost. His gaze met the Lion's across the fray, and he felt a surge of anger when remorse fleeted across those amber eyes. His tattoo gleamed in the gloom, nearly identical to the safi's.

Benyamin's friend, once. Who repaid kindness with death.

Nasir heard nothing but the soft whirr of Benyamin's breathing.

People had dreams, thoughts, ideas. Nasir had facts. When he had stepped upon this path the sultan had lain for him, he had always known there was no one left to love him. No one to liberate him.

Some fates were made easier with acceptance.

Yet here lay Benyamin. An immortal safi, vain by nature, embittered by knowledge. Nasir's hands shook as he regarded the wound. There was so much blood he didn't know where it began and where it ended. Altair dropped beside him. Kifah shouted out as she fought back to back with the kaftar, but she was too far, too overwhelmed by ifrit, to be of assistance.

Nasir found the point of impact. He sat back on his heels, hope leaching. "It is fatal," he said, hands drenched in red.

Dark steam wafted from the stave.

Benyamin spoke lightly. "Now I know what it is like to live as a mortal. Death"—he pressed his lips together against the pain, his brown eyes soft—"is a welcome truth."

His white keffiyah was smeared with blood. It slipped from his head and Nasir righted it, perfected it as the safi would. Altair clasped Benyamin's hand, drawing him close. "Oh, akhi, akhi, akhi."

My brother, my brother, my brother. By a bond stronger than blood.

Nasir had never seen Altair cry. His raw sobs racked his whole body, desolate in the din. Nasir had never thought someone else's tears could hurt him so much.

"Why? Why did you do this?" Nasir whispered. Something fisted in his throat, hindering his speech.

Altair kept murmuring the word "akhi" over and over, anger and pain shattering his voice.

"Sacrifice," Benyamin bit out.

Nasir knew sacrifice, but for him, the Prince of Death?

"For you. For her. For the ones who deserve to see another day. Your story remains unfinished, Prince."

Something cleaved in Nasir. The children in the camel races. The rebels in Sarasin. Zafira. Kifah. *They* deserved to see another day. *They* deserved sacrifice. Not Nasir, whose hands had felt the last breath of countless souls. Not the Silver Witch, who had made her mistakes.

"Remember me, eh? Say hello to my beloved, but not my sister," Benyamin whispered.

Altair sobbed a laugh.

Benyamin struggled to smile. He cupped Altair's face. "I seized it, brother. Strength was mine. But it turns out"—he coughed and more blood spurted from his wound—"the price of dum sihr is always great."

A tremor shook his body. Benyamin did not shed a tear. He did not cry out in pain. He entwined his fingers upon his stomach, posture at ease.

Nasir watched the light fade from his eyes, a death that wasn't his doing, a final breath he hadn't captured. A sacrifice. He couldn't move, even as the sounds of battle wound around him.

Slowly, he closed Benyamin's eyes. Skeins of black leached from his fingers, bidding farewell. He pulled a feather from his robes and touched it to Benyamin's blood before tucking it between the folds of the safi's thobe. The black vane glittered red. One last gift from the Prince of Death.

"Be at peace, Benyamin Haadi min Alderamin."

Altair clasped Nasir's hand and helped him to his feet. Never had Nasir seen the general so weary, so shattered, streaks of grief staining his golden skin.

Together, they faced the Lion of the Night.

"You have dealt your hand upon one of ours. There will be retribution." Nasir's voice was cold. Low. The Prince of Death drew his scimitar, a hiss through the sands, echoed by Altair's own swords.

Again, Nasir saw that flicker of remorse. A sorrow the Lion did not deserve.

"You've come a long way, Prince. But you will always serve the dark," said the Lion.

The ifrit swarmed, fortified by the shadows Nasir had unleashed.

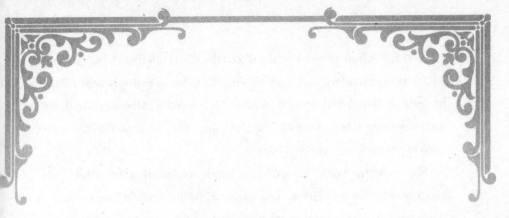

CHAPTER 87

THE WORLD SPUN BLACK AND CHAOS RAN RAMPANT. THROUGH it all, Zafira saw the exact moment Benyamin's body went still, one with the earth. Pressure built in her throat. This wasn't Deen or Baba. This was someone else she had come to know the little things about. The things that made Benyamin the safi he was: his penchant for naps, his extraneous words, his silly pride. The value he placed in trust and truth.

You didn't need to know someone's darkest secrets to wish for their life. *In this moment, we are two souls, marooned.*

But what happened when one soul marooned the other? When death decided to stand between them?

The last time she'd spoken to him, it was to tear him apart. Hateful, bitter words she wished she could draw back. Words she could never, ever atone for.

She would never again see his umber eyes or his feline smile. Hear the drone of his endless voice, the rue when he spoke of his son.

"Zafira!" Altair yelled over the din of the shrieking ifrit. "The Jawarat!"

Soldiers of shadow took up every empty pocket of space, nearly invisible because of Nasir's billowing darkness. They howled, staves of fire flaring and swooshing. There were too many of them. There was no way the zumra could fight their way through this.

She found the book. Wrapped her hands around the soft leather, pulse settling with the reassuring heartbeat of the Jawarat. *We are the past*, it whispered. It was everything they needed to return magic, but not magic itself.

She felt the steady beat again, thrumming beneath her boots. *The Sisters gifted us their good hearts.* It was a line every child of Arawiya knew.

Sweet snow below. It wasn't the heartbeat of the *Jawarat* she felt. It was that of the—

She lifted her gaze up. To the five trees surrounding them, protecting the Jawarat in one final stand.

—the Sisters.

Their actual, beating hearts were vessels of insurmountable power. *Magic.* And those vessels were buried beneath each tree, housed in a rib cage of roots. The trees were the Sisters.

She needed to retrieve the hearts, untether them from Sharr, and, in so doing, lift Sharr's curse. The Silver Witch's strength would return. With the guidance of the Jawarat, they would return the hearts to the royal minarets.

Restore magic to the caliphates.

But freeing the hearts meant freeing the Lion, too.

"The hearts," she whispered, unable to hold the words inside anymore. They rose in her chest, clawed at her mouth, made her speak. "The hearts are in the trees. *Magic is in the trees.*"

The zumra heard her.

There was a sudden burst of movement as they struggled to fend off the ifrit while moving toward the trees. But the Lion had heard, too. He swept toward her. He didn't need the hearts just yet—the Jawarat was more important to him. To him, knowledge trumped all.

Destroy him. He has served his purpose. The Jawarat's words echoed in her heart. They were not the words of the Sisters. They were a result of the years the book spent festering in darkness.

Zafira backed away, ducking from an ifrit's stave. Another swooshed behind her, but Kifah hurled one of her lightning blades, felling the ifrit in its tracks. Altair appeared with raised scimitars, but the Lion deflected with ease, hurling him into the path of the rushing ifrit.

"Huntress!" Kifah yelled.

Zafira saw Kifah running to where Benyamin's body lay, saw her bending over the fallen safi, their friend, but she couldn't react. Her vision dipped darker and the book trembled in her hands. She was not atop the stone, her only protection. Distantly, she heard Kifah shout and Altair answer with orders, the general in the battlefield.

The Lion snarled, skeins of darkness trailing him. Zafira ducked away, trying to see in the chaos that pelted from all sides. Trying to listen over the demands of the Jawarat. She heard Benyamin's voice, telling her to remain calm. To think. To trust. *We are stronger as one.* But he was dead now.

Screams pierced her eardrums, followed by the howl of wind before a body crashed into hers and the Jawarat was ripped from her grasp.

This time, she felt its loss like a seam tearing in her heart. She felt its call, its panic as it called for the one it was bound to.

The whisper of the Lion's lips caressed her ear, and she knew she had failed.

CHAPTER 88

NASIR WRENCHED HIS GAZE FROM TREE TO TREE. They were massive, their boughs old and weary, veined in white like the Silver Witch's hair. He counted five.

This was what had become of the Sisters.

He hurled knives at oncoming ifrit, their shrieks numbing his eardrums as he slowly fought his way toward the first tree. The Silver Witch was nowhere to be seen. Nor was Zafira, but he trusted her to stay safe and protect the Jawarat.

They all did.

Without it, they would have nothing more than five bloody hearts locked with power beyond imagination.

He reached the tree, even more enormous up close. The heart could be anywhere, hanging from some limb, tucked within the trunk—no. He paused.

A steady beat pulsed at his feet.

The roots. He cut his scimitar across a line of ifrit, giving him a moment to hack at the twisting roots. Another ifrit howled, the heat of a stave licking Nasir's neck. He turned and put down another horde, hurling knives to hinder the next wave. *Come on*, he gritted, digging beneath the dirt, nails turning black, fingers going cold. The beat grew louder the farther he dug.

There.

He nearly recoiled as he drew the organ from the ground, insides lurching at its pulse, at the rubbery softness. Strains of blood mixed with the dirt on his hands.

Kifah appeared at his side and barely flinched at the sight before she barked, "Four more to go. Yalla, yalla."

More ifrit hounded forward in black waves, fiery staves flashing, and Nasir quickly wound the inner cloth of his robes around the pulsing heart, leaving it hanging at his hip.

He locked blades with an ifrit, shoving with all his strength before hurling the last of his knives at the surrounding creatures. He made way for the next tree, but Altair met him halfway with a panicked look, another pulsing heart held gingerly in his palms. Nasir took it and tucked it into the folds of his garb.

Kifah felled ifrit upon ifrit as she headed to the next tree, her spear a moving shield and weapon at once. Nasir fought off another horde and looked up in time to see the pump of her fist as she retrieved another heart.

Two more to go.

He retrieved another, suffering a gash across his leg before he shoved his sword through the ifrit's throat. He stumbled to the next tree, stopping when Altair rose from its roots, the final heart in hand.

The ground rumbled.

A stillness fell over them. The land sighed and groaned in relief. An exhale of contentment, finally liberated from what it was not. Sharr was free.

Which meant that across Arawiya, the Arz had begun unfolding into the ground.

Rimaal. Nine decades of encroaching darkness. Of a forest that stripped them of their sea. Of caliphates cursed to suffer endless snow, darkening skies, and dying lands. Of hostility gnashing razor-edged teeth.

It had ended.

It was over, and Nasir had been a part of it. He nearly swayed with the realization. He had been a part of something *good*.

The elation in his chest fell when an ifrit nearly decapitated him. He saw a flash of silver as the Silver Witch slowly rose to her feet, her power no longer receding.

But there were two sides to this coin: The Lion was no longer tethered to Sharr. They had to move quickly.

"Gloomy weather you've gifted us," Altair called as he stumbled toward Nasir, blood across his brow. He seemed to be bracing himself before he turned back to the surrounding din, where ifrit swarmed, trapping them. The dark creatures were thriving, drunk on the shadows Nasir had unleashed. Retrieving the hearts meant nothing if he and the others died in these endless hordes.

"Eh, old tomato!" Altair yelled.

The Lion paused mid-stride, robes billowing in the wind.

"The retribution promised begins now."

"What are you trying to do?" Nasir snapped. "If you die, I will kill you myself."

"Akhh, I love conundrums. Careful, little brother, I'm beginning to think you're worried for me." Altair patted Nasir's cheek with a bloody hand before Nasir could wrench away and then strode toward the Lion of the Night.

Altair heaved a dramatic sigh. "I'd been saving for a special occasion, something with more flair. You know, a wedding or my beloved Nasir's coronation or—akhh, words fail me. But beggars can't be choosers, can they? I suppose this, uh, the Skirmish of Hearts, is just as special—"

"Shut up, Altair," Nasir growled against the twitch of his lips.

His half brother only winked, and Nasir realized what he was doing. Drawing attention to himself, for Altair's every action was done in deliberation, carefully calculated.

Then Altair al-Badawi lifted his hands to the skies, a crooked grin upon his face, and Sharr exploded with light.

CHAPTER 89

ZAFIRA PAUSED HER DESPERATE SEARCH WHEN LIGHT ERUPTED across the world of marble and wood. It took her a moment to find its source amid the blinding white: Altair's outstretched hands. This was his affinity. He truly was the light to Nasir's dark. *As Deen had been to mine.*

Panicked screeching filled the silence as the ifrit skittered to the shadows of the ruins. She saw Nasir, Kifah, and the kaftar snatch at what Altair had given them—a distraction—and returned to her task.

Her fruitless task.

She dropped to her knees and grabbed fistfuls of sand. Digging, searching. Looking. *Begging.* The others trusted her to keep the Jawarat safe. She swiped sweat from her brow as Altair's light began to fade. But even in the dim she could see: sand upon sand, no bolt of green.

Her fingers snared against something beneath the sand, and her heart clambered to her throat. *Please.* She wrenched it free—but it was only a stone. She hurled it away with a cry. The island mocked her even now.

Someone grabbed her wounded hand and ran, pulling her along. Fear pounded in her eardrums.

"We have to go," the voice said, and for a moment, she thought it was Benyamin before she remembered he was dead, and it was only Kifah.

The cut in her hand throbbed. She had been a fool, and that gash was the reason she had inadvertently bound herself to the Jawarat, body and soul. She had failed.

Some must be given for us to succeed. She startled at the Jawarat's words. She hadn't been a fool. She was suddenly glad for the gash in her palm that had gifted her this connection. That had given her such immeasurable knowledge.

But the Lion was nowhere to be seen. Which meant he had the Jawarat.

"We have to go back," she protested, wrenching free from Kifah's grip.

The warrior grabbed her hand again. "For what?"

"I dropped the Jawarat. The Lion must have it!"

"Oh, keep your wits," Kifah snapped, and leaned close, her whisper almost lost in the din. "I'm a miragi, remember? I have the blasted book. I took"—her voice cracked and she drew in a steadying breath—"I took Benyamin's book and illusioned it to match the Jawarat. Then I grabbed the real thing from you and threw the decoy onto the sand. The Lion grabbed it in the frenzy."

Zafira nearly wept with the realization. *Safe.* The Jawarat was safe.

"It won't last long, though, now that Sharr's magic is gone," Kifah said with a slight frown before spearing another ifrit. "So grab your bow, Huntress."

"Wait, what about the kaftar?" Zafira said as her mind slowly cleared from the haze of panic.

Kifah shook her head. "They fought well. I offered them passage back to the kingdom, but they refused. Sometimes, when you live a life of captivity, trapped for so long, freedom becomes a thing to fear."

Zafira understood that. It was how she feared the defeat of the Arz. The loss of her cloak. A life where she wasn't the Hunter.

They joined Nasir, who limped as he slashed at the ifrit brazen enough to step into Altair's fading light. Slowly, they battled their way out of the confines of the towering palace of marble and stone with the help of the Silver Witch. As Zafira, biting her tongue against the pain in her hand, nocked arrow after arrow, she guiltily recalled how she had lashed out at Benyamin for trusting the witch.

Without the sorcery of Sharr, the shore was not so far from them now. Dawn returned to the island, a beatific sight after the depthless dark skies they had been cursed with these past days. They were soon rushing past the island's gates, prim between the towering hewn stones of the wall. Benyamin and Kifah had come in from that front entrance, the one Deen had wanted to find.

Loyal, softhearted Deen. *There is no man in Arawiya more loyal to the Hunter than I.*

He had believed in her until his very last breath, and now he was all but a ghost in her thoughts, a fragment of her past. What would she tell Yasmine?

Yasmine. *Oh, Yasmine.*

They hurried through the gates, steadily nearing the ship. An arrow whizzed past Zafira's ear, and everyone froze. It had come from the ship. Another volley headed for them, and Zafira ducked. The Silver Witch hissed as an arrow struck her.

Kifah sighed and shouted, "Oi, Jinan! Quit firing at us."

"Cease!" someone yelled, and the arrows stopped. A waif of a girl stepped to the rail, a checkered turban on her head, an ochre sash at her waist. "About time. Wait—where's Effendi Haadi?"

"Dead," Nasir said in the silence.

Something cracked on the girl's face before she nodded and ordered for the plank.

The ship was as extravagant as expected, with gleaming golden rails and sails of cream emblazoned with the tiny diamonds of Alderamin. It reminded Zafira of Benyamin, and a wave of grief crashed in her chest.

Even in death, the safi was assisting them. They would have been stranded without him.

Kifah pivoted her spear. "Yalla, zumra. Let's get off this damned island and start making sense of all this."

Even the Prince of Death smiled at her words.

——◆——

Nasir surveyed Benyamin's ragtag Zaramese crew as they studied him back.

More than a few went slack-jawed as the Silver Witch swept on board, and Nasir noticed that Kifah never acknowledged the witch's aid. Nasir hadn't either, for that matter—no one had. They were still reeling from the battle. From Benyamin's death.

The girl who had ordered the plank—Jinan, the captain, he guessed—stepped forward and shooed the others back to their posts. "Everything in order?" she asked Kifah.

Kifah nodded, removed the turban that had been knotted around her waist, and began spreading the cloth on the gleaming deck. She took out the Jawarat and he noticed Zafira lurch forward, barely holding herself back when the Pelusian laid it in the fabric's center. Then Kifah held up the heart she had collected.

"Let's see the rest," she said to Nasir.

He carefully unwound the red organs from the folds of his robes, gently laying them atop the cloth.

"There are only four," Zafira puzzled, leaning over them. They gleamed in the early sun, steadily beating. Pulsing, red, and *wet*.

"Oi, Altair has the last one. Where is that bumbling fool anyway?" Kifah asked, wiping sweat from her scalp and leaving a smear of blood behind.

Everyone looked up when the general gave no response. Nasir called for him, unease creeping into his veins in the answering silence. Realization swept the deck.

The general had vanished.

CHAPTER 90

LTAIR WAS GONE. THE ZARAMESE CREW EVEN SEARCHED
belowdecks, but he was nowhere to be seen. Zafira had been so
engrossed in reuniting herself with the Jawarat that she hadn't
even noticed his disappearance.

"We're going back for him," Nasir said in the silence.

"What if he's dead?" Kifah asked, forever optimistic.

"I know Altair, and he won't die so easily," Nasir said. "He'd crawl out
of the grave if he had to."

The prince produced a wooden crate he had picked up during their
search of the ship. With a nervous, jittery energy that Zafira hadn't seen
in him before, he placed the four hearts and the Jawarat inside. The book
called to Zafira from the confines of the box. *Do not forget us.* It spoke only
to her, she knew. No one else had cut a gash across their palm and bound
themselves to it. It pulsed in time to her heart; it breathed in her.

Nasir hefted the crate toward Captain Jinan. "Protect this at all costs.
Or I'll put your head in one of these boxes."

Kifah shot him a glare.

Zafira glanced at the captain apologetically. "That's his way of saying please."

"I'm not sure I want to know how His Highness repays favors," Jinan said, taking it from him. "You're lucky Effendi Haadi paid me well."

Something swelled in Zafira's throat, and she swallowed it against the burning in her eyes. She could never think of Benyamin without remembering how she had pushed him away after everything he had done. Because he had put her mental state first. When she closed her eyes, she was in the dreamwalk again, on that gilded balcony in Alderamin, at ease and at home, Benyamin's grin broad and his tears raw.

Her first and only dreamwalk.

Kifah tugged her arm as she and Nasir turned to leave, but the Silver Witch stepped between them and the plank, her cloak blinding in the early sun.

"No one is going back."

"It's a bit too late to impart counsel, Sultana," Kifah said.

Though Zafira thought the Pelusian's words were harsh, she agreed. The Silver Witch *was* too late to be frank with them. Even if she had fought on their side.

Even if, without her aid, they would have perished as Benyamin had.

"We can't lose one more of ours," Zafira said.

"I don't intend to lose my son," the Silver Witch said curtly. Before Nasir could protest, she continued. "You forget I know the Lion more than most. If we want to keep the hearts safe, we cannot fight him here. He has one heart, one of five of what he so terribly desires, but without the Jawarat as a guide, it is useless to him. A vessel of untapped power. He will follow us to the mainland and use Altair as leverage."

Kifah pursed her lips at this, seeing the sense in the witch's words.

But Nasir was not yet ready to acquiesce. "Maybe so," he said, jaw clenched, "but there is no guarantee that Altair will be left whole."

"That is a risk we have to take," the witch said, looking to the sea. "I'm not losing both of you in one day."

"I am not yours to lose," he said coldly, but Zafira heard the hurt in his voice.

There was a touch of remorse on the Silver Witch's face before she said, "And you are not yours to lose, either. Like it or not, you belong to the Arawiyan throne."

Nasir held her gaze, a vein feathering in his jaw before he whirled around and half-limped to the prow of the ship, skeins of black trailing in his wake. He was like the Lion, Zafira realized. A study of darkness, a profile of shadows.

The last time Zafira had stood so close to him, she had pressed a dagger to his neck. Before that, her hands had fisted in his hair, her mouth on his.

She followed him after a moment, and he turned at her approach. His eyes were gray like the world fresh awakened from darkness, but they were shuttered and dim, just like when the Lion had pressed the poker to his skin. When she had tended to his wound and he had bared his soul.

This means nothing.

"Are you all right?" she asked, extending an alliance.

"Define 'all right,'" he said quietly.

She reached for his arm, expecting him to pull away. He stilled when she tugged up his sleeve, where rivulets of shadow crept up his golden skin, swallowing the words inked upon his arm. His hand was warm in hers. "'All right' is when you're bleeding black but it's not as bad as bleeding red. When the world crashes but you're not alone when it does. When the darkness is absolute but you hunt down the smallest flame and coax it brighter. When you carve the good out of every bad and claim it a victory." She released his arm, but he didn't move. "If Sharr has taught me anything, it's that every breath is a victory."

One side of his lips curled into a smile before he stopped himself. "I suppose I am then. All right."

Waves crashed upon the side of the ship as the crew readied to set sail. The Silver Witch idled in silence, eyes trained in the distance. Zafira couldn't imagine how she felt, losing a son she had never claimed, reuniting with a son she had shown a different face. Being used and used and used by the man she loved.

After a moment, Nasir sighed. "I can't leave him."

"We're not leaving him. We're recouping," Zafira said, knowing of whom he spoke. "Altair knows we'll come back for him."

"You don't understand," he said, and he sounded tired. "If our situations were reversed, he would have fought tooth and nail for me. But he knows I was sent to Sharr to kill him. He knows I don't disobey orders."

Zafira thought of Altair, in some dank place, imprisoned by the Lion, hopeless. Helpless. He would endure it, he *had* to. So she said what he would: "We'll just have to surprise him, then."

"Optimism suits you." Nasir smiled then, a true smile.

It looked foreign as they stood before the sea, tumultuous and wild. But like everything that had come to pass on this journey, it was laced in sorrow.

They had lifted the decades-old curse and freed magic from Sharr, even if they had freed the Lion in the process. They had salvaged four hearts, even if they were leaving one behind. They had triumphed over the Lion's hordes, even if they had lost Benyamin for good and Altair for now. The safi would never be buried with his son, but he would forever rest with the Sisters. Zafira had succeeded in her quest to find the Jawarat, even if she had lost Deen.

They had magic now, even if she no longer felt the rush of it through her veins. And until they returned the hearts to the royal minarets again, she never would. The hearts were merely hearts.

A gain for every loss.

CHAPTER 91

THE CAPTAIN SHOUTED OVER THE DIN, BARKING orders from the helm. They were all young, Nasir realized. Arawiya was being brought from the brink of ruin by a handful of youth. Jinan saluted two fingers off her brow when she saw him looking. "Sultan's Keep awaits, Your Highness."

Sultan's Keep. Home. He wasn't certain if the Lion's hold upon the sultan remained, now that his tether to Sharr's obsolete magic was destroyed. He supposed he would find out soon enough.

His dark thoughts scattered when Zafira laughed.

It freed him. Reached into that crevice between his rib cage and gave him life. A vial of light undeterred by the dark, a sound he would burn down cities to hear again, wild and free. She stood differently now. Shoulders pushed back, dark hair adrift in the wind. Taller. Stronger. A woman, through and through.

The woman he had believed to be a man, the Hunter he was sent here to kill. She caught him watching. "I will make sure no woman fears herself. Like in Zaram, and Pelusia, and Sarasin."

"I have no doubt, fair gazelle."

She met his eyes, and Nasir felt a jolt in his chest when diffidence darkened her cheeks. She stepped closer, and Nasir remembered the marble columns, those moments before she held the Jawarat, when *he* held *her*.

This means nothing. He wished he could take back his harsh words. It hadn't meant *nothing*, no. Nor had that moment before, when she had cared for him with a gentle hand, without a hint of repulsion on her open face. It had been the culmination of his life, to be looked at the way Zafira Iskandar had looked at him. If only she knew.

But those three words lingered between them, lifting a guard behind her eyes as she regarded him now.

"And you? What will you do, Prince of Death?"

He didn't say what he wanted to say. "If I live past this journey, I'll see then."

"You'll live, Prince," Kifah said, joining them. "The Huntress will make sure you do."

The Huntress in question scoffed softly. "The Arz has fallen. I'm not a huntress anymore."

Kifah shot her a look. "There's still a Lion to hunt down and a general with a penchant for conundrums. Don't tell me you're hanging your hat up so soon."

She smiled. "I suppose not, then," she replied, relief toning her voice.

They did not look behind, to where Sharr wavered, a scourge on Arawiya's map, a place of shadow and death. They had lived in the past for far too long. Yet Nasir would always carry a souvenir of the island in his soul, another scar to mark his suffering.

"We will raise dunes from the earth, and rain death from the sky," Zafira said.

"And then some," Nasir promised.

Kifah gave a sharp nod.

It was time for change to sweep across Arawiya, this zumra at its helm. He had a brother to save and a father to liberate, through death or otherwise. There would be more walls to hurdle, battles to triumph, and victories to glean. But walls were nothing for a hashashin.

And the Prince of Death never left a job unfinished.

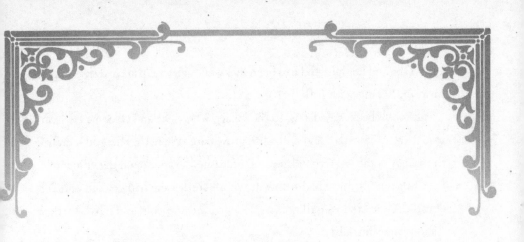

الخاتمة

EPILOGUE

THERE WERE ONLY SO MANY TEARS A SOUL COULD shed before weariness and fatigue dragged her to an endless pit of grief. Yasmine had seen too much.

She no longer felt the joy of her marriage. Dread and defeat bittered her tongue. A place ravaged by war was no place for happiness.

"This isn't war," Misk had said, lashing out in a voice that promised retribution. "This is butchery. Cold-blooded and heartless. It will not stop with us. Zaram will be next, then Pelusia, and then his crimes will come full circle, Arawiya under his black crown."

They were already under his black crown. She didn't understand what more the sultan wanted.

The men had been there, wearing the black and silver of Sarasin, waiting in the shadows between houses and trees. When the ship carrying Zafira and Deen had vanished from view, they came. Misk had friends, she learned, and so she and her husband had been lucky enough to slip aboard the caliph's caravan, fleeing with little Lana.

She went back, days later. To the village where she and Deen had distributed meat. Where they and Zafira had grown up. Where the men had scorched the homes of the western villages and unleashed a vapor upon the vulnerable.

Children Yasmine had tutored, whose smiles she had coaxed and celebrated, now lay in small coffins, the ground too cold and hard to allow them proper burials.

Their deaths were bloodless, but the pallor of their skin spoke of hours of suffering. The few who survived told of the colorless poison.

There was no escaping something that killed through the cardinal act of inhaling.

Now Yasmine stared from the window of the caliph's palace in Thalj, far, far away from the forsaken village she once called home. She *had* no home. And if the Sarasins continued under the sultan's orders, no one in Demenhur would, no one in *Arawiya* would. What was the purpose of such slaughter?

"She will come," Misk said. He rubbed warmth into Yasmine's arms and pressed a kiss to her head.

Zafira. The sister of her heart. There was no way to send news to Sharr, and no way of retrieving news, either. She did not know if Zafira still lived, but she did know that her brother did not.

She would have learned more, if Misk had let her wander farther into the Arz when she had been in that senseless, helpless state. She would have died, too, but she had remained there long enough for the dark forest to show her something too vivid to be false.

The vision had gripped her: Deen dying by the hand of a golden-haired man who had attempted to kill Zafira.

Yasmine vowed to kill him. To bring to him the same level of suffering he had brought to her.

She didn't know how she would, for between her and Sharr was her husband, the Arz, the Baransea, and possibly a thousand and one other things she didn't know of. She was no Huntress, but she was Yasmine Ra'ad, and she would find a way. She didn't even know if the golden-haired man still lived, nor did she know his name. *One donkey at a time.*

Misk was still rubbing her shoulders, silently awaiting her response.

"For what?" Yasmine asked him.

What Zafira faced on Sharr was surely better than this. Yasmine didn't want her to return. First they had suffered from the cold, then the loss of their parents. Then Deen. Now this.

"Suffering is our fate."

Misk made a sound in his throat. "Have faith, Yasmine."

"It's hard."

"That's why I said have *faith*, not have a sweet."

Yasmine gave him a look.

He laughed. "What? All of your terrible jokes are catching up with me." He wrapped his arms around her, his chin on her shoulder, his voice warm in her ear. "Zafira will return with others in tow. Including a man I trust with my life and that of my mother's. Deen knew of him, too."

"And he will end our troubles with his oh-so-great powers?"

Misk let her mocking slide. "Not alone. But he will be part of it."

The maids had brought her kanafah and mint tea, but the tray sat untouched, the tea long since cooled. Yasmine couldn't stomach the sight of food or comfort. Everywhere she looked, she saw the bruised skin and still chests of the children. Small coffins and screaming mothers.

She was tired. So very tired, but she gifted her husband a small smile. "Does your mysterious savior have a name?"

Misk kissed her cheek. "Altair al-Badawi."

⸻ ◆ ⸻

He never did like the darkness. It was too heavy on the eyes, left too much to the imagination. It was where he had been shoved, confined, while his

467

mother doted on his brother. While Arawiya celebrated the birth of a prince.

He preferred light. The dizzying kind that hung above the feasts he had once frequented with Benyamin.

Another sob slipped from his parched tongue.

Benyamin, who had risked his life for decades by acting as the one heading Altair's treasonous gossamer web. His brother by choice, his friend by fate. Who lived with the guilt of his people's negligence, with the guilt of his own kindness, embarking on this journey and not once expecting to die.

He was dead now. A lonely, honorable death, where he would rest with the Sisters of Old for eternity.

Altair watched the zumra leave. He saw the fall of Zafira's shoulders, knowing what this battle had cost her. He saw Nasir, felling ifrit after ifrit, leading the others to the Alder ship. He saw his mother, weakened by Sharr.

None of them looked for him. Not while they boarded the ship. Not when they loosened their sails. Not when they left him. Even the lonely kaftar had pitied him before dispersing into the ruins.

Leaving him shackled by the Lion's shadows, unable to escape. He had helped the zumra, released that dizzying distraction of light. And they had left him.

Then he was thrown on his hands and knees, forced to work alongside the chittering, shrieking ifrit as they salvaged a ship from Sharr's ruins. Now, days—weeks?—later, his chains rattled as the ship heaved across the Baransea.

He knew why the dark creature hated him and the prince: *Because we have what you do not. We tumbled from the womb with all that you strive for.*

They were descendants of one of the Sisters of Old, with magic in their veins. They were vessels of power, even if they weren't as powerful as the full-blooded Sisters. They didn't need a magical heart or the light of a royal minaret. The land needn't host magic for them to wield it.

The shadows stirred, alerting him to a visitor. Waves crashed against the ship, roiling the insides of his stomach. While his brother trailed shadows on another ship, he tossed an orb of light to the cabin's ceiling.

His visitor's amber eyes glowed, tattoo gleaming bronze, elongated ears tucked beneath his ebony turban. Ears much like Altair's own.

"Hello, Father," said Altair. His voice was rough. "Come to gloat?"

The Lion of the Night smiled.

ACKNOWLEDGMENTS

THERE'S MAGIC IN WORDS, I KNOW, BUT THERE'S A particularly different kind of magic in the bond between blood. And this story could never have happened without my family. My greatest thanks goes, first and foremost, to my mother and father, for giving me courage and strength, and most importantly, for putting faith at my core. There is no greater gift.

To my sisters, Asma and Azraa, I owe you both the bulk of my smiles, my love, and my sanity (and insanity, if we're being truly honest). Thank you for lending your brains so that *We Hunt the Flame* could be the greatest it could be. For being my biggest fans and my favorite critics. I love you both more than any alphabet can allow me to express. And yes, Nasir and Altair are yours before anyone else's. To my brother, Abdullah, for sometimes being the worst, for being my earliest friend, and for reintroducing me to the world of books.

To my agent, John Cusick, for being kind and supportive and for always,

always being there with the right words precisely when I need them. You found my book the perfect home.

My endless appreciation to my editors: Janine O'Malley, for seeing something special in my words and for being my greatest champion from the very first day; to Melissa Warten, who answers my hundreds of emails with enthusiasm and love. Thank you both for asking "why" countless times, and for making the rough stones of my work shine.

To everyone at Macmillan: Thank you for being the publishing home of my dreams and working tirelessly to make this book all it can be. To my brilliant publicists Brittany Pearlman (fellow displaced-Californian) and Shivani Annirood: Thanks for putting up with my mumbling and endless questions. To Molly Ellis: Your lengthy emails will always be a bright spot of this journey. To Melissa Zar and Jordin Streeter in marketing: It's because of you two that I had to sign my name so many times, and I'll forever be grateful for that and all else. To Hayley Jozwiak, for reading over my words a hundred thousand times. A much-needed thank-you to Elizabeth Clark, for putting up with the designer in me—and I don't say that lightly.

Special thanks to Joy Peskin, Jen Besser, Jon Yaged, Allison Verost, Katie Halata, Mary Van Akin, Kathryn Little, Tom Mis, and Gaby Salpeter. To Melissa Sarver White at Folio Lit, for taking *We Hunt the Flame* abroad. To Virginia Allyn, for the gorgeous map, and Erin Fitzsimmons, for the typography. To Simón Prades, for the amazing cover. To Jenny Bent for your never-ending support and love, and agent extraordinaires Molly O'Neill and Suzie Townsend. To Sharon Biggs Waller and Leigh Bardugo, for empowering me from the very beginning, and V. E. Schwab for answering my many questions about how to get published. To Stephanie Garber, Lee Kelly, and Rachel Bellavia, for steering me in the right direction during my querying days, and Jessica Khoury, Ron Smith, Margaret Rogerson, Beth Revis, Evelyn Skye, Sabaa Tahir, Robin LaFevers, and Roshani Chokshi, for the love and support.

To Kerri Maniscalco, for teaching me how to appreciate every moment in the crazy world of publishing. To Katie Bucklein, soul twin and fierce fighter. Thank you for always having my back. To Joanna Hathaway, dearest friend and loving soul who keeps me going. Britta Gigliotti, principessa and the other half of this old couple. To Marieke Nijkamp, generous heart and mentor, thank you for being one of my earliest readers. To Joan He, partner in crime, agent sister, and debut friend. I heart you, goat friend. To Jessica Brooks, who kept a list and believed in me. To Beth Phelan and the #DVpit squad, you guys rock. To Brittany Holloway, my favorite mega fan. To the amazing fans with dedicated accounts supporting the world of Arawiya. To Lisa Austin, Kalyn Josephson, Jenna DeTrapani, Ksenia Winnicki, Heather Kassner, Mary Hinson, Sara Gundell, Korrina Ede, Noverantale, Ashelynn Hetland, Amanda Foody, and Michael Waters: Thank you, thank you, thank you.

To Amy Georgopoulos and Jenny Ethington, the librarians who were my pathway to the world of publishing. Thank you for helping teen-me out of her shell and for introducing her to the magic of book blogging.

To Catherine Gnoffo, mentor and friend, gone too soon. To my grandfather, whom I miss every day, who pressed crisp dollar bills into my palms so I could buy that new Harry Potter book at the fair. I wish you were both here to hold this book in your hands.

And last but not least: My deepest gratitude goes to you, dear reader. For picking up this book, devouring my words, and supporting a dream. None of this would have been possible without you. Thank you for being a part of Zafira's journey, Nasir's quest, and my adventure. *Shukrun.*